A MESSAGE FROM HIS NATIVE AMERICAN PAST . . .

Link came partially awake, aware suddenly he'd been speaking aloud in his sleep. The beside clock showed it was almost midnight.

As he attempted to return to sleep, he tried to remember the words he'd been muttering. As he drifted closer to slumber they came to him. *Come home.*

Glimpses of the dream returned in flickering snapshots. The Grandfather had been at his side, but he had difficulty recalling the subjects of his ramblings and the images they'd brought.

"Come home."

There'd been a crow in a thicket of trees. There'd been a dark man, thin, with a pencil-lined mustache.

"Prepare yourself."

The dream came to him more clearly. The next image was of the dark man, whose head erupted in a spray of red.

"A knowledgeable writer."
—Mark Berent, author of *Rolling Thunder*

"Wilson is every bit as good as Coonts, Brown, and Clancy." **—Colonel Glenn Davis, USAF (ret.)**

Black Wolf

TOM WILSON

A SIGNET BOOK

SIGNET
Published by the Penguin Group
Penguin Books USA Inc., 375 Hudson Street,
New York, New York 10014, U.S.A.
Penguin Books Ltd, 27 Wrights Lane,
London W8 5TZ, England
Penguin Books Australia Ltd, Ringwood,
Victoria, Australia
Penguin Books Canada Ltd, 10 Alcorn Avenue,
Toronto, Ontario, Canada M4V 3B2
Penguin Books (N.Z.) Ltd, 182–190 Wairau Road,
Auckland 10, New Zealand

Penguin Books Ltd, Registered Offices:
Harmondsworth, Middlesex, England

First published by Signet, an imprint of Dutton Signet,
a division of Penguin Books USA Inc.

First Printing, September, 1995
10 9 8 7 6 5 4 3 2 1

Printed in the United States of America

PUBLISHER'S NOTE
This is a work of fiction. Names, characters, places, and incidents either are the product of the author's imagination or are used fictitiously, and any resemblance to actual persons, living or dead, events, or locales is entirely coincidental.

Prologue

London, England

The apartment building was a block off Regent Street, facing a street no wider than an alleyway. Four months ago their employer had leased two adjacent flats. One form showed two male tenants. On the second a single name was listed—but it was not his name. In private others called him Ghost. The two men in the neighboring apartment would visit him during the course of each day to listen to his instructions, which they performed without hesitation. They carried Jamaican passports, and in public all three spoke in the clipped, melodic cadence of Caribbean islanders.

They were gathered in Ghost's second bedroom, with six cheap and use-beaten suitcases opened about the room. Each was neatly filled with 120 brick-shaped objects. All but one brick in each case were sealed in black plastic, with a white number at one corner showing the burn rate of the compound inside. The bricks were arranged in such manner that the explosive blast would be funneled forward. At the top center of each case was a single green brick containing a radio receiver and fuzing circuit, with fine wires that spider-webbed to detonators embedded in the bricks. A dark-tinted wire extended from the receiver through a hole in each case and ran the length of the top: the radio antennae. Each brick weighed 250 grams, and together, when added to the weight of the suitcase, summed up to 30.5 kilos, or 67 pounds.

The two men watched intently as Ghost carefully snapped two of the cases closed, then secured each with a length of cotton rope, the sturdy kind sold in London shops as clothesline. When he'd finished, Ghost placed them on the floor and motioned to the slighter of the two men. He had him lift the cases by their reinforced handles.

The slight man strained with the effort. "Heavy."

Ghost shrugged, expressionless. "We won't want to make two trips." His voice emerged in a richly timbered American accent. He sounded differently when he wished by changing his tones. He was good at it and tutored the others to do the same.

The slight man blew a breath, then gingerly put down his load.

The next two suitcases had phosphorous-coated titanium plates at the forward ends, scored so they would fragment into a shower of fiery, half-inch projectiles. When he'd secured the cases, Ghost had the darker and more muscular man heft those two, which weighed eighty-four pounds each. He handled them easily.

"Those are yours," the man called Ghost told the men. "Take them to your rooms when you leave. Get accustomed to carrying them. Now, let's go back to the map." He looked at his watch. "At nineteen hundred we'll take the taxi and look over the objective again."

He spoke with the crisp voice of authority, of one accustomed to being in charge, and did not ask for questions. Ghost treated them not as accomplices but as he might a brace of obedient hunting dogs.

"Be glad when it's over," Rashad muttered as they walked into the small living room and leaned over the map. He'd complained often the last few days about the seclusion and the fact that he needed a woman. Ghost demanded isolation when they were on an operation. This one, like the others they'd performed, would be accomplished with precision, with no outside influences clouding their minds.

Ghost pointed to the detailed chart of the objective. "The suitcases must be positioned exactly *where* and precisely *as* I've shown." He'd told them that many times, but wished to emphasize the point.

The slighter man was frowning. "What if someone picks one up?" He'd asked that question before, and just as before, Ghost ignored it.

"Study the map, Charlie," Ghost said. Then he began to go over the operation once again.

BOOK ONE
Ghost

1

Friday, January 13th

5:00 P.M.—Boudie Springs, Montana

The town was nestled at the foot of mountains so picturesque that even longtime residents drew breaths of wonder as they approached from Kalispel. At six thousand feet Boudie Springs was the epitome of the high country, and local entrepreneurs advertised it as God's offering of respite.

The earliest settlers had been migratory peoples called Salish and Flatheads, who endured harsh winters and devastating raids by fierce Blackfeet to remain near hunting grounds with abundances of moose, elk, deer, and bighorn sheep. Then came white trappers attracted by the beaver—and later, raucous, hell-raising miners drawn by the lure of gold. Except for ventures to trade, buy whiskey, or steal horses, the People stayed out of the white men's way. A Flathead chief, unlucky enough to be born after the whites had come in sufficient numbers to impose their will, had agreed to give up land promised to the People in perpetuity and become known as a good Indian. The whites named the valley after him. The town was founded by a squaw man named Boudie, who set up a trading post beside a hot springs lying smack between the soaring Lewis and Whitefish ranges of the Rocky Mountains.

In the high country, seasons are moods and colors. Spring is a time for renewal, as fawns, saplings, and tender grasses emerge from the snow like children who cannot suppress their delight. Summers are discovery and maturing, warm days and temperate nights, when the sun's mysterious processes turn things to darker shades of green. Autumn is the quiet time, when leaves become medleys of flashy reds and yellows, and is too short-lived. Winter arrives with a harsh blanket of snow, and from the onset is morose. Although the locals are prepared, and though that is the season when ski tourists flock into town to fill hotels and condominiums and toss money at storekeepers, they grow weary of five long months of black and white.

January is especially stark and often includes a week of temperatures that hover near forty below, regardless of the thermometer you look at. European tourists are confused by Fahrenheit readings, for they use the centigrade scale where water freezes at zero. At forty below zero the two scales cross, so that extreme reading is the same. Regardless of your origin or hardiness, forty degrees below either zero is cold.

For the previous three days the temperature had varied from thirty-eight below under the hazy afternoon sun to forty-four below in the pitch-black of early morning.

Although life was sometimes harsh, Abraham Lincoln Anderson liked Boudie Springs. The air was good, there was work, and with few exceptions the town was populated by no-nonsense people who held the belief that you should leave another man's business to himself. His battered, forest green, four-wheel-drive pickup had a hundred and sixty thousand honest miles on the odometer and was only fifteen years younger than Link, thirty-one, but it was surefooted, mechanically fit, and paid for. The two-bedroom cabin at the northeast edge of town was efficient, snugly insulated, and also paid for.

Tall, intense, dark-haired, and gaunt, Link Anderson was a quiet man who'd come to Boudie Springs for anonymity and a chance to grow comfortable with himself. He'd achieved the first goal. The second was elusive. Through strenuous activity, he maintained himself at the peak of physical condition. In the summer he cut and hauled firewood in the pickup. In snow season, he worked on the safety patrol at Borealis Mountain, a nearby ski resort on the western side of Glacier Park. There he sometimes stared out where distant Siyeh Mountain loomed: dark, enigmatic, and brooding. An odd feeling of serenity settled over him whenever he looked there.

As he drove home in the growing winter gloom, an inner voice urged him to hurry. He ignored the impulse and reduced speed as he entered the town. It had been snowing off and on, an oddity when it was this cold, and clear ice gathered in unseen patches on the town's roadways despite the prodigious amounts of cinders and salt put down by municipal works trucks.

Link slowed to a crawl, then stopped at the mouth of his snowpack drive, pulled an assortment of flyers and bills from the mailbox, then eased down the fifty-foot driveway, still fighting the strident voice. He believed in an orderly world of explained sciences and reason, unadulterated by intuitions and inexplicable urgings.

As he approached the cabin a motion sensor activated outside floodlights. He regularly came home late, and automatic lighting made things easier. Link parked beside a two-foot mound of white, then emerged and deftly brushed away snow, exposing a wooden stand with an electrical receptacle. He unwrapped an electrical cord from a rack above the winch, recessed into the grill guard he'd fashioned from angle iron and a slab of steel, plugged in, and listened for the sound of the pump that circulated warmed coolant through the engine. Another wire electrified a battery blanket. It was all necessary. If the electricity went out and the engine wasn't periodically started, it could take hours to get a sluggish engine turning over.

Link walked to the cabin, thermal boots crunching through crisp snow, picked up the shovel leaning beside the door, and began to clear the path with deft and practiced strokes. The driveway would wait until morning when he'd use a snowplow attachment that bolted to the truck's grill guard. He heard the telephone ringing inside, but did not hurry.

Satisfied with his work, he stomped snow from his boots and went in. "Cold out there," he muttered as he pulled off gloves and the blue-and-red ski parka, thankful that the fireplace insert still knocked off the chill in the room. Again the telephone began to emit its shrill sound.

Link placed two fresh logs into the stove, opened the draft, and turned the circulating fan up a notch. The answering machine made a clicking noise. His voice sounded, followed by a tone. As he closed the door to the stove, Myra Bourne's voice came over the speaker, saying something about a rescue effort in progress.

Jim and Myra Bourne operated the most popular tavern in town, a trendy place frequented by mobs of ski tourists, especially when the weather was bad and the ski hill was shut down, as it presently was. Jim also headed the North County Search and Rescue Team, and the previous year he'd cajoled Lincoln Anderson into joining his group.

"Hell," Link muttered. He walked to the telephone on the kitchen counter and answered.

"Anderson." He was not a man of profuse words.

"Finally," Myra said. Link could hear noise from the bar in the background. "Jim radioed in about an hour ago and asked me to call you."

"What's this one about?" Link asked, trying to keep fatigue from his voice. It had been a hard day at the ski resort. He'd blown two potential avalanche buildups and surveyed another for tomorrow morning.

"Four tourists insisted on going cross-country skiing this morning," Myra said. "They were supposed to be back before noon. When they didn't show, their friends were concerned."

"They ought to be. It's too damned cold to try something like that."

"Amen. At two this afternoon the hotel manager called us. Jim took a few members of the team out, and they still aren't back. He radioed for me to get hold of the rest of the SAR team and you in particular."

Link was beginning to thaw and didn't look forward to returning to the cold.

"Where are they from?" he asked. If they were residents of places like upper Michigan or New England, they might be pros at winter survival.

"Chicago. Members of a singles athletic club."

"Men or women?" he asked.

"Two of each. The youngest is a woman in her early twenties and the oldest is a guy about forty. They started on the Tweedie, but Jim said the team's already taken snowmobiles around the trail and up a couple of side paths."

Tweedie Trail was a nine-mile hiking and cross-country

ski path that looped around the town, put in the previous summer to attract year-round tourists.

Link glanced at the clock. It was twenty past five. After this long in the frigid air, if the foursome hadn't yet found shelter . . .

Chicago? *Damn.*

"The weather station at Kalispel airport says it's supposed to warm up tonight."

"I heard the same report," Link said. He decided to take the Jones down and wolverine-fur parka. The Canadians knew how to make winter wear.

Link double-parked in front of Jamie's Pub, leaving the engine running, went inside, and pushed his way through the crowd.

Myra was in the back office. "Talking on the radio," the bartender said.

Link rapped once on the door and went in. Jim Bourne had set up the room as a combination business office and communications central for the rescue team. Myra was speaking on the base station radio. "Link, just came in," she said.

He took the mike. "Anything yet, Jim?"

Bourne's voice sounded dog-tired. "No sign of them so far, Link. There's been a couple of inches of fresh snow since they went out, and it's damned difficult tracking."

"Where are you?"

"Out at the old Crowder Ranch."

Link eyed the spot on the wall map, five miles distant. "I'll head over."

"Myra's got up some food and hot coffee. Don't forget 'em."

"See you in a few minutes." Link went to the charger rack and removed a handheld radio, tested it, then shoved it into one of the parka's pockets.

Myra passed him thermoses and a sack of sandwiches.

"What are the tourists' names?" For some reason Link wanted the names. Something to do with the urgings that had been nagging him.

Myra transcribed, pulled off a stickum note, and handed it to him.

He took his armful through the barroom, she leading the way. Myra was tall, endowed with tremendous breastworks she carried so boldly that customers stared in awe, but her cool gaze and no-nonsense demeanor made them step aside.

Outside Jamie's Pub, a black-and-white Bronco with light bar was pulled up behind Link's pickup, emergency lights flashing. Deputy Ernie Gilchrist saw him emerge and waved from the cab. Link nodded, silently thanking him for making sure a tourist hadn't smacked into his double-parked truck—although it had easily survived past such encounters. A tourist's Mazda sedan had once slipped on clear ice into the Ramcharger's path. Link had stopped, and the Mazda had decelerated to five miles per hour when they impacted. The sedan had been totaled. Link had done his repairs to the bumper guard with a couple of hisses from a can of spray paint.

The deputy sheriff cracked the Bronco's door. "You headed to Crowder's?"

"Yeah."

"I'll lead the way."

Inside the truck's cab, Link switched on the dome light and read from the list Myra had provided. John was a first name. "Where are you, fellow?" he asked conversationally. Another was Linda, the same as his mother's. Knowing the names made the search seem more personal.

Gilchrist pulled around in front, blue-and-red lights flashing in the gloom. Link eased out the clutch and followed. They accelerated to a moderate speed.

"John and Linda," he muttered aloud. A chill ran through him, although the heavy-duty heater was going full blast. He stared intently at the road, and at Deputy Gilchrist's taillights a hundred yards distant. It was no longer snowing. The evening air was crystal clear. The radio crackled from his parka pocket; Jim Bourne querying a couple of his SAR team members. They didn't have a clue.

Gilchrist was drawing ahead. "Where are you, John and Linda?" Link repeated, and wondered if they were alive. He geared down to second and slowed even more. Deputy Gilchrist was a quarter of a mile ahead, approaching the turnoff to the old Crowder Ranch.

Don't turn.

He frowned, creeping now. Gilchrist turned left onto the Crowder road.

Link squinted into the semidarkness beyond the turnoff.

The inner urging continued—telling him to proceed on the highway.

Crazy.

He turned and accelerated toward the distant taillights of Gilchrist's Bronco.

A mile down the Crowder road they found an assortment of pickups and snowmobiles parked in a ragged row beside one of the bunkhouses. Twenty years earlier the Crowder Ranch had employed scores of cowboys to tend more than five thousand cattle on the holding. Now the place was owned by a development company headquartered in Los Angeles, and was in the process of being sold off as five-acre *ranchettes* to land-hungry Californians. The original house, barns, corrals, workshops, and outbuildings were abandoned.

Inside the bunkhouse lanterns had been suspended from hooks, and fires had been built in the potbelly stoves at either end of the long, open room. Members of the rescue team stood about in parkas and mittens, blowing clouds of vapor from under hoods.

Link placed the sandwiches and thermoses on a dusty tabletop, and walked over to Jim Bourne. "Any idea where they are?"

"Nothing but guesses. I've got two crews out in snowmobiles, going around the trail. There's no telling where they got off. We're beginning to think they decided to cut directly toward town and got held up by something—then maybe holed up in a gully to keep off the windchill. If that's right they could be anywhere between the loop and town."

"Makes sense." Link cocked his head thoughtfully, remembering the urging to continue north on the highway. Jim's idea made more sense. Why would they go away from the town?

The radio sounded; a woman's voice—one of the snowmobile crews—said they'd found a broken fence rail a mile west of the Crowder Ranch.

"Any ski tracks?" Jim asked into the mike.

"Everything's under fresh snow."

"Which side of the trail?"

"North, away from town. That's why we were wondering."

Jim examined the map, then shook his head. "Keep looking in the other direction."

Link wanted to encourage him to look to the north, but he held his tongue. There was no basis for his feeling, and there weren't enough resources to search everywhere.

Jim motioned to another two-person team, both bundled warmly, black nylon masks protecting faces and woolen knit hats pulled low. One wore a pink snowmobile suit and ornate parka, the only way to tell she was female. Jim pointed out their search route on the map—east on the Tweedie Trail—and they went to the door. Seconds later snowmobile engines cackled to life. The team made radio contact and said they were beginning their search.

10:40 P.M.

Lincoln Anderson came into the bunkhouse and stamped his feet. Clinging ice fell from his trousers. He'd helped another team member replace a bent skag rod on a snowmobile.

Jim Bourne put down his radio and regarded him wearily. "Looks like a long-term operation, Link. I'm splitting us into two groups. One will keep searching, the other will rest and take over in the morning. How about taking the second shift?"

"Sure," said Link.

Jim raised his voice to the others in the bunkhouse. "Listen up!" He told them about his decision and that Link would be in charge of the morning shift. They'd bunk at the far end of the room. Jim said he'd wake them before the sun peeked over the mountains in the morning.

Link pulled a foam rubber mattress and sleeping bag from one of the big rescue kits and trudged to the opposite end of the bunkhouse. Six others did the same. Annie Bright Star, a Flathead Indian from a reservation a few miles to the south, made her nest not far from Link's.

"Now we're sleeping together," she joked.

Annie worked with him on the Safety Patrol at Borealis, and consistently volunteered to team with him on the avalanche patrol. She was ever-pleasant and friendly, and had an obvious crush on Link. He generally tried to avoid her.

Link crawled into the bag and settled, wishing he'd been able to return to the cabin. There were times when his nightmares became so intense he found himself yelling aloud in his sleep. He closed his eyes and tried to focus his thoughts, and not to think of the men in the armored personnel carrier who had dominated his nights for the past several years.

Dead men.

The pilots in his flight had killed them. He'd been their flight leader, and as such had been responsible.

Stop it! Forget them, at least for the night. Concentrate on the rescue effort. Four people were out in the vicious elements and hopefully not yet beyond help—unlike the men in the APC.

He rolled the names John and Linda about in his mind and tried to rationalize the inner urgings to search to the north.

Why there? It made no sense.

Had they holed up—or kept going until they fell? If they'd decided to find shelter, what kind had they looked for? What was available in the stark, rolling rangeland?

Link's mind slowed, but the questions continued until he fell asleep.

2

Saturday, January 14th

2:00 A.M.*—Crowder Ranch, Boudie Springs, Montana*

He is a child, sitting naked on an earthen ledge, surrounded by darkness and warmth. Steam wafts about the enclosure, issuing from wetted hot stones in a small pit at the center of the place. A familiar man is seated beside him, humming in a quiet, pleasant voice.

The Grandfather.

The old man leans forward, draws moist heat into his aged and scarred chest, holds it there, then whoofs it out in a great breath. He mutters pleasantly as he regards the boy, and although the words are odd ones the boy understands.

"Come home."

The words echoed and receded as Link almost aroused, then again descended into deep slumber. He was pleased yet uneasy that the Grandfather had returned.

After a time he dreamed again.

The pleasant expression on the Grandfather's wrinkled face has changed to sadness as he speaks in a grave tone. Unpleasant images appear—incomprehensible yet vivid flickers seen through the Grandfather's description.

There is the mouth of a great, dark cave. People are inside, screaming in pain and terror.

"Come home. Prepare yourself."

Link heard himself grunting and felt himself moving—

almost awake, then wafting—and even in his reverie he knew he must concentrated on his present task.

"Where are John and Linda?" Did he speak the words as he drifted back to the pleasantness of the Grandfather's companionship?

The old man nods his understanding.

New words build a new image. There are two trees, one thin, the other fat.

Link's mind played with the image, building different types of trees.

Beneath the trees people huddle together—ice-chilled and terrified that they are in the process of perishing.

Link lingered in the shadowy world between dream and awareness, shifting uneasily, mouthing words. He came partially awake, drifted back, reemerged. With effort he opened his eyes, looked about through gritty eyes, and realized he was in the bunkhouse.

Snapshot memories of the dreams lingered. *A cave. People screaming in pain and terror.*

But those were from the first dream. What of the second? *Two trees, one thin, the other fat. People huddled together beneath, cold and miserable.*

Link stretched his muscular body as his limbs slowly came to life.

The Grandfather—that was what he'd called the taciturn old man of the reassuring dreams he'd had as a boy. When his parents had first adopted him, he'd been terribly lonely, missing someone he could no longer remember. An only child, there had been no one to play or talk with—until the Grandfather had begun visiting in the night. He recalled being careful not to tell his mother for fear she'd send him back to . . . somewhere. The orphanage? He'd not yet realized how tenaciously his new parents loved him, and the idea of rejection had troubled him, so he'd not spoken of the nightly visits. Later, when there'd been friends and things to do, he'd suppressed the dreams of the Grandfather until—finally—there'd been no more of them.

The next time he'd thought of the Grandfather had been in a psych course at the Air Force Academy, when an instructor discussed how the human brain offered escape for troubled minds. Men in combat would blank memories of friends being killed. Lonely children would invent playmates, often protectors, mother or father figures, and those would come alive for them. Link had thought it interesting, for it explained the old man who had been his companion. He'd had no real grandfather that he could remember, so he'd invented one.

The dreams of the reassuring old man had not returned. Not until now.

Some dreams, Link knew, were manifestations of the subconscious. There'd been times at the academy when he'd pored over difficult subjects, and answers had come to him during the night. He'd found that the same happened to other cadets, that sometimes when they'd drop off to sleep concentrating on a problem, solutions would come to them.

Had that just happened? He'd gone to sleep thinking of the lost tourists.

He tried to focus on the dream, the details of which were no longer clear. *A cave?* There'd been people inside, but they'd been different from the tourists they searched for. *Two trees?* People huddled beneath, miserably cold, like the ones they searched for would be—if they still lived.

Link withdrew from the sleeping bag carefully so he wouldn't disturb the others resting nearby. The bunkhouse was warm enough to go without a heavy jacket.

He walked quietly to the other end of the room, where Jim Bourne spoke to one of his teams. Someone had made a trip to town and retrieved a fresh stainless steel jug of coffee. Link picked a paper cup from a stack and poured as he listened in on the conversation.

There was still no sign of the tourists. The teams were now searching between the trail and town. The people finished their report and went to the stove to warm themselves.

"Couldn't sleep," Link muttered as he studied the map. "I've been trying to think of places they might use for shelter."

"Me, too," Jim said. "Trying to recall all the shacks and range sheds between here and town. Can't think of any we haven't searched." Jim knew the area better than most.

"How about trees, say . . . two or three miles north of the trail?"

"It's flat and barren. No trees. Just sagebrush and prickly weed." Jim turned and spoke with the search crew warming by the stove.

Link wandered to an old single-pane window that was solidly frosted over.

"Still colder'n a whore's intentions," Jim said, approaching from behind. "Weather people are as screwed up as ever. Better get back to sleep, Link. It's doubtful we'll find them until morning light, and you'll want to be alert."

Link nodded vaguely, unable to shake the thought of the four tourists. Maybe shivering in the miserable hut under two trees like he'd visualized in the dream.

There aren't any trees there.

Link was a nonbeliever of the occult. He chuckled at descriptions of UFO's and kidnappings by aliens. But this was different, and he became increasingly convinced that his subconscious had pieced together bits of logic and was trying to provide a solution.

He went to his bedroll and retrieved the parka, then the handheld radio and flashlight. Returning to the SAR kit, he pulled out a flare kit and a pair of aluminum bear paw snowshoes.

"Where are you going?" Jim asked.

"I keep getting this wild notion that someone ought to look to the north."

"They'd have been crazy to take off in that direction."

"Yep. But I can't sleep, and I'm going to take a look." Link pulled on his parka, then stepped out the door into bitter cold. He hurried to the pickup, placed the snowshoes in back, then crawled into the cab. The moon was down, the night pitch-black.

The engine growled sluggishly, but caught. As soon as the temperature needle quivered off the post, Link drove back toward the highway. When he reached it, he turned north.

After a couple of minutes on the deserted roadway, he pulled to the side and stopped.

Where are you, John and Linda?

A flashing yellow light identified a snowplow coming up the highway shoulder. Link made a U-turn, and waited, engine idling, until the snowplow rumbled past. Then he began to crawl along, heading back toward the Crowder Ranch road, looking out at fields so dark that had there been a tree he could not have seen it. He'd be better off at the bunkhouse resting for the morning shift. Jim Bourne knew more than he about this sort of thing.

If the tourists were that close to the road, surely they'd have seen passing car lights. Yet there remained the conflicting feeling of certainty that they were there.

Ridiculous.

He drove along the highway shoulder until he came to a snowpack road bisecting the open range. It was in the area—north of the Tweedie Trail and west of the highway—where he'd had his urgings. Link selected low range on the transmission and turned off the highway, letting the pickup wallow along the ill-defined roadway through a fifteen-inch accumulation of snow. After a few minutes he stopped and turned off the lights. While most of the sky was obscured, he could see Polaris and the stars of the constellation Cassiopeia to the north.

He shut off the engine and crawled out. After latching the snowshoe bindings, Link shuffle-walked a few feet in front of the pickup. He shone the flashlight beam, carefully observing what was there, moving the light, periodically stopping and staring.

Jim Bourne had been right. There were no trees—nothing but sparse, rolling prairie.

Link continued observing. When he was looking at the left-forward quadrant he stopped, for he'd glimpsed something in the distance. A gust blew up a sheet of fine snow, and it was gone. When it was this cold, the snow was like grains of sand, pelting his face like grit.

He shuffled ahead for fifty feet, then stopped and listened, using the flashlight to illuminate the area ahead. He was about to turn off the light when he glimpsed it again; a tall, man-made shape. Link kept the flashlight on as he shuffled forward, heard a periodic creaking sound of boards chafing against one another. The shape took form—an old windmill. He stopped when he was within a few feet and studied another structure beyond.

The windmill creaked louder, but another sound drew his attention. A human utterance?

"Hello," Link called, and moved the beam about, now looking at an aged wooden water tower just beyond the windmill. He fumbled in his pocket and pulled out a pen-gun flare kit, snapped a cartridge into place, aimed forty-five degrees above the horizon, and released the plunger. Red light streaked upward.

"Here!" shouted a high, frightened voice.

A figure emerged from a mound at the base of a water tower—a range shed. Link trotted forward, pulling out the handheld radio.

An hour later, the four tourists had been packed aboard two ambulances and were on their way to the hospital in Kalispel, thirty miles south of Boudie Springs. All were suffering from various degrees of frostbite. They'd been huddling in a storage shed at the foot of the old water tower.

As the search and rescue team watched the ambulance depart down the highway, Jim Bourne shook his head. "I'd have never guessed they'd come this way."

"Wasn't smart of them," Link said.

"What made *you* so positive?"

"Just a gut feeling that anyone dumb enough to go cross-country skiing in forty-below weather might be silly enough to go the wrong way."

"Some guess." Deputy Ernie Gilchrist had been at the bunkhouse when Link had called in, and had been acting like Link had accomplished some sort of miracle. Ernie was the foremost town gossip, and Link wondered what he'd make of this one to spread about.

Link walked to the pickup, feeling good about what he'd done. The rationale he'd given Bourne was true. His subconscious had placed everything neatly together and presented them in the bizarre fashion. The only things that continued to puzzle him were the water tower and windmill, for in the night they resembled a fat and a skinny tree.

He thought back on the dream and tried to remember more. There'd been something about a dark cave and people inside screaming in pain and terror.

Those parts of the Grandfather dream had been totally wrong.

11:00 A.M.—Piccadilly Circus Station, London, United Kingdom

The underground station was busy that Saturday morning. Three men wearing Rastafarian dreadlocks and dressed in unkempt greatcoats went unnoticed as they examined a large and colorful route map with suitably puzzled expressions. One pointed to a destination and determined the fare. Another purchased tickets at a vending machine, then doled them out. Each hefted two inexpensive suitcases, ropes binding them for added sturdiness, and joined a queue leading to a turnstile. Once through they melted into the crowd, going separate directions.

Precisely twelve minutes later, they emerged together from the underground station into the drizzling rain. They carried no umbrellas, and now no luggage, and were pushed along by the chattering swarm of humans. After fifty meters they paused at an occupied telephone booth. The shortest, most compact of the men nodded to the others. They moved to one side to watch the crowd and talk in low tones. He waited patiently as a woman with two small children spoke into the receiver handset. The girl examined the West Indians somberly, especially observing their sodden dreadlocks.

A group of spike-haired teenage boys passed, and one intentionally jostled the compact man. He gave them a humble, apologetic look. The boys laughed and jauntily continued toward the entrance of the underground.

The woman finished and gathered her children. "Thank you for waiting," she said, tying a plastic kerchief over her hair before venturing from the booth. She took each child by hand and hurried toward the overcrowded underground station. The little girl looked back over her shoulder. The dark-skinned, compact man formed a smile.

He dialed, dropped the correct amount into the slot, and spoke to the receptionist at the *Times,* asking for the city news desk. Another voice answered and told him the editor was tied up. Could he call back later, or perhaps leave a message?

He glanced at the two other men, huddling into their coats to ward off the chill, water dripping from chins and hair. "Tell him it's Ghost," he said into the receiver.

After a few seconds the city news editor came onto the line, his voice cautious. "Hello?"

"Hi," said Ghost. "It's been a while. What? Six weeks now?"

The newsman's voice betrayed his anxiety. "Where are you?"

"Out of the rain for the moment, thank God." He

changed to a clipped English dialect. "Truly *beastly* weather, isn't it, old sport?"

"Where are you?" the editor repeated.

He chuckled. "Weather here matches the British temperament, don't you think? Bland and cruddy, as my Irish friends say. They'll be giving you a call in a few minutes, like before."

"For Christ's sake, where are you?"

"This one's bigger. You'll become a part of modern history just by taking this call."

The editor pulled in a breath and spoke evenly. "Please, where are you?"

"Let's see now. Regent and Piccadilly, the signs over there say. Not far from the underground station. The place was absolutely mobbed."

It's Piccadilly Station this time, they'd be whispering at the *Times,* and someone would have the police on another line.

"Are you still there?" he asked over the phone.

"Yes." The *s*-sound was hissed nervously.

"Dreadful," Ghost said, reverting to the British accent. "People everywhere. But then, we'll thin them out some, won't we old sport?"

"God!"

"Well, I must be going. Nice to chat with you again."

"Wait!" the newsman almost shouted. He'd obviously been told to delay him as long as possible. "Think of what you're doing, Ghost. Think of the innocent lives."

"I am, of course. Actually, I'm paid quite well to think of this sort of thing."

"Don't do it. This one time, don't do it."

He watched a happy young couple disappear into the mouth of the underground entrance. "Gotta go, old buddy. Like I said, you'll go into the history books. There's six of them this time."

"For God's sake, Ghost!"

"Whose god? There are so many it becomes wearisome to attempt to distinguish them." He hung up, stepped out to allow a waiting Oriental man into the booth, then ambled over to his companions.

They shielded him from view as Ghost removed an electronic device from his pocket that looked like a television remote control. He depressed the first button. A second later a green light began to intermittently flash: the feedback signal that the repeater had sent the transmission for the bombs to arm themselves. Ghost looked at his watch, waited for ten full seconds, then depressed the second button. The light came on steady. The detonate signal had been transmitted on a second frequency. He nodded to the others, noting that Rashad could not suppress a grin, and replaced the device into the overcoat pocket. He'd used delay fuzes that would take thirty seconds for the first to be activated. Ghost turned, and as they began to walk down the street, heard the annoying sound of a distant siren.

They waited patiently at the intersection to cross to Regent Street. When the light changed, they surged with the flow of pedestrians. The siren was closer, now joined by others. Halfway across the walkway, there was a rumble from beneath.

"What the bloody hell?" a man exclaimed. Others looked about with widened eyes. The three men continued, although Charlie could not resist a look back. People about them began to ask questions. The men continued walking, now on Regent Street, at their unhurried pace. There were more rumbles and shakes.

People were looking about with inquiring expressions, some staring in the direction of the underground station. Shrill screams began to emanate from behind them. The sirens were closer, obnoxiously loud and persistent.

A taxi pulled to the curb; one of the two that had dropped them off precisely thirty-five minutes earlier. They crawled in, and the driver wordlessly proceeded down Regent. He glanced into his mirror several times, Ghost noted.

Minutes later, in Ghost's apartment, all three began to shuck out of wet overcoats and pull off wigs. "Channel four," Ghost said, nodding at the telly. Charlie switched it on—a woman was wilting as a ridiculously handsome man kissed her. An American soap opera. After four long minutes the scene evaporated—a still shot flashed onto the screen, words that an important bulletin was to follow—a ditty of music—"*You get the latest news on channel four.*"

The three men stripped, tossing clothing into a corner, eyes fixed to the television screen. An announcer's face appeared, staring into the camera.

"An explosion has been reported at Piccadilly Circus Station. Thus far there are no reports of injuries, or cause for

. . . please wait." He took a sheet of paper from someone off-camera. His voice faltered. "It is now confirmed that there have been a series of explosions. The underground station was filled with weekend shoppers, and there have been casualties . . ."

A short while later, television crews were reporting from the scene, although citizens were being told to avoid the area so emergency personnel and vehicles could get through. Alternate reports of four and five explosions were mentioned, for people near the scene had heard the rumbling sounds and felt earthquake-like tremors. As a reporter spoke, a woman screamed incoherently.

The three men finished changing their clothing, pulling on neat slacks, shirts, sweaters, and loafers. They took seats on the sofa opposite the set, and Ghost told Charlie to fetch a bottle of bitter lemon from the refrigerator.

An hour after the initial explosion, it was apparent the tragedy was of immense proportion. Emergency teams had emerged with some eighty bodies, and ambulances, police cars, and private automobiles were transporting large numbers of soot-faced patients to surrounding hospitals. Officials were pleading for blood donors to report to their nearest British Red Cross facility.

Urgency continued to mount. Hundreds of people were feared to have been killed. The Provisional Irish Republican Army had telephoned a newspaper, taking responsibility and demanding that all political prisoners held in British jails be immediately released.

The men watched. Rashad pointed out one of the wise-ass kids who'd passed them at the telephone booth, the same one who had jostled Ghost. "Punk," he said, with satisfaction. The dazed youth was staggering drunkenly, head hanging and an arm held askew.

The camera pulled back to a panoramic view from atop a nearby building, showing a lingering pall of dust and smoke, tendrils of the stuff still issuing from the maw of the underground station. Ambulances and fire trucks filled the lower portion of the screen. Medics toiled on the living under the canopy of a portable first-aid station. Bodies were laid out neatly to one side. A steady line of emergency personnel streamed into the dark cavern's mouth—others emerged with people on litters or supporting walking wounded. A team assembled in the square, carrying air tanks, and the announcer guessed it was a rescue squad of firemen. They donned gear in unison, adjusted straps, and filed down the dark stairs wielding electric torches.

New reports told of the horror below. There'd been nothing like it in London since World War II at the height of the bombing. An unofficial toll was totted up—more than two hundred dead, but BBC speculated it would be awhile before accurate figures could be derived.

Charlie settled beside Ghost on the couch and began a question.

"Watch," Ghost barked, eyes glued to the screen.

He envisioned the gloomy interior of the station. They'd strung emergency lighting by now, but it was a large area to illuminate. There'd be upward of a hundred emergency personnel inside, trying to get to the victims, just as he'd anticipated. Ghost looked at his watch, then back to the television.

A cloud of dark smoke belched from the entrance, accompanied by a sharp report. People near the dark mouth were swatted from their feet and hurled outward. The bodies and the medical station were obscured. The picture shuddered and became a series of fluttering lines.

"There's been another explosion," cried someone from the safety of the television station.

Rashad laughed like a delighted child.

"Silly twits," said Ghost. "I told them there were six."

No one had moved the bombs. He'd placed large strips of tape on the sides of the shoddy suitcases and crudely written: AIDS PATIENT.

"Twits," Ghost repeated as he took a last sip of bitter lemon and turned off the set.

The two other men followed Ghost into the corridor. A moment later they were outside, crawling into the waiting taxi. The driver motioned to four women waiting in a nearby van. The cleaning crew would scour both apartments thoroughly and eliminate all traces of their stay.

1:00 P.M.—Floor Three, Department of Justice, Washington, D.C.

Interdepartmental Task Force number four (ITF-4) had been formed by presidential order in 1990, when Saddam

Hussein threatened to unleash terrorism upon any country that dared to challenge his newly expanded nation. The task force, unanimously concurred with by the House and Senate Intelligence Committees, was comprised of members from all U.S. government intelligence and policing organizations, with the mission to identify and intercept Iraqi-sponsored terrorists before they could reach American shores. Saddam's threats had been taken seriously, and the secretive ITF was assigned far-reaching authority. Representatives from Justice, State, Treasury, Defense, and their various bureaus and agencies worked long hours and brought their considerable capabilities to bear on the problem. One by one, five different terrorist groups had been systematically discovered, intercepted, and neutralized.

After the foul-smelling, smoke-filled desert dust of the Mother of all Wars had settled, and the immediate threat to the United States of America had diminished, the task force remained in being. Since they'd done their initial assignments so superbly, the President ordered ITF-4 to continue, its job redefined to guard against all terrorism that threatened the country.

ITF-4 was lean, with only seven senior members and a small support staff, and their mission was clearly defined. Since their budget was modest by Washington standards and there was no publicity to be had due to their secrecy, they remained one of the most efficient units in the capital city. They achieved numerous successes and suffered few failures. Credit for their coups were claimed by other government agencies whose leaders did not shrink from announcing achievements. Due to that rare efficiency, others in government were covetous. Thus far ITF-4 had resisted all efforts to be absorbed by various agencies, bureaus, and departments. The current suitor was the new director of the National Security Council, who wanted to bolster the image of his organization after an endless series of international blunders.

Marian Sarah Lindquist had been a federal judge for nine years before the present administration had come to power in the Year of the Woman, and her work on the bench had been deemed daring, outstanding, and innovative. While hers was regarded as one of the finest legal minds in Washington, she'd been overlooked for higher office because she refused to be categorized as pro-life or pro-choice (she considered it a private matter) for or against the death penalty, or even liberal or conservative. She'd denounced politics in the courtroom, judged each case on its individual merit, and been unafraid to make unpopular decisions. When the first woman attorney general asked if Judge Lindquist would take the chair of the previously male-dominated ITF-4, she'd accepted.

Manuel G. DeVera, deputy chairman of the task force, had been number three in the State Department's Bureau of Intelligence, with a staff of forty. Now he had a staff of only four, but he felt the mission of ITF-4 was important. He also lusted after the tall, trim body of the chairman who'd been assigned there only weeks before himself.

He'd met Judge Lindquist at a cocktail party given in her honor by mutual friends, Linda and Paul "Lucky" Anderson, at their Falls Church home. Manny had been drawn by her pleasant smile and obvious intelligence. He'd also admired her full-breasted, high-waisted figure, which, although hidden under a simple yet tasteful dress, he'd somehow *known* to be spectacular.

He'd waited until her insignificant other—a stuffy law professor from Georgetown University—had gone to fetch a drink before approaching her. After a few words she'd politely turned away, as if something across the room caught her interest. When he'd gallantly persisted, she'd continued to ignore him.

"How about another time?"

She'd pinned him with a suffering expression, looking down, for in heels Marian S. Lindquist was slightly taller than Manny. "Not if you were the last remaining male on earth," she'd said quietly, and haughtily strode away.

He was drawn to women who knew their mind. The next week, when Manny had shown up at her office and introduced himself as the new representative for State, which meant he'd be deputy chairperson for ITF-4, she'd not mentioned the meeting in Falls Church. He'd interpreted that as giving him a new opportunity. After getting his things unpacked, he'd sauntered across to her office and casually mentioned dinner, maybe talking over the job and finding out what she expected? Judge Marian Lindquist had smiled as if she'd anticipated his offer, rose from her desk, and physically propelled him outside her office door before slamming it in his face.

He'd liked that about her, too. She was no pushover.

Four months had passed before she'd accepted his invitation to dinner, but by then the stuffy professor no longer escorted her about the city. Six months later he'd discreetly moved his things into her brownstone home in Georgetown. That had been two years earlier. Now things had come full circle. She hated him again, this time for making an injudicious statement over dinner that he could not even remember.

Judge Lindquist opened the meeting with her normal slap on the table, cutting off discussion between Cyrus White, representing CIA, and Slocum, from Treasury.

"Let's go to work," she announced. Marian was not in a good mood. "Where's the colonel?"

Manny lounged in the cheap armchair provided by the General Services Administration to masquerade as overstuffed leather and appear comfortable. "Got me," he said, looking to his right at Cyrus White. "He give you a call, Serious?" Manny called him "Serious" because it upset the technically minded analyst from CIA.

Cyrus White glared on cue, then turned to Marian. "He's at the Pentagon. Said he had something to attend to there."

"Damn it," she exploded. "When I call a meeting I want *everyone* here."

As if answering her call, Colonel Pershing C. Sloan, U.S. Army, entered the room and took his seat. He smiled at Judge Lindquist. "Weekend traffic was atrocious," he said.

Sloan held himself stiffly erect. He was prone to agree with all official edicts. Although somewhat of a pain to work with, he was also hardworking and tried to do the right thing.

Marian nodded for the young man at the front of the room, one of several agents who manned their small communications center, to proceed. Their official titles were Intelligence Duty Officers, and they remained astutely informed by gleaning information from national and international government organizations. IDOs were handpicked from the various agencies and were very good at their jobs. Those who were not, the judge sent packing.

The IDO launched into details of the explosion at Piccadilly station that had occurred six hours earlier. There were now 186 deaths by official count, and the number was expected to rise much higher. The Provisional IRA had taken credit for the bombing, their second since the fragile cease-fire had broken down in Northern Ireland.

Judge Marian Lindquist raised a hand, and the briefer paused.

"I've been in touch with Scotland Yard and the British Security Service. This one's confirmed as Ghost's doing. He made his phone call to the *Times* before the first explosion. I also received a call from the council, and they're upset." She referred to the National Security Council, now headed by Leonard Griggs, the President's buddy from his college days.

"We're getting involved," she added.

"Should we?" asked Colonel Sloan. "There's no threat to America."

"We'll stretch our charter," said Judge Marian. It wasn't the first time they'd become involved when Ghost's terrorists had performed atrocities in foreign countries. An American-born individual was known to be a member of the group.

Manny started to speak. "I'd like . . ."

"Later," the judge snapped meanly, and nodded for the duty officer to proceed. The IDO told as much as they had, which was little more than had been reported on CNN.

She dismissed him and turned back to the group at the conference table. "Ghost's modus is to depart the scene quickly. Department Five has their people monitoring all major air and seaports, but they're not hopeful. Picking Ghost's crew out will be next to impossible."

"Perhaps I can help." Cyrus White cast a look down the table. "I just received this from Langley. They took the video sequence from the Leonardo Da Vinci airport and came up with an acceptable computer enhancement." He held up an eight-by-ten glossy photo. "Charlie."

Marian Lindquist cleared her throat. "What's the probability it's him."

Cyrus smiled smugly. "They're sure he was one of the people shown in the image. When the enhancements were made, the others were too unbelievable. I'd say it's a sure thing."

As the photo was handed past, Manny intercepted it and stared. When Judge Lindquist received it, she also took a long look. Her eyes raised and caught Manny's. She'd noticed the same startling thing.

Marian drew in a calming breath and nodded to Cyrus White. "Fax and then send a hard copy to Department Five and the Anti-Terrorist Unit." Department Five of the British Security Service was popularly known as MI-5. The ATU was a subunit of Scotland Yard. Marian gave Cyrus names of the people she'd been working with.

Manny tried again. "I'd like to go over and give the blokes a hand."

Judge Lindquist frowned.

Manny continued quickly. "I'd like to take J.J. Davis along." Supervising Agent Davis ran the explosives investigations course at the FBI National Academy for law officers, and had a well-deserved reputation as the best at his business in the U.S., perhaps in the world.

Judge Lindquist suppressed an angry sigh. "Arguments?"

There were none. She paused for a long moment before giving a nod. "Approved. I'll forward the request to the Hoover Building and get them to spring Davis."

Manny knew she hadn't wanted to grant permission, but it made too much sense to deny him. They must be seen as doing everything possible to help the British. One of the senior staff members should go if only to wave the flag, and he was a logical choice.

He tried to smooth things. "After I learn what's going on, I'll call back with a report."

The discussion continued. Where would Ghost and his people hole up? They'd surely avoid Ireland, for the P-IRA was involved and a search would be underway there. Marseilles and Sicily were choices they explored, and Judge Marian said she'd speak with agencies in those countries. There was also Iraq, Libya, Sudan, and Iran, whose doors were always open to Ghost's group, but contacting their officialdom would be a joke.

As the meeting broke up, DeVera followed Marian, hoping her anger had subsided.

"We should have a . . . ah . . . certain matter looked into," he said.

"I suppose you're right."

"You should use your FBI people on it, Marian. We'll want it done quickly."

"I don't want it getting out that we're investigating him."

"Just a background check like he's going to work for the government."

A man resembling an obese, grinning Buddha waddled down the hallway toward them. Supervising Agent J.J. Davis had another man in tow.

Manny felt a moment of panic. He'd wanted to talk with J.J. before they saw Marian.

J.J.'s huffing voice was cheerful. "Judge, Manny. Well, we're packed and ready to go."

Marian Lindquist arched an eyebrow. "How did you know we'd call on you?"

"Soon as Manny phoned, I grabbed Jonesy here and hightailed over."

DeVera tried his winning smile on Marian. "I . . . ah . . . called the Hoover Building and got it cleared when I heard about the bombing. I thought you'd approve, and . . . you know."

Judge Lindquist's secretary came into the hall, smiling nicely at Manny. "I've got reservations for three at the Green Park Hotel in London, Mister DeVera."

"Thanks, Mimi," Manny muttered.

"You presumptuous ass!" Marian's face flushed hotly, growing redder by the second. She glared at Manny for a long, smoldering moment, then stalked into her office on wooden legs.

"Did I do something wrong?" Mimi asked.

"She's not been herself lately," Manny said forlornly.

3

Tuesday, January 17th

12:25 P.M.—The Farmhouse, Falls Church, Virginia

The Farmhouse presented an imposing appearance, situated some three hundred yards off the road on a gentle hilltop. A home had first been built there in 1770 for a Custis-Lee, an amalgamation of the two families who had been as close to royalty as Virginia could muster. That structure was burned in 1861 by Union soldiers returning from the ignominy of defeat at the First Battle of Bull Run. The current home had been built in 1885. It had been located in the rural countryside then. It was now at the periphery of an urban sprawl stretching to Baltimore.

Linda had looked for the right home in the Washington area when her husband returned to Southeast Asia in 1972. He'd commanded a combat wing, flying F-4 Phantoms from northern Thailand. Since she'd known that bullets didn't differentiate between colonels and lieutenants, she'd worried—and prayed for his homecoming. They'd learned he would be stationed at the Pentagon, and since she'd received a new position in the State Department hierarchy, Paul—she seldom used his nickname, Lucky—had given his approval to buy a house.

When the Farmhouse had caught her eye, Linda had hoped he would like it. She needn't have worried. On his first day home Lucky had taken Lincoln, then nine, and walked the twenty-two acre parcel as if it were a kingdom, planning where the barn and cross-fencing should go. Lucky had been enamored with the grounds, she with the ninety-year-old home, and young Link with the prospect of owning a horse.

The Farmhouse had contained seven bedrooms, but they'd converted one into Lucky's study and another into a studio where Linda painted and read. There was also a "great room" where they entertained, and a large kitchen, complete with its own fireplace, where they lived.

Their son's coming-of-age and their retirement had brought subtle changes to their lives. They'd sold the horses, an aging mare and gelding, for Link had been the equestrian of the family. They kept the two English setters that Lucky still took to the Blue Ridge on grouse hunting forays with air force cronies, but the agreeable canines now spent most of their time lounging near the kitchen fireplace and very little in the kennels behind the house.

Lucky and two friends had started a VIP flying service, and kept a Gulfstream, two Learjets, and three King Air propeller-driven aircraft sufficiently employed to continue the endeavor. The aircraft were hangared at Washington National. Lucky periodically took a turn on the schedule to keep his pilot's skills alive, but he was always happy to return home.

Linda spent her free time nurturing roses and trying to capture them in still life with oils or watercolors. Some paintings she displayed and sold at local art shows. A few she kept or gave to friends. Most she destroyed, for she felt she seldom captured their true beauty.

Altogether they led a pleasant and relatively uneventful life at the Farmhouse.

Earlier that blustery morning, Marian Lindquist had called to say she had a free afternoon and would like to drop by. Linda had answered that they'd be delighted to receive her. When Linda answered the door, she led Marian into the studio that was her private domain. Then she brought a pewter salver with a pot of hot tea from the kitchen and poured.

"Thank you," Marian said politely, and sipped from the teacup. "It's delightful and so *different.* What in the world do you use?"

"Loose Earl Grey, mixed with a splash of what Paul calls

his 'sun-brew.' He's secretive, but I believe it's a mixture of rhubarb and crushed berries."

"Delicious!"

Linda decided upon the direct route. "How are things with you and Manny?"

"I've never met a man who infuriated me *half* as much as Manny DeVera."

After listening to a full minute of diatribe against Manny and most of maledom, Linda decided she'd been right. She spoke in her gentlest voice. "You've got it bad, huh?"

Marian hugged a sigh. "He's the best thing that's ever happened in my life."

Linda lifted an eyebrow. "What did he do to upset you?"

They'd spent half an hour in Linda's studio when Lucky rapped on the door. He'd made sandwiches. The housekeeper took Tuesdays off, and they traded turns on meal preparations.

They ate in the kitchen, at the rustic table in front of the crackling fire. The sandwiches were wafer thin strips of corned beef piled on rye, topped with Swiss cheese and a dollop of homemade sauerkraut. They washed them down with homemade chowder made from fresh Chesapeake clams. The stuff was thick, with chunks of tasty vegetables and nuggets of clams.

He measured Marian's reaction with a critical eye. Between spoonfuls of chowder, she wagged her head at Linda. "How in the world do you stay thin with this guy around?"

"Easy," Linda responded. "I prepare every other meal, and I'm an awful cook."

Lucky grimaced. "That's what she says to try to get me to do *all* the cooking. No way."

Linda was preparing a repartee when Marian mentioned that her niece would visit during Easter vacation. She adored children, and had always been sad she'd had none of her own.

"You're fortunate," Marian said quietly, "to have a son like Link."

Linda agreed. "From the moment we saw him, there was no question. He was the one."

"How old was he?"

"Four. With big, expressive eyes and an alertness about him that was simply precious."

Marian smiled.

"The timing was perfect for him to enter our lives. Paul and I were going through a difficult period. We'd wanted children, but I was in my early thirties by then, and we knew we had to get on with things. When the doctors told us I'd be unable to give birth, we were devastated. Within a month we'd contacted an orphanage in Helena, Montana and flew out to take a look at an available child." Linda laughed. "It was love at first sight. When we walked out an hour later, Paul said we weren't going home unless he was with us, and I agreed."

"You made up your minds that quickly?"

"There was absolutely no question," Linda said softly. "Lincoln made us well. He made us a family. Of course that wasn't even his name then."

"Oh?" Marian was obviously interested.

Since her son was a favorite topic, Linda had no trouble continuing. "His name was shown as Black Albertson on the birth certificate. That's all. Black, like the color. It was a *horrid* name for a child. That night at the hotel, Paul said he knew what he wanted to change it to, and that was before we'd even signed the petition for adoption."

"My childhood hero was Abe Lincoln," Lucky said.

Their guest finished her chowder with appropriate gusto. "That was great!" Marian announced. "I wish Manny would cook."

"Men are hunters, women the keepers of the hearth," Lucky said in his friend's defense.

"Baloney," Linda snorted.

"Are you still upset with Manny?" he asked Marian. "Last time I saw him, he told me he'd said something the night before that he couldn't even remember and you were angry."

Linda shook her head sternly. "Paul, that's a topic between us girls. Stay out of it."

"He asked if I'd try to find out so he could apologize."

"Paul?" Linda chided.

Marian silently finished the last of her sandwich and dabbed her mouth with her napkin.

Lucky looked at her as if still hoping she'd tell.

She changed the subject back to Link. "Was the adoption process difficult?"

Linda shook her head. "Not at all. We'd inquired in several states and found nightmares of red tape involved. But in Montana, and especially with Indian children, we believe, it was easier. After only three weeks we were able to take him home to Virginia. Within six months the process was complete: adoption, name change, and all."

After a few minutes of idle chatter, Marian asked to see the adoption forms.

Linda hesitated thoughtfully, then said she'd retrieve them from her office safe. As she went there she wondered what Marian was about. Then she smiled to herself as she twirled the the dial on the recessed safe. She decided she knew the answer.

Linda brought out photos as well as the documents, then sat beside her friend.

First the folder with the official judgment, birth certificate, and name change form.

The birth certificate seemed alien for the son Linda cherished. *Name: Black Albertson—Date of Birth: (Est.) July 4, 1964—Place of Birth: Near Peshan, Montana Blackfeet Indian Reservation, State of Montana*—the block showing time of birth was left blank. *Father: Albertson* (no first name was shown)—*Mother: Sarah Layton.*

Marian examined the certificate. "It's certainly vague enough. *Estimated* date of birth?"

"All the sisters at the orphanage would tell us was that he was at least part Indian."

"Blackfoot, we assumed from the birth certificate," said Lucky. "We pressed for answers, but they either couldn't or wouldn't tell us more than you see there."

Marian picked up another form, this one changing the name from Black Albertson to Abraham Lincoln Anderson.

Lucky looked on inquisitively as Marian went through the papers, as if searching for something, but Linda gave him a small shake of her head so he'd hold his tongue.

"And that's all you know about his former family?" Marian asked.

Linda nodded. "When Link graduated from the academy, I gave him a copy of everything, thinking he might want to learn more about his origins. He didn't seem interested."

Lucky smiled. "All he wanted to do at the time was learn to fly fighters."

"That wasn't the only reason," Linda said. "Link was ashamed of being Native American. We tried to raise him without such prejudices, but it bothered him. When a friend of Paul's visited, a colonel who was a Cherokee Indian, Link refused to act civilly toward him."

"It was embarrassing," said Lucky. "Entirely out of character for him."

"He was a friendly child. I don't think it was something he could control," Linda said. "I believe it was a reaction from his past."

As Marian replaced the papers into the folder, Linda brought out photographs. Her heart warmed, as it did each time she showed them. First the earliest ones of Lincoln as a child. Next one in his Little League baseball outfit. A shot of a teenager with a grin and a football helmet under his arm. A posed photo of Link and his date on their way to the senior prom. Next several of him in his Air Force Academy cadet uniform.

"He graduated second in his class," said Linda, "and the competition was stiff. The commandant of the academy told Paul that Link's leadership potential was unlimited."

"He excelled in flight school, too," said Lucky. "Top in both academic and flying. His last instructor pilot rated him the best student he'd ever flown with . . . a natural pilot."

One of their favorite photos was of Second Lieutenant Lincoln Anderson standing stiffly at attention as Lieutenant General "Lucky" Anderson pinned silver wings on his chest.

There were several of Link as an air force pilot, wearing a gray, multi-pocketed flight suit. In one he stood beside a sleek F-16 jet fighter with a wide grin, in another beside an ungainly A-10 Warthog attack fighter, where he posed with a comic leer.

Lucky explained one where Link was awarded a trophy for winning a gunnery contest. "That was at Gunsmoke 90, at Nellis Air Force Base. He won the Top Gun award for bombing accuracy, which means he was the best in the air force. Hell of an achievement. Like I said, he's a good pilot," he said, "but he was also a fine officer. Junior officer of the year at his first operational assignment. Outstanding evaluation reports across the board."

"You must be very proud of him," Marian said softly.

"More than he or anyone else can imagine," said Lucky.

They were looking at their newest photo of Link. In that one he was not smiling. The eyes were narrowed, brooding, and hawk-like. It had been taken after the strafing incident in the Iraqi desert.

"Self-doubt is a cruel enemy," he said grimly. "No one can remove it but yourself."

Half an hour later, after Marian had made her excuses and departed, Lucky Anderson cast a curious look at his wife. "Why's she so interested in Link's past?"

Linda collected the photographs from the tabletop. "I believe she and Manny are getting serious about their future and considering adoption."

"I didn't think of that."

"We should give Link another phone call. It's been weeks since we spoke with him."

7:30 P.M.—Goodwick, Wales, United Kingdom

Ghost went to the window, pulled the curtain aside, and stared into the darkness. Charlie and Rashad Taylor were in the kitchen playing gin rummy, with Charlie winning as usual. Rashad didn't give much of a damn about games, and he presently had a bad case of cabin fever.

It was their fourth day in the cottage. The next morning they'd be secreted in the bowels of the auto ferry that traveled daily across the Irish Sea to Rosslare Harbor. After a short stay near Dublin, they'd proceed to the safe haven.

He watched a car pull up, then a man emerge and walk with a pronounced limp toward the cottage. IRA Major Jock Donovan cast cautious looks about as he approached. He didn't like working with Ghost's deadly crew, even though he was immune from their "cleanup" practices. Other than a single agent of each employer, few humans had seen their faces and survived.

Ghost let him inside.

Jock Donovan was rawboned and florid-faced, the kind of man who shouldn't grin because it made his face become uglier. Prominent, crooked teeth, and foul breath didn't help. He limped badly, the result of taking a bullet in the hip during an ill-conceived ambush on a British convoy in Ulster. He was not likable, but since he was their conduit, Ghost was forced to deal with him. In the course of his profession, he had worked with worse.

"I got news," Donovan hissed in his conspiratorial whisper, so Ghost called for the others to join them in the living room.

"Go ahead with it," Ghost told the Irishman.

"The bleedin' British are goin' crazy," Donovan said, flashing his ugly grin. "Got half o' their people in uniform searchin'. More'n three hundred dead at Piccadilly an' they's still findin' 'em. A couple newspapers are callin' for the government to negotiate for a new cease-fire, but most are screamin' for revenge."

Ghost nodded impatiently. "We got all that from watching television."

The toothsome grin. "The brigadier wants ye t' do another. Ye got their bleedin' attention. He's thinkin' one more big un might do the trick."

"You've got money for another?" Ghost's services didn't come cheaply.

Donovan's grin faded some. "We'll have it." The old IRA had made it a practice never to pay for atrocities. Those had been done for Mother Ireland by IRA martyrs, most of whom languished in British prisons. During the cease-fire, the disastrous agreement and the Ulster Defense Force had decimated the P-IRA's fighting capacity. When they'd resumed their militancy, they'd turned to Ghost. The success of Piccadilly showed the wisdom of their decision.

Ghost considered. "Maybe in a few months. I'll be in touch."

Jock Donovan hesitated. "A woman found a plastic bag floating in the River Wye."

Ghost's eyes narrowed. "And?"

"They was arms an' a man's head in th' bleedin' thing."

Ghost turned his gaze on Rashad, who mumbled, "Shoulda put more rocks in the bag."

"Yes" was all Ghost said, but his look was cold. During the trip from London, he'd told the IRA lieutenant posing as a London cabbie to turn into an empty field. Rashad had taken three plastic trash bags with him as he'd urged the sobbing man toward the river at knife point.

Cleanup. The man had looked into the rearview mirror too often. Their employer should have briefed him that Ghost did not like his men to be observed close-up.

Ghost turned back to Donovan. "What else?"

"We're gettin' attention from other countries as well.

There's a to-do in Europe lookin' for ye, an' the Czech Republic's sendin' some kind of chemical analyst."

"Their people made the explosives. It's an embarrassment for them."

"Even Dublin's sayin' it was too much."

"That's just words. Is your brigadier nervous about the attention?"

The IRA man's grin widened. "Not bleedin' likely. It's what he was after. Like I said, he'll be wantin' another contract."

"And the investigation in London?"

"Goin' nowhere we know of, but our boys are keepin' their heads low."

"The reaction in the States?"

"Th' President sent a message to the Prime . . ."

"Damn it, we know that," Ghost interrupted. "What's happening we *don't* know?"

Donovan grinned nervously. Although he tried to be chummy, he was frightened of Ghost and his crew. Fear made the rotten odor from his mouth more pronounced.

"How about ITF-four?" Ghost prodded. Like Ghost, the Provisionals knew about the task force. Irish-American contacts within the United States government reported on their activity.

Donovan motioned his head at Rashad. "The President's people was bleedin' upset when they learned a Yank was in on Piccadilly. The ITF sent a team to Lunnon."

"Go on."

"A guy named DeVera's in charge."

"How many total?"

"Just three. There's DeVera, another named Davis, and a black nigger . . ."

"An FBI agent named *J.J.* Davis?"

Donovan wrinkled his brow. "He's FBI, but I'm not remembering a first name."

Ghost had heard only vaguely of DeVera, but he knew about Davis. He'd been called in after other of their operations and would not let go. On two occasions sources of explosives had been traced and intermediaries arrested. Davis had once tracked Ghost's group to a safe house in Paris, and they'd only escaped in the nick of time.

"Where's J.J. Davis staying in London?" Ghost asked Donovan.

"The Yank team's in a hotel next to Green Park."

"I see." Ghost continued to think about the agent. Davis didn't hesitate to bend laws. His doggedness and the fact that he didn't respect rules made him doubly dangerous.

Donovan continued. "The Canadians are sending a team to help, too. They got . . ."

"I'm going to my room," Ghost said abruptly.

Donovan grew his nervous grin. "I'll drop back in a couple of hours an' take ye to the boat."

"Stay here until I return." It was not a request.

Ghost entered the dark bedroom and closed the door behind himself, brooding about the FBI investigator. He lay upon the bed, evened his breathing, and closed his eyes, thinking about J.J. Davis and the hazard he posed.

A short while later his eyes blinked open. Ghost took a deep breath, which he released in a slow sigh, then rolled catlike off the bed. When he returned to the living room the others were still seated, Rashad talking about how he needed a woman, Jock Donovan promising they'd have one for him when he got to Dublin.

"Charlie," Ghost called quietly. Rashad became silent as Charlie rose from his seat.

"You're going back," he said. "They won't expect that." He explained what he wanted done and told Donovan to provide necessary support.

"I dunno," Donovan said dubiously. "It takes time to set up somethin' like that."

"It must be done immediately. They won't expect us to return." Ghost looked evenly at the IRA conduit. "This one's free. Your people can take credit, and it won't cost a cent."

"I'll see what the brigadier says, but I'm not bein' hopeful."

"If he refuses, this will be the last contract we perform for him." He let that sink in. There were other leverages he could use, but he doubted he'd need them. The incomparable success of Piccadilly made them invaluable to the IRA—and to a dozen similar groups.

"I'll be getting back with his answer," Donovan said, still whispering.

Ghost continued as if it was agreed upon. "Rashad and I will go on to Dublin."

"I'll tell the brigadier what you want," said the crippled IRA man.

After Donovan's departure, Ghost spelled out details for Charlie. "All three of them, but especially J.J. Davis."

"I understand."

Ghost told him how and when to contact him next, and repeated the number until Charlie had it memorized. He went to his valise and retrieved an identity packet, complete with passport, international drivers license, and credit cards.

"When are we going home?" Charlie asked wistfully.

Ghost's voice softened. "I'll tell you on Friday. It won't be much longer."

8:40 P.M.—Boudie Springs, Montana

Jamie's Pub, the town's favorite watering hole, had been discovered by the latest crop of skiers and was filled to overflowing. A would-be cowboy crooned in nasal tones from the stage, accompanied by guitar and fiddle, obscured from view by a mob of Texas two-stepping couples.

Link was seated in the farthest corner of the room, sipping on Coors and tomato juice and trying to ignore the riot scene. Deputy Ernie Gilchrist sidled through the crowd toward him; bending awkwardly to avoid a young woman who squealed as she was twirled by her partner, excusing himself when he bumped into an arm-waving tourist.

Ernie looked as Link envisioned Ichabod Crane: tall, skinny, and seemingly disjointed. He wore a grin that stretched his mouth and looked forced, but was not. He liked people and was friendly with most, but just watching him somehow made observers grow uneasy.

The deputy arrived and hovered. "How ya doin', pardner?" He screamed the words so they were heard over the music.

Link nodded his response.

Ernie arched an eyebrow as if he knew something. Link didn't ask, knowing if he waited Ernie would be unable to contain his secret. Deputy Gilchrist could talk about inconsequential things for hours. If he had news, it would quickly bubble its way through his lips.

"You hear about two guys askin' questions?"

Link waited.

"Not s'posed to tell you . . . at least I don't think I am."

Link sipped his drink.

"This morning these two FBI guys showed up, flashed their badges, an' said they were checking up on . . . somebody." He leered, awaiting a response. Getting none, he nodded to himself, then carefully looked about the room. Satisfied the FBI agents weren't lurking nearby, he turned to Link. "They wanted to know how long you'd been here, where you work, what you've been up to the past few months, things like that."

FBI? Link wondered. Myra had mentioned that someone had been asking about him.

"I tol' em you were just doin' the normal things like everyone here. Runnin' drugs, robbin' banks, shootin' people, stuff like that." Ernie chuckled.

Link nodded his thanks. If the agents wanted their inquiries to remain secretive, they'd come to the wrong town. The year-round residents of Boudie Springs welcomed the money brought by outsiders, but they remained a clannish group.

"I tol' em how you found those tourists the other . . . *damn!*" A scuffle had begun on the dance floor, and Ernie did not appreciate his gossiping to be interrupted. He stretched and peered over heads, then started there, demanding in his megaphone voice for the fight to stop.

As Link wondered about the agents, Annie Bright Star's moon-shaped face loomed.

"Mind if I sit with you?"

He nodded, which she took as an invitation.

"Sure is crowded," she said.

"Yeah."

She leaned forward conspiratorially. "Two men were at Borealis asking about you."

"Oh?" Link watched as the scuffle became something more serious. One of the tourists turned toward Ernie Gilchrist and punched a finger into his chest. The other pushed his face into Ernie's and both men began venting their anger on the intruder.

"You were on the mountain setting off that last charge," Annie was saying. "They talked to a couple of guys on the ski patrol, then to me."

Link continued to observe the situation on the dance floor.

"They said it was a routine background check. Asked where you go, are you on drugs or a heavy drinker, things like that."

Link nodded. The pugilist with his finger in Ernie's chest was shouting, the other nodding agreement and urging him not to back down. Both were middle-aged. Probably friends who'd had too much to drink and gotten into a squabble Ernie should have left alone.

Annie looked at him with a nervous smile. She sometimes grew tongue-tied around Link. Others at work joked about the way she cast puppy dog looks in his direction.

"Can I ask something?" Her voice held a trill. "You look like one of the People, Link."

"The people?"

"You know. Native American?" Annie noted his frown, and blurted. "I didn't mean anything *bad* by that."

"Hey!" Gilchrist's voice sounded. The man pointing the finger had pushed the deputy against a table. His cohort began to grapple with Ernie Gilchrist, who had to learn to stay out of a shuffle-and-shove between friends.

Annie was observing the melee. "Ernie's about to lose his pistol," she commented. Gilchrist's revolver threatened to drop out of his unsnapped holster.

Bullshit! Link gained his feet and pushed his way through the crowd. A beefy onlooker refused to move aside so he pushed hard, sending him sprawling into the finger-pointer.

The tourist and Ernie were still wrestling when the pistol fell and skittered on the floor.

Link's moves were lightning quick. With his right hand he scooped up the revolver—with his left he grasped the pugilist's collar and dragged him off Ernie.

"Watch it!" someone yelled to Link. Finger-pointer was launching a roundhouse swing.

Link shifted the man in his grasp—the fist smacked into the side of his head. When Link released him, he dropped to his knees. Finger-pointer held his hand before himself, grimacing.

Link brought the revolver down medium-hard on Finger-pointer's bruised hand. He yelped and backpedaled, cradling the hand as if it was a child as Link hauled Ernie to his feet and shoved the revolver into his holster.

"Thanks." Ernie huffed, eyeing the subdued tourists.

"Keep your damned pistol strapped down," Link said angrily. "Someone could get hurt." He turned, slipped through the crowd, and headed toward the door.

With the temperature back to a normal twenty above zero, the snowfall was heavier and there were more potential avalanche buildups at the ski resort. Those kept Link busy at work. The snows also meant more to shovel and plow, and that occupied much of his time at home.

He pulled into the driveway, wallowed through the stuff until the truck was in position, then shut off the engine. After plugging into the electrical receptacle, he went inside, high-stepping and deciding to put off his snow removal chores until morning.

After he had the fire blazing and the fan blasting heat into the room, Link's thoughts returned to the FBI agents. He eyed about the room suspiciously, wondering if they'd been there, then realized they couldn't have approached the cabin without leaving tracks. Not even federal bureaucrats could do that.

Their presence in Boudie Springs likely had something to do with the tragedy—strafing the friendlies in the desert—and none of the locals knew about that part of his life. Link wanted to be angry, shout that he was putting in his penance, but he could not. He deserved whatever was handed him. Regardless of inquiry findings and the excuses his government had mouthed, he'd always be damned by the eight doomed men in the armored personnel carrier.

There were messages on the answering machine, one from Lucky asking him to call, another from a neighbor telling him about FBI agents asking questions.

Too late back east to return his father's call, he rationalized. Link had ignored their recent pleas, telling himself he didn't want to saddle them with his concerns.

After his return from Saudi Arabia, his mother had suggested that he visit a therapist to help with the terrible guilt. Although she was trying to help, the advice had hastened his decision to seek his own solutions. Link idly wondered if he was indeed going mad. In the past nights there had been more dreams about the men in the desert, more accusations from within. He'd found himself yearning for the return of the comforting old man he called the Grandfather.

As he prepared for bed, Link thought of Annie's question. As a child he'd been uneasy that he was part Indian, no matter that his parents encouraged him to take pride in the fact. He'd wanted to be precisely like Lucky Anderson. When he learned that his real father was listed as only a last name, and that his mother had obviously abandoned him, he'd known there was something less than desirable there. By the time he was a teenager, Link felt he was likely the result of a casual union between a drunken buck and squaw. He'd come to think of Native Americans as weak-willed aborigines. When questioned about the dark hue of his skin, he'd tell schoolmates he had Hispanic blood from his mother's side.

When one of his father's friends had visited the Falls Church Farmhouse—a colonel named Billy Bowes whom Link learned was full-blooded Cherokee—he'd acted a brat. After Bowes had left, Lucky had asked what in the world had possessed him. Link hadn't responded for he'd known his father would never understand.

His father said Bowes had saved his life in combat and described the man's heroism. But even after Link apologized, he'd not altered his disdain for Indians . . . Colonel Bowes included. Yet his earliest memory was of the somber and comforting man called the Grandfather, and *his* face was dark, haphazardly streaked with dull red paint. Was he the image of an Indian? It was all very confusing, then and now.

He dropped off to sleep thinking of the Grandfather's odd visage.

Link came partially awake, aware he'd been moving about the bed and talking in his sleep. He peered at the bedside clock; it was almost midnight.

As he attempted to return to sleep, he tried to remember the words he'd been muttering as he'd awakened. As he drifted closer to slumber, they came to him. *Come home.*

Glimpses of the dream returned in flickered snapshots. The Grandfather had been at his side, but he had difficulty recalling the subjects of his ramblings and the images they'd brought.

"Come home."

There'd been a crow—a thicket of trees. There'd been a dark man whose head oddly changed to bright red.

"Come home. Prepare yourself."

He recalled the dream more clearly. The dark man had been thin, and he had a pencil-line mustache. In the next image his head had erupted in a spray of red.

None of it made the slightest sense, but of course dreams seldom do, and the still photo scenes were soon forgotten. When he slept again, he did so soundly and the dream did not return.

4

Thursday, January 19th

7:05 A.M.—Green Park Hotel, London, United Kingdom

Women! Manny trotted down the stairs of the old hotel, wishing he'd gotten more sleep. He'd been up late speaking with Marian on the phone, and for the hundredth time had pleaded for her to tell him what he'd said to make her that angry.

She'd said if he was so insensitive that he didn't know, she wasn't about to tell him. Then she'd bade him an imperious *good night,* and abruptly hung up. He'd repeatedly and in great detail gone over the events of the dinner where he'd made his faux pas, but could not for the life of himself remember anything he'd done to so arouse her.

He paused at the edge of the dining room, still brooding about Marian.

"Over here" came a loud voice. J.J. Davis motioned from a table against the far wall, where his bulk dwarfed and abused a straight-back chair. Hiram Jones, his younger and much leaner assistant, was seated at his side.

"You look like hell," J.J. said cheerfully as he approached.

"Good morning to you, too," Manny replied.

The waiter took orders. Coffee and juice for all. Continental breakfasts for Jones and Manny. Four poached eggs, a double order of ham, potatoes, and breakfast scones for J.J. Davis.

"Anything new?" Manny asked as they launched into their morning discussion.

Davis and his assistant were working with the British Security Service. The previous morning J.J. had reported that they were cooperative and seemed pleased about his assistance.

"Yeah. You hear the television announcements?"

Manny nodded as he swigged orange juice. The evening's airwaves had been full of MI-5's findings. A Security Service spokesman had pointed out placement of the bombs on a diagram of the underground station. This morning he'd made a new announcement, for a search team had discovered appropriately scorched fragments of inexpensive luggage material. The explosives, the spokesman said, had been packed in suitcases.

"Do you agree?" Manny asked.

J.J. shrugged. "Probably, but they're too quick with the announcement. There's pressure to come up with answers, and they're so anxious to give them they're prone to make mistakes."

Davis treated each investigation as a personal challenge. The current FBI director called him outrageously independent, thoroughly insubordinate, and the best explosives investigator in the business. When J.J. Davis made a statement, you could put it in the bank.

His assistant, a slight and eager black agent with a thin mustache, said he'd examined the electronic device taped to a sign at the mouth of the station. "It was professionally done," Hiram Jones said. "A compact, dual frequency receiver transmitter."

"Not *that* professional," Davis corrected. "It was supposed to self-destruct five minutes after the firing signals were relayed."

"It would have," the agent said, "except wind from the explosions jarred it and broke the trigger wire. The electronics worked just fine."

J.J. huffed. "Still a screwup." He looked at Manny. "Jonesy's Ghost's latest admirer. Thinks he's infallible."

"I didn't say that," Hiram Jones said defensively. "I just said he was damned good."

"So am I," Davis responded, then quickly corrected himself. "So are we. We'll find them." There wasn't the slightest doubt in his voice.

J.J. Davis was not modest. He despised terrorists, knew what their explosives could do to human innocents, and was determined to stop Ghost. While he'd not been able to do so in the past, he'd succeeded in drying up sources of explosives and running intermediaries to ground.

"Nineteen more bodies yesterday," Davis said. "Brings the total to three hundred seventy-six. That'll grow when they find they've got more pieces than they need to fill caskets."

"Still think it was plastique?" Manny asked.

"I can smell the stuff. You read about Semtech being odorless, but that's bullshit. Semtech smells like dirty socks, which is why the shitheads have to make sure it's sealed. Soon as I get a spectral breakdown, I'll go to the plant and start tracing it."

"The Czechs sent an analyst."

"A government chemical engineer. I want to talk to company people. Back when they were commies, they passed out explosives like it was candy. After Ghost used it on the Uffizi Gallery, they tightened up their record keeping."

Hiram Jones frowned at Davis. "I don't see how you'll get batch identification. All six bombs fully detonated. If one had gone off with a partial, maybe . . ."

Davis raised his hand to silence his assistant. "Jonesy, learn to listen more and talk less."

Hiram grew silent, but didn't appear convinced.

J.J. snorted. "I know more about high explosives than you'll pick up in a couple lifetimes. Like the fact that since '92 the Semtech plant's added spectral-coded variants so they can tell the production run. Did you know that?"

"No, sir."

"You weren't supposed to. If every blabbermouth junior agent around knew that, the word would get out. But you won't be a blabbermouth, right Jonesy?"

"Of course not, sir."

"Anyway," J.J. said, "if the plastique was manufactured in the past couple years, I can track its history and find out who was involved along the way. Ghost prefers mercury-flow fuzes, so we'll check those sources, too."

The waiter brought breakfast. Manny sipped the watery stuff the English insisted was coffee and broke open a sweet roll.

"How about you, Manny?" Davis poked a poached egg

into his mouth, followed by half a blueberry scone and a chunk of ham. J.J.'s eating habits were not delicate.

DeVera had been working with Scotland Yard's Anti-Terrorist Unit. The two agencies, Scotland Yard and British Security Service, were aloof rivals, battling for publicity and credit—to help justify ever-dwindling budgets from Parliament—but both went out of their way to cooperate with the Yanks from ITF-4 who would let them take credit for their findings.

"ATU's looking for the safe house and interviewing everyone who was around the phone booth Ghost used to make his call to the *Times*."

"Anyone see him?"

"A lot of people think so. A merchant watched two blacks arguing with an Arab outside his shop. Two men were looking out a window above the square before the first blasts went off. A couple punkers bumped into a guy in dreadlocks. A pickpocket lifted a wallet off a Hindu. He turned it in, trying to do his part. A woman saw two men standing on the sidewalk, looking back at the station. Those are a few of the useful sightings. Some of the others are real lulus."

"And the safe house?"

"They're looking at places vacated the day of the bombing."

The three men continued talking, J.J. sputtering bits of eggs and ham when it was his turn. By ten minutes of eight, they'd finished eating.

Manny paused in the lobby to pick up a morning newspaper while the others went out to hail a taxi. GHOST SIGHTED IN MARSEILLES, the banner shouted.

The story, however, consisted of secondhand accounts from citizens swearing they'd spotted Ghost's gang checking into different hotels, one of them dressed as a rather svelte female. "Bullshit," Manny muttered, but he continued reading as he pushed through the door and emerged onto the street.

J.J. Davis had his hand up, summoning the next taxi in the nearby lineup.

"You see this?" Manny called to him, and held up the paper.

"What's that?" Davis asked, and turned.

Manny's brain hardly registered the next image. Davis's

jaw slewed sideward, and a spray of white issued from his mouth. J.J. staggered as the crack of the rifle sounded.

"Get down!" Manny yelled. As he propelled himself toward the nearest parked vehicle, his eyes shifted to Jones, whose head was swiveled, mouth drooped in amazement as he stared at Davis. There was a flash of red as the front portion of the black agent's skull exploded.

As Manny continued his downward movement, a third round narrowly missed him. He knew, for he felt the rush of air as it passed his ear.

8:00 A.M.—ITF-4 Offices, Department of Justice, Washington, D.C.

Judge Marian Lindquist was entering the conference room to open the emergency meeting when Mimi hurried in to tell her she had a call from Leonard Griggs, director of the NSC.

At first Marian thought of calling him back. She prudently reconsidered, even though it had been a nightmarish morning, and returned to her office.

"Judge Lindquist," she said into the telephone, trying to maintain a reasonable tone.

Griggs didn't pause for niceties, but immediately launched into a tirade about the shootings of the two FBI agents on loan to ITF-4. "Didn't you think of the possibility something like this might occur if you sent agents to be placed in jeopardy?"

The day before, Leonard Griggs had demanded that ITF-4 take stronger action.

"For Christ's sake, those agents were Americans. Americans! Yet you placed them in harm's way without proper protection."

Marian found her voice. "That's ridiculous. We didn't purposefully place *anyone* at risk."

"Learn to think, woman. Use your head for something more than a place to swab makeup. We will *not* have a replay of the embarrassment in Waco."

"There is absolutely no parallel. This time . . ."

"*This* time I am not going to stand for it." He paused, and his breathing was harsh over the line. "I'm withdrawing all FBI support from your task force."

"If you'll examine our charter, you'll find FBI support is required by presidential order."

"Not *this* President. *This* one's not a swaggering fool."

"*All* police and intelligence agencies are to support us. We don't have the manpower . . ."

"We'll see about that charter, too," Griggs spat out, and the line was disconnected.

Marian paused for a moment, collecting herself before placing a call to her immediate boss, the attorney general, and relating what had transpired.

"Don't worry about it," the attorney general said. "Len gets hostile whenever he feels someone may be about to criticize his empire. If you want, I'll speak to the President about it."

"I'm not asking for that," Marian said. "I just wanted to make sure you knew about a potential problem."

"Your charter's intact. We need you right where you are, Marian. Brief me as soon as you've got something on the shootings."

"I will."

When she hung up, Judge Lindquist knew the matter was not closed. Leonard Griggs, the former antiwar firebrand and college buddy of the President's, had only held the post at NSC for four months, replacing a serene-natured academician who'd become a liability for the presidency by being labeled a thorough wimp.

Griggs could not, by his worst detractor, be called a wimp. The first time she'd briefed him, he'd decided the task force should be a subcommittee under control of the NSC. The idea made sense to a growing number of presidential advisers, regardless of Marian's arguments that it would dilute the task force's independence and therefore their effectiveness.

She reentered the conference room, trying to conceal the emotion the call had created, opened the meeting, and called out to Mimi that they were ready for Mr. DeVera's call. A moment later his voice sounded over the speaker before her, and Judge Marian S. Lindquist's heart fluttered happily. He'd escaped injury! She calmed herself enough to answer.

"We hear you loud and clear, Manny. Give us a rundown on what happened."

"Three shots were fired," he said. "All in rapid succession with less than two seconds between. Two hits, one miss. I went out there as soon as I had medical help for Davis, but the shooter was long gone."

"Damn it, Manny, we don't need any John Wayne theatrics."

"The bobbies closed the park and interviewed everyone inside, which wasn't many because it was so chilly. A lady said she'd seen a man in an overcoat with a guitar case, and we got a description. It was pretty general, but I'm sure it was Charlie."

"How's J.J.?" she asked, unable to keep concern from her voice.

"He's got a badly shattered jaw and lost some bone and teeth. If he hadn't been moving, he'd be in worse than serious condition. I'll talk to him this afternoon if he's lucid. Make that sign language or something. They're still working on his jaw at the hospital."

Colonel Pershing Sloan raised his voice. "You really think it was Charlie?"

"Yeah. The shooter was two hundred and fifty yards out, in a thicket of trees. I got a look at the casings before Scotland Yard collected them."

"He left the casings? That's unusual."

"He had to get out of there in a hell of a hurry, Colonel. Bang, bang, bang, and go!"

"How about the casings?"

"Similar to a .22-250, like Charlie prefers, but these were necked down .308 cartridges. They had marks like an autoloader leaves. Makes sense, with the shots coming that fast."

Cyrus White spoke up. "Why are you so sure it was Charlie?"

"Everything fits, Serious."

The CIA representative visibly bristled at the nickname, and Marian suppressed a smile as Manny continued.

"Long-distance head shots. Great accuracy. And it makes sense that Ghost doesn't want us here. Especially J.J. Davis, because he almost caught him once before."

"I don't think we should *automatically* assume it was Charlie," said Cyrus White. "Charlie hasn't missed like that in the past."

"J.J. and I were moving targets. Everything considered,

it was great shooting. Tell you what, Serious, you come on over here and stand still, and we'll see if he does better."

Cyrus glared at the speaker. "In the past, Ghost's people haven't stayed around after an operation to shoot anyone. Why are you assuming they remained there this time?"

"I'm not, Serious. I don't know if they're on their way to Pago Pago. But Charlie was sure as hell here this morning."

The colonel spoke up. "How's the manhunt going?"

"There's a massive search. Roadblocks everywhere, and the motor police are checking every automobile leaving the city. Scotland Yard's making a sweep of hotel rooms and apartments, and reinforcing surveillance at all airports and seaports in the British Isles."

Marian broke in. "Thanks, Manny. Stay on the line, and I'll talk to you from my office."

"Will do."

Marian switched off the speaker and turned the meeting over to Colonel Sloan, who was her deputy in Manny's absence. She hurried to her office and grabbed up the telephone.

"You're okay?"

"Just a few pavement burns from crawling around and whimpering."

"Damn it, watch out for yourself!"

"I will." He paused. "I miss you."

She blew an angry breath. "I wish you hadn't gotten your testosterone up and decided you had to go on this one."

"I'll be fine, Marian."

"I got the report back on Link. He hasn't left Montana during the past two years."

"Good," Manny said. "That clears him early, before others might want to take a look."

"I talked with Lucky and Linda, wondering if Link might have a look-alike relative."

"You told them?"

"Of course not. Anyway, their records don't tell much. I had the bureau send an agent to Helena, Montana and check with the orphanage where they found Link, but they aren't cooperative. It took a court injunction to determine what other records they had, and they turned out to be nil. Link was a foundling, Manny, and there's nothing more to learn."

"That's okay. Our objective was to clear him early, and

we've done that. I've got another idea bouncing around in my head. I'll share it when I get home."

"When will that be?"

"A few more days. I've got a feeling Ghost may have finally screwed up. Charlie's in town, and we've got an acceptable photo of him."

"I've got to return to the briefing."

"I'll call tomorrow."

Marian bristled. "You'll phone me tonight at home."

"There's the time difference, and . . ."

"I don't care if it's three in the morning there. Call me at home."

His voice became lighter. "I thought you were mad at me."

"No, I hate you. There's a difference. That doesn't mean I don't expect a call every night, or that I don't worry." Marian slammed down the receiver and returned to the meeting.

5

Friday, January 20th

1:30 A.M.—Boudie Springs, Montana

Eight young men are crowded into the rear compartment of the armored personnel carrier, bouncing along as they continue across the desert, apprehensive because they haven't yet engaged the enemy and are unsure of their responses when they come under fire. Joking nervously and snickering at anecdotes that seem funnier than usual.

The attack is sudden. A hail of 30mm projectiles slice through the armor plating as if it is butter, the depleted uranium bullets creating deadly gas that fills the interior. Three men, the lucky ones, are killed instantly. The others are severely wounded by flying debris and shards of shrapnel. Their deaths will be more agonizing and much slower. Shrieks from the . . .

Link was crying out as he bolted upright, tense, eyes wide, trembling. He slowly relaxed, sighed deeply. The nightmare came nightly. The same scene, with little variation.

He slid his long legs out of the bed and sat hunched over, wet with perspiration that glistened from his heavily muscled chest in the dancing reflections of the fire. After a moment he rose and padded to the living area. Although there were two bedrooms, in winter months he closed them off and used a pull-down bed opposite the fireplace. It was easier to heat that way.

Link stared at the flickering light of the fireplace, still apprehensive about returning to bed. He'd tried pills to aid his sleep, but they only made the nightmares appear more vivid.

Link refilled the insert stove with two small aspen logs. The room was sufficiently warm that he turned down the blower. He paced for a while, and finally took a seat in his overstuffed chair, eyes still drawn by the flame, his mind busy with anything other than the dead men.

He was tired—so damnably tired—and knew he must rest, but he was fearful of the nightmare, and . . . His eyes closed, and he drifted into a sleepy reverie.

The wood smoke is mixed with steam from rocks piled at their feet in the center of the brush hut. The Grandfather is there—serious as always—looking at him kindly—speaking words that are strange yet understandable to the young child. There are vague and meaningless visions.

Something about a wolf. A small dark bird. Something about honor.

"Come home."

"Prepare yourself."

Link blinked himself awake. He grunted in his sleepiness. This time the Grandfather had appeared, but he'd provided little of the solace Link had come to expect.

9:20 A.M.—Manor Kilhooney, near Ballyboghil, Republic of Ireland

After the ferry docked in the slip at Rosslare Harbor on Wednesday, they'd waited for darkness. Then Donovan had driven Ghost and Rashad into the Irish countryside, avoiding main roads and urban areas. After four hours, he'd taken them through the gates of an estate he said was the property of a *friend*, and pulled up to a modest-sized guest house set discreetly away from the manor. The place was adequate. They'd be there for no more than three or four days.

Rashad was unhappy nonetheless. He had to stoop at the doorways and complained the low ceilings made him feel like a "fuckin' midget." Jock Donovan explained that the guest house was two hundred years old. The Irish had been shorter then and built them like that to conserve warmth. It hadn't helped Rashad's temperament. His displeasure was due to another matter.

When they'd entered the safe house, Rashad had looked vainly for the woman Donovan had promised. He'd grumbled about it continuously ever since, and his looks became especially dark whenever their host visited.

They were in the small living room, Ghost reading the Dublin newspaper. The results of Charlie's lone-wolf operation had made page one. Nothing like the banner headlines of Piccadilly, but prominent enough. One American FBI agent killed and another badly wounded, the article read in a neutral tone. Killings of Americans weren't normally well-received, for Irishmen felt close kinship with the United States, but these men had been helping the British—and regardless of official rapport, Dubliners regarded the Brits as usurpers of Irish soil.

No names were given in the article, so Ghost had to wait and hope that it had been J.J. Davis who'd been killed.

Rashad was testing the keenness of the thick-bladed, heavy knife he carried in a sheath strapped to his keg-size calf. It was his favorite weapon, a present from Ghost, and he kept it razor sharp. Taylor was good with knife work, had demonstrated how it could be used to delicately filet living muscle cleanly from a bone or, with application of pressure, cleave through a man's leg joints.

Ghost looked up at the sound of voices, then frowned as Donovan limped into the room, pushing a reluctant teenage girl before himself.

The colleen was no more than fourteen, and darted a wide-eyed, frightened gaze between the men in the room. She had an upturned pug nose, large, light blue eyes, and an oval face sprinkled with freckles. She was overweight, and only beginning to develop breasts and widen in the hip. Moisture bled freely onto her cheeks from crying.

Donovan shoved the girl forward, and she uttered a sharp whimper. Rashad regarded her with a tentative expression. She stood very still, eyes fixed on the knife. Taylor placed it on the tabletop, then wordlessly stood and reached for her hand. She held back, so he grasped her arm and pulled her roughly toward his room.

As the bedroom door partially closed behind him, Ghost

turned to Donovan. "I told you to bring her blindfolded. I expect you to do as you're told where security is involved."

Donovan made his death's-head grin. "Guess I forgot."

Ghost glanced at the door. "She's a kid."

"She's the bleedin' daughter of a British major in Ulster."

They heard the sound of a loud slap, then the girl crying.

"I tol' her if she pleases him, I'll turn her loose. Kep' whining about being a virgin all the way comin' over." Donovan licked his lips, nervous about Ghost's displeasure.

Ghost dismissed the girl from his mind. "How about London? Did you get names?"

"The dead man's Jones, the black nigger. Davis was shot in the jaw, but he's alive. T'other missed."

Ghost's eyes narrowed. He glanced at his watch and stood. "I'm going to take a drive."

"Need me along?"

"No." Ghost went to his room and retrieved a holstered Walther 9mm from the bedside table, clipped it to his belt at the small of his back, and pulled on a windbreaker. As he entered the living room, there were noises of movement from the bedroom. Rashad grunted loudly, and the girl cried out. Donovan sat staring at the partially closed door, his face a taut mask, lips drawn to expose his badly stained teeth. He scarcely noticed as Ghost went out.

The Irish road was in poor repair, but improved some as he bypassed Dublin Airport. A few miles farther he parked the Fiat on a side street of Ballymun, a suburb at the northernmost sprawl of the Irish capital city. Ghost prudently locked the vehicle, then walked two blocks until he arrived at a telephone booth at a quiet intersection.

The booth was empty, the telephone in working order.

He'd waited for only eight minutes when the bell jangled. Ghost picked up. "Go ahead."

Charlie introduced himself as Doctor Spencer. He spoke in their code, and said the police were swarming about the area but hadn't yet visited his new apartment.

"I expected better results, Doctor," Ghost admonished.

Charlie paused. Finally, "Do you want me to meet with the patient again."

"It's time to go home. Use the southern exit." Since Charlie's safe house was in Bromley, Ghost had just told him to fly out of Gatwick rather than Heathrow. "You'll be first to operate . . . as usual, Doctor. Do you foresee any problems?"

"No." Charlie's voice was contrite.

"Give me a call as soon as you get there. Say at . . . noon?" He'd told Charlie to subtract three hours from whatever he told him on the phone.

Ghost hung up, looked about casually, then crossed the street, nodded amiably at a grocer merchant sweeping the walk in front of his small store, and walked back toward the Fiat.

Charlie would proceed to their safe haven using the identity Ghost had provided. Which meant he would call the day after tomorrow at nine to tell him the way was clear and the cabin secure. Ghost and Rashad would follow.

Charlie always went ahead. The authorities didn't have a good description of any of them, but Charlie was likely the least known of all.

He heard a voice hailing from behind, and turned. A florid-faced policeman was hurrying toward him. Ghost's body tensed as he formed a bashful smile.

The copper stopped before him, giving a stern look. "And I suppose you're thinking you can cross the street any place you please?"

Ghost's look turned more sheepish. "I ver' sorry, sor." He spoke with halting difficulty.

The policeman pursed his lips. "And where are you from, lad?"

"Sout' America, sor." He fished in his pocket and came up with a card that read he was Victor Gomez, representing an import corporation headquartered in Brazilia. Ghost worked his mouth energetically, having trouble forming the English words. "I visit wit' de trade show, sor."

The policeman examined the card, then handed it back with a nod. "Use the walkways or ye'll be hit by an auto."

Ghost nodded contritely. Spittle flew as he got out his reply. "I s-sortinly will, sor."

The copper backed off a step. "Get on with you, and have a pleasant stay."

Ghost beamed his gratitude and hurried away.

Twenty-five minutes later he pulled through the gate at Manor Kilhooley, parked beside the guest house, and went inside.

Jock Donovan grinned from a chair, motioning his head

toward Rashad's door, which was now cracked several inches. There was a steady sound of bedsprings and an occasional thud—the sound of the headboard striking the wall. "She was cryin' like a babe till he thumped her an' tol' her to stop."

Ghost ignored him as he took a seat on the sofa.

"He be a bleedin' machine," Donovan said in his confidential whisper. "He be givin' it to her for the third time."

Ghost vaguely nodded. He'd heard Rashad's rutting sounds in more cramped quarters. He opened the newspaper he'd purchased in Ballymun and began to read about measures the police were taking throughout Great Britain, looking for terrorists they called Ghost's Gang.

In the other room the girl began to grunt in cadence with furiously squeaking bedsprings.

Donovan shook his head in admiration. "He don't wait much in between. She sure as bleedin' hell can't complain about bein' a virgin."

To Rashad Taylor, foreplay was ordering a woman onto her hands and knees. He was insatiable and rough with his female toys, but that wasn't particularly bothersome. Rashad did his job. Ghost thought of other times, when other employers had provided women. Rashad had his fun after each operation, and Charlie also liked a bit of enjoyment, so the provision of females had become a part of Ghost's contract negotiation. Their employers saw to it that the women they supplied were free of disease and, as importantly, that they didn't talk. As a precaution, Ghost demanded darkness in rooms where Charlie and Rashad met with their prizes.

An especially loud thump came from the other side of the door. Donovan's eyes had become slitted, his breathing reduced to shallow wheezes.

Ghost turned to remembrances of Charlie, whose sexual encounters were quite different from Rashad's. Charlie was tender with women. He treated them considerately, regardless if they might be a lowlife, ten-dollar prostitute. Charlie searched for something deeper than the terrified females could begin to understand, yet alone provide.

Rashad spoke to the girl in a guttural voice, ordering her to roll over. She whimpered, and they heard a smack of flesh on flesh.

Rustling sounds. The girl squealed, and Rashad slapped

her again. She was quiet. Rashad grunted, and the girl uttered a bleating sound. Donovan turned and whispered. "Her pudgy arse ain't no virgin either now." He grinned the ugly look, turned, and leaned closer to observe.

Ghost became moody, wondering if he'd done the right thing by sending Charlie from a British airport. They'd be watching those closely. He wondered if he shouldn't have him brought to Ireland—perhaps have Donovan provide him a girl as he had Rashad, and wait until they could all disembark at their leisure.

The thumping sounds commenced, and with each the girl released a new bleat.

"Sounds like a bleedin' sheep," Donovan whispered in wonder as he watched.

Ghost paced to the window, staring at the brooding, clabbered-milk sky that matched his present temper. The girl in the room began to cry in great sobs, and then the thumps became different, more muffled, and with each she'd wail in pain.

"Christ and Mary be damned," Donovan whispered in awe, "if he ain't rammin' her head against the wall."

Ghost decided that trying to contact Charlie to change plans might be more dangerous than allowing things to continue. Suspected IRA collaborators would be closely watched by Scotland Yard, and perhaps they'd be led to Charlie.

The cries and thumping of flesh grew even louder. "He be rammin' her right through the bleedin' headboard!" Donovan whispered excitedly.

The wailing accompaniment stopped.

"He done knocked the silly bitch senseless."

The creaking and muffled thumps continued for another long minute, then diminished, and Rashad emitted a long grunt of pleasure as he finished again.

Charlie and Rashad Taylor were the only two humans Ghost trusted. He'd trained them well, and their skills complemented one another's. He'd also promised to take care of them and not allow them to be taken, and Ghost never lied. It was part of his honor, learned during his special tutoring as a child. He understood and knew how to deal with the Italian Mafia leaders who'd once employed them, for their code closely matched his own. They knew what obligation was about—unlike the Arabs who lied incessantly to one another as well as to outsiders.

Rashad came into the room wearing a terrycloth robe, a pronounced swagger to his step. He brushed past Donovan and went to the kitchen to pull a bottle of lager from the refrigerator.

"You done with her?" Donovan asked when he returned.

Rashad snorted. "I ain't even got started." He turned to Ghost, and his voice changed to subservience. "You want a turn? Don't have a clue how to use it, but she's got a tight puss."

"Later perhaps." He'd sometimes enter one of their rooms and push the man aside to have a session with his woman. It was an infrequent biological urge, never an emotional one.

"Maybe I oughta," Donovan said, looking in through the opened door.

Rashad eyed him as he took a swig of beer. "Get out of my fuckin' way," he growled, and went back into the bedroom, this time pulling the door closed.

10:30 P.M.—Gatwick International Airport, United Kingdom

Manny DeVera called Judge Lindquist at her ITF-4 office, pleased to catch her before she left for home. He could hardly contain himself and did not waste words. "I'm at Gatwick. Three hours ago a man matching Charlie's description was seen on one of the airport video monitors."

Her voice went quiet, as if she didn't dare believe their fortune. "You think it's him?"

"I'm staring at the video right now, and it's the same guy in Serious's photo. Even the same getup, dressed in a turban and suit. An airport security officer noticed the similarity while he was reviewing the tapes. Scotland Yard's got people swarming all over the place."

Sounds of Marian's breathing betrayed her excitement. "Is there a chance he's there?"

"Probably not. We're guessing he either beat it out of the terminal or made it through one of the security gates without being recognized. Don't know which airline he used, so they're circulating Charlie's photo to the ticket agents."

"Any luck?"

"We think he's on an airplane," Manny said. "Three different agents say they sold tickets to guys who looked like him. We feel he's either on his way to Barcelona, Frankfurt, or Bogota. All of those flights are airborne, and Scotland Yard's making notifications to appropriate security people at the destinations."

"I'll keep my fingers crossed. Anything else I can do?"

"Not that I know of. We're . . . Just a second." A security guard handed Manny a slip of paper, which he read. A grin crawled across his face.

"Add Chicago to the list," he told Marian. "An American Airlines agent says he sold a ticket to a man who looked like Charlie's photo. The airplane took off at nine-fifteen local time, more than an hour ago."

"Flight number?"

"American one-oh-one-two. Just a minute and I'll get a landing time at O'Hare."

"Don't bother. I'll have it covered from this end. Every FBI agent in Chicago will be waiting for him. If he's on the flight, he's ours."

Manny laughed, unable to contain an outburst of elation. "Ghost screwed up, Marian. I can *feel* it."

"I certainly hope you're right."

"I'll take a flight to wherever Charlie's taken into custody. I can't wait to look this guy in the eye and ask a few questions. Like why he thinks he can shoot my friends and get away with it."

"Pray it's Chicago," she said. "I want him here on American soil."

"Yeah," Manny agreed. "Me, too."

6

Tuesday, January 24th

9:00 A.M.*—Ballymun, Republic of Ireland*

It was the third day he'd waited near the telephone booth, the fourth since he'd heard from Charlie. Ghost looked at his watch as the second hand swept past the designated time for contact. Less than a minute had passed when he impatiently looked again.

He would wait for ten minutes, as he'd done the previous two days. Longer and his presence might be imprinted in the minds of merchants and other denizens of the area.

After five minutes, he wondered if Charlie had remembered to subtract three hours as he'd been told? Or perhaps had misunderstood and *added* three hours? Or adding nothing and called at noon? Or used local time from where he was calling rather than Dublin time?

An automobile pulled to the curb and an elderly woman emerged from the passenger's door. She approached, eyed Ghost with distrust, and entered the booth to make a call. When she found the slot jammed by an oversize coin, she glared about for someone to accuse, then returned to the auto and climbed inside.

After ten minutes, Ghost walked briskly from the booth, this time using proper crosswalks as he returned to the Fiat. Something was definitely wrong, and Ghost did not believe it was Charlie forgetting the simple time calculation. He climbed into the Fiat, then sat for a while, thinking.

Charlie was to have ticketed himself on a nonstop flight to Chicago, then transferred to another international flight using other identification. At the destination he would be met and driven to the safe haven. The entire passage should have taken no more than fifteen hours.

He and Rashad were to follow via Lisbon. Jock Donovan reported daily that their transportation was ready. All they awaited was Charlie's call. Was there treachery from within the employer's organization? He felt that was doubtful. They were more than pleased with Piccadilly, and Donovan said they wanted another operation mounted in the near future.

He'd tried meditation, but his helper had not provided insight about Charlie. Ghost drove northward slowly, well within the speed limit. As he continued past the airport exit, a light drizzle began to fall. He switched on the wipers and found the frantic clip-clop sound irritating.

He planned operations meticulously, down to the smallest detail and least plausible surprise, paying equal attention to the four phases: preparation, insertion, execution, and withdrawal. Few humans knew what they looked like, and even then they practiced constant changes in appearance, mannerisms, voice tones, language, and dialect.

It was unlikely anyone had a description of Charlie, and his identification papers weren't flawed. Yet something was obviously amiss.

Ghost drove through the opened gate of Manor Kilhooney.

Rashad was seated before the television. Ghost went directly into Rashad's bedroom where the girl huddled miserably at the end of the bed, staring with one slitted eye, the other swollen and discolored the same purple-blue hue as other bruises on her body. She seemed much older.

"Wipe the snot from your face," Ghost said, and began pulling off his clothing, stacking them neatly near the door. It had been months since his last release. Perhaps it would help.

She whispered something as Ghost finished unclothing and started for the bed.

"I'm hungry," she whimpered louder.

He stopped cold.

"Please?" she asked woefully.

Ghost backed away from the bed, stared for a moment,

then reached for his trousers. He dressed quickly, then went out.

"Feed her," he said in an angry hiss.

Rashad looked up, then scrambled to his feet. "Give her something to eat?"

"Jesus. Don't you listen?"

"Sure. Sorry." He started for the kitchen.

"You trying to starve her?"

"She was sorta pudgy. I thought maybe . . ."

"And give her something to drink besides the warm beer you leave in there. You're having your fun. No use to starve her." Ghost waited. A couple of minutes later Rashad passed through the living room carrying a sandwich and jug of water.

Ghost went into his bedroom and lay down. He could not stand the idea of humans being hungry, refused to watch programs about famished people in Africa or anywhere else.

It was not a good time to meditate since he'd fouled himself by lusting after the girl. He'd made contact the previous night, though. While he'd not received help on Charlie, there'd been another message.

It was time to live out his destiny.

He had no idea what that meant, but it would come to him. It always did. He was the chosen one. But first he must make sure Charlie was safe, as he'd done since they were children and had been starved and treated like just two more scrawny head of cattle.

Ghost willed his body to relax. He'd trained himself to rest in the most difficult of times and was able to slip into a reverie of half sleep—yet even then the sense of foreboding about Charlie would not go away.

After half an hour, Ghost returned to the living room. The door to Rashad's bedroom was closed, the television turned off. Sounds of fornication came from the room, but the girl was quiet. She'd been brutalized beyond complaint.

He heard a sound outside, went to the door, and admitted Donovan.

"I got news," the crippled IRA officer said. "We got connections in the States."

Ghost nodded impatiently. The IRA had tentacles across America. A fund raiser from the Shamrock Isle could go into a Brothers of Erin hall anywhere there, whistle a couple bars of "Moon Arisin'," and find a smiling Mick sidling up to see what he needed.

"What happened to Charlie?"

Donovan told him Charlie had been arrested as he'd deplaned in Chicago, then taken by police convoy to the maximum security area of the Cook County prison facility. Charlie remained under massive and close guard, and there'd been no releases to the press.

Although it had been his greatest dread, Ghost had known something like that had transpired. He knew what he must do. It was time to live out his destiny.

"Charlie will tell them nothing," Ghost said coldly. He inhaled deeply, lest he show the emotion that coursed through him. The extent of his bitterness and concern for Charlie surprised even himself. He would use his rage to advantage. Ghost worked best when his mind was charged and he was faced with great challenge.

"We'll leave in two hours," Ghost told Donovan.

"I'll arrange it." Jock Donovan did not appear unhappy that they were going.

"I'll need a contact." Ghost told him where.

Donovan reacted with surprise at mention of the destination. "You're going there?"

Ghost shifted his cold gaze to the man.

Jock Donovan's eyes widened at what he saw. "I'll be leaving," he blurted, and fled.

Ghost used a call booth in the nearby village of Ballyboghil. He dialed the international operator and gave a charge card number, then the number he wished to be connected with. The man who answered represented another who was once said to be the single-most powerful figure in the world. The *capo di capi*.

Ghost had worked for him in Italy, with such success the boss of bosses had wanted him to continue in another country.

He used as few words as possible, told the voice that they must meet and when, and that he'd need a large amount of "supplies." He would call back to confirm. The man acknowledged and abruptly broke the connection.

Ghost paused for only a moment before connecting with a second number.

It was time to live out his destiny.

The man who answered was expecting his call, although they'd not spoken for months.

"This is the chosen one. It is time," Ghost said simply into the phone.

"Yes," the elder replied in the antiquated language that was difficult even for Ghost. "Contact us when you get to your destination so we can pass your telephone number to the wayfinder."

The connection was broken. The code name "wayfinder" echoed in Ghost's mind.

As he drove toward the manor, his anger over Charlie festered and grew, but the emotion did not show. Whenever someone looked at the Fiat, he smiled pleasantly, yet by the time he drove through the gates of the estate, cold fury was pulsing through his veins.

Ghost went into Rashad's bedroom. His lieutenant was leaned back against the headboard, his hand entwined in the girl's hair, pressing her face down as she labored.

"We're leaving."

Rashad grinned.

"Time for cleanup." Ghost went to his own room.

He was packed in less than ten minutes, and carried the single bag out. Then he went to the bathroom where Rashad and the girl waited, both still naked, Rashad holding her so she was on all fours in the tub. Garbage bags were stacked outside; his knife rested on the rim of the sink.

Ghost nodded. Rashad grasped her hair and pulled back hard, until she would have stared at the ceiling if her eyes hadn't been swollen closed. She made a gurgling sound. Ghost picked up Rashad's knife and positioned the point at the side of her neck. He pressed until he felt contact with bone, sliced outward, and Rashad held her head ever lower to ensure the red gusher was confined to the porcelain tub. The girl thrashed but Rashad held her firmly in place.

"Hurry with it," Ghost said simply, placing the knife handle in Rashad's free hand. He often participated in cleanup killings. At first it had been to ensure it was properly done, so he could be positive no witness would survive to identify them. It had grown to be a ritual.

"She's a good one," Rashad exulted as the girl's body continued to buck and fight. He positioned the blade for the first dismemberment, oblivious that he was grinning from ear to ear.

Ghost started to remind him that there was no honor gained in the killing of a helpless person—especially a woman. He decided against it and left the room.

An hour passed before Donovan arrived. Ghost and Rashad were packed, watching CNN to determine the latest news concerning the Ghost Gang.

"The plane's ready," Donovan said cheerfully, looking about with his ugly grin. As they picked up their bags, his eyes shifted to Rashad's bedroom. "The girl in there?" he asked.

Rashad snickered. "Takin' a bath."

"Let's go," Ghost said.

"The girl . . ." Donovan began.

Ghost beckoned impatiently. "You can come back for her. She'll be here."

On the drive to Dublin Airport, Donovan gave Ghost the name of the IRA contact at their destination. Ghost wrote the encoded telephone number and slipped the paper into his wallet.

When they'd entered the airport and were approaching the executive jet, Rashad decided on a last bit of fun with Donovan. "The girl's got a tight puss. You oughta try it."

Jock Donovan's eyes glittered in anticipation.

10:10 A.M.—Chicago, Illinois

Manny DeVera stood outside the cell, staring at the prisoner. The man lay on his back, and it was difficult to tell if he was asleep. He appeared composed, guileless, more like a child than an adult, although he was estimated to be thirty.

The man called Charlie remained an unknown, for he'd not responded to their questions. Video cameras were set up in two corners of the room, tracking his movements, recording his sounds. His movements about the cell and when he was taken to and from interrogation had been observed. A few words of denial and contempt had been captured. They'd recorded the way he stood, walked, stretched, ate sparingly, urinated and defecated, belched and released gas. Those frugal bits of information were all that had been learned about Charlie. Yet a plan was growing within DeVera's mind that would put his utterances and movements to good use.

Manny sensed a hesitation, a subtle change in the rise and fall of the prisoner's chest. Charlie's eyes became slitted, and DeVera knew he too was being observed.

A smile crept across Manny DeVera's face. He wanted the prisoner to know he was pleased. They'd worked long and hard to get their hands on one of Ghost's group.

It was time to go after Ghost and Rashad. The plan developing in Manny DeVera's mind continued to take shape. This afternoon he'd fly to Montana and take the next step.

Airborne over the Atlantic Ocean

They were in a private jet owned by a wealthy IRA supporter, flying to the first destination of a busy day. Ghost held his opened valise on his lap and examined an identification packet. He handed it to Rashad and repeated procedures he was to follow after they deplaned. Rashad listened attentively, periodically asking questions to make sure he had everything memorized.

When he was satisfied with the responses, Ghost latched the valise's false bottom into position and carried it with him as he went forward to another seat. He leaned back in the plush leather and closed his eyes. When his mind threatened to drift, he willed it back into focus. His rage was undiminished; a fire that stoked and fueled him.

From early childhood, he'd promised to watch over Charlie.

Memories of Charlie and the time at the cruddy hardscrabble ranch when they were worked like mules by the lean, unsmiling man. He remembered how his hatred had welled each time they were beaten with fists and boots for slacking off in the impossible tasks set for them.

American and British women mewled about child abuse. They didn't know what abuse was about, believed a child was abused when a relative patted their butts or got their way using threats. Ghost snorted. Where'd the ladies groups been when Charlie had been knocked to all fours during a whipping with a horse harness, begging for it to stop, telling the old man he'd do better next time, getting a boot job on his frail body for the effort? Then, when Ghost would begin to recover from his own stomping, the old man would turn his attention back to him. Never with glee or a grin of anticipation, though. Neither he nor Charlie could remember the old man smiling after his florid-faced wife had died in her own alcoholic haze.

That's the only thing your kind understand, old man Weiser would say after he'd whipped them and promised to withhold another meal. It had seemed they would never stop, the old man's nightly drunken beatings and the starvation. Sometimes they'd become so hungry they'd dip into pig slop that reeked so badly it seared their nostrils, so foul they'd puke it up. When the old man caught them at it he'd beat them for stealing from the swine.

The man with the wandering eye, the one Ghost came to know as the traveler, had come to the ranch so stealthily that old man Weiser never knew he was there. Ghost had been twelve, and was suspicious when the traveler first approached him.

The traveler told him he'd searched for a long time and had come to take Ghost back. Trust him or not, Ghost had decided to go with the man, but he'd made a condition since the traveler had said he should come alone. When they'd left, he'd had nine-year-old Charlie in tow.

He'd told the traveler that he'd sworn to protect Charlie, and the man with the wandering eye understood. He knew about vows and how they must be honored.

The jet landed at Lisbon's Portela Airport at 3:00 P.M. The ritual with the Customs people was brief, and Ghost went directly into the sprawling, busy terminal to find a pay telephone.

He used a new telephone calling card number from the list, and was connected with the switchboard of a London hotel. Ghost identified himself as a previous guest, calling from Bern, Switzerland, and said he'd misplaced the proper phone number. Since it was a matter of some urgency, he asked if they'd be so kind as to connect him with the editorial office of the *London Times*. The operator was pleasant and immediately shunted the call through. Following another short delay, Ghost spoke with his telephone pal.

The city editor was shaken, as he always was when Ghost called. The conversation was brief, lasting little more than a minute. As he hung up, Ghost heard the first boarding call for Rome. He gathered the valise and carry-on bag, and hurried.

7:55 P.M.—Boudie Springs, Montana

It had been a sunny day with the temperature hovering in the high twenties, and the ski lifts at Borealis had been running at capacity. Link had been kept busy dealing with everything from broken legs to cajoling skiers down expert hills they'd tackled without the skill or confidence to get down. He'd returned to the cabin dog-tired. He had slept little the previous night—or the ones before. The dreams had him constantly awake during the long nights.

Come home. Prepare yourself. The Grandfather's words plagued him at night, echoed in his head through the waken hours. There'd been images of a small bird.

He rebuilt the fire, then went to the kitchen area to survey what he might prepare for dinner. He was standing in turtleneck, jeans, and stocking feet, staring woefully into the empty refrigerator he'd forgotten to stock, when he heard the sensor click on the floodlights outside, then sounds of an automobile in the driveway.

Link had settled on tuna fish and stale bread sandwiches—no mayonnaise because he was out—and was pulling out the ingredients when the knock sounded at the door.

"It's open," he yelled. Jim Bourne dropped in some evenings to chat when he wanted to get away from the pub.

The door cracked a few inches.

"Come on in," he grumbled. "I can't heat the entire state."

"Jesus, it's cold out there," a deep voice said. It was not Jim Bourne.

"Take off your boots and leave 'em at the door," Link told him.

The man removed his footwear. Street shoes, Link noted. He looked closer. "Colonel DeVera?" he asked incredulously as the man pulled off his overcoat.

"How you doing, tiger?"

Link hurried over and took the overcoat, then led him to the living area. DeVera wore a dark suit with a white shirt and tie, not at all appropriate for winter in the high country. His shoulders were hunched, and he was shivering.

Manny DeVera had been a close family friend since Link's earliest recollections, one of the pilots who'd flown in his father's unit in the Vietnam air war before he'd moved to intelligence. When Link had been stationed in Arizona, DeVera had been a colonel at their headquarters in Austin, Texas. When Link's squadron deployed to Saudi Arabia for Desert Storm, Colonel DeVera had already been there, working for Lieutenant General Ben Lewis, who had run the air war for General Schwarzkopf.

After the fateful mission involving the British armored column, Manny had flown to the forward base to debrief Link and the pilots in his flight. Three months later he'd appeared at the Pentagon inquiry and played tapes of the radio conversations recorded by the AWACS airplane. He'd displayed gun camera film of the British column and shown the lack of panel markings on the tanks and APCs and how they'd had their cannons pointed the wrong direction, which was the final determinant of positive ID. DeVera had proved that Captain A. Lincoln Anderson had made the proper decision when he'd left in his battle-damaged airplane—that his flight had done their best—that it had been a tragic accident. The board had had no alternative but to agree.

Link owed him.

"Good to see you," Link said as he shook the older man's hand.

DeVera looked about the cabin with a neutral eye as he hovered by the fireplace insert, hands held out, trying to soak up every BTU of heat.

"Get you something to drink? No hard stuff, but there's a couple of beers."

"Anything hot," DeVera said, and shivered violently.

Link busied himself with spooning instant coffee into cups—he was out of ground coffee—and heating water in a kettle. "Be just a minute, Colonel."

"No more colonel. I'm one of the government bureaucrats I used to make fun of."

"Still working in Mom's old organization?" Linda had mentioned she'd offered him a job in State Department Intelligence.

"Something like that," DeVera said, meaning he was with another clandestine agency.

"How're Mom and Dad?" Link asked.

"I was at the Farmhouse last week. They were fine." Manny turned from the stove and looked at Link. "From what I heard, you don't phone home very often."

"That why you're here, to check on me?"

DeVera shook his head. "Business."

Link smiled. "There's nothing except cattle ranches, Indian reservations, and ski hills within a hundred miles, Colonel."

"My *business* is with you. Your parents don't know I'm here, and for the present I'd appreciate it if you didn't tell them."

The kettle was starting to growl.

"I haven't seen you since the inquiry," said DeVera, and Link had the uncomfortable feeling he'd brought it up purposefully.

"Did I thank you for that? Bringing in the tapes and gun camera film and all?"

"That's what friends are for. There was no need for a formal board in the first place."

"Eight allied soldiers were killed. I know who was responsible."

"You didn't do anything wrong. Your airplane took battle damage, and you flew it home. You could have been any other flight leader in that situation."

"I should have told the others to make another identification pass before they strafed. You can tell the difference between Soviet and British armor if you look closely enough."

"Your airplane had been shredded by a ZSU. The AWACS bird didn't have the Brits on their screens, and the Brits didn't have their panel markers in place. Your pilots thought it was the same column that got you. It wasn't your fault, and it wasn't your flight's fault."

Link didn't respond. The kettle began to whistle louder. He switched off the burner, poured two cups of coffee, and carried them into the living area.

Manny took his and sipped, sighed appreciatively. "We need your help, Link."

"You're offering me a job?"

"Maybe. We want you to perform a task for your country."

"Why me?"

"Let's just say you're uniquely qualified."

Link thought about that. Uniquely qualified? With all the cutbacks there were hundreds of ex-fighter pilots around the country. It was more likely that his father had asked his old friend to make the offer so Link would be closer to home.

"I've already got a job," he said.

Manny snorted. "A guy with an aeronautical engineering degree hauling wood and working at being a ski bum?"

"Is that what Dad calls me?"

"He's not overjoyed at what you're doing with your life, but I didn't come here because of him. We need you for a difficult and potentially dangerous contract."

"Doing what?"

"I can't tell you until you come to Washington and listen to what we've got to say. You can back out later if you don't like the sound of it."

"And neither Dad or Mom knows you're here, right?" He spoke the words with sarcasm.

"There's a group of people we've got to stop or they'll keep on killing innocent people."

Link motioned around. "Maybe this doesn't seem like much, but I like it here. Tell Dad I'll stay for a while longer. Then maybe I'll be ready to come home for a visit."

Manny tried to argue that his father wasn't involved. After a while he stopped and released a resigned sigh.

"Mind if I use your phone? I've got to check in."

"Be my guest."

As Manny spoke on the kitchen telephone, Link wondered if DeVera didn't truly need his help. It took effort to push away the thought that he'd turned down a friend to whom he owed so much.

Manny DeVera hung up, looking grim-faced. "Things just got worse. Pack your bag. I've got a government bird standing by at the Kalispel airport."

Link dropped the sarcasm. "I'm sorry, Colonel, but the answer's still no."

Manny used his trump card. "You owe me that much, Link. Come out and listen, then make up your mind."

"I can't just leave. There's my job and . . ."

"To *hell* with your job!" DeVera exploded. "I'm talking about stopping a monster. A sick man who takes human life with contempt. Women, children . . . anyone who gets in his way."

Link looked at DeVera.

Manny's voice was firm. "Two days to hear me out, *then* you can tell me to go to hell, come back here, and brood all you want."

7

Wednesday, January 25th

8:15 A.M.—Hotel Americana, Washington, D.C.

Following the flight, Link had checked into a hotel room that had been reserved for him and spent the sparse remainder of the night. After breakfast an unmarked staff car arrived on schedule and transported him to the huge Department of Justice building on Constitution Avenue.

Link passed a group of loud demonstrators waving posters and chanting slogans to abolish the death penalty, then another demanding tougher laws, and hurried up granite steps under the watchful eye of Madam Justice.

DeVera met him at the north side of the lobby and vouched him past a guard station.

"Sleep well?" Manny asked as he led him toward a bank of elevators.

"Fine," Link said, although he had not. It had been days since he'd felt rested.

They took an elevator to the third floor, proceeded around a busy ring to an inner concourse, then encountered another security desk where Link was scrutinized for a second time. Here the permanent staff wore special, blue-striped identification badges. Link filled out a data sheet and was issued a white one, with bold red letters reading: VISITOR, ESCORT REQUIRED AT ALL TIMES. Manny signed the form, and they continued down the hall.

"Lucky and Linda will be happy you're in town," Manny said.

"It might be awkward if I can't tell them why I'm here."

He was led into a small, sparsely furnished room with four chairs and a standard government-issue table. The walls were soundproofed.

DeVera pushed a stack of forms across the table. "Look those over and sign the appropriate ones. I'll be right back."

On top was a Department of Justice form explaining that Abraham Lincoln Anderson had been summoned as a witness for the government. He was to save all receipts for food, lodging, and transportation, and document expenses for the trip. A travel voucher was stapled as a second page, his name and social security number typed in at the top.

The second set of documents were in a folder. His top secret security clearance had been renewed, showing that his most recent FBI background investigation had been completed two days earlier. He signed the form on top, attesting that he understood the penalties for revealing classified information that might be injurious to the United States of America.

The third set of papers were a contract for A. Lincoln Anderson to "perform prescribed services" as directed by the deputy attorney general of the Department of Justice. The time period was left blank. He would be provided the benefits and privileges of a GS-14 government employee, and receive $136 per day of employment plus appropriate living expenses.

Link did not sign the contract.

The door opened and a neatly dressed woman with rust-colored hair peered inside, then offered a smile. "There you are."

Link gained his feet. "Judge Lindquist?"

She grasped his hand warmly. "Don't make plans for lunch. We'll go to a place nearby. You'll have to tell me what you've been up to, Link."

"Yes, ma'am," he said, wondering how she was involved.

Marian looked at the stack of forms, then evenly at him. "Make sure you know what you're getting into before you agree to anything, Link."

He started to respond, but she smiled again and departed.

Manny DeVera came back in with a large manila folder, a secretary trailing with a tray. A steaming cup of coffee was set before Link.

DeVera lifted the security clearance from his stack, checked that he'd signed it, then took a seat across the table. "The briefing's classified. No mention of any of it to anyone, okay?"

"Sure."

"What do you remember about the Piccadilly Circus bombing two weeks ago?"

It took a moment for the incident to register. "Not much," he admitted.

"Surely you heard of it. It's been in all the news."

"This is our busiest time of year at the ski hill. All I heard was that there was an explosion and a large number of deaths."

"Three hundred and seventy-nine fatalities, the worst terrorist atrocity of the decade."

"There was something about an American being involved."

"He's one of those we'll be talking about."

Link mused. "Am I supposed to know him?"

"I doubt that very much."

"Then why . . . ?"

DeVera interrupted. "Let me take it from the beginning. There's a sequence I'd like to maintain. By the time we're done tomorrow, you'll understand."

Link settled back to listen.

"The leader of the terrorist group," DeVera began, "calls himself Ghost."

Link remembered hearing the name in the news. "He's an American?"

"We don't know. The DGSE, the French spooks, speculate he's South American. He's dark and stocky like Carlos, the Venezuelan terrorist. Mossad says he's Palestinian. We also have reports that he's Georgian, Khazak, Algerian, and a half-dozen other nationalities."

"Then you don't know his background."

"Nothing except somewhere along the line he became an explosives expert, and I don't mean a nutcase who's learned to mix diesel and fertilizer or make a Molotov cocktail. He's good. Think back to your military days. Do you remember hearing about shaped charges?"

Link nodded. "Explosives configured so they focus their blast."

"Yeah. The army uses them to clear mine fields and for neat things like blowing up enemy soldiers. Claymores, for instance. Ghost's forte are focused-effect bombs. He knows the burn rates of explosives. He can assemble an electronic trigger to detonate blasts at millisecond intervals. He tailor-makes bombs for specific objectives. Ghost is the best in the world at what he does. He's also amoral and doesn't care who he kills or how horribly they suffer.

"The Israelis got wind of him in '83, when the U.S. and French sent peacekeeping forces into Beirut. Mossad received information that an expert was in town helping a group of Muslim radicals, the Hezbollah, build a truck bomb. Their informant said he was very young, despised Americans, and went by the name of Ghost. Unfortunately they didn't pass the report on."

"Jesus," Link said, remembering. "The marine barracks."

"That was Ghost's debut. Three hundred U.S. Marines were killed by the blast, and both France and the U.S. withdrew their forces from Lebanon.

"Enter, Rashad Taylor." DeVera pulled out an official U.S. Army photograph and pushed it across the table. A uniformed black youth stared insolently at the camera.

"He's big and tough. A onetime martial arts instructor who's good with a knife."

"He's the American?"

"From Detroit, but he's not nostalgic about the place. Beat up his mother and declared incorrigible at age eleven. Raised by a string of foster parents, and on the streets. There were a few arrests for petty theft, but not enough to keep him out of the army. Enlisted in 1982. Made PFC twice and busted back to private both times for fighting. In '84 he was stationed near Munich and got into a row with two German nationals at a *gasthaus*. Killed one and carved the other up so badly his mother wouldn't recognize him. Rashad was fingered by a guy from his unit, and the MPs tossed him in the stockade until they could turn him over to the local authorities.

"His first night in the stockade, Taylor killed a guard and escaped. The next week the soldier who'd identified him was murdered. Not just killed but horribly mutilated. Shortly afterward, we think he hooked up with Ghost.

"In 1985, he and another guy were seen leaving a GI dance hall in Berlin before a bomb went off. Seven Americans were killed. A month later a bomb was hidden in a truck before it entered a German air force base. Three Luftwaffe airmen died in the blast. Ghost called the local newspapers before both bombings. The Red Army Faction took credit, their swan songs before their last leaders were arrested, but Ghost's reputation was made. He and Rashad were put on Interpol's wanted and dangerous list.

"They dropped out of sight . . . location unknown until the next year when they were reported at a training camp in Libya. By then a man we know only as Charlie had joined up, and they'd become a triple threat. Ghost knows explosives. Charlie's a shooter. Rashad uses a knife. They came out in 1988 to bomb an Israeli police station in Jerusalem. Four killed in that one. Then a Ghaddafi-sponsored execution in Paris—vaporized the guy with his family."

DeVera held up a glossy photo. "That's an automobile, man, wife, and three kids."

Link studied a mass of bloody, twisted metal and slowly shook his head.

"That time we almost got them. An FBI agent named J.J. Davis caught up with them near Paris. The local gendarmes underestimated Ghost and lost two men . . . and they got away.

"The group went underground again. The Berlin Wall fell and communism began to crumble. Without places like East Germany to run to, everyone thought their days were numbered. They were wrong. In 1990, they were in Iraq hobnobbing with Saddam's brother who ran their secret police. The next year Ghost supervised the bombings of hospitals, buildings, oil wells, and water desalination plants—you name it—as the Iraqis pulled out of Kuwait."

DeVera showed photographs of the destruction.

"How can they be so sure it was Ghost?"

"Too professionally done to be the work of Saddam's military yokels. Also, he left his signature, which we'll discuss later. The agencies kept it close to their vests. I was running the targeting intelligence shop in Saudi, and I never even heard of him. You may have flown over Ghost on one of your missions. Too bad we missed him.

"After Iraq, the Israelis had a report that Ghost was in Port Sudan. Mossad infiltrated four agents—three men and a woman—to take them out. The Sudanese captured the agents coming ashore and gave them to Rashad. He raped the female for a couple of days, then butchered her and the men. Ghost shipped the remains to Jerusalem. We have photographs, but you don't want to see them. Ghost and crew disappeared again, with most of the world looking for them.

"While they were gone, the Soviet Union folded. Bad guys running everywhere. Ghost's gang was reported in Colombia. The RCMP thought they spotted them near Calgary. Three non-Orientals were said to be in hiding near Chiang Mai, Thailand. Local authorities cooperated on all of those, but they came up empty. Like the other times, no one knew where they'd holed up.

"Eighteen months after Desert Storm the Cosa Nostra's boss of bosses was arrested and the Italian Mafia began to fall apart. They hired Ghost. That was when I joined this organization. My first briefings were about Ghost killing an anti-Mafia newsman in Rome, and the well-publicized bombing at the Uffizi Gallery in Florence.

"Charlie was busy, too. He made three spectacular killings, ex-Mafia collaborators he took out with long-distance head shots."

He showed two photos of sprawling dead men with open eyes. They lay in pools of blood and brain matter, their skulls shattered by impacts of bullets. The third photo showed only a small dark hole in the center of a man's forehead.

"That was from six hundred fifty yards, using a .22-250 target rifle."

"Damn," said Link. It had been a spectacular long-distance shot.

"No one's safe if Charlie's within half a mile. That made it impossible for the carabinieri to protect witnesses unless they kept them hidden indoors, which was what they finally did."

DeVera showed another photo, gorier than the others. "Rashad's work. He cut this guy's legs off at the knees while he was alive and left him to bleed to death."

Another photo. "He flayed the muscle off the man's

arms—held him down and filleted him like a fish. The stuff next to him's his tongue, penis, and testicles."

Link found himself mesmerized by the terrible photographs, not wanting to acknowledge what his brain was registering.

"Understandably it became difficult for the Italian government to get more witnesses or collaborators to come forward." DeVera replaced the photos in a manila folder. "The Cosa Nostra paid ten million dollars for their work. Ghost is the highest paid terrorist of all time, including Carlos and Abu Nidal. The Serbs wanted his group for a job on the Croat leadership, but Ghost turned them down because they offered too little. Same for a contract in Moscow and another in Egypt. They were in demand. They not only did the tough jobs, they did them either without trace or with maximum publicity, as their employer wished. They'd made the top of the most-wanted list for Interpol and seven European countries."

Link made a guess. "Then they hid out again."

"Yes, and we were scrambling to find them because every time Ghost recharged his batteries, he'd come roaring back with more outrageous atrocities. There were sightings, but none were real. We held our breath and expected the worst, and we weren't disappointed. Last year the Provisional IRA were on their knees because the Ulster Defense Force had decimated them during the cease-fire, so they hired Ghost. Charlie kicked off the campaign with a long-range assassination in Belfast. Next came a bombing in Essex, England. We knew it was Ghost because he left his signature."

DeVera reached across the table and drew two wavering parallel marks on the pad.

"He draws those squiggles on bomb components so we'll know who built them. That's close hold. We keep a lid on it to avoid copycat bombers. When he wants publicity, he makes a phone call to a local newspaper. We've got tapes and voice analyses in five languages. He's so good at changing tones and speech patterns that he damn near fools the experts."

As Link took notes, DeVera spent the pause taking out more photographs. "Ghost began this year with the Piccadilly station bombing, the worst terrorist disaster in modern history."

He slid photos across the table. Humans inside the underground station were so mangled it was impossible to tell which limbs belonged to whom.

DeVera described the timing. Five focused-effect bombs detonated in sequence . . . a final blast when the rescue attempt was under way.

He showed a photograph of the exterior of the underground station. Before he could go on, Link held him up. He'd seen the image. The maw of the station looked like the dark entrance to a cave. In his mind he could hear echoes of humans screaming in pain and terror.

"Something wrong?" DeVera asked.

Where had he seen the photograph? A newspaper?

The door opened and Judge Lindquist leaned into the room. "Time for a break. I made reservations for twenty minutes from now, and it's going to take that long to get there."

The restaurant was upscale, with rich paneling and linen tablecloths. Marian Lindquist said it was the latest "in" place for government movers and shakers, and they'd likely see a few. Link noted that Manny DeVera was very correct in her presence, as if he was trying to impress her. For his own part, Link felt more than a little self-conscious, dressed in the sheepskin coat and Western boots that had seemed sensible when he'd left Boudie Springs.

Marian said the chef was superb. Link took her advice and ordered a bowl of European-style goulash soupen, followed by a bountiful salad garnished with strips of prosciutto, different cheeses, roast beef, and anchovies.

She delved into his life at Boudie Springs, seemed interested when he spoke about his work at the ski hill, and finally brought up the subject of his parents.

"You should visit them while you're here, Link."

Manny DeVera spoke up. "He's concerned about mentioning why he's here. Hell, Link, tell them I called you in for a meeting. Just don't bring up the subject."

As they chattered, Link remembered where he'd seen the entrance to the Piccadilly station. The dark maw of the cave. The screaming people.

The Grandfather dream.

He'd obviously seen the photo in a newspaper, and the image had triggered the dream Link had experienced in the old bunkhouse when they were looking for lost tourists. DeVera said the disaster had occurred two weeks earlier.

When they'd returned to the building, Marian Lindquist insisted he use her office to phone his parents, and he could think of no good excuse.

When she heard his voice, Linda was breathless with happiness, then became more excited when he said he was in town and could come to dinner. He'd have to drop by his hotel room to clean up after he finished what he was doing, but he could be there around seven.

"Is that too late?" he asked.

"You just get here," she said. "We'll hold dinner."

He left Marian's office feeling better for calling yet apprehensive about seeing them.

As DeVera led the way back to the small briefing room, Link told him he'd be going out to the Farmhouse.

"I'll arrange transportation." DeVera closed the door and took his seat across the table. The folder of briefing material was before him, and Manny bent over to organize it.

The security forms had been taken from Link's stack. The blank expenses sheet, unsigned contract, and pad with his scribbled notes remained.

Link spoke to DeVera's lowered head. "I've got a question. When was the bomb set off at Piccadilly?"

DeVera did not have to look it up. "Eleven twenty-eight a.m., on January fourteenth. It was a Saturday."

Link released a silent sigh. The Grandfather dream had come earlier. He'd had the vision, *then* it had taken place—the worst terrorist disaster in modern times.

Link knew there was a rational answer, but he certainly wished it was more apparent.

There was the Grandfather's message: "Come home." Did he mean here, to Washington?

"What is it you want me to do?"

"For now just get a feel for Ghost's group. I have my reasons for presenting things in the order I'm using."

Link tried to quell his growing irritation.

DeVera laboriously recapped all they'd gone over that morning, showing the photos for impact, making sure Link knew of every movement and awful act the terrorists had committed.

"Ghost is the man in charge—period. Rashad and Charlie do as told. They're scared of him. Ghost is vindictive when they screw up the slightest thing. On the other hand, he takes care of them. For instance, Ghost isn't especially drawn to women, but after each operation he makes sure they're around for the other two. Rashad is insatiable. Charlie falls in love easily."

"You seem to know a lot about them."

"U.S. intelligence, Mossad, MI-6, the DGSE, and a dozen other country's clandestine services have tried to learn everything possible about them. We thought we had a good photo of Rashad. We also had a composite of Ghost from two members of the Red Army Faction trying to get their sentences reduced."

DeVera pushed across a drawing. Ghost's face was dark, the smile thin but confident, and he looked vaguely familiar. An emotion welled in Link that he couldn't identify.

Link examined the photo of Rashad and drawing of Ghost. "These aren't clear enough?"

"Out of hundreds of surveillance photos, some of sequences we believed they were in, no one was able to get a match. We now believe Ghost and Rashad underwent extensive reconstructive surgery in Teheran . . . there was an Iranian doctor who was very good at it . . . which means we haven't known what they've looked like for the past several years. We have computer-generated variants made up by the FBI lab. Some may be accurate. We have no idea."

"Fingerprints?"

"Rashad's were probably altered in Iran using an acid-etch procedure, but we could still make a positive ID. Our problem's physical identification so we can get our hands on them."

Link tried an obvious tack. "How about descriptions from the women?"

"They keep them in the dark, and they're told if they get even a glimpse, they'll be killed. The ones we've talked to are scared, even years later. The only things we've learned is that they all change appearances, voices, and mannerisms. Long hair, sometimes medium or short. Rashad sometimes wears a beard, sometimes a stubble or a mustache. They slouch or limp, shuffle or take long strides. They're chameleons.

"They're uncanny about blending with locals," DeVera

went on. "They're at home in a desert, jungle, or urban environment. They're good at languages, and Ghost with dialects. Finally, Ghost has connections he's built over the past ten years who help them in Europe, the Middle East, and North Africa. Ghost's an irreplaceable asset, so they take pains to hide them."

"How about Charlie? Could he have been in the army like Rashad? Maybe in their sniper program, where he learned to shoot?

"We don't know anything about Charlie before he showed up in Libya. He and Rashad are the only people Ghost trusts. He's protective of them both, but especially Charlie."

"You showed likenesses of Ghost and Rashad. What about Charlie?"

"Until recently we had nothing except a series of fuzzy images from a surveillance camera. One was believed to be Charlie, but we didn't have the technology to improve it enough for use. Recently the lab computer programs were improved. They enhanced the photos, morphed two shots together, and the result was impressive. I'll show you tomorrow."

DeVera glanced at his watch. "It's after four. I've got things to do in my office, and you've had enough to digest for one day. We'll continue in the morning."

"I'll need a lift to the hotel, if you don't mind."

Manny scribbled a number on a slip of paper and handed it to him along with a set of keys. "That's my parking spot. Take my car. It's not much, but it's transportation."

"How will you get home?"

"I'll ride with Marian," DeVera said with a smile.

4:30 P.M.—Kennedy International Airport, New York

The two men arrived on flights half an hour apart, bearing passports and papers proclaiming them to be delegates to the United Nations; one a priest representing the Vatican, the other a Kenyan in dashiki on a flight from Cairo. They took taxis to different hotels in Queens, then transferred to other cabs to take them to a high-rise condominium complex in Manhattan. There they waited in the lobby until a limousine pulled to the curb.

When the bags were loaded, they crawled in back and were met by a small man. Martin Cherone introduced himself as if they'd not met. He politely asked about their trips over, and both said their flights had been uneventful. Silence followed as they were driven across the George Washington Bridge and into a six-story parking building. There they transferred to a nondescript 1992 Chevrolet station wagon with dark-shaded glass, and Cherone took the wheel.

There were no discussions as he drove to a modest home in a quiet Teaneck, New Jersey suburb. Martin Cherone pressed a button, then pulled into the garage. He lowered the door before they stepped out and followed him into the house.

Inside they were met by a middle-aged, pleasant-countenanced man and shown to a small living room. Two men, wearing sports jackets and alert eyes, followed them closely.

Ghost knew the pleasant man's identity. In 1993, Salvatore Riina, the Cosa Nostra's *capo di capi,* had been arrested in Italy. Joseph DiFazio had succeeded him and deftly combined the embattled Sicilian, Italian, Georgian, French, and American branches under his sole control.

Twenty years earlier, many would have considered the boss of bosses to be the most powerful man in the world. Now federal antiracketeering task forces and local district attorneys picked off his men. The streets were controlled by gangs, mindless fools who didn't care if the person they killed was a kid, housewife, cop, union organizer, or Mafia soldier, only if they threatened their operation.

It was the responsibility of the boss of bosses to halt the deterioration of power, as others had dealt with similar threats since the thirteenth century. Thus far DiFazio had not succeeded and was increasingly desperate. Ghost had known that when he'd chosen him as employer.

Joseph DiFazio gazed at Rashad. "If you don't mind," he said quietly, motioning toward the kitchen. Rashad looked at Ghost, who nodded. He left, followed by the two men. Cherone remained behind, sitting in a chair near Ghost's.

For a full minute Joseph DiFazio remained silent, studying his guest. Ghost did not feel threatened. It was not the first time he'd been closely scrutinized by a potential employer.

"You've done well recently," said DiFazio.

Ghost didn't answer. Achievements spoke for themselves.

"One of your men is being held in prison."

"For the present." For the next few minutes Ghost outlined his plan.

Joseph DiFazio took a deep breath. "Outrageous," he whispered. DiFazio took a sip of bloodred Valpolicella, then held the glass thoughtfully to his lips. "You are ambitious."

"Some underestimate me. Do you?"

Joseph DiFazio watched him closely. Finally he tipped and drained the wine, as if he'd decided upon something. He waved the glass toward Martin Cherone, who refilled it from a nearby bottle. A common brand, Ghost noted.

"You met Martin when I sent him to you before."

Ghost nodded. He'd dealt with Cherone when he had contracted to eliminate Italian Cosa Nostra informers in 1993 and '94.

"Now other thorns are festering."

Ghost waited. He did not want the man's contract, but he needed other things from DiFazio and they would have their price.

"There are those determined to destroy my organization in this country. Others help foreign governments bother my people abroad. Thorns." Joseph DiFazio mentioned names and explained the difficulties involved in dealing with each. He motioned with his head. "Martin can provide details. Do you foresee a problem?"

Ghost spoke quietly. "I will remove your thorns, and no one will notice. They'll be . . . preoccupied."

"I would not wish for publicity, especially considering what you intend to do."

"That's understandable."

"What will be your fee?"

"The support of your organization. There are things I'll require."

"Martin will provide you with transportation, a place to stay, and protection."

"I'll need detailed information about my objectives."

The *capo di capi* looked at Martin Cherone. "Give him what he needs. Use all of our resources."

"I'll also need . . . supplies."

"We've anticipated that."

Martin Cherone spoke up. "Semtech compound can't be obtained in sufficient quantity—since Piccadilly it's closely monitored. Would you prefer cyclonite, tritonol, or C-4?"

Two hours after they'd arrived, Cherone drove them southward. Ghost and Rashad had changed to casual sports wear.

In the backseat, Ghost closed his eyes. After a short while he blinked and came awake, and placed a hand on Cherone's shoulder.

"When we get to Washington, take us to a hotel."

Martin Cherone frowned. "The house is ready."

"Just do it," Ghost snapped.

Cherone's jaw worked angrily; he was unaccustomed to arguments. Finally he sighed. "Which hotel?"

"I'll give directions when we get closer." Ghost did not know the name of the hotel or why he had to go there. He only knew he must. The rest would be revealed soon enough.

8:10 P.M.—The Farmhouse, Falls Church, Virginia

Lucky was pleased that their son was home, even if he was being evasive about why he was visiting Washington. They'd spent an hour talking before they finally sat down to dinner. Linda flashed her smile about the table, looking happier than she had for months. She'd spent the afternoon preparing the pot roast, fresh snow peas, new potatoes and rich gravy, which were Link's favorite meal.

Between bites, Link told her it was wonderful.

"Are you eating well?" Linda asked in an accusatory tone. Each time they'd visited him after he'd left home, she'd been appalled at his barren cupboards.

Link grinned. "Nothing like this."

"So what did you do today?" Lucky asked. All he'd told them so far was that Manny had asked him to come out. Something to do with an investigation Manny was working on.

"We just talked," Link said again. "I had lunch with Judge Lindquist."

"Marian visited last week," Linda said.

"She's an intelligent lady," Link responded, and Lucky realized he'd steered the conversation away from the purpose of his visit.

When they'd finished dinner, topped off with Linda's Dutch apple pie, the men helped clear the table. Finally she shooed them out, and Lucky led his son to the bar in the great room. He poured cognacs, and they sat quietly.

Lucky broke the silence. "We wish you'd call more. We feel you're avoiding us."

Link was quiet.

"We're the ones who love you most in this world, son."

Link looked up. "That's not one way. I love you both, too."

Lucky set down his drink. "Is it the strafing incident? Still?"

Link shrugged.

"Tell you a war story?"

"Sure."

"It regards something that happened almost thirty years ago when I was a flight commander stationed in Thailand, and we were flying combat missions over North Vietnam."

"In Phantoms?"

"Nope. This was the first time I went over, in the F-105 Thunderchief. The Thud was an honest lady—tough as hell, and lightning fast down on the deck. I had an assistant flight commander named Turk Tatro. A feisty little guy with a burr cut and a big grin. He liked to say, 'it ain't the dog in the fight that counts, it's the fight in the dog.' I'd known his wife and two daughters from before. Turk called them his little women, and he doted on them."

Link was leaned forward with both elbows on the bar.

"There was this target the brass decided we should go after; a big bridge in downtown Hanoi. Somehow the word leaked out, and the North Vietnamese concentrated antiaircraft artillery and surface-to-air missiles around it. The smart thing would have been to go after another target while the defenses were moved, but that wasn't the way it went. We were ordered to attack the bridge using wire-guided Bullpup missiles."

Link frowned. "On a bridge?"

"A big, sturdy bridge, and the missile weighed less than six hundred pounds."

"The warhead's not big enough."

"That's what Turk and some of the other pilots said. Manny DeVera gave part of the mission briefing, and before we went out to the airplanes, he told me he didn't feel good about it. But we took off, and when we got there the flak and missiles were as bad as we'd thought they'd be. We pressed in, and two of us hit the bridge. Of course it didn't go down. Every airplane but one was shot up. Two of the eight pilots were lost, including my friend Turk Tatro."

"Did he survive?" Link asked.

"At the time, Glenn Phillips was a prisoner of war in the Hanoi Hilton. Another P.O.W. recognized Turk's voice yelling when they brought him in for interrogation. They heard screams for the next couple of hours, and finally a pistol shot."

Link was quiet.

"Every man who's seen combat has regrets. While I was writing my condolence letter to Turk's wife, I had some heavy ones. One was that I should have complained more about the weapons. Another was that when I saw all the flak, I should have ordered the others to pull off the target high and dry. But I did neither of those things and had to live with the fact."

Link studied his brandy snifter.

"I finally turned to some advice I'd gotten from an old warhorse. It went like this. 'When you run into a challenge, try to do the right thing. Once it's done, learn from it but don't spend valuable time worrying about *could* have been. There are too many important things to concern yourself with for the present and future.'

"Take your case in Iraq. You were hit and kept your airplane flying. No one can change what happened after you limped away for home base and your pilots attacked the wrong column. The tacticians learned something and changed the guidelines. Now it's time for you to make a choice. Either you continue worrying about what could have been, or turn your mind to things you can do something about."

After a pause his son spoke. "Sometimes it isn't that easy to forget."

They sipped cognac and were quiet.

"How about you, Dad? Do you think about Turk Tatro?"

"Sometimes," he admitted. "But I don't let myself dwell

on it." Lucky realized his son was not entirely alone. He thought of Turk at the damnedest times.

Linda came in to join them. "I wish you'd spend the night," she complained.

"It's handier at the hotel. I would like to pick up some clothes, though." Link grinned. "I felt a little out of place wearing boots and a sheepskin coat to a nice restaurant."

"Everything you left is still in your room."

It was another hour before Link left them, carrying a half-filled military hang-up bag. At the door he solemnly shook Lucky's hand, then hugged his mother.

"I love you both," he said, and the words came freer than they had in years.

10:30 P.M.—Georgetown, Washington, D.C.

As they prepared for bed, Manny brought up the subject of Link Anderson again, trying to overcome Marian's objection. "He's the best chance we've got to lure Ghost in."

"I wonder if we shouldn't tell Linda and Lucky what we're doing."

"Lucky might not stand for it," Manny said. He felt guilty about keeping it from his friend, but he was driven in his determination. It had become a personal agenda that they stop Ghost from further killing.

"J.J. Davis telephoned from London," Marian said as she got into bed. "He had a nurse call, anyway. He's on his way back—should be in the office tomorrow morning."

"He should take sick leave."

"He thinks we should be on lookout for thefts of large quantities of explosives that might somehow end up in you-know-who's hands."

"This soon?"

"He doesn't want to take chances. I've prepared a message for all explosives importers, manufacturers, and storage facilities to watch after their stock especially closely."

Manny yawned, then put a tentative arm around her.

"Go to the other bedroom, Manny. Good night."

He tried to stroke her breast through the nightgown, but she pulled away.

"It's been a long time," he tried.

She hesitated. "Not long enough," she finally said.

8

Thursday, January 26th

4:50 A.M.—Rocky Mountain Arsenal, near Denver, Colorado

The Mark-37 Mod 1 thermonuclear weapons had once been carried in the bellies of B-52 Stratofortress bombers that roved about the perimeter of the Soviet Union on continuous airborne alert. Now contractors worked around the clock to disassemble them.

Radioactive materials and electronic components had been removed by Department of Energy technicians. All that remained were aluminum casings and high explosives.

The dismantlers followed the steps described in their contract precisely, for the worst thing that might befall a government contractor was a nuclear safety violation. The fact that the nuclear material had been removed was inconsequential. Two government safety monitors were assigned to watch over the process. Signs were posted about the building, reading: SAFETY IS YOUR RESPONSIBILITY. Every man and woman assigned to the contract had been thoroughly briefed on the volatility of the explosives involved.

Nose and tail sections were removed and placed in large waste containers, leaving only the center portions with the high explosives. Those were held securely as cone-shaped segments of cyclonite and tritonol were withdrawn and carefully placed into non-ferrous aluminum-alloy tubs.

Each cone weighed forty-four pounds. Each filled tub weighed more than half a metric ton.

Four such tubs of tritonol cones, together weighing more than six thousand pounds, were carefully tamped and covered, then hoisted onto a flatbed trailer and securely cinched down. A government inspector checked off the amounts and waved to the tractor driver.

The dangerous cargo was to be taken eight miles across the big base, and the trailer left in front of an earthen bunker called an "igloo." The tubs from that trailer, as well as from several others, would be moved into the igloo at the close of the day. They had been working around the clock to finish on time and avoid the penalty specified in the strict government contract.

The Peterbilt's diesel engine surged, and the tractor-trailer moved slowly out of the building into the early morning darkness. Seven minutes later the driver turned off at gate three, where a pair of civilian guards waved him through.

Sixty-five thousand dollars had exchanged hands for their services. Twenty thousand to the contractor's on-site supervisor, fifteen to the driver, ten each to the guards and the woman at the igloo who was maintaining the records there.

After sixteen minutes of negotiating the deserted streets of the immense but unfilled industrial area, the driver pulled into a truck stop adjacent to Interstate 80 and drove to a darkly shadowed area. There he hurried from the cab, chocked, and disconnected the trailer. Less than four minutes after he'd entered the lot, he steered the unladen tractor back onto the roadway and accelerated toward the arsenal.

As the Peterbilt was moving out of sight, another diesel-powered tractor was pulled into position. The driver's assistant opened a case of flat-black spray-paint cans and methodically began to cover the government-owned flatbed's markings. Plain mud flaps were removed and replaced with others showing silver silhouettes of nude women. Yellow tarps were pulled in place over the tubs, each imprinted with a triangular logo reading: Oregon Building Industries.

In the cab were six different bills of lading, to be used at weight stations en route. The cargo was nontoxic concrete/plastic building materials. One showed the correct destination.

9:00 A.M.—Department of Justice, Washington, D.C.

Link reentered the briefing room, wearing a sport jacket, slacks, and dress shirt with tie. The same papers—the expense voucher and unsigned contract—were still in place on the tabletop.

As DeVera settled into his seat, Link handed over the keys. He'd been impressed. Manny's parking space was one of those reserved for high-ranking officials.

DeVera poured a cup of coffee for them both.

"What's this organization?" Link asked, referring to the sealed-off portion of the concourse, obviously set aside from other Department of Justice activities.

"It's an interdepartmental task force called ITF-4. One of those spook operations the public's not supposed to know about." DeVera handed coffee to Link. "After you sign on board, I'll set up a briefing to give you everything, including sources and methods. That means your name will go to a list, and you'll be monitored for life. For now be content knowing our purpose is to capture Ghost and his men."

"How about Judge Lindquist?"

"She's boss. I'm number two honcho. Made your decision about joining us?"

"Not yet," he replied.

"Then there'll be no more answers about the organization, okay?"

"I understand."

"Let's go back to the Piccadilly disaster." DeVera began to outline what they knew about Ghost's operation in London, which was considerable. They'd stayed in an apartment house off Regent Street, not far from the underground station. Dressed and acted like Jamaicans, and were good at it, fooling everyone.

Manny described the bombs, then showed a photo of a scrap of suitcase lining with the two squiggles. "The psych profile describes Ghost as an egotist. He likes to leave his mark."

Ghost's group had left the apartments clean, with no prints or evidence of their stay. The three men had likely left town, and then Charlie had returned for the shooting. They'd lost a good FBI agent, and Supervising Agent J.J. Davis had been wounded.

"Sounds like you were almost a casualty yourself."

"I saw flak over North Vietnam, like you did over Iraq. There's no such thing as accurate flak unless it hits you. I moved at the right time, and Charlie missed."

Link was reminded of the philosophy his father had mentioned. Manny didn't seem concerned about could-have-beens.

"Once we knew Charlie was back in London, we grabbed at the opportunity. Sending him back was Ghost's first big mistake. Scotland Yard put heavy surveillance in . . ."

The door opened and Marian Lindquist interrupted. "Guess who's in town?" she asked Manny. A corpulent man followed her into the room, his lower face swathed in bandages.

DeVera scurried to pull out a chair. "Damn, J.J., you shouldn't be here."

"He's as mule-headed as ever," Marian said with a concerned look.

Davis sat heavily, then motioned to DeVera, who pulled up beside him. He pulled over the pad Link had been using and scribbled words, then looked inquiringly at Manny.

"Come with me, Link," said Marian. "Bring your coffee, and we'll go to my office."

Link followed her from the room and down the hall. The secretary in Marian's outer office smiled nicely as they passed through.

"Watch out for Mimi," Marian said when the door was closed. "She's asked a hundred questions about you. One of the first was whether you were married."

"Sounds like my mother."

"You had dinner at the Farmhouse?"

They talked briefly about Lucky and Linda, then she asked, "Have you made up your mind about coming aboard?"

He tossed her a challenge. "Should I?"

She hesitated. "The men Manny's telling you about must be stopped," she finally said.

The intercom buzzed and the secretary's voice sounded. J.J. Davis had left, and Mr. DeVera was ready for Mr. Anderson.

The briefing resumed. The previous week, Charlie had been picked up coming into O'Hare International dressed as a Pakistani.

DeVera didn't seem as pleased as Link would have thought.

"That's great," Link tried.

"Now the bad news. Two days ago Ghost made a phone call to the *London Times*, saying if he wasn't released, the United States would go into mourning."

Link stared. "What does that mean?"

"Who knows? We're sure as hell taking it seriously, though."

"That's all he said? That the U.S. would go into mourning?"

"We've got it on tape. He said that, then added some words we're having trouble with." DeVera read from a sheet of paper: *"Akah-ee o-match ee kay mosa."*

"What language is it?"

"We've got every reputable linguist we can find working on it. So far no one knows."

"Say it again?"

DeVera did so, reading the words slowly.

"Sounds like gibberish." Link frowned. "Do you really think Ghost might come to the States with his terrorism."

"We've never known him to make idle threats. There seems to be some kind of warped honor involved. We've had several psychological profiles made up on all three of them, and while some differ greatly—on that one part they agree. Ghost's never made a statement that wasn't true, and they don't believe he'll change. He's a compulsive *non*-liar."

"So you think he's coming?"

"That's a possibility, but then he might attack American interests abroad. There are a lot of them. Consulates, businesses, tourists, and so forth. We've sent bulletins to all the embassies."

"How much time do we have?"

DeVera picked up on the *we* and darted a look. "It's taken him anywhere from three weeks to two months to mount an operation. He's got to establish safe houses, get his hands on explosives, do his planning . . . all that. Ghost moves carefully. We've established a minimum window starting three weeks from the call."

"And if he comes to the States?"

"We should have even more time. Analysts at CIA and FBI agree it'll likely take Ghost a few days to slip into the

United States and a *minimum* of four or five weeks to set up. He'd have to get explosives, and we're tightening up sources. Then he's got to study his target and build a bomb. Both the agency and the bureau feel we'll have at least a month. They open the minimum probability window on February twentieth."

Link felt a chill run up his spine. "What kinds of targets would Ghost pick?"

"We're preparing a list of potentials—places like New York's Holland Tunnel, which was on the agenda of a Muslim extremist group. Then there's large-scale sports events, rock concerts, and such. We think he'd go after people like he did at Piccadilly."

"Damn. Can't you get something out of this man Charlie?"

"He's not talking. Just sits in his cell and stares at walls."

"What makes you think I can help?" Link asked the question quietly.

"Ghost has always promised his men that if they were captured, he'd come for them."

DeVera looked evenly at him, then slid an eight-by-ten glossy photograph across the table. "That's Charlie."

It was a full-color police mug shot with name and number placard. The face was impassive, the features those of Link Anderson. As he stared at Charlie's image, stunned at the similarity, Link felt the same emotional tug he'd experienced when he'd seen Ghost's photo.

DeVera began to detail what he wanted from him.

Americana Hotel, Washington, D.C.

After lunch in the building cafeteria, Manny DeVera drove Link to the hotel. He had more than an hour to pack and check out before leaving for Baltimore–Washington International, where Mimi had him booked on a flight back to Kalispel, via Denver. After shaking hands, Link crawled out. Manny gave him a last wave before driving away.

Link stood at the curb for a moment, watching him depart with mixed feelings. DeVera wanted to use him as a lure, to draw Ghost so they could capture him. There would be two efforts. The first would be in the States. If that one didn't work, a second attempt would be made in Europe.

Link had not signed the contract. He'd said he would think it over, and Manny had been careful not to apply pressure. They had a month—Link had promised an answer within a week. He knew he would do it. What other response could he give? Still, he wanted some time to himself before he made the move from the cabin and the simpler life he'd made for himself.

He went up to his room and packed, changing back into jeans, boots, and western shirt. They'd become a sort of uniform during the past two years, and he felt comfortable in them. He might look odd at BWI, but when he deplaned at Kalispel they'd be appropriate.

Before leaving the hotel room, he phoned the Farmhouse and spoke with his mother. When he told her he'd be returning in a week, she was pleased. The conversation made him feel better about himself and the decision he would make.

As Link hung up he detected a faint, unpleasant odor that he'd not noticed before. Disinfectant? He shucked into the sheepskin coat and hefted the bags. As he went down to the lobby the acrid smell persisted.

At the desk Link encountered a rush of people preparing to check out. He entered the rear of the queue, thinking about what he'd learned during the past two days.

DeVera and Judge Lindquist were right. Ghost must be taken . . . his killing stopped.

The pungent odor intensified, and he grew the uneasy sensation that he was being observed. He glanced around and saw no one looking, but the odor and the feeling persisted as he moved forward in the line.

"How was your stay, sir?" asked a dapper black man as he stepped to the front of the line and handed over his room key.

The odor and the uneasiness remained. "Good enough," he found himself answering, pulling a credit card from his wallet. "There should be a phone call on there."

"We've got it," the man said brightly. His machine made a sputtering noise and spat out an itemized form. "If you'll sign there, you'll be done."

As he bent over the form, Link frowned, then glanced up into a mirror behind the clerk. A compact, dark man was staring. As their eyes locked, an emotional wave swept over him.

The face was unfamiliar, yet was indelibly etched in his mind. It was a feeling of déjà vu—he'd stared into the same eyes before—he knew the man. Yet who was he?

The man he knew but did not recognize moved . . . and was gone.

Link spun and pushed through the crowd. The man had melted away somehow. Link continued to the door. As he stepped outside the odor returned.

There were several people near the entrance. Beyond them the compact man was twenty yards down the street, walking at a brisk pace. Link hurried after him.

A violent blow struck him in the side, and he reeled, staggered, and almost fell. When he came upright, there was no one near . . . and both the odor and the sensation were dwindling.

He fingered his tender kidney area and looked. The compact man was gone.

A cabbie lounged nearby, watching him. "Did you see who hit me?" Link asked.

The cabbie shrugged. "Better check your wallet, man."

He did. Then he remembered he'd left it on the counter.

As he returned inside, the bruise still throbbing, Link wondered. The compact man's face was unlike those he'd seen in DeVera's photos, yet he'd experienced the same odd sensation of familiarity. Had it been Ghost?

Hadn't DeVera said that Ghost couldn't be in the country yet?

Link shook his head at his folly. Whoever it had been was now gone.

As he pushed his way to the counter, he tried to return his thoughts to the checkout and concentrate on getting to BWI on time—yet Link could not stop thinking of the compact man and the emotion he'd aroused. The fact that he'd fled was equally puzzling.

Link's wallet lay opened on the counter. "Sorry about that," he mumbled to the still-surprised desk clerk. "I thought I saw someone I knew."

9

Friday, January 27th

6:55 A.M.—Boomtown, Washington, D.C.

The run-down house was on the northeast side of Washington in a neighborhood the DEA called crack heaven, for there were more than a hundred known crack houses there. The police called it the combat zone, and seldom ventured there at night unless they took at least three patrol cruisers and were on a specific mission of mercy. But the local residents called it Boomtown because of all the shootings—drive-by and otherwise—in the past ten years.

The house was small, once white on the exterior, now faded and covered with artless graffiti. Inside, the four main rooms were adorned with ancient wallpaper sporting various flora, but they were well-scrubbed and the appliances in the small kitchen were in operating condition. A ten-year-old van was in the garage. A black Ford was parked at the curb. They didn't worry about thieves or vandals. Three burly black men lolled about the area, ignoring dealers and watching over things during the daytime. At night their numbers were doubled.

Ghost lay in bed, staring at the dark wall and thinking of what must be done. The previous day he'd called his tutors. An elder had taken his cellular telephone number, then uttered a single word of guidance and hung up.

The number would be passed to the man code-named

Wayfinder. The word of guidance the elder passed on had been reinforced in his meditation.

His idea had been to take things cautiously, to plan carefully, and to wait until every condition was perfect. Part of his mind still argued that was the rational thing to do.

But the new word that reverberated in his mind was "relentless."

The bedside phone warbled. "Yeah?" Ghost said, using a sullen ghetto voice.

"I got the information on the cowboy," said Martin Cherone's quiet and sleepy voice. "I'll be by in a few minutes." He hung up.

Ghost lay back and began to modify his original plan with the new guidance.

Be relentless.

The first target was so audacious that they'd be thrown off balance. Joseph DiFazio had thought Ghost would fail. He didn't understand it was audacity that would make it work. Ghost would have their full attention—and their panic—on his side. Be smart. Be thorough. Now also be relentless. He'd continue with his list: *bam . . . bam . . . bam.* They wouldn't expect it. They'd think he'd have to take time to set up, to plan and prepare between one target and the next.

Make them bleed. Keep at it until they blinked. Keep on until they agreed to his terms.

It was time to live out his destiny.

He remained troubled by yesterday's eye contact at the hotel. At first he'd sworn it was Charlie. The men were that similar in appearance, down to the western clothing Charlie wore when he was at home. But there was a difference. This one was huskier, taut as a drawn bow, his eyes hawk-like and observant. A danger flag had flickered, the helper's warning, but Ghost had felt an odd tug of emotion. Not for Charlie, but for the new man. As if he'd known him.

Ghost had been perplexed even after Rashad had rejoined him. When Martin Cherone had arrived to take them to the Boomtown safe house, Ghost told him to learn more about the man in the boots and sheepskin coat. He might be a hazard to the operation.

He'd gone to his bedroom as soon as they'd arrived at the house, and—after long reflection—realized that he'd known of the man's existence. There were dim memories of another who looked like Charlie.

He'd been directed to the hotel by the helper, who had wanted Ghost to meet his enemy.

Enemy? Ghost wondered. Perhaps Martin Cherone could tell him more.

Ghost went to the bathroom. He was efficient with his toilet. He'd relieved himself, showered, shaved, and dressed within twenty minutes. He waited in the living room, watching the gloom outside brighten as the sun peeked through early morning overcast. Waiting, wondering.

Martin Cherone arrived with the two men who'd accompanied him the previous evening.

"Jesus but it's early," Cherone complained as he opened the door. He motioned the others toward the kitchen so they could talk.

Ghost nodded impatiently. "What did you learn?"

"A government sedan dropped him off. He was registered as A. L. Anderson, from . . . ," he pulled a note from his shirt pocket, "Boudie Springs, Montana."

Ghost waited. Finally he frowned. "That's all?"

"If you want more, it'll take time."

Ghost sighed. "I do the planning, like I did last time we worked together. You get what I need, when I need it. That's our agreement. I need information on A. L. Anderson."

Cherone's face tightened with irritation.

"Something else. I told you last time we worked together and I told you in New York. One conduit to the employer. That's you. No one else sees us up close. You had those two with you last night, but at least it was dark. Now they've seen me in the light."

"I'll vouch for them."

"You don't understand. I won't work with those who can't listen."

Cherone's face flushed. "They're my people."

"I don't care if they're your mother and father, your priest or rabbi. *No* one sees us. That's the way I work. If you don't want to cooperate, we'll walk now."

Cherone's eyes narrowed as he thought it over. Ghost knew what his response would be. He would not dare go against Joseph DiFazio's wishes.

"Tell me," Ghost said evenly, "so I won't waste any more of my time."

Martin Cherone blew out a breath. "I forgot the way you work." He looked toward the kitchen, frowning. "What do you want done?"

Ghost made a decision. With the size and fury of the operation, he might need the extra muscle. "I'll make an exception. But just those guys. No more." Rashad would silence them later, when the operation was cleaned up.

Cherone brightened. "Sorry."

"I need more information about A. L. Anderson."

Martin Cherone's attitude had changed. "One of our assets is the second biggest credit bureau in the country. We can find out anything about anyone. Anderson used a card at the hotel, and we got the number. That'll access his social security number. One phone call, and the credit people will punch a few computer buttons and tell us what kind of tennis shoes his mother wears. Where he is, where he's been . . . everything. And it's legitimate."

Ghost shook his head in feigned interest.

Cherone smiled, as if he was Ghost's buddy. "That's better than flying out to Bumfuck, Montana, where it's probably so cold the roaches wear warmers."

"Tell them I need information as quickly as possible, then to stay on him."

"I'll call now." Cherone started toward the kitchen telephone.

"One moment," said Ghost. He handed Martin Cherone an envelope. Inside was a list of things he'd need. Electronic equipment and precision tools. Components like mercury-flow fuzes, radio transmitters and relay units, detonators and explosive squibs. There were also requests for information. Military unit and government agency disposition and procedures. VIP aircraft flight paths and routines. Individual addresses and lifestyles.

"Like before," Ghost said, "I'll give you a list every morning."

Relentless. The word echoed in Ghost's mind.

10:00 A.M.—Boudie Springs, Montana

Link had spent the night in Denver, grounded by a snowstorm—had landed only an hour earlier at Kalispel and driven straight home. He'd been greeted by a foot of fresh snow.

He sat in his living room, thoughtful as the fire flickered brighter, pondering over Manny's briefing and the face he'd glimpsed at the hotel. He remained in gloves and coat while heat from the stove made a dent in the harsh chill.

The previous night he'd dreamed of the Grandfather again. As always, it was difficult to remember the subject. Again there'd been something about returning home to prepare himself.

He was home. What was there to prepare? Eggs and bacon? He tried to make light of it all, but his effort fell flat.

A question reared suddenly, and he wondered if it wasn't a vestige of the Grandfather dream. *Who am I?* The message was strident.

Link went into one of the closed-off bedrooms, opened a closet, and searched through a cardboard box until he came to the folder his mother had given him years before. He quickly left the cold room to return to the heated area.

He sat at the table and opened the old folder. Inside was a sheaf of stapled papers, on top a collection of State of Montana forms filled with bureaucratese. They'd been issued to the Sisters of Joseph Foundling Agency, Helena, Montana, dated August, 1968, and contained little information. Next were adoption papers, a birth certificate, and a name change form—Black Albertson to Abraham Lincoln Anderson—all appropriately stamped and sealed.

What kind of first name was Black? for God's sake. Lucky and Linda had given him the new name. He had no recollection of life with the other.

Link sorted through the rest of the papers. There was nothing new to derive from them.

He thought of Charlie. The physical similarity was uncanny.

With the dearth of information about his childhood, he wondered if Charlie might not be a relative. Possibly also from the reservation. He'd been hesitant to look into his past, expecting to dislike what he found. It certainly didn't please him that he might be related to Charlie. Yet Manny might be able to use whatever he could discover to help capture and stop Ghost.

DeVera said they had weeks before Ghost could begin his terrorism. Link had decided to take a few days to put things in order before agreeing to help.

Link opened a kitchen drawer, delved out a Montana road map, and spread it onto the tabletop. He found the Blackfeet Reservation and looked for Peshan, the town shown as his place of birth, but couldn't find it. There was no listing for it in the index at the side of the map.

The reservation was just across the mountains from Boudie Springs, the largest town there was called Browning. As much as he disliked the idea of confirming he was the cast-off of a drunken squaw, he decided to find out just who the hell Lincoln Anderson—or more accurately the child born as "Black Albertson" thirty-one years earlier—really was. And, if he was damnably unlucky, he'd learn something about Charlie.

Link called the ski patrol captain at Borealis Mountain and told him he'd be temporarily leaving the area on personal business. The patrol captain liked his work, and after a short argument said Link would have a job when he returned. He asked how long he'd be away. Link guessed at a month or two.

He went to the local bank, where he pulled out half of his savings, $5,600, and put all but five hundred in traveler's checks. Next he dropped by Jamie's Pub and gave Myra Bourne the extra set of key to the cabin, saying he'd be out of town for a while. She said Jim would drop by periodically and check it. He gave his parents' telephone number in case she needed to get in touch.

Link kept the pickup in good running condition, so there was nothing to do there. He stopped by the post office and had his mail forwarded to his parents, then the phone company to have his number placed on hold. Link returned to his cabin and repacked the carry-on bag with fresh underwear, jeans, and shirts, then put it and the hang-up bag with the city clothes near the door. Finally he sat at the table again, to study the papers closer and glean every possible clue.

Tomorrow he'd head south, then east on U.S. Route 2. The "Going to the Sun" road, directly across the high Lewis range, was closed in winter due to heavy snows. He regretted having to go around because the direct route would have taken him past Siyeh Mountain, and he always felt a rush of warmth when he looked upon the craggy, brooding massif.

2:00 P.M.—Washington, D.C.

Prudence befit the scholarly image he'd picked. Since the sky threatened rain, Ghost slumped inside a dun-colored raincoat. He wore a plaid porkpie hat, horned-rim eyeglasses, sport jacket with shoulder padding removed, green shirt with blue bow tie, and a bulky sweater. He was a studious tourist, perhaps a schoolteacher, without the slightest threatening mannerism.

He'd driven about the area several times to get the traffic flow fixed in his mind, and was now walking on New York Avenue where it turned onto Executive Boulevard. He approached the front of the objective, then stopped and stared as a number of other tourists were doing. A woman with children in tow bumped against him. He smiled kindly, then stared again at the huge home, thinking of the lifestyle of the people who lived there.

It was not difficult to despise them.

He remembered how he and Charlie had lived like animals when they'd been with old man Weiser. Not at all like the family who lived in the big home. He wondered what they'd think if a slice of moldy bread were tossed onto the floor and they were told that was all they'd get because they'd not finished the day's impossible chores.

He estimated angles and distances with his eyes, and although he was good at such mental calculations, knew he must have more precise measurements. He'd bought a detailed map of the house, gates, lawns, and driveways for two dollars at a souvenir stand. It would be sufficient for his purpose. Security at the mansion was thorough, but a focused bomb could reach out to such a target. All Ghost needed were proper materials and knowledge of the building to construct an appropriate device.

He began to walk again, picked an appropriate place to park the car bomb, stopped, and surveyed it. As he examined, Ghost muttered *Akai omachk kai mohtsah* under his breath.

4:55 P.M.—ITF-4 Offices, Department of Justice, Washington, D.C.

Manny sat at his desk, wondering what his next step should be. He'd been relieved of all other duties, but it was still difficult to know the best direction to take.

There'd been no sightings of Ghost or Rashad, not even the normal false ones, and Charlie remained tight-lipped in Chicago. The silence lent to wild speculations, but without firm knowledge of what Ghost might do—and where—perhaps those were necessary. Where would they strike? When and how? Who were the potential victims?

He examined the two typed sheets of paper laid out before himself and reread the words spoken during the telephone call Ghost had made to the *London Times*.

Transcript of TeleCon—23 Jan, 1538 GMT

"This is Ghost. I've got something for you."—Source verified.

[Background sound. Human coughing—Unknown source.]

"Where are you?"—Source verified as John L. Dye, London Times

"Don't be concerned about that. This time it's about Charlie. They've got him."—Ghost

[Background sound. Laughter—Unknown source.]

"Who's they? Who's got him?"—Dye

"The Yanks took Charlie hostage at the Chicago airport."—Ghost

[Background sound. Voice speaking Portuguese words: flight, seven are distinguishable—Unknown source.]

"Where do they have him?"—Dye

"Don't worry about that part of it. I know where they took him. I know what they're doing with him. Have you got your recorder on?"—Ghost

"Yes."—Dye

"Good." [Sounds of breathing.] "Give the fucking Yanks a copy of the tape. They'll want to hear what I've got for them."—Ghost

"Where are you?"—Dye

[Background sound. Child crying. Voice speaking French words: the automobile in the parking lot is distinguishable—Unknown sources.]

"Maybe I'm at the hotel next door. I won't be here long. [Sounds of breathing.] The Yanks will be sorry they took Charlie. Their fucking government is going to be flying a lot of flags at half mast if they don't let him go. Tell them that. Tell them it won't be worth it to them. If Charlie's not released immediately, the United States will go into mourning."—Ghost

"What does that mean?"—Dye

"Akah-ee o-match ee kay mosa."—Ghost

"What was that?"—Dye

[Sounds of telephone hang up.]

"Are you still there, Ghost?"—Dye

End of TeleCon. Total Time: 1 Minute, 11 Seconds

Manny stared at the transcript. Ghost had been upset—angrier than he'd ever been on previous tapes. He'd only been specific about one thing: that the United States would go into mourning. Which meant American deaths and suffering if he could not be found in time.

He thought again about the strange words. There'd been nothing from the linguists.

The security desk called from the downstairs lobby. There was a General Anderson who wished to see him. Manny told the guard to have Lucky brought to the third floor. He'd meet him at the security station there. He pursed his lips, wondering.

As he rose to leave, DeVera pressed an intercom button to tell Marian about their visitor.

Manny was waiting at the ITF-4 checkpoint when Lucky Anderson arrived. He'd already completed the form and had the visitor's badge in his hand.

He ushered him to his office. As soon as the door closed, Lucky asked his question. "What's going on with Link?"

"Have a seat."

"I want to know how my son's involved in whatever you're doing."

Manny sat, chin propped gloomily on his hand, studying his friend but not responding.

"My clearance is current. I still receive briefings concerning national security."

"I'd trust you with my life. I've done that, and I'd do so again. That doesn't give you the need to know. I can't tell you, Lucky. I don't have the authority."

"Will you be placing him in danger?"

Manny didn't respond.

Marian Lindquist came in and closed the door behind herself.

Lucky spun on his heel. "And *you.* You came to our home and wanted to know about Link, then he's suddenly called in for a briefing? We thought you were our *friend*, Marian."

"I am." She nodded at Manny. "So is he."

"Then tell me what the hell's going on."

"Okay."

Lucky's voice shook. "I want to know . . ." He stopped himself as her word sank in, looked back and forth between the two of them, then slowly took his seat.

"Give him the briefing," she told Manny.

When Lucky rose to leave two hours later, he did not reveal his emotions. He'd not agreed to help persuade Link, but he understood their problem and felt more grim than angry.

"One thing," he said. "If Link decides to help, promise you'll look out for him."

"That goes without saying."

Lucky squinted out the window at the dark courtyard. "Sometimes kids grow up, and you can't do a damned thing about it."

"Your father likely said the same thing."

"Probably." Lucky looked at his watch. "It's nearly eight o'clock. Let's go somewhere for a drink before I drive back to the Farmhouse."

Manny reached for his coat. "Why not. I'm already in trouble with Marian."

10

Saturday, January 28th

9:15 A.M.—Department of Justice, Washington, D.C.

On evenings and most weekends a skeleton crew of two intelligence duty officers manned the ITF-4 offices. Yet when Judge Lindquist and Manny had arrived at nine, Colonel Pershing Sloan was already in his office, working on a report. He labored fastidiously on such things and would also come in on Sunday. A widower without children, Sloan's work had become the most important thing in his life—the task force people the closest thing to family.

Marian had just finished reading the overnight message traffic when the colonel came in with a Flash priority fax. "Just picked this up at the comm center," said Sloan.

It was from FBI headquarters at the Hoover Building, specifically from Supervising Agent Davis. He'd shunned medical leave and was working out of an office there. Like them, J.J. was working overtime.

She turned the page and read, and felt her muscles involuntarily stiffen. An inspector at the Rocky Mountain Arsenal had discovered a discrepancy. A large amount of high explosives had either been taken or misplaced on or after the morning of January 26th, two days before.

Marian tried to reason that it had happened too quickly, that the explosives couldn't be intended for Ghost. But J.J. Davis was obviously not convinced:

I intend to fly to Denver to check on the matter. If theft is verified (it may be an administrative error, i.e., explosive misplaced into another bunker), we are presented with a grave problem. Tritonol is a volatile and versatile compound, well-suited to construct focused-effect devices.

Marian called Manny DeVera over the intercom and asked that he come to her office. As she waited her telephone buzzed.

Leonard Griggs, director of the NSC, came on the line. "Time to get off your butt," he growled in the unpleasant voice reserved for people who refused to toady to him.

She immediately bristled.

"Be here at nine o'clock Monday morning for the briefing," he told her, "and be prepared to tell the council what you're doing about Ghost."

"Director Griggs, this is an unclassified line," Marian cautioned. ITF-4 and Ghost were words not to be mentioned.

"Jesus. I didn't ask for a fucking sermon. The boss will be here, and the Vice President thinks he may want the briefing, since you alerted his office the fucking sky's about to fall."

She set her lips firmly. "I'll be there."

"Don't be late. This isn't a fucking beauty shop appointment." He abruptly hung up.

She'd been briefing them weekly, each time enduring Griggs's harassment. He was especially aggressive when the President was present.

When the previous NSC director had served, the administration had been plagued with criticism that the soft-spoken man preferred to study problems rather than act on them. The President hadn't looked far for a more forceful personality. Leonard Griggs had been the most volatile of his antiwar university acquaintances and had mellowed very little. No one could accuse Griggs of being reticent. His first act at NSC had been to change the membership—Marian had been among the original group—replacing them with incompetents who never questioned. The second had been to expand the council's attention to such issues as subjugation of America's military to UN control, and domestic inner city violence. Members of the cabinet were in full rebellion. The result was growing paralysis and chaos.

The President had been overheard saying that Len Griggs had charged the administration with new vitality. They were such good buddies, Griggs and the President, that Marian often wondered why her group hadn't been subjugated to the NSC as Griggs wanted. She was wearying of the battle. When Ghost was apprehended, she was seriously considering giving her notice and saying to hell with government work.

Manny entered with a smile. His expression faded as he read the fax from J.J. Davis.

In the ITF-4 communications center the senior intelligence duty officer read an item on the INTELNET computer screen that had been placed by the FBI's criminal division. A federal prosecutor named Harold Ringold had charged that a large number of very large, legitimate businesses were owned and controlled by organized crime. Two of those shown were a credit assurance company and a firm that installed security systems in homes and businesses.

The IDO prudently read the entry for a second time, for he was a careful man. Since he could see no possible connection with international terrorism, he went on to the next entry.

9:55 A.M.—Bethesda, Maryland

Ghost stood with Rashad and Martin Cherone, observing from shadows inside the small warehouse as the heavily laden flatbed trailer was chocked in place at the loading dock.

A work crew removed tarpaulins, exposing four large metal tubs, then backed away to make way for a heavy-load forklift. One by one, the tubs were brought into the warehouse, where the crew began to remove and stack twelve-by-eighteen-inch cones of concrete/plastic building material into wooden bins. Thirty cones were placed in three bins, twenty-five in the fourth—a total of one hundred and fifteen cones, each weighing forty-four pounds.

The empty tubs were returned to the trailer, lashed

down, and covered. Finished, the crew foreman herded his men outside and pressed a switch to lower the heavy warehouse door.

The three men approached the pallets. Cherone stood aside, watching. Ghost examined what he had to work with, then had Rashad carry a single cone to a worktable.

From outside they heard the roar of a diesel engine as the lightened rig was driven away.

Ghost withdrew a pocket knife and carefully stabbed the amber-colored substance, then carved out a walnut-size chunk. He lifted and smelled it—it gave off an acidic aroma more pungent than Semtech plastique. He worked it with his fingers.

Ghost shaped the piece into a square with his fingers, then changed it to a pyramid. The compound hadn't dried. Although it was old and had been exposed to air for the past two days, the burn rate would be undiminished. Tritonol was extremely volatile when properly triggered, yet was stable and would withstand considerable abuse. If he wished, he could drop a cone to the floor and nothing would happen. If exposed to a low temperature flame, it would melt.

Ghost was pleased with his choice.

He'd meditated that morning and again been told that he was about to begin what all of his life had been leading up to. He was the chosen one. He felt heady with emotion.

When ITF-4 had captured Charlie, they'd provided the catalyst. He might despise them, but he could not fault them, for they'd done what they had been formed to do. In turn, he would do what he'd been born to do. That was why the traveler had searched for and found him. That was what all that had gone before was about.

"Is it the right stuff?" asked Martin Cherone, eyeing the cones with respect.

"Yes." Ghost said to the Cosa Nostra conduit. He motioned for Rashad to begin bringing out the tools and electronic test equipment.

Ghost turned to Cherone. "I only have one thing on this morning's list. A vehicle."

"You name it." Cherone had been agreeable since the discussion in Boomtown.

"A late model black limousine? Split seats in front and

two bench seats in back." It would appear appropriate, parked near his objective.

"I'll have it here by afternoon." Cherone walked toward the side exit.

Rashad was placing the test equipment and toolboxes on the bench. Ghost watched him for a moment, then opened the manila folder, the first installment of exhaustive information he'd demanded from Cherone.

On top were schedules for several individuals. He leafed through, then paused.

Abraham Lincoln Anderson, a leaf of paper read, and gave his social security number. *DOB: 4 July 1964.* He settled down to read what they'd provided.

Why had Ghost's helper drawn him to meet the man who looked like Charlie? Was he truly a threat? The computer readout did not tell him those things, but it revealed other information about Anderson that interested him. For instance, he was preparing to take a trip.

12:30 P.M.—Browning, Blackfeet Indian Reservation, northern Montana

Link stepped from the pickup and walked toward the motel room. Halfway there he stopped and looked out at the snow-covered countryside. Browning was located in flatland at the base of the Lewis Range, a series of soaring peaks to the west. To the north and east was big sky country.

He pulled the battered, curled-brim hat lower over his forehead and huddled in the sheepskin coat as he cast his gaze about the small town.

Browning was vastly different from Boudie Springs, with its alpine setting, trendy restaurants, and upscale condos. Here the town's core was a collection of weatherbeaten stores, with modest homes scattered about. Stark and windblown were good descriptives for Browning.

The girl at the motel desk had told him he'd picked a poor day for his inquiries, for the reservation administrative offices wouldn't reopen until Monday. When he'd asked about Peshan, the place of his birth, she'd said she had no idea where it might be. There was a community college with a good library on the east side, she'd said, and he'd likely be able to find it there if it wasn't closed. He could also check with the people at the Museum of the Plains Indians on the west side. He remembered passing it on his way into town.

Link hauled his bags into the room, placed them unopened in a small closet area, and went back out. As he crawled into the pickup's cab, he questioned why he'd come. There'd been no dream the previous night. No message from the Grandfather—no nightmare about dying men in an APC. He'd slept well, and awakened refreshed and ready for the day.

He drove to a service station, topped off the gas tank, and again wondered. The rationale that he might discover information about himself that it might somehow lead to a clue about a group of international terrorists seemed increasingly ridiculous.

He ate lunch at a small restaurant in town, then drove to the museum—a large red-brick structure built in the thirties—and parked in the almost-deserted lot.

As he walked along a sidewalk, Link paused to study a stone that had been brought there from elsewhere. The legend read that Indian warrior parties had once stopped off at the stone—had touched it for good luck in their endeavor, whether hunting, raiding for horses, or just traveling past. There was nothing unique about the stone. Link stared, wondering what kind of mentality he was dealing with, then trudged on toward the entrance.

Inside, Link looked about the foyer until he spotted an open door. A dark-haired woman was seated in the small office, nibbling at a sandwich from a brown-bag lunch and writing on a pad of paper. The desk plaque read Marie S. LeBecque. She looked to be in her mid-twenties. Long hair shimmered with blue-black highlights, framing delicately sculpted features. She might have been considered beautiful if not for the distraction of a scar. Pale, gnarled skin marred the left side of her cheek and extended down her neck, disappearing under the fabric of a sky-blue dress. She'd been badly burned. The remainder of her skin was tawny, as if she had a well-tended suntan, but that seemed unlikely in the gloom of winter. He decided she was from a Mediterranean country. Italy? He considered the name. More likely southern France.

She glanced up. "Could I help you?" Her eyes were deep

brown and widely set, giving her an exotic look. Animation and intelligence glistened. When she smiled, as she was doing, her eyes sparkled. Link felt an immediate attraction.

"I'd like to ask about records of people living in the area."

"What time frame?"

"The 1960s?"

"Most of our records are much older. You'd do better looking in the agency office."

"They're closed today."

She studied him with the bright eyes, the smile playing at the corners of her mouth. Finally she pointed beyond him. "There's a display in the next room you might be interested in. Why don't you take a look while I finish a small project, then I'll try to help."

"Sure." Link turned and looked about. To his left was a gift shop, beyond it a sign showing the way toward something called the Native American Crafts Association. Directly before him was an arched doorway with a banner reading: 19TH CENTURY HERITAGE OF THE BLACKFEET PEOPLE. He entered and scanned a large room filled with exhibits and collections of artifacts. There were only two others, an Indian couple who were leaving.

Link paused at a placard near the entrance:

THE BLACKFEET NATION IS COMPRISED OF THREE RELATED TRIBES: THE SIKSIKA (BLACKFEET PROPER), KAINAH (BLOODS), AND THE PIKUNI (PIEGANS). THE THREE TRIBES HAVE BEEN RIVALS AT TIMES, BUT NEVER ENEMIES. THEY HAVE HISTORICALLY SHARED LANGUAGE, CUSTOMS, DRESS, AND RELIGIOUS BELIEFS. THROUGHOUT THE PAST THEY INTERMARRIED AND JOINED TOGETHER TO HUNT OR BATTLE ENEMIES. TODAY ONLY THE PIEGAN RESIDE IN LARGE NUMBERS IN WHAT HAS BECOME THE UNITED STATES. THE REMAINDER OF THE BLACKFEET PEOPLE LIVE IN PRESENT-DAY CANADA. ONCE EACH YEAR THE PEOPLE GATHER FOR A SUN DANCE CEREMONY, HOSTED BY ONE OF THE TRIBES TO CELEBRATE THEIR UNITY AS A COMMON PEOPLE—AS THEY HAVE DONE SINCE THE BEGINNING.

In the large room were mannequins dressed in traditional garb and headdresses. Men sporting spears, bows and arrows, and old firearms. Women in deer and elk-hide dresses, adorned with porcupine quillwork and profusions of silver bells. To his right were buffalo hides and paintings that depicted the various ways the great animals had been hunted. There was a rendering of a herd being driven over a cliff, with women waiting below to butcher them. A series of watercolors showed vast seas of buffalo with horseback-mounted Indians in their midst.

At the end of those displays was a sadder portrayal. A scant dozen animals were shown huddled together. The caption:

IN 1879, THE BUFFALO DISAPPEARED FROM THE CANADIAN PLAINS. IN 1884, THE PIEGAN KILLED THE LAST OF THE WILD BUFFALO IN MONTANA. THE PEOPLE WERE CHANGED FOREVER. WHEN THE SNOWS OF 1884 ARRIVED, 'STARVATION WINTER' BEGAN. IN THE NEXT MONTHS MORE THAN ONE-FIFTH OF THE PIEGAN TRIBE DIED OF SMALLPOX AND HUNGER.

Link worked his way around the room, examining displays and reading captions. The exhibits were professionally done, the collections laid out meaningfully. A good way to waste a few hours . . . if he'd been interested in such things.

He arrived at a collection of old photographs, protected inside a long, glass-covered case that extended the length of the rear wall. Link examined them, killing time until the woman in the office was freed from her task.

A photo showed a group of blue-clad men on horseback, armed with rifles and revolvers, wearing round-crowned black hats: MEN OF THE MAD DOG SOCIETY ARE INDUCTED INTO THE AGENCY POLICE FORCE—JUNE, 1894.

Scruffy white men lounged about a clapboard building, staring sullenly at the camera: INDIAN BUREAU ADMINISTRATORS AT OLD AGENCY, CIRCA 1881.

He'd obviously begun at the wrong end, for the dates of the photos were chronologically reversed—becoming earlier as he continued moving down the length of the showcase.

A clapboard storefront, with a small, stern-faced man staring at the camera. At his side was an Indian woman in a high-neck dress. HENRI J. LEBECQUE OPENS HIS TRADING POST AT OLD AGENCY, 1876. It was the same surname as the woman in the office. If she was related to the trader in the old photograph, she was likely a mixed blood—like himself. He felt an irrational twinge of revulsion, and consciously fought to quell it.

Link returned his attention to the next photograph. A large number of mounted Indian men, with women and travois in a separate group: GOING TO THE HUNT, 1874. AN ESTIMATED FOUR MILLION BUFFALO ROAMED THE NORTHERN PLAINS. TEN YEARS LATER THERE WERE NONE.

Two Indians were stiffly posed, with stoic faces and trade blankets draped about their shoulders. CHIEF LITTLE DOG AND HIS SON AT FORT BENTON—CIRCA 1865. BOTH MEN WERE FOUND MURDERED NEARBY IN 1866. WHITES ACCUSED THAT PIEGANS HAD KILLED THEM FOR BEING TOO FRIENDLY WITH AUTHORITIES.

The next prints were very old, taken at the dawn of photography.

A grim-faced man stared out at him, cradling a long-stemmed pipe.

LAME BULL (OF THE HARD-TOP-KNOTS BAND), CHIEF OF THE SOUTH PIEGAN, TAKEN AT THE GREAT COUNCIL WHERE 'LAME BULL'S TREATY' WAS SIGNED BY 26 CHIEFS OF THE BLACKFEET NATION AND U.S. GOV'T REPRESENTATIVES. THIS CALLED FOR PEACE WITH THE U.S. AND ESTABLISHED THE BLACKFEET RESERVATION, BOTH IN PERPETUITY. THE AGREEMENTS WERE EVENTUALLY BROKEN BY BOTH PARTIES. PHOTOGRAPH TAKEN OCTOBER, 1855.

Beside that one was a retouched photo of a man with his hair harshly drawn into a cone on his head. Someone had written *October 15, 1855* in flowery script across the bottom.

An odd tingling sensation formed as Link stared at the photo.

He read:

BLACK WOLF, WARRIOR AND HOLY MAN—SPIRITUAL LEADER OF THE COMBINED PIEGAN FROM (CIRCA) 1829 UNTIL 1835. SPIRITUAL LEADER OF THE SOUTH PIEGAN FROM 1835 UNTIL HIS DEATH IN 1867. THIS PHOTO TAKEN AT THE GREAT COUNCIL THE DAY BEFORE THE SIGNING OF LAME BULL'S TREATY.

Link became stone still as emotion continued to stir him. He examined Black Wolf's somber face closely. There was no doubt. He was the Grandfather.

"See something that interests you?" The voice came from his side.

"Hi there," he managed, embarrassed at being caught with the astonished expression.

She smiled and held out her hand. "I'm Marie LeBecque, curator of the museum."

They shook. "Link Anderson. From Boudie Springs, just across the mountains."

"We put a lot of work in on this exhibit. A number of the photos are from the Smithsonian in Washington. That's what the SI stands for on the captions. The ones marked HF are on loan from the Heye Foundation's Museum of the American Indian in New York."

He pointed. "How about this one?"

She smiled. "Black Wolf's from the Smithsonian."

"I've seen it before." *Something* had triggered the Grandfather dreams. He assumed it was an association with the old photograph. Since they'd lived near Washington, D.C., his parents had taken him through the various Smithsonian museums on several occasions as a child.

"Are you sure?" She sounded dubious.

"Pretty sure."

"I wrote my thesis on Black Wolf."

"You've got a degree in this stuff."

"You can say that. I have a masters in cultural anthropology, and I've finished some work toward a doctorate."

"I'm impressed."

"Do you know the story of Black Wolf?"

He shook his head. "I don't know about any of this."

She observed him. "Are you part Piegan?" She pronounced it "pay-gan."

"Maybe." He sighed. "Look, I'd never heard of Piegans until I read the sign at the door."

"And you don't know if you're one of them?" Her voice was reproachful.

"I was adopted when I was young. I know very little about my origins." He motioned at the photo. "Tell me about this guy."

"To understand Black Wolf, you have to know at least

a little about the Blackfeet people. It would take a few minutes." She had a low, melodic voice.

"I have the time, and I really would like to know about him."

She began in her pleasant voice. "Until the mid-nineteenth century, the Blackfeet were the most powerful of the American Indian plains nations . . . probably in North America."

She went to a map showing Montana and southern Alberta. "They controlled an empire stretching hundreds of miles east from the Rocky Mountains, and from the Yellowstone north to the Saskatchewan River. The Confederation consisted of the three tribes listed over there, the Siksika, Bloods, and Piegan, but the Piegan were the largest. They had hundreds of lodges and owned so many horses that they were easily the wealthiest of all Plains Indians.

"The Piegan wielded so much power that no other tribe could successfully challenge them. The Shoshoni, Assiniboine, Dakota Sioux, Crow, and Cree would invade from time to time, but they were always defeated and pushed out of the area Old Man had told them to . . ."

"Old Man?" Link interrupted.

"The creator of mankind. The Sun. The one who made it all."

"The Blackfoot deity?"

"Yes . . . well, sort of. It's complex. Anyway, Old Man had given the vast area to the Blackfeet and told them to keep all others out, which they did very effectively until the white man came along with their smallpox, whiskey traders, and worst of all"—she made an ogre's face and spoke in an ominous tone—"Washington politicians."

Link released a chuckle.

"The story began during the 1820s, when the Blackfeet nation was still strong. It started with an argument. On one side was a young warrior named Lame Bear, the only son of Walks Alone, who was the great chief of all the Piegan. On the other side was young, articulate Black Wolf, destined to become the most powerful medicine man of his time—perhaps of *all* time. The animosities festered until one day Lame Bear stole Black Wolf's youngest wife and, with a number of his friends from the Bull Clan, took her away to the north.

"Even worse, the story went around that he gave her to a warrior of the Snake tribe, a Shoshoni, who were the despised enemy of the Piegan. Supposedly the Shoshoni passed her around to his friends and then killed her. When Black Wolf heard about it he was outraged, so he asked Chief Walks Alone for warriors to pursue Lame Bear. The great chief, who loved his son dearly, refused. Black Wolf went to the mountains where he prepared a dream house, spread his medicine about, and fasted until he received guidance. Black Wolf came down from the mountains weak from hunger and thirst, and told the people what he'd learned. If the Piegan were to remain prosperous, Lame Bear and his Bull Clan friends must be banished forever."

"That sounds appropriate."

"Oh, but there were those who supported the other side of the argument. Lame Bear was popular, a great warrior, and there were stories that Black Wolf's youngest wife wasn't quite the innocent he proclaimed her to be."

"Did you get all that from books?"

"Except for the times when whites visited, there were no written accounts. And those the whites wrote were presented from their viewpoints, not the People's. I took my information from oral histories and drawings on buffalo skins to mark events during the various years and seasons. The different tribes and bands had slightly differing stories, but they generally agreed."

"It happened so long ago, I'm amazed you got anything at all."

"It was definitely not easy at first," she agreed. "But then the pieces started coming together like a jigsaw puzzle."

"What happened after Black Wolf told the boss he should banish his son?"

"Chief Walks Alone despaired. He couldn't disregard Black Wolf's dream or he might bring on drought or drive the buffalo away. He also couldn't stop loving his only son. He meditated for many days and nights, and decided he must do what was best for the People."

Link found himself listening intently; out of interest but also because he enjoyed watching Marie LeBecque and listening to her voice.

"Walks Alone gathered those who would follow and sent out the wayfinders . . ."

"Wayfinders?" Link asked.

"Scouts. The ones-who-go-ahead. The warriors who showed the way. Walks Alone and his group went north to join his son, Lame Bear. When they arrived there was a great celebration, but also sadness. The People were split forever. The North Piegan still live in present-day Canada, near Calgary, and we South Piegan remain here in Montana."

"We? You're Piegan?"

"Mostly. An Acadian from Maine named Henri Le-Becque came to set up a trading post in 1858 when the first reservation agency was opened, and married an Indian woman. He moved to Old Agency when the headquarters moved, then here to Browning. During the last fifty years, most of my family migrated to points south, but when I finished college I came home."

"Come home," the old Grandfather had told him in the dream. Was this the place he'd meant? Or Peshan, the town shown as his birthplace? Link abruptly rejected both ideas, refusing to accept the words of a make-believe character manufactured by a lonely child.

He returned to her story. "So the quarrel between Black Wolf and Lame Bear split the Piegans into northern and southern groups."

"That's what my research found. There are people here who say the division was made because the white men's government sent the Piegan to different reservations, but they're wrong. Some of us tend to blame everything on the white man. Some—especially ranchers and agents—exploited the Blackfeet, but by the time of the treaty the Piegan were already split."

"So Walks Alone and his son ran things up north, and Black Wolf was in charge here?"

"Black Wolf never became chief, but he remained the most influential man of the tribe with the most powerful spirit, and the chiefs spoke with him before making decisions. For instance, in 1854 Black Wolf had a vision and announced that the Piegan must make treaty with the whites, although most of the warriors felt they should continue fighting to keep them out. Black Wolf quickly lost patience. Those who wouldn't agree, Black Wolf banished to join Walks Alone and Lame Bear up north. Those who stayed agreed to his terms. The chiefs signed the treaty the following year, in 1855."

"Black Wolf was a powerful man," Link observed.

"He certainly was. In the north, Chief Walks Alone died brokenhearted because his people were split. His son, Lame Bear, blamed Black Wolf for his people's troubles, but whenever he tried to bring warriors to invade the South Piegan, Black Wolf would have visions that forewarned him and have even more men waiting to turn them back."

Link frowned. "You believe that? That his dreams warned him?"

"I'm telling the story of Black Wolf," she admonished, "not what I believe or disbelieve."

He offered a contrite smile. "Sorry. I won't interrupt again."

"When Black Wolf grew very old he went to Peshan, where the People erected an Okan lodge—that's another name for the medicine lodge—for a Sun Dance ceremony."

"Peshan?" The word burst from his lips.

"That's the old gathering place north of here. The South Piegan invited all of the Blackfeet nation. On the fourth day of the Okan celebration, Black Wolf withdrew into a sweat house to meditate. Lame Bear was waiting nearby. He sneaked into the sweat house, interrupted the sacred time with a shout, and attacked Black Wolf with an ax."

Link grimaced theatrically, making her laugh. He liked the sound of her happiness.

Marie continued. "But Black Wolf's spirit was great, and although his body was old and he was severely wounded, he crawled from the sweat house. A dozen holy men and warriors fell on Lame Bear and killed him, but Black Wolf also died."

"It sounds like a Greek tragedy."

"Doesn't it? There's great drama in the old stories. Anyway, the South Piegan began a great mourning. The medicine men and holy women carried Black Wolf's body away to a secret place, as he'd told them to do. In the meantime, members of the Bull Clan took Lame Bear's body away to the north.

"The South and North Piegan were never reunited. Some say the spirits of Black Wolf and Lame Bear still struggle in the area around Peshan."

Link grinned. "And some might think that's a pretty tall tale."

"Don't say that. It got me a masters degree, and I'll

probably use it for my doctorate." She smiled, and again Link was warmed by her radiance.

He grew silent for a moment. "My birth certificate reads that I was born at Peshan."

"Oh?" She seemed interested.

"What's it like there now?"

"There's nothing left except a few abandoned buildings and an old burial ground. The council limits access for fear outsiders will disturb things."

"Where is it?"

"About thirty miles north of here, near the Canadian border." She raised an eyebrow. "You're not thinking of going there, are you?"

"Maybe. How hard is it to get to?"

"It's well off the highway. You'd never find it unless you knew where to look." Marie LeBecque was studying his face. Perhaps the magnetism wasn't all one-way, he thought, then decided it was her professional curiosity that was aroused.

"Have you heard of a woman named Sarah Layton?" he asked.

"*Sarah* Layton?" She became thoughtful. "It doesn't ring a bell. Why?"

"That's the mother's name shown on my birth certificate. How about a man named Albertson? He was listed as my father."

"I'll look in our files. Let's go to my office."

He followed. She was petite, several inches shorter than he, and there was a sensuousness about her, a promise that an extremely appealing body lurked beneath the modest dress.

She sat at her desk. "What were the names?"

"Sarah Layton and a man named Albertson. No first name was given for the latter."

She wrote them down. "And your birth date?"

"Sometime in the summer of 1964. The certificate *estimates* the date to be July fourth. I've wondered why it wasn't more accurate."

"Some of the People aren't that interested in specific dates. If you were born to one of the farm families up there and they didn't get around to reporting it to the officials for a while, they may have been unsure about just when the event occurred."

"Think you'll be able to find anything?"

"Perhaps. I've got an uncle who knows a lot of people. He's been the town's general practitioner for the past thirty years. If anyone knows about them, he likely will."

"How soon can you talk to him?"

She cocked her head. "You've gone an entire lifetime and now you're in a hurry?"

"It's important to me."

"I'll see what I can find. When will you be back?"

"I'm staying at the Outlaw Motel. I can drop back by whenever it's convenient."

"Maybe in the morning," she said. "It's almost closing time. I'll talk to my uncle tonight."

Link had an idea. "There's something else you can do," he said, knowing he was being presumptuous. It was important that he not press his luck and alienate her.

She raised the eyebrow, forming the cute expression.

"I'd like you to show me the way to Peshan tomorrow."

She didn't appear as surprised as he'd thought she would. "Take you there, you mean?"

"I've got a four wheel drive pickup. It would be nice if you could show me the way, though. Or maybe suggest someone who might be willing to go."

"There's only a few old buildings and the burial ground. What would you look for?"

"I'm not sure," he admitted. He hesitated, then looked at her squarely. "I've been troubled by dreams recently." He surprised himself. She was the first human to whom he'd mentioned his secret.

"Oh?" The look of interest again.

He gave a lame shrug. "I thought I might find answers there."

"What sort of dreams do you have?"

"Some are pretty bizarre." He nodded back at the other room. "The photo of Black Wolf in there? Some of the dreams involve an old man who looks like him."

"That's interesting."

"I probably saw the photograph during a visit to the Smithsonian when I was young. My parents took me there several times. *Something* triggered the dreams."

She nodded abruptly. "We'll talk about it on the drive to Peshan," she said.

He grinned. "Great."

"You've piqued my curiosity. Sort of like when I was trying to put together the jigsaw puzzle I told you about, trying to dig up the old stories. There's a problem with your having seen the Black Wolf photo. Last year the Smithsonian people let me delve around in their archives. I found the photograph in a box that was sealed in 1895."

He released a breath. There were too damned many mysteries.

"One of the primary differences between European and Piegan cultures was the Indian belief in dreams."

"I'm not much for mysticism."

"Not many were capable of having meaningful visions. Only a few, and they became the great warriors and the holy men and women."

"I have trouble accepting that sort of thing."

"Saint Thomas was a doubter, too."

"But you believe it?"

"I keep an open mind. How about meeting here in the morning? We'll leave at eleven sharp, if that's okay," she said.

As he left the museum, Link wondered about what he'd learned, and whether any of it had anything to do with his search. He was sure of only one thing. He looked forward to seeing Marie LeBecque again, and to her presence during the drive to Peshan.

After dinner, Link went to a small bar at the edge of town for a drink before returning to the motel room. He sat at the counter, sipping tomato-beer and thinking about what he'd heard. Thus far he'd discovered nothing about his past, except that he'd identified the Grandfather.

Marie LeBecque was wrong. At some time in his childhood he'd seen a copy of the photo, or one similar to it, and had been so impressed that the image had become his nocturnal companion. It was the only logical explanation.

When he glanced to his side, a man wearing an expensive Stetson hat was looking intently at him. Link ignored him and returned to his thoughts.

Tomorrow he'd go to Peshan, take a look around, and return. It was unlikely anything could be found there. The following day, Monday, he'd drop by the administrative office and see what they had. Look up everyone named Albertson and try to find something about Sarah Layton.

While he was about it, he might as well see if they had anything on Charlie, although without a last name he didn't know how to begin.

"Captain Anderson?"

Link turned. The man who had been observing him slid his drink down the bar and came closer, his eyes fixed on him. "Your name's Anderson, right?"

When Link nodded, the man proffered his hand. "I'm Jack Douglas. I was a flight line chief at Davis Monthan in eighty-nine and ninety. I worked on your airplane a few times."

Link took the handshake. "I remember you."

"I was also in Saudi when you were there." He shook his head. "That was a bum rap you took, about your flight strafing the British armored column."

Link shrugged.

"We crew chiefs got the word from the other pilots," Douglas said. "There were tanks everywhere, and the Brits weren't marked. It was a wonder it didn't happen more often."

"Maybe."

"I saw your bird. You were lucky to make it back."

Link changed the subject. "What are you doing in Browning?"

"I'm from here. I made senior master sergeant, and ended up retiring last year. The air force isn't the same after the cutbacks. I miss the old air force, but not what it's become."

"So you live here now?"

"I've got some acreage not far out of town where I run a few head of cattle." Douglas drained the last of his drink and motioned at the bartender. "Let me buy you a drink, Captain."

"To hell with that," Link said. "I owe you and every one of the crew chiefs. You guys did the work . . . good work . . . and we got the credit."

Jack Douglas grinned. "My daddy told me to never turn down a free meal or a free drink. Now, what are *you* doing here?"

Link hesitated, then wondered what he thought he was hiding. "Looking up my past," he said, then added, "And finding out what I can about the Piegans."

Douglas nodded. "I knew you looked part Indian. I

didn't know you were Blackfeet, though. Learning anything?"

The drinks arrived and Link paid. "I went by the museum and picked up some."

"Talk to Marie LeBecque," Jack said. "She's sort of standoffish, but she's smart. If there's anything known about Piegan heritage, she's probably got it cataloged."

Link said he'd met her. They talked about the days they'd spent at the base in Arizona, then about Saudi Arabia.

"One thing you'll find out," Jack said. "We may act a little more civilized about it now, but we Piegans still like to strut around and play warrior. Probably two-thirds of the men around here have spent time in the military services. Any time there's a war brewing, all the young guys join up." He grinned. "Someone's got to fight the white eyes' wars for them."

Link chuckled.

"If you need anything while you're here, give me a shout. I'm in the book. We've got a lot of guys around from Vietnam and Desert Storm, and we support one another."

"I'll remember," Link said. A short while later, he left the bar to return to his motel room, feeling somehow better about himself after talking to Jack Douglas. He was also looking forward to tomorrow and seeing Marie LeBecque again.

11

Sunday, January 29th

7:30 A.M.—Rocky Mountain Arsenal,
near Denver, Colorado

Supervising Agent J.J. Davis arrived early at the sprawling weapons maintenance and storage site. He was met by Colonel Rash, project officer for the special weapons dismantling and disposal effort, who would answer his questions then accompany him on a tour of the facility.

The colonel was articulate and knowledgeable. He began by explaining the dismantling process. As he finished, Rash looked contemplatively at the FBI agent.

So U deal with HE last? J.J. wrote on his pad. He was getting better with his scribbled communication, worse with his moods. His jaw would remain wired for several weeks. He ate often to nourish his considerable bulk, but the process was time-consuming—liquids and mushy pap were introduced through a gap left by newly missing teeth—and he was perpetually hungry. The reason for the inquiry—that five thousand pounds of explosives were either misplaced or stolen—didn't help his disposition.

"Yes," Colonel Rash responded. "After the nuclear material and fuzing systems are removed, the remainder is taken to the dismantling shop. The aluminum casings are salvaged for recycling, and the explosives taken to igloos where they're stored until they can be neutralized."

How nutralize? J.J. wrote.

The colonel explained how the compound was immersed in alkaline solution until it became saturated, its volatility reduced to that of the chemically boosted fireplace logs sold in supermarkets. The resulting mush was then burned in closed-loop incinerators so toxic gases couldn't be released into the atmosphere."

Had missing HE been nutralized? J.J. wrote hopefully.

"No. The discrepancy occurred somewhere between the dismantling shop and the igloo."

U have 2 kinds of HE?

"These older weapons used cyclonite and tritonol. We've accounted for the cyclonite. It's tritonol that's missing."

J.J. Davis hmphed. He was out of questions that might bring good news responses. A thorough reinventory of the igloos had brought no answers.

"I'm still hopeful it might show up," the officer offered.

Do U believe that w/be the case?

"No." The colonel looked evenly at him. Whatever had happened to the explosives—whether it had occurred by error or purpose—his military career was ruined.

Davis nodded. *Go over process again*, he wrote.

As the colonel went through the details, J.J. began to mentally zero in on possibilities. Of those, and they were considerable, at the top of his list were the contractors and gate guards.

8:00 A.M.—Bethesda, Maryland

The previous day and evening Ghost had toiled on the Lincoln limousine. He'd begun by removing the center and rear doors on the right side. Next he'd removed all but the driver's seat and replaced the void with frameworks of steel rods that he'd arc-welded into position.

He began to place cones into the frame, fitting them in their respective channels like building blocks until the first layers were wedged in place. The cones were held firmly by the steel rods, the apexes of the cones directed at a common point to the right of the vehicle.

Ghost remeasured angles, then nodded, pleased with his work. He motioned to Rashad. "Bring the others," he told him. "One at a time."

As Ghost worked, he hummed a low tune, obsessed with

thoughts of Charlie. He remembered a time old man Weiser had beaten Charlie until blood ran down his back, all the while calling him a *goddam heathen.* Ghost had tried to stop him and received an even worse beating for his effort. But he'd successfully diverted the old man's attentions—he was older and stronger than Charlie and could endure pain better.

He remembered the period after they'd been taken north by the traveler, the strange-looking man with the wandering eye—how joyous Charlie had been at their new freedom—then how he'd tried to play like other nine-year-olds, but could not. He'd never lost his fear that Weiser could come and take them back.

Ghost had never known that kind of fear for the old man. Only hatred. Ghost remembered when the men of the secretive Bull Clan had told him how he'd been conceived, then lost. How they'd searched until the traveler had found him laboring at the hard-scrabble ranch.

They'd briefed him about the beginning, about Lame Bear and Black Wolf, then about the injustices wrought upon the People more than a century before.

He'd been initiated into the Bull Clan and tutored in the old beliefs. Be strong and honorable. Never lie. Mutilation of victims was proper. The men of the Bull Clan believed in vengeance. They'd called it covering . . . The painful deaths of five enemy might *cover* one of the People who'd been murdered.

It would take a legion of deaths to cover the great wrongs brought upon the People.

He was the chosen one, the People's instrument of retribution. He would accomplish feats no other warrior would dare. His spirit was stronger than that of any human, and no man would be able to defeat him.

When the time came, the Bull Clan tutors said the wayfinder would be in place to help him. The wayfinder had his telephone number. He wondered when he would call.

Ghost took another cone of tritonol from Rashad and slid it into the frame.

11:00 A.M.—Browning, Montana

When Link drove into the museum parking lot, Marie LeBecque was waiting in a white Jeep Cherokee wagon.

She got out and waved, then pulled a picnic basket from the rear.

He parked and went around to open the passenger's door, gratified that he'd cleaned the vehicle's interior that morning. He helped her into the cab, then handed in the basket.

Marie loosened the zipper of her Kelly-green woolen parka as he crawled into the driver's seat. "I thought we'd want a bite to eat," she said, nestling the basket at her feet.

"Good idea. Which way?"

She pointed westward. "Out to highway eighty-nine, then north toward the Canadian border. I'll show you where to turn off."

"You're the navigator," he said, placing the Ramcharger in gear.

The sun was out, peeking past cumulus puff clouds. "Nice day," he remarked as they pulled onto the roadway.

"It's lovely."

"I met a guy named Jack Douglas last night. We were stationed together in the air force. He spoke highly of you."

"Jack's one of the good guys. He retired from the military last year and came back to take over his family's ranch east of town, just beyond my uncle's place. Biggest spread in the area. They're well-to-do, but you'd never know it."

"Were you able to find out anything about the names?"

"I went through our records. There's nothing about anyone named Albertson, and no mention of a Sarah Layton."

"Damn," Link muttered.

"I called my uncle and he couldn't remember them either, but he reminded me of something I already knew. There was a *Henry* Layton."

"Did he live near Peshan?"

"Layton wasn't one of the People. He was a historian who came to the reservation in 1960, hired for the job I now have . . . curator of the museum. Henry Layton played a major part in modernizing the place. He instituted an artifact inventory system, interviewed a lot of the old-timers to update our oral history bank, and built a number of the displays that are still shown."

"Was he married?"

"A bachelor. I asked my aunt, and as far as she could remember he didn't even have a steady lady friend. Layton was dedicated. He went out on field trips around the reservation, taking photos of old encampment grounds and talking with people, especially the full-bloods. He gathered a lot of oral history. I've read some of it, and it was good. He didn't embellish or try to add anything, just recorded what they said and tried to put it in perspective with other accounts."

"I'd like to talk to him."

"You're too late. In 1963 he began to visit one area more than others, like he was onto something interesting at the northern part of the reservation. He kept going back periodically for the next three years—always alone—and sometimes spent several days on a single trip. Then he went out one day and didn't come back."

He glanced at her.

"That's all. He vanished ... just disappeared. Agency police nosed around up there, but they never found him or his vehicle. There was simply no sign of him."

"The northern part of the reservation," Link mused. He glanced at her. "Peshan?"

"Somewhere in that area. No one was sure just where. He'd take off with his camping equipment piled in the back of his Bronco without telling anyone where he was headed, and come back a few days later. Then that last time he just didn't come back."

"Layton's not a common name," Link mused. "Makes you wonder."

"We'll turn off in a couple more miles. The road isn't marked, so I'll have to show you."

They exited onto a rough road made marginally better by snow and ice that packed the potholes. Link slowed to a crawl, not wishing to bounce Marie too violently. It was noon before they approached a small collection of wooden buildings.

"This is it," Marie murmured, staring out at the open-sided shed and two long-neglected structures that adorned the bleak landscape.

"Not much," Link observed.

"Peshan was a gathering place where the tribe set up their annual Okan ... the Sun Dance. There was a small trading post built here, where supplies were brought in during the summer for the Okan celebrations." She pointed to their right. "There's a creek over there."

A grove of willows and cottonwood trees poked their heads out of a depression.

"The burial ground's in the thicket on this side of the creek. It's very old."

"You haven't been there?"

She smiled. "I try to approach my job scientifically, but I'm not one to rile the old spirits."

"You believe in that sort of thing?"

"I just don't enjoy hanging out in spooky places. There's not much to be learned from a bunch of old mounds. Maybe if they were opened there'd be something of interest, but the council wouldn't allow it. Peshan is a special place from the old days."

"Mounds? The Piegan buried their dead?"

"Not back then. Some of the bodies were placed in trees, like the Crow people did. Important men were laid out on sleeping robes in their lodges, with their favorite horse tied up outside and killed. The idea was that their spirit would ride off to the Sand Hills. No one knew how long it might take for the spirits to do that, so they didn't disturb them. Over the years the lodges collapsed. Blowing dust and dirt covered them, and the mounds formed."

He nodded toward the burial ground. "Is that where Black Wolf's body was taken?"

"No. They took him to the mountains. He'd been specific about where he was to be laid to rest, but it was a secret known only by the holy people. They were gone for six days. I studied different robes that showed major events for the various years, and Black Wolf's murder was certainly the biggest happening of that time. They all showed six small lines, and next to those the sign of a powerful spirit."

"So his body was left in his lodge somewhere in the mountains?"

"A lodge would have been too bulky and heavy. They were great to haul around prairies, but it would have been impossible to move one up there in that short period. Like I said, no one knew how his body was handled or where it was taken except the holy people.

"Black Wolf's body was well hidden. The holy people were concerned that the Bull Clan, friends of Lame Bear, might find and desecrate it."

"You mentioned this Bull Clan before."

"The men were separated into societies, sort of like men's clubs you find today . . . Elks, Masons, Moose, Rotary, and such. They performed various functions, and had secret ceremonies. The Bull Clan's duty was to keep the Blackfeet culture intact. Today they'd be classified as ultraright wingers. They hated Black Wolf and the white man's government equally. You can see why the South Piegan medicine men were determined to keep his body out of their hands."

"Perhaps they passed the secret down to other holy men. Are there any still around?"

"Yes, but it's not the same. My uncle's a general practitioner. He's also a medicine man and weather dancer at the annual Sun Dance, but they're just honorary titles for the ceremonies."

"Another dead end," Link muttered.

"If the secret *was* handed down, the most likely sources are gone. It was a special honor to be descended from Black Wolf. All of them were trained as holy people, and *maybe* they knew, but the line died out. The last descendant's a woman who's certifiably insane."

"Maybe we should talk to her."

"She can't speak coherently. She's called Crazy Woman. Every now and then she'll show up at a farm and wander around babbling nonsense. People are afraid of her. I wanted to interview her when I was researching my thesis, but my uncle warned me away. Anyway, why are you so interested in locating a hundred-and-thirty-year-old body?"

"I guess I'm looking for anything I can, and it sounds like another mystery."

"There are certainly enough of those."

"Let's look around," Link said, tired of butting his head against dead ends.

Outside, Marie led him to the largest of the shacks. "This was the trader's store," she said. "I believe it was last used in 1921."

"Mind if I look inside?"

"Be careful. I wouldn't trust these old structures."

Link pushed his way past a door that drooped from rusted hinges. Inside were collections of refuse and animal droppings. The main room was small, with a fallen counter at its back. He peeked into an open doorway and found an empty storeroom with more cobwebs and droppings.

"Pretty bad," Marie said from the outer door.

"Yeah." Link took a last look around and went back out. He walked toward the second, smaller building.

"What's this one?"

"Since there's no windows, it was likely a warehouse of some sort. Or maybe where the trader slept when he came out from Browning."

Link tried the door but it was firmly closed. He walked about the exterior. Unlike the trading post the smaller structure had no missing boards and he couldn't peek inside.

"Someone's made repairs," he said. Odd-shaped pieces of plywood were nailed in place.

"Recently?" Marie asked, looking puzzled.

The nails were old and rusted. "I don't think so. I'd like to look inside."

Marie gave him an unsure look. "There's talk of preserving Peshan. Especially the area where they held the Okan, but likely here, too."

"I've got a hammer in the truck. I'd repair any damage I make."

She made up her mind. "Go ahead. I'm curious, too."

Link pulled the hammer from the toolbox bolted into the back of the pickup, returned, and carefully pried at a piece of plywood nailed over a rent in the side of the building. A screeching sound issued as the wood came free. He peered but saw only darkness, so he went for a flashlight he kept behind the pickup's seat and looked again.

The interior was free of cobwebs and droppings. In his narrow line of vision he could see tattered, threadbare blankets, neatly folded and stacked in a corner.

"I think someone's staying in there," he announced uneasily.

"That's odd."

"If it's true, there's an easier way in." He walked to the front of the structure and stared at the door, then felt about its circumference until he found a leather thong protruding from a small hole. He gave a gentle tug. A latch was pulled, and the door swung inward.

"Yeah," he said. "Someone been here recently." There were three small wooden crates resting on their sides, their contents hidden from view by the angle.

Marie peered in from his side. "My uncle didn't think anyone lived within miles of here."

Link gingerly stepped inside, then knelt and looked into the crates. There were a few rags and two old water glasses, one of them cracked. There was also a pop bottle half-filled with water, a small stuffed animal, and a pocket knife. Everything was positioned very neatly.

The feeling grew that he was invading someone's home, and he'd started to rise when a shiny, metal object caught his eye. He carefully raised a heart-shaped golden locket with a broken chain. Link inserted a thumbnail and it popped open, revealing a faded photograph of a woman's face. He stared for a moment, then closed it and looked at the surface.

The impression was faint, but he could make out the ornately engraved initials: S.A.L.

"Sarah Layton?" Marie was kneeling beside him.

"But you said there was no record of her."

"None I could fine. My uncle couldn't remember anyone by that name, either."

"The initials could be for Sally Long or a hundred other names."

"It does seem to be an odd coincidence, though."

Link carefully replaced the locket where he'd found it, then stood and glanced about. "I feel like I'm intruding where I don't belong."

They left the building together, and he pulled on the door until he heard the latch fall.

"Let's have a bite to eat," she said.

"I have to replace the plywood first. I get the distinct feeling someone's staying there. Did you notice there was no dust on the floor?"

"It was very neat and clean."

Marie returned to the pickup while he recovered the hole.

The temperature remained ten degrees below freezing. They sat in the pickup cab, marginally warmed by radiant heat cast from the bright sun.

"So what do you think?" he asked, staring out toward the grove of willows. He'd thought he'd seen movement. Likely a coyote or other prairie animal, he decided.

"I think you like stacked pastrami on rye. At least I hope so."

He told her he did. While he munched on a sandwich, she produced potato salad, crunchy dill pickles, and a thermos of hot tea.

"Great!" he announced, then glanced her way, wondering. "I envy your husband."

She bit into a pickle, held up a bare left hand, and regarded the countryside.

"Fiancé?"

Marie LeBecque rolled her eyes, took a small bite of the potato salad. "I love this stuff. My aunt sends me home with dishes she makes. She feels sorry for me because she thinks I'm on the verge of becoming an old maid."

"Are you?"

"Nope. I plan on finding a hunk and settling down. Two kids. House with a view. All that mundane stuff."

"Any prospects?"

She took a bite of sandwich and chewed thoughtfully. "Maybe."

"I'm not that far along in the process. My mother's beginning to believe I'm a hopeless bachelor. I don't think she'd forgive me if I didn't produce some grandkids for her to spoil."

"My parents died in a fire when I was eleven. They were in back of the house, and I was in my room in front." Marie motioned at her scarred neck. "That's how I got this."

Link grimaced in sympathy.

"I spent the rest of my childhood with my grandparents in Billings. My aunt and uncle here would pick me up every summer to visit. They sent money, and then paid for my college. When I was in grad school, I decided to write my paper on one of the old Blackfeet legends and came back to do my research. Now I'm stuck."

"You don't like it here?"

"I love it: dust, wind, blowing snow, and all. It's my roots. Everyone needs to know about themselves. You, too, Link."

"Maybe."

"So what's your story? How does a guy like you end up in Boudie Springs? I don't know exactly why, but it doesn't seem to be a match."

He told her about himself from age four to the present. He even spoke of the Grandfather, whose nocturnal presence had helped him through the difficult times of his childhood. Link mentioned, but did not dwell on the strafing incident. He described his present life and how he enjoyed the physical challenges. The only part he omitted was the briefing at ITF-4.

She listened intently but politely, and didn't interrupt.

"That's it," he concluded. "I went to Boudie Springs to get away for a while, and came here to find out more about myself."

Marie looked at the small building. "It seems eerie, you wanting to get information about Sarah Layton, then coming here and finding the locket. Like I said before, it's almost too much for coincidence. I've done a lot of research, and it's just not that easy."

"What do we really have? Someone stays in the shed, and they've got an old locket with what *might* be the right initials."

"You don't think that's eerie?"

"Maybe. I just wish we had some real answers." Link smiled. "Thanks for bringing the food. I'm stuffed."

"Too bad," Marie said, taking out another container. "I brought this blackberry cobbler my aunt cooked, and that's *really* her specialty."

He ate that, too. When he finished he was filled to bursting.

"Now what do we do?" she asked as she placed everything into the basket.

"Show me the rest of it."

They climbed back out of the pickup cab, and Marie resumed her explanations. "Canada lies five miles to the north. Not many people live around here. There are a few farms on both sides of the border, but it's not good for much besides grazing cattle."

Link turned and looked again at the grove of willows three hundred yards south of the buildings. He seemed drawn, as he'd been to that other desolate area the frigid night the tourists had been lost. He remembered Marie had said it was forbidden. Yet . . .

Marie showed where the Piegan had set up their medicine lodge in the old days when they'd gathered for the annual Okan . . . the Sun Dance ceremony. "Over there the men would build sweat houses, and they'd strip down and go in to purify themselves."

"No women?"

"They were sacred to maledom, sort of like men's locker rooms at a football game. The old guys could go in and tell their tall tales to one another, and the youngsters would listen."

"Hot rocks in a pit in the middle?" he asked.

"Yes." She stopped. "I thought you didn't know about these things?"

He started to tell her he'd been in one in his dreams, but stopped himself. How *had* he known? What could have triggered such knowledge in a child. He argued with himself again. There must be a plausible reason. It had been described to him as a youth . . . or something.

"The sweat houses were relatively small," she said, "but the Okan lodge was very large, built just as Old Man had told them. The Okan was the most sacred ritual of the Blackfeet. The holy woman would open the ceremony, then the weather dancers would do their act to make sure they weren't rained out, and everyone had a great time. It was like Christmas, Mardi Gras, and Thanksgiving rolled into one. If a man had done something great that year, like get a coup on an enemy, he'd be given a new name, then shoved out into the world with it."

"Men were given more than one name?"

"Yes, and that really screwed things up for whites who dropped by. One year they might meet a guy named Black Kettle, and the next time they came, a man who looked just like him was named Big Bull. It was pretty confusing to them, but to the Blackfeet it made perfect sense. You knew a man named Big Bull had either seen something in a vision or in real life that had to do with a damn big buffalo. That was a lot more interesting than a guy who owned a pot."

Link grinned. "How about the women?"

"They were stuck with their names unless something really . . ."

"Look," he interrupted, staring toward the distant gully. A woman with long gray hair stood rock-still at the edge of the willows, watching them.

He felt the urge again, drawing him, and took a tentative step.

"Wait," Marie said in an awed whisper.

The old woman stared for another moment, then turned and was lost to their view.

"Who was she?"

Marie caught a breath. "The one called Crazy Woman. The purebloods say it's bad luck to look at her for long. She walks among the dead."

Link continued staring at the willows where the woman had disappeared.

"She's the last descendant of Black Wolf. As a girl she was prepared as a holy woman. She went into the mountains to seek guidance, and disappeared—like what happened with Henry Layton a few years later. People thought she'd likely frozen to death or been killed by an animal, but several years later she was discovered near here, demented and ranting nonsense."

"She looked hungry."

"She was emaciated when they found her that time, too. The agency police took her to Browning so they could nurse her back to health, but she escaped and came back. After doing the same thing a couple of times, the police decided to leave her alone."

Link cocked his head. "I wonder . . . could she be the one living in the shed?"

"I should have thought of her when we found it."

He remembered the locket. "What were her initials?"

"She had a traditional Piegan name. I remember it had a pretty sound, but I don't think the initials were S-A-L. Anyway, the woman in the photograph wasn't Piegan."

"I'd like to get a closer look. Maybe talk to her and ask a few questions."

"That might not be wise, Link. The people fear her, especially the full-bloods. They say she walks in the sacred grounds and talks to spirits."

"She looked like she's starving. There can't be much food out here. There was none in the place she's staying. Only the bottle of water."

"I've got another sandwich and some salad. I'll leave them behind." Marie gave a visible shudder, and Link knew it wasn't from the cold. "Let's go, shall we."

Link was stepping out of the shower when the telephone rang. It was Marie, whom he'd dropped off at the museum parking lot half an hour earlier.

"How about dinner?" she asked.

Link smiled. "Sounds great."

"I'll drop by your motel, and you can follow me to my uncle's house. I spoke with him on the phone a few minutes ago, and he's interested in what we found."

"Sure," he said, wishing they could be alone. He said he'd be in front in twenty minutes.

Marie was on time. She opened the Cherokee's door. "No use taking two vehicles."

Ten minutes later she pulled into a well-tended driveway half a mile off the highway east of town. The home was white, with gables, larger than most of the others he'd seen in the area.

"My uncle's name is Benjamin White Calf. He was my mother's older brother," Marie said as she shut off the engine. "He's very protective. If you make a move on me, he'll probably track you down, shoot you, and then string you up."

"Okay, no moves."

"If my aunt likes you, she'll stop him. She believes I'm drying up like a prune. She was seventeen when they married, and she felt *that* was too old."

"Then I'll make a move."

Marie pursed her lips thoughtfully. "Not yet." She slid out her door.

He dismounted and followed, smiling to himself.

Benjamin White Calf met them at the door. He was a large man, white-haired and thick of chest, with a prominent Roman nose.

When her uncle took Marie's parka, Link couldn't suppress a lingering stare. The green silk dress shimmered and clung, and there were no more doubts about the curves and hillocks of her body. She hurried away toward the kitchen.

"Your coat?" Ben White Calf was repeating, and Link came to life. He shrugged out of the sheepskin and gave his host an apologetic look.

The doctor smiled vaguely as he hung his coat and ushered him into the living room.

"Your home's very nice," Link said, and received a casual nod.

"Care for a libation before dinner?" his host asked. His look was appraising, and Link felt the same pangs of discomfort he'd suffered when fathers of high school dates examined him when he'd come for their daughters. He had a beer, Ben White Calf a soda—he didn't drink alcohol—and the conversation was confined to the various issues faced by the council. One of those was whether to open a casino in Browning, which the doctor vigorously opposed.

A short while later they were called into the dining room, where Marie and her aunt served a feast of succulent pork roast with all possible trimmings. There the discussion was about the museum and the new exhibit. Marie said the numbers of visitors were disheartening. Her aunt counseled her to be patient. Ben White Calf groused that the younger generation didn't give a damn about heritage. In another couple of years they'd be a bunch of homeless bums who gambled their money away at the casino they wanted to build.

When they'd finished, having topped off with fresh apple pie with ice cream, the doctor pushed his chair back and pulled a pudgy cigar from his pocket.

Marie's aunt glared. Ben White Calf ignored her, and lit the cigar with a match. He puffed once and sighed, then put it out and turned his gaze on Marie. "So you think Crazy Woman's living at Peshan."

"Someone lives there, and she was the only one we saw."

He became thoughtful for a moment, then turned his attention to Link. "You're searching for someone named Albertson?"

"He's shown on my birth certificate as my father."

The doctor shook his head. "There's been no people here named Albertson. No Sarah Layton, either. May have passed through, but they didn't live here."

They all went into the living room together. After a few minutes of polite conversation, Marie said she had to work tomorrow and must get home.

Link thanked his hosts and told Mrs. White Calf the meal had been delicious.

"You'll have to come back for another," Marie's aunt said, and Link noted a shrewd glimmer in her look.

When they were outside, walking to Marie's car, he said they were nice people.

"I think so."

On the return trip to town, they talked about the day's events.

"Thanks for everything," he said as she pulled up to the motel.

"I enjoyed it. It's like one of the puzzles I told you about."

He dawdled, trying to think of an excuse to see her again.

"What will you do tomorrow?" she asked.

"Check with the reservation administrative office for records, then go back to Peshan. All today did was rouse my curiosity. Maybe I can find something more concrete." He didn't tell her about the inner urgings.

"I don't know what you could find there," she said.

"Probably nothing. It's just a hope that there's something more." He looked evenly at her. "Care to come along?"

"I've got to work. There's a new project with . . ." Her voice trailed off, then she looked at him and sighed. "Oh hell. This is ridiculous. I'm interested in your search. I could try to get off early, say three-thirty or four. Is that too late?"

He smiled, uncaring that he revealed his pleasure. "I'll drop by the museum at three."

12

Monday, January 30th

3:00 A.M.*—Washington, D.C.*

Ghost looked to their left as Rashad drove past the spot where the limousine would be parked. There were two sets of signs on the side street. The first told motorists they were entering a restricted area, and parked automobiles would be promptly towed. The second signs issued a more terse warning: absolutely no vehicles were allowed. Security planners had considered car bombs. Since the mansion was substantial—with thick walls and shatter-resistant windows—they did not consider vehicles parked in the restricted zone to be as much of a hazard.

The public thought of bomb makers as cartoon characters wielding bowling balls with sputtering fuses. Or a guy lighting a bundle of dynamite sticks. They weren't entirely wrong. Most car bombs were rudimentary. If their makers wished to kill more people, they added explosive, like the buffoons who'd tried to take out the World Trade Center by stuffing a van with a home-brewed compound of diesel–fertilizer–gunpowder.

But Ghost was neither mad nor foolish. He considered himself part engineer, part artist. Given appropriate conditions and time, he could construct a focused device that—at two hundred yards—could take off a man's head and not dirty his suit. By varying burn rates, shapes, and fusing, he could reach out and destroy virtually any target within a reasonable distance.

This objective was difficult, and the device was not precise, but it would suffice to accomplish his purpose.

As they drove on, he memorized shadows and features as they'd appear at that hour. He stared especially hard as they passed the objective, trying to imagine the people who slept soundly there. *"Akai omachk kai mohtsah,"* Ghost whispered.

"You say something?" Rashad asked.

"Turn right up here, then we'll go to the warehouse."

Rashad switched on the overhead lights as Ghost approached the bench. Much had been done in the past two days. The limousine was almost ready. Twenty-one reshaped cones of tritonol were contained in the frameworks replacing the mid and rear seats. More than 900 pounds of it: focused upon a common point 270 yards to the right, perpendicular to the limousine's prow.

He leaned in the opened front right door, and knelt over the mechanism. Even the best bomb was nothing without a proper fuzing mechanism. Improperly fuzed, the blast effect would be diverted, the bomb a spectacular fireworks display rather than an instrument of destruction.

Ghost examined the color-coded wires. Minuscule time delays had been set, then checked on the oscilloscope for a plus and minus tolerance of microseconds, for the various cones must be initiated precisely together. A wire bundle ran from the rear—twenty-one wires, each attached to a detonator embedded in a cone.

He began to fasten the color-coded wires to their appropriate gold-plated terminals on the master timer. Once done he would recheck everything, then begin on cosmetics: form and paint sheets of thin aluminum to be fitted into the void left by the removed doors.

When set off, nine hundred pounds of explosive would be focused upon a pinpoint, reaching out like a fire bolt to the first objective.

Retribution. But there would be much more. *Akai omachk kai mohtsah.*

9:05 A.M.—Subbasement of the White House, Washington, D.C.

The President of the United States was, arguably, the most protected person in the world. A shift of "presidential detail" secret service agents always lurked nearby. His official residence was defended by a variety of light and heavy weapons. If a threat was perceived by the agent-in-charge, the President was moved to the nearest "safe room," blast-resistant vaults with self-contained life-support systems, located in the President's various sleeping quarters and work areas. If the agent-in-charge determined there was sufficient time, the President was hustled down to the subbasement, built to withstand a nuclear blast on the structure above.

Heavy steel doors in the White House subbasement opened onto a subterranean tunnel interconnecting with other key government buildings. The subbasement also contained offices, and the first large room encountered when you stepped off the main elevator was a conference room used by the National Security Council.

Until late the previous year, the chairman of ITF-4 had always served as a member of the NSC. When Leonard Griggs had taken over the council, he'd made changes he'd called "streamlining" and "reorienting." Judge Lindquist and several others were changed to "adviser" status. New members—all of whom incessantly agreed with Griggs—had taken their places.

White House insiders were increasingly talking about how indispensable Len Griggs had become to the President, saying he added "balance." Marian was less charitable. Griggs had created an "us-versus-them" atmosphere, with *them* being anyone Len Griggs could not influence. With the reelection effort looming, he was also increasingly inferring, "You tend to your campaign while I watch after the store." The President seemed to be blind to the fact that Griggs was destroying the already uneasy rapport within his cabinet. State and Defense were favorite targets, but others were also feeling Griggs's wrath and scorn.

The eleven senior NSC members sat about the conference table, awaiting the arrival of the President, who often sat in on the Monday morning drill. Marian Lindquist occupied a chair in the "peanut gallery" at the side of the room along with several others, the folder with her presentation beside her on the floor.

The Vice President entered the conference room quietly, looked about, then came over to the peanut gallery and leaned toward her.

"We're having a get-together a week from Friday. Don't make other plans, okay?" He grinned boyishly and took his seat at the conference table without waiting for an answer.

Marian knew the Vice President and his vivacious wife reasonably well. Following her appointment to ITF-4, he'd congratulated her and said that if things went the way he felt they would in a few years, she would certainly be high on his list of appointees. Thereafter, he'd gone out of his way to be pleasant.

They all stood as the President entered, talking animatedly with his Chief of Staff. When he slouched into his chair, the others also sat.

"I just saw the First Lady off. She said to make sure we don't get in trouble while she's away. No more scandals or invasions, that sort of thing."

Sounds of mirth tittered through the room.

"I've got a tight schedule this morning. What have we got?" he asked.

"Scandals and invasions?" joked the Chief of Staff.

Leonard Griggs took his feet. He was a short man with flat-black button eyes. His head was elongated, with shock-straight black hair severely swept back. A couple of years back he'd eliminated his trademark pigtail and earring, yet those had somehow seemed more fitting.

"Before we begin," he said, "I'd like to announce that I've added a domestic terrorism panel to the council. Their task will be to look hard at the continuing violence within the country and make suggestions on firearm control and such."

The President made an impatient gesture for him to continue.

"We'll open with three presentations. First a problem with Ukrainian wheat production that State *wrongly* believes will impact their long-range economy. Next a look at what's going on with the UN rapid reaction force and why our military should be placed under their command like the rest of the world. Finally a sit-rep on what's happening in Korea vis-à-vis the Chinese."

The President nodded abstractly, then formed his I-know-something-you-don't look. "The First Lady's working with a group of special education specialists this week. Teachers for the mentally retarded. Anyone have any idea how many kids like that we've got in the country?"

"Far too many," said Leonard Griggs with a sad shake of his head.

The President nodded. "As more crack babies come of age, there'll be a regular deluge. It's a topic we've got to keep in front of the public. *No* one can argue against helping children."

"It's a natural," said the Chief of Staff. "Good opportunity that the opposition can't attack without taking flak. I think it should go front-burner into the campaign."

Marian took her feet. "Mr. Chairman?" she said, looking at Leonard Griggs. "I have a presentation concerning a potential problem with the terrorist called Ghost."

"We heard it last week," Griggs grumbled.

"There's a new development. The theft of explosives at Rocky Mountain Arsenal has been verified. We're concerned it may be intended for Ghost."

"Have you confirmed he's coming to the States?" the Vice-President asked.

"I read the report she's talking about," interjected Leonard Griggs. "An FBI investigator *believes* the explosives *may* have been stolen."

Marian shook her head. "No, sir. The report reads that he's now relatively *certain* the explosives were stolen and transported out of the Denver area. He'll be interviewing more people at the site today, trying to determine how it was done and who's involved."

"One person being *relatively* sure doesn't *verify* anything. And there's absolutely no reason to believe this . . . Ghost . . . is in the country."

"It's the kind of explosives Ghost prefers. My concern is that things may be moving faster than we anticipated. If so we should act quickly to apprehend Ghost. That's the focus of my presentation . . . a way to lure him so we can capture him."

Griggs smirked. "Last time you weren't sure he was coming to the U.S., and if he did, it would take him a month to get established. Do you change your reports to meet the occasion?"

Several NSC members formed smiles. Leonard Griggs was known for his ability to put others in their places. The most recent recipient of his sarcasm had been ITF-4.

Marian turned to the President, trying to draw his attention from a whispered discussion with the chief of staff. "We're not positive of anything concerning Ghost's intent or location. He's elusive. But he's threatened American citizens, and now there's the fact of the theft. We'd like to try to neutralize him before he can do his damage. Our plan involves disinformation and the cooperation of more than one cabinet post, so I'll require executive approval."

Leonard Griggs sighed. "Leave your brief. I'll have the domestic terrorism panel study it and get back to you."

The President laughed at a joke whispered by his Chief of Staff as Marian set her mouth and started to sit down.

The Vice President was regarding Marian. "Do you feel there's an imminent threat?"

"We don't know, sir, but we're dealing with one of the most dangerous men in the world, and there's a possibility that he's been provided with explosives. My people have come up with an operation designed to draw him into a trap."

"I'd like to hear Marian's suggestion," the Vice President said.

The President had listened to the last part of her plea. He turned to the Chief of Staff.

The Chief of Staff shook his head. "No time. We've gotta make an appearance at a Kennedy Center benefit and get back for a one o'clock with the reelection committee."

The President regarded the Vice President. "After this meeting's over, you and Len listen to what she's got and give me your suggestion."

Browning, Montana

He is a young boy, naked and seated on an earthen ledge. The Grandfather is sad—sadder than he remembers him being, and speaks in the strange yet understandable tongue.

"There is no more time. Prepare yourself."

"Why, Grandfather?" the boy asks.

"You must stop him."

The words and image changes, and he sees an illuminated mansion. A sudden blinding flash hurts the boy's eyes. The light dwindles. There are cries of terror and agony.

The Grandfather's face is resolute. "You must hurry."

"What must I do?"

"Your duty. Stop him."

Duty . . . Stop him. The words echoed. It was the second time the dream had been repeated during the night. Link found himself sitting up in bed, his breathing loud in his ears.

"Jesus," he muttered, trying to calm the thumping in his chest. He purposefully filled his lungs with air and exhaled. He did it again—then waited as his heartbeat subsided. His eyes were grainy and he was logy with weariness, but there was no way to return to sleep. Too much was swirling in his head—too much adrenaline continuing to flood and charge him.

Link slid out of bed, switched on a light, and went to the bathroom for a glass of water. He drank it down, still feeling shaky. With the recurrences of the same Grandfather dream, there was no doubt what it had been about. A large home was destroyed by an explosion.

He'd foreseen the tragedy at Piccadilly. Was this one also real?

Stop him.

A flash of irritation swept over him. Why did the Grandfather plague him? No—the Grandfather was a whimsy created by his mind. What game was his *subconscious* playing? Was something actually wrong and his mind trying to alert him? If so, what was it trying to tell him?

Answer: he'd been thinking about the atrocities in Manny DeVera's briefing.

He stretched and worked shoulder muscles, then hmphed a weary sigh as he switched on the television, careful to keep the audio low. Link searched the channel guide, found the listing for CNN, and turned to it. After twenty minutes of watching the plight of Rwandans, Haitians, Cubans, Ethiopians and Bosnians, he decided there was nothing about a disaster at a mansion.

Link turned off the set. He wondered again about the dream. *A mansion. A bright flash of light. Voices crying out in panic.*

Duty. Stop him.

It was all bullshit. Smoke and mirrors generated by his mind.

It was growing light outside. He started to dress, deciding on an early breakfast. It would be a busy day.

* * *

The reservation administrative building wasn't difficult to locate. Link parked in a visitor's space and leaned into a stiff wind as he went inside.

The receptionist listened to him with disinterest, motioned vaguely down the hall, then pulled earphones in place and began to nod to an unheard beat as she fiddled with a Rolodex.

In the records office a plump-faced Indian girl took his request, disappeared into a back room for a moment, and returned with the original birth certificate for "Albertson, Black." He found no difference from the copy he'd brought with him.

He asked about records of his natural parents. She looked—there was nothing listed under the name of Sarah Layton and, except for himself, no Albertson.

An inexplicable rush of relief flowed through him. "There's no *Charles* Albertson?"

"There's no Albertson but yourself."

Although they looked alike, he and the terrorist called Charlie hadn't shared a last name.

She suggested that he try the Community College or the museum on the west side of town. They both kept some old records.

Link left the building half an hour after he'd entered it, no better off than when he'd arrived. As he opened the pickup door, he felt an icy gust. The sky was blustery. It would snow.

4:10 P.M.

Link waited in the parking lot with the heater blasting. He'd spent two frustrating hours at the Community College library and found nothing concerning Sarah Layton or anyone named Albertson. By the time he'd emerged, the temperature had dropped to near zero. There'd been intermittent snow flurries all afternoon.

Twice he'd gone in to check on Marie. Both times she'd been meeting with people in her office and motioned helplessly.

He saw movement at the museum door. The people she'd talked to came out and left. A moment later he watched as Marie LeBecque emerged, raised the hood of her parka, then bent into the blowing snow as she hurried. He got out and waited at the passenger door.

"Sorry I was so long," she said as she climbed in.

He went around and slid into the driver's seat, and immediately set the truck in motion. He didn't want to be later than necessary. Nightfall would come early in the winter gloom.

Link motioned at a house they passed. "Never seen so many American flags. Looks like every other house is flying one."

"We Piegan are patriotic. Whenever there's a war, our young men are first to join."

"That's what Jack Douglas said."

"Let me tell you an old but true story. You've heard how the Sioux and Cheyenne killed General Custer and his men. There's a local footnote. After their victory, the Sioux sent a pipe of tobacco to the Piegan, who were known as the fiercest light cavalry warriors of them all, asking them to join their fight. Our chiefs sent it back, saying they'd made treaty with the Americans. They felt it was no honor for two thousand warriors to defeat so few soldiers. Our people are still proud of that."

As they drove out of town, she told more vignettes about the Piegan, but his mind was elsewhere. Finally he interrupted. "Marie, I've got something I'd like to share with you."

As he drove, he told her what Manny DeVera had cautioned him to tell no one. He went through the briefing he'd received, explaining Ghost, Rashad, and Charlie, and what they'd done. The only detail he omitted was the fact that Charlie had been captured.

She listened raptly.

He'd turned off on the dirt road and driven almost to Peshan by the time he finished.

Marie shook her head. "I heard Ghost's name on television when they were talking about the tragedy at Piccadilly. Your story makes him come alive. He's worse than I imagined."

"Charlie and Rashad aren't much better."

"And you look like Charlie?"

"We're very similar. I'm an inch taller and ten pounds

heavier. His face is thinner, but we share the same features and facial structure."

"And no one knows anything about his background? Not even his nationality?"

"Neither Charlie's nor Ghost's."

She hesitated. "Have you considered that you might be related to Charlie?"

"Right from the moment I saw his photograph. I checked. I'm the only Albertson in the administrative office files, and there's nothing about anyone with that last name in the college library."

She was quietly thoughtful. "There are the buildings," she finally said.

He parked in front of the smaller one, which they now knew was inhabited—likely by Crazy Woman—and shut off the engine.

"Link?" she asked softly. "Why did you tell me all of that?"

"I wasn't supposed to. I wasn't supposed to tell anyone. I guess I felt I could trust you, and I needed to share it." He felt awkward. "I probably shouldn't have."

"You mean, you need someone on your side?"

He nodded. "Something like that."

"I'm glad you picked me." They were silent for a moment. She looked out at the building. "There's no stove or heater. She must freeze when it gets bitter cold."

"Yeah."

She turned to him. "I'm glad you told me about Ghost. They want you to help find him?"

"That's what they said a couple of days ago."

"Maybe they don't need you now," she said, and he heard a hopeful tone.

"I still want to find out what I can about myself . . . and about Charlie if he's related."

"I'll keep searching records and asking around."

Link looked out toward the old burial ground. "I want to go there."

She stared with him. The dreariness of the day added to the deepening gloom. "We really shouldn't," she said.

He got out. "Coming?"

When he opened her door she got down, still looking at the dark trees, then drew an apprehensive breath. "There's nothing there," she tried. "Just an old burial ground."

Link nodded. "Stay here if you want. I've got to take a look. Something's . . ." He stopped himself from saying he was being drawn by an inner emotion he didn't understand.

"Don't disturb anything," she cautioned.

"I won't." He began to walk toward the trees, she following at a distance.

He paused at the rim of the depression, then went on. The shadows were growing longer and darker. He flinched then, realizing he'd almost stepped on an old tepee—they called them lodges, he remembered—that had fallen in and was collecting dirt. She'd told him the place hadn't been used since the early 1920s. The lodge looked at least that old, now just a collection of crumbling hides. A musty smell pervaded the place.

There were other fallen lodges, most in even worse condition. The oldest were only mounds, as Marie had explained. He walked on, raised his eyes to the trees, and drew a breath. Several had bundles tied in the deepest vees of their branches. Small skeletal bones protruding from the nearest one—obviously a child.

"Hurry," Marie urged. She was walking closer, wearing a worried expression.

Link was drawn to continue, although he had no idea what he might look for.

He heard a gasp from Marie and half turned.

Crazy Woman had appeared behind them, dressed in the same rags as before. Her face was more youthful than he'd imagined, but gray hair hung in strings to her waist and her skin was gnarled like old leather. She approached—looked at him closely for a moment—then walked on. He followed. She moved slowly, as if each movement was painful, leading them ever deeper into the burial ground. She stopped abruptly, then slowly sat beside a mound and stared.

Link knelt close by. Marie stood behind him, scarcely breathing.

Crazy Woman made a long, low crooning intonation—a forlorn sound, like wind blowing through treetops. She was silent for a moment, then began to chant alien words in wavering but distinct tones. He'd heard the language, but could not remember where.

"Can you understand her?" Link asked in a low voice.

"Yes." Marie's response was even quieter. "It's Algonkian," she whispered.

The chanting continued.

"What's she saying?"

"She is Bright Flame, daughter of the son of the grandson of Black Wolf."

The woman's voice became youthful, as if she was assuming a role, and she began to rock back and forth as she chanted, eyes never wavering from the burial mound.

Marie whispered. "As a young girl, she became a holy woman. When walking in the mountains searching for herbs, she was taken by Ah-but-ochsi and brought to Peshan."

"Ah-but-ochsi?"

"North Piegan Indians."

The woman released a single low sob. Her voice caught as she continued.

Marie blanched, and paused before interpreting. "She was mated with an old man who was a descendent of Lame Bear. The . . . the act was made to capture Black Wolf's powerful spirit." Marie turned to him. "Oh, God, Link. She was held down and raped."

"Don't stop," he told her.

Marie listened to the chants. "They kept her in Peshan, and she was mated again and again with the old man. When she was pregnant, they kept her here and watched over her until she bore a son. The Ah-but-ochsi men named the child 'Spirit of Lame Bear.' They brought food and blankets, then told her to stay and rear him as a warrior until they returned. She remained here in old Peshan, too frightened to do other than she'd been told."

Crazy Woman . . . Bright Flame . . . looked at the sky and uttered words, her voice a plaintive cry.

"She repeated that the son of the old Ah-but-ochsi was named Spirit of Lame Bear."

The woman chanted a short phrase, then turned and stared at Link, dark eyes glistening with moisture. She drew a sharp breath, stifling a sob.

"Akai omachk kai mohtsah," she said again. Her body convulsed with weeping. Then, with suddenness, she rose and hobbled into the darkness.

Link had heard the phrase. It came to him then, for he'd repeated them himself. The same words had been spoken by Ghost to the London *Times* editor!

"What did she just say?" he asked Marie.

She told him, and he lurched to his feet, looking into the shadows. "Wait!" he cried out to the departed woman.

Marie placed her hand on his arm and shook her head. "She's tormented. That was enough for one day." She tugged at his hand, and led him back toward the pickup.

Before they departed for Browning, Link removed a cardboard box and several sacks from the bed of the truck, and left them beside the door of the small shack.

"Food?" Marie asked. Her voice was uneven. She was still shaken by what they'd heard.

"Food, warm clothing, and I tossed in my down sleeping bag," Link said.

She smiled wistfully.

They started back, and were quiet for a long while. Marie broke the silence first, explaining that the last phrase had been oddly spoken. "Bright Flame speaks Algonkian Blackfeet very well, but those were like someone with a poor understanding of the language."

"They're the same words Ghost used when he spoke with the London *Times* editor."

"When he made the threat to bring grief to Americans?"

"Yeah." Link's mind was also troubled with another matter. "Did you notice how she looked so oddly at me when she talked about the child named Spirit of Lame Bear?"

Marie quickly shook her head. "She couldn't have been talking about you. For one thing, the timing wasn't right. She disappeared several years before you were born in 1964. She's demented, Link. I don't know how much of her story we can believe."

Link nodded, then a new frown crept across his face.

"What is it?" she asked.

"If Ghost's words were spoken in Blackfeet Algonkian, how did he become familiar with the language unless . . ." He left the word hanging.

"Unless he's Blackfeet?"

"They don't know what he is, or was. He hates Americans. That part doesn't track, but it's odd that he'd speak a Native American language."

"It was very poor Algonkian. It could have been taken from the Calgary dictionary."

"What's that?"

"The North Piegan came up with a dictionary of Blackfeet Algonkian words. It's rudimentary, but it's the only one I know of."

"Maybe." He nodded. "It makes sense. He somehow got hold of the dictionary."

They rode in silence for a while before he voiced another thought. "Let's say the locket in Bright Flame's hut did belong to Sarah Layton. What happened to her? Was she at Peshan, too"

Marie just shook her head. The puzzle was growing more complex.

He arrived at the highway and turned toward Browning. "How about dinner? I'll buy."

"As long as it includes a stiff drink, it's a deal."

Link dropped Marie off at the museum parking lot to retrieve her car, then went to the motel to clean up. They'd agreed to meet at a restaurant.

In his room he found the light on the telephone flashing. The desk clerk read off a number with a 202 prefix. The message was to call as soon as possible.

Judge Marian Lindquist answered.

"This is Link Anderson. Is Mister DeVera there?"

"He's right here. We've been waiting for your call."

Manny DeVera came on the line.

"How did you know where I was staying?" Link blurted.

Manny ignored the question. "Make up your mind about doing the job for us?"

Link didn't hesitate. "I'm aboard."

"We were counting on that. Some odd things are happening, and we have to move more quickly than we'd anticipated. Can you start tomorrow?"

Link almost put it off. Then he realized the delay would only be to see more of Marie LeBecque. "Tomorrow's fine."

"Be at the Kalispel airport for a six-thirty morning flight to Chicago. You'll be met there and briefed. Four hours later you'll leave for Washington. The timing's important."

"Six-thirty in the morning? It's a two-hour drive to Kalispel."

Manny chuckled. "It'll be good for you. You need some discipline back in your life."

"Why Chicago?"

DeVera responded with silence.

Charlie! They were holding him in jail there. "Oh, yeah, I remember."

"Observe the subject closely and study his mannerisms. Find out anything you can. He hasn't opened up with anyone else, but who knows."

Link thought. "I'd like to speak with him one-on-one."

"I'll arrange it. As soon as you arrive here in D.C. we'll put him on television."

"I don't understand."

"You will when you get to Chicago."

Link took in a breath. "I've learned something you'll be interested in. The meaning of the words you were trying to have interpreted?"

"You're *kidding,*" Manny said excitedly.

"It's in the Algonkian Indian tongue." Link spoke slowly and clearly as he repeated the translation: "Many great chiefs shall die."

BOOK TWO

Many Great Chiefs Shall Die

13

Tuesday, January 31st

10:00 A.M.—Chicago, Illinois

Link had risen early to drive to Kalispel. On the flight to Chicago he'd slept and dreamed. He'd seen a hazy, softer image of himself as the Grandfather had spoken in his alien tongue. Something about a small bird. *A dark bird.*

The face had reappeared, and the Grandfather had repeated the words, as if he was patiently trying to get something across. Dark bird. Small bird. *Small dark bird.* He'd jolted awake with images of himself and the bird swirling incomprehensibly in his mind's eye.

When he deplaned at O'Hare, Link was met by a tall, serious woman who introduced herself as Special Agent Josephine Stickley. He hefted his carry-on bags and followed her down the concourse into a VIP lounge, where they took seats at a secluded table. She handed him a closed manila folder, then ordered from a hostess as he opened it.

A note inside said the folder had been forwarded from Manny DeVera.

"There's something for you to sign," said Stickley, "before you read the rest of it."

It was the contract he'd looked over in the ITF-4 briefing room. He scrawled his signature onto the last page, then at the bottom of an identification card form, and handed them over. She placed them in her briefcase and sat back, eyes averted from what he was reading.

When the hostess returned, he closed the folder. As she left, he reopened it and sipped black coffee—Stickley's brew was chocolate-curl topped cappuccino—as he read about a gamble to lure Ghost out of hiding. Link was the bait, the magnet to draw Ghost, who had promised to free Charlie if he were ever captured. If there was no response in Washington, he would be shuttled to France where the scam would be repeated.

He read it through twice, then looked back at the short note Manny had penned.

Link,
We're awaiting executive approval for this plan. If it's not granted by your takeoff time, stay in Chicago and learn more about Charlie's mannerisms—and we'll try again tomorrow. When we get a go-ahead, you become Charlie. Good to have you aboard.
M. DeVera.

Link looked up at the agent. "What do you think?"

"I have no idea what you've got. My instructions are to get you in to see the prisoner and have you back here for a two-o'clock airplane. That's where my need-to-know begins and ends."

He drained his cup, then pushed to his feet. "I'm ready."

On the drive through the city, Link thought about Bright Flame's words the previous evening. In the light of the new day, the entire conversation seemed wild and improbable.

The FBI agent pulled into a reserved space beside a large brick building.

"The Cook County facility's got a section for federal prisoners. Your guy's there, with a guard assigned at all times. They're moving him to an interrogation room where you can talk privately. It's just you and him. All monitoring equipment's to be turned off."

Link looked at his watch. It was 10:35. "How long will I have?"

"Two and a half hours. Then I've got to get you back to O'Hare." She opened her door.

Special Agent Stickley had prearranged things. Fifteen minutes after his arrival, Link was admitted into a stark room with chipped and stained green walls. His mirror image was seated at a barren table. Link had known what to expect, but Charlie had not. His eyes bulged as the door behind Link was closed and he took his seat.

Link examined the deadly terrorist before him. Charlie's face was more boyish than his, yet the resemblance was so strong Link could be staring into a mirror.

The images of the Grandfather dream returned. A thought bubbled its way to the surface. "Little Crow," Link murmured.

Charlie's mouth drooped in further astonishment. He was slow in recovering.

His name was Little Crow. Somehow Link had known that.

Charlie pulled back his head. "Who are you?" he blurted.

Link felt the sensation of familiarity he'd experienced when he'd first looked at the man's photograph. Like he was someone special he'd once known.

"Who the hell are you?" Charlie repeated in an awed, shaken voice.

"I'm from Peshan," Link said softly.

Charlie started again, as if jolted by electricity. After a moment he averted his eyes, but Link knew he was striking chords.

He tried another tack. "Where's Ghost? I'm looking for him."

Another glimmering. "You can't . . ." Then Charlie's eyes narrowed. As suddenly as it had been opened, the channel into Charlie's awareness closed. Charlie's jaw became firm, and he stared blankly at the opposite wall.

"You're Little Crow," Link tried again, but there was no response; not a misplaced breath or flutter of eyelids. He settled back to study the man before him.

12:15 P.M.—ITF-4 Offices, Department of Justice, Washington, D.C.

Marian leafed through the plan, a synopsis of which had been forwarded to Link Anderson in Chicago. It was too fanciful for her straightforward mind. She would not have let it proceed if the analysts hadn't agreed there was a chance it might work.

The elements were ready. Participating military, FBI and U.S. Marshal's office personnel were prepared. All that remained was approval. The last time she'd seen the Vice President, when she'd briefed him and Leonard Griggs after yesterday's NSC meeting, he'd told her he'd get back as soon as possible with the President's response. She'd asked for an answer by eleven o'clock, more than an hour ago.

The project would probably be rejected. Leonard Griggs had hardly listened to her presentation, and the President was likely to heed his advice. The only carrot she'd been able to offer was that the National Security Council could take credit for any success that came of the plan. It had obviously not been enough.

Mimi buzzed from the outer office. "The Vice President's secretary is on line twelve."

Marian hesitated, drew a breath as she picked up. A moment later the Vice President's familiar voice came over the secure line. "Marian?"

"Yes, sir." She steeled herself for rejection.

"I apologize for being late with my answer, but I had trouble getting in to the boss. He had a full plate yesterday, and this morning wasn't any better."

"I fully understand, sir."

"About the plan. Do you really think it can work?"

"I have no idea, sir. As I said yesterday, it's something we developed after we discovered the look-alike and restudied Ghost's psychological profile. Estimates of success vary from one analyst to another, but they average about fifty percent."

"The boss left it up to Len Griggs and me. Len thinks it's foolish, but I feel it's worth a try and he's going along." He paused. "What's the source of the animosity between you two?"

"I really don't know, sir. Mr. Griggs has been hostile since our first meeting."

"Let me offer a word of caution, Marian. The President has great confidence in Len. With the campaign for reelection on front burner, he's relying on him to handle some of the tough decisions. Others have let him down, but Len's been reliable and he feels comfortable with him."

The Vice President's next words made his point. "If you want to be effective in this administration, you'll have to learn to work with Len Griggs."

Marian suppressed her argument. The Vice President was trying to be helpful. "You're in agreement, then? We can activate the plan?"

"Conditionally. Len wants you to keep the lid on about the possibility of Ghost coming to the States. He believes it might unnecessarily alarm the public."

Marian frowned. Griggs had deleted an important objective. "Is that wise, sir? Part of our purpose was to educate the public and warn them to be on the lookout for Ghost and Rashad."

"I'm going along with Len to keep his feathers smoothed. You can mention Charlie, but not Ghost or his message. That's the condition. Half a loaf's better than *nada*, Marian."

"Yes, sir." She sighed bitterly. "We won't say more than's necessary to bring it off."

"Good. Then everyone's in agreement."

"Another subject, sir. What was the President's reaction to this morning's memo?"

"The interpretation of the words spoken by Ghost?"

"We felt it was quite chilling." The ITF-4 members had agreed the translation should be immediately disseminated to the executive branch.

"The words were supposed to be American Indian . . . Algonkian you said?"

"It's one of the major Native American languages."

"So we learned. Len Griggs's people called a professor at the University of Wisconsin, one of the nation's foremost experts in Algonkian, and had him listen to the tape. He denied the translation and wasn't even sure the words were American Indian."

Marian winced hard. She should have verified the damned translation.

"Perhaps you should check your source." The Vice President's tone was reproachful.

Marian was abashed. "We will. Thank you for your help again, sir."

"Good luck. I hope to hell it works." He chuckled. "Let me rephrase that. I hope Len's right, and this Ghost character's off in some foreign desert having second thoughts about threatening the world's foremost superpower."

After she hung up, Marian brooded for a moment. The mistranslation was an embarrassment for ITF-4. Whatever his faults, Leonard Griggs was thorough, as she should have been. There was no room for such errors in her profession. Then she wondered about working with Link Anderson . . . they could ill afford a loose cannon on deck.

She had to decide quickly whether to continue with Link or make major revisions to the plan and go without him. There was little time. With the condition imposed by Leonard Griggs, they'd already have to make extensive deletions to the announcements they'd prepared.

Manny wanted to get them into the Justice Department's afternoon news conference. A spokesman for the U.S. Marshal's office would reveal that Charlie had been captured and was being flown into Andrews. They'd pass out photographs of Charlie, but not the newly enhanced drawings of Ghost and Rashad as they'd intended.

She decided to go ahead with their choice and cross their fingers that Link didn't make another error. Marian called out to Mimi and told her to summon Mr. DeVera to her office.

5:00 P.M.—Andrews Air Force Base, Maryland

The aircraft was an Air Force C-140, a military version of the Boeing 727. Link sat in front, just aft of the crew compartment, staring out the window as they neared the field.

He'd nodded off for a few moments and dreamed—the vision of the large home and the flash of light again—but he didn't allow himself to dwell on the Grandfather's growing urgency.

He recalled the interview and how the name Little Crow had found its way to his lips.

The words had struck a chord. Charlie was Little Crow, which was obviously an Indian name. Piegan? Was there a connection with the story told by Bright Flame? It didn't track. The Ah-but-ochsi had named that child Spirit of Lame Bear, not Little Crow. In the old days, warriors had sometimes been given new names at the Sun Dance. Could that be the case? He wondered.

How had Ghost known the Blackfeet words? Through Charlie? Why did Link and Charlie look so much alike? Who was Black Albertson? He was no closer to learning who he was than when he'd begun the search.

As the airplane turned on final approach to Andrews, Link wondered again how he'd known Charlie was Little Crow. The Grandfather was a contrivance of his mind, but he had to admit he was a powerfully analytical one. Somehow Link must have deduced the name from things he'd heard and learned during his visit to Browning.

When the landing gear kissed the runway, Link judged it a nine. Military landings were rated from one to ten, and this one was close to perfect. He watched the runway markers rushing past and felt a familiar yearning to be at the controls of an airplane—to fill his mind with understandable things. He was a good pilot. Could he be a good actor as DeVera wanted?

The C-140 was taxied into an isolated parking area at the far end of the runway, stopped, the avoidance lights shut off and the engines set to idle. Link felt the pressure being equalized, and a moment later heard the sound of the passenger hatch being opened.

Manny DeVera boarded and immediately saw him. Behind him came a younger man carrying a metal suitcase, and behind him a woman and four military policemen.

Manny shook his head. "You know what to do?" he asked.

"It sounds easy enough." Link took the gray prison uniform from the suitcase and held it up. It was too large, as Charlie's had been. As he began to strip off his clothing, the woman set a tape recorder and a large cosmetic case on a nearby seat and began removing items she'd be using. She turned and watched impassively as Link pulled on prison trousers and shirt.

She had him stand before her. "Walk," she said, and motioned down the aisle.

He went to the bulkhead and back.

"Too positive," she said. "Move more hesitantly and drop your shoulders some."

"She's watched six hours of tape of Charlie moving around in his cell," Manny told him.

Link tried it as she'd said.

"Better, but slouch even more," she said.

After a fourth try, he did better. She had him sit and pulled a wig into place, looking back and forth at him and photographs of Charlie's longer hair.

"After you left him," Manny said, "we moved Charlie to an isolated area of the prison."

Link nodded.

"Please remain still," the woman said. She went to work applying cosmetic to highlight his features for the cameras.

After a couple minutes she examined. "That's all we can do," she said. She motioned. "Try walking one more time."

She was satisfied. "Now the voice," she said. "Say 'I don't know.' "

"I don't know."

She punched a button on the high fidelity cassette recorder. "I don't know," a voice said.

"Like that," she said.

Link mimicked the voice that was slightly higher in pitch than his own: "I don't know."

She nodded. "That's good. Again."

He repeated the words. She played two more utterances, and he tried them.

She motioned. "Now walk and talk."

That took two tries before she was satisfied.

"Do you get stage fright?" she asked.

"I don't clench up when I give briefings."

"This is different. Put yourself in the guy's shoes. You are Charlie. You're close enough in appearance to be his twin. Be him. From now until the game's over, you are Charlie."

Link nodded. "I'm Charlie."

"Almost. One more time."

He gave her an uncharacteristic, almost bashful look. "I'm Charlie." His voice was softer, his tone slightly higher.

She stared, then nodded. "Yeah. Hi, Charlie."

DeVera motioned toward the hatch. "Time for us to go." The younger man had placed Link's clothes into the suitcase. He took that and Link's luggage to the hatch and deplaned. The woman followed. Seventeen minutes had passed since they'd come aboard.

Manny was still watching him. "See you at the other end, Link."

"Who's Link? I'm Charlie." He gave the bashful look,

then slipped into the non-expression he'd seen on Charlie's face in Chicago.

DeVera stared, took a breath as if he had to convince himself who he was with, and left. As the hatch closed, two military policemen slipped cuffs over Link's wrists and secured his ankles. One looked hard at him and gave a sharp tug to make sure they were properly attached. "Bastard," he breathed. He was a burly, black master sergeant, and did not smile.

Link looked expressionlessly at the window. *I'm Charlie,* he kept thinking.

The black MP settled into the seat beside him as the airplane's engines surged and they began to taxi. Link saw a flicker outside as the avoidance and taxi lights were turned back on. They seemed brighter in the growing gloom of evening.

The guard yanked on his chain for no good reason.

Link watched the bulkhead before them. *I'm Charlie. I'm Little Crow.*

"Rat fucker," whispered the burly guard.

"Leave him alone," said a lieutenant seated across the aisle.

"The fucker killed an FBI agent and wounded another. He's an asshole. Shoots people from long distance like a fucking coward."

"We just transport 'em. He'll spend his life in jail."

"Wish they'd leave me alone with the fucker for half an hour," the sergeant muttered.

Link felt his animosity grow. He remained impassive.

The C-140 taxied into a well-lighted area.

"Jesus," said the black MP in a disgusted tone. "The fucking television cameras are set up like he's some kind of hero."

Link looked past him. A dozen TV camera's were manned and positioned, getting footage as the airplane taxied into position and stopped. There were fifty-odd onlookers, some in uniform, most cameramen or reporters speaking into microphones.

A crew member came back from the flight deck and nodded at one of the military policemen, then opened the forward hatch. A boarding ramp was positioned, and the lieutenant went to the hatch and peered out. He saw something and motioned.

"Move the car over here," he called out.

Unseen by the officer, the black MP jerked on Link's chain.

I'm Charlie.

"Come on, asshole," said his tormentor. He pulled hard, dragging Link to his feet.

The lieutenant motioned. The MP pulled Link along, the two others trailing along behind.

I'm Charlie. Ghost will be watching. I want to be freed. I want to get word to him where we're going. He promised to keep me from harm.

"Come on," the black MP urged, and gave a final harsh yank before they reached the door and the bright glare.

Link tried to shield his face from the light. When he raised his hand too quickly, he tugged at the binding on his ankles and stumbled. The black MP stabilized him.

"Ought to let you fall on your ass," he hissed.

Ghost is watching. How do I get him word. I want to be freed, Ghost.

Link was out the hatch into the lights. He paused, but the MP firmly pushed him onward. He took the stairsteps cautiously because of the chain between his ankles.

He looked up, squinting. "Keep moving," said the MP at his side.

How do I tell him where to come for me. How do I tell him it's really me and not a trick?

They reached the bottom, then he was led forward, not looking at the cameras but not avoiding them. A reporter approached with microphone held out, hopeful he'd say something.

"Fort Myer," he blurted. *Now Ghost would know their destination.*

"Quiet," barked the black MP, leading him on.

"Little Crow," he said, mouthing the words distinctly. *No one but Ghost would know that. No one but Ghost and Charlie. Little Crow did as Ghost told him to do, and Ghost would know he'd said nothing to the authorities. Now he'd know where they were taking him . . . that it was surely him and he'd not talked.*

"What did you say?" asked the reporter.

"Fort Myer . . . Little Crow."

The black policeman moved between Link and the reporter.

The lieutenant MP blocked the reporter's way. "Stay back, please."

They approached a blue-and-white police car. The burly MP pushed down on Link's head. He grunted and ducked, and was shoved inside. The MP crawled in behind and closed the door. The lieutenant got in front.

"Go ahead," muttered the black man.

As they drove away the lights shone through the rear window until another car fell in behind and blocked it. They went only two hundred yards down the parking ramp and pulled up beside a helicopter whose blades were clop-clopping at idle.

Link was dragged from the vehicle and rushed aboard the helicopter. The black man slid in beside him. The lieutenant and the other two MPs sat opposite them. The doors were closed.

"Hold it until I say go." The black sergeant pulled on a set of earphones and checked in on a handheld radio, then waited.

The lieutenant leaned toward Link. "They're reviewing what they got on the cameras. If something's fishy, we'll do it all again. That would give it away to the press, and we don't want to have to bring the reporters in on the scam."

The sergeant responded to something on the headset, then nudged Link. "DeVera wants to know if you made a mistake saying what you did back there. Something about a crow?"

"No mistake," Link said. "That was part of it."

The black master sergeant spoke into the radio, waited for another second, then pulled off the headset. "Take us to Fort Myer, driver," he yelled happily to the pilot.

The tempo of the blades increased.

They flew toward Arlington. The army post had become an elaborate trap for Ghost. He'd be able to get in to rescue Charlie but not get out.

Fort Myer, Virginia

They'd played it out after landing at the army post adjacent to Arlington National Cemetery and only a mile from the rear of the Pentagon. From the helipad, Link had been taken directly to the stockade, escorted inside, and placed in a solitary confinement cell.

Link sat on the bunk, as he had since he'd entered the small room. He'd not spoken since he'd been brought there, not even to answer if he was hungry.

Charlie would have done the same.

The black sergeant swung open the unlocked door, carrying the metal suitcase Link had seen earlier. The charade had ended.

"How does it look?" Link asked.

"This is a low security post, so it's not difficult to get through the gate. That's what we're hoping for, that they'll know that and move quickly to get Charlie out."

"How quickly?"

"According to how close they are. Ghost knows the score; the best time to set up an escape is as early as possible during a movement. Still, he likes to plan everything, then double and triple check it, so it'll take a while. The press was told you're only being held here for a couple of days. If he's in-country, that'll give Ghost time to get here, but not too much time to do his planning. So . . . I'd guess he'll move tomorrow night."

"And you'll be waiting."

"When his people come, they'll see the place is easy to take."

"But not really."

The sergeant smiled. "We've pulled the military staff out of this entire side of the post and replaced them with our people. We're ready for anything he wants to try."

"You're FBI?"

The question went ignored. "We've got surveillance set up all over the post. Hidden cameras everywhere and a central monitoring post. There's a dozen shooter teams with twilight scopes, two rapid reactor teams, and a helo gunship on standby alert."

"How long do we wait?"

"We'll remain set up until noon day after tomorrow, but we're taking you out tonight."

"I'd rather stay."

"Ghost will be able to get close. We want him close. You've got friends who want you out of here, and they outrank me all to hell." The black man removed a shoulder-holstered automatic pistol from the suitcase and handed it over. "You know how to use that?"

"Yes," he answered simply. Link handled the weapon, a

Beretta Model 92 in 9mm caliber. He pressed the release button, and the clip dropped into his hand. It was loaded. He slapped the clip in place and pushed the pistol into its holster.

The black man handed him a black leather case with a laminated identification card showing A. Lincoln Anderson as an employee of the Department of Justice.

"Your clothes are in the suitcase. Go ahead and change while I check everything again. DeVera will pick you up in a couple hours, when everything's cocked and ready."

The sergeant left. Link stared after him for a moment, then stripped off the prison garb and pulled on clothing he'd removed earlier. He strapped the nylon-web shoulder holster over his shirt and slipped on the sport jacket, then settled on the bunk to wait.

He was weary from the long day and lack of sleep, and although his mind fought to stay awake, Link Anderson dozed off.

Bethesda, Maryland

They were in the warehouse, Ghost examining the various radio relays and fuzing devices he'd put together. Two had barometric chambers. Three were elaborate precision timers. There'd been more of them on the bench that morning.

The limo, cleaned, waxed, and gleaming in the dim light, was ready for use. Yet Ghost was increasingly angry as his confusion mounted. The previous night's meditations had been unclear. Normally they were easily interpreted, orderly visions, but it had been as if his helper had been unsure. Then, in mid-afternoon, he'd watched a news release revealing that Charlie had been captured in Chicago and was being flown to Washington.

The fact that Charlie would be nearer should have pleased Ghost, but something about it made him uneasy.

The cellular telephone buzzed.

"Go ahead," Ghost responded.

Martin Cherone's voice: "Channel two's about to show a report you'll be interested in."

Ghost punched the END button, walked to the glass-cage office, and switched on a portable television set.

Rashad came into the office and stood silently nearby.

After a commercial, the news item aired. A terrorist known as Charlie had been moved to Washington less than an hour earlier. Charlie's prison photo was shown. A newswoman said he was charged with murder by the governments of France, England, Israel, and Italy, and there was speculation that he might be extradited to one of those countries.

Extradited? Ghost pursed his lips. If they weren't going to release Charlie as he'd demanded, it made a smattering of sense that Washington would pass their problem to others. Yet twenty-four Americans had been among those killed at Piccadilly station—would they forget that and try to eliminate the threat to their country by flying Charlie out?

He didn't think that was likely—the leadership was not sufficiently frightened. Not yet.

The television image changed to Andrews Air Force Base—of an airplane taxiing in.

"Charlie was apprehended at O'Hare International as he got off a flight from London, England, where he was suspected of shooting two American FBI agents, one of whom was killed. Surprisingly, no charges of that crime have yet been filed by the Department of Justice."

Maybe not so surprising if they really did want to extradite him.

The airplane came to a stop; the entrance hatch became bathed in light.

"Charlie is said to be a member of the Ghost Gang, believed to be responsible for a number of atrocities throughout Europe and the Middle East. A Justice Department spokesman declined to comment on the location of the remainder of the group."

The aircraft's hatch was opened, and a ramp pushed into place. An army officer with an MP brassard came out, motioned. A moment later Charlie emerged, chained ankle and wrist. He stumbled once, then laboriously began to make his way down the stairs.

Ghost waited, realized he was holding his breath, and released it.

"That's him," said Rashad.

Charlie stared straight ahead with a blank expression. The movements were familiar. He was at the bottom of the stairs, then being escorted toward a waiting police car. As he passed near the camera he looked directly at the lens and spoke.

Ghost nodded to himself. Charlie hadn't answered the authorities' questions. The Bull Clan had taught them—Little Crow must always be obedient to Ghost.

"Fort Myer . . . Little Crow," Charlie mouthed again.

"What did he say?" Rashad asked.

"Fort Myer," Ghost said. "Near the Pentagon."

"They'll probably take him to the post stockade."

"Probably." Ghost watched as Charlie was driven to a waiting helicopter. The nagging feeling that something was wrong continued. His confusion grew.

"There isn't a military base in the world we can't get into," Rashad boasted.

The announcer said Charlie would be held for two nights in the Washington area before being transferred elsewhere.

Likely to a high security prison, Ghost thought. Then he wondered again about the possibility of extradition.

As he watched the helicopter lift off, he replayed in his mind what he'd seen on the screen. Finally he dialed Martin Cherone's number.

"We'll need weapons, a good map of the post, and a military decal for the car," he told Rashad as he waited. "We'll hit them tonight, so fast and hard they won't be able to react."

Relentless, his mind told him. It would be a tremendous gamble. Yet Ghost had promised Charlie that he would keep him from harm . . . and Ghost did not lie.

8:50 P.M.—Fort Myer, Virginia

"Pull over," Ghost said when they were still two hundred yards from the poorly illuminated side entrance to the post. Rashad turned into a pullout, parked, and shut off the headlights.

A Honda sedan slowed as it approached the entrance. A female guard stepped from the gate shack and scarcely glanced before waving it through. She yawned as the car drove past, then peered at her watch, visibly sighed, and reentered the shack.

"Dumb cunt," snorted Rashad. "Doesn't care who gets on post."

Ghost had applied a yellow DOD sticker to the Ford Escort's windshield, showing that the vehicle was owned by a noncommissioned officer. He'd also acquired a green DD Form 2 identification card, complete with altered photograph.

He looked at the gate and wondered at how easily the Honda had passed through.

He'd studied the map of the base for more than an hour before deciding to take a firsthand look. He'd rejected the idea of bringing Cherone's goons, feeling they'd only get in the way. If the situation was appropriate, he and Rashad would act. If not, they'd depart the post.

"I don't see a problem gettin' on," Rashad said. They could not pass an automobile inspection. Under a blanket in the Escort's rear seat were two time-fused tritonol cones, a Colt CAR-15 assault rifle, and an M-79 40mm grenade launcher. In the trunk was an M-60 .30 caliber light machine gun with bipod and six one hundred round belts of ammunition. Martin Cherone had proven his ability to provide supplies on short notice.

Ghost mentally went over the map of the army post again, remembering the location of the provost marshal's office and the adjacent stockade.

An automobile left the post, not slowing as it passed the gatehouse. There seemed to be no obvious problems, certainly no heightened security. He started to tell Rashad to drive on in, but again the wave of uneasiness washed over him.

On the way over he'd tried to meditate but there'd been only confusion again.

The cellular phone buzzed. Ghost answered. "Go ahead."

"This is the wayfinder. Fort Myer's a setup." The voice was crisp and abrasive.

"Understood," Ghost said, and punched the END button, severing the connection.

Ghost's mind spun furiously. "Get out and take a piss." he hissed to Rashad.

"What?"

"Damn it, just do it."

Rashad dismounted, went around the van to a shadow, and urinated. When he'd finished he climbed back inside.

"Now turn around and let's get out of here." As they headed back toward the main road, Ghost felt his tension subside. They were back to the original plan.

Link looked about groggily, and checked his watch. Two hours had passed. It had not been the dream that awakened him but an offensive smell. The odor was pungent and clinging, and evoked an unsettling sensation. At first he thought it might be smoke, but it was different.

He rose from the bunk as the black master sergeant returned.

"Ready to go?"

"Yeah," Link said. "Anything happening?" The sharp odor was diminishing.

They walked toward the exit. "A car pulled off outside the side gate, and the surveillance crew got excited. Turned out it was some poor guy who had to pee." He chuckled. "We're already goosey and it's just beginning."

A familiar sedan was parked on the street. Link slid into the passenger's seat. Manny DeVera nodded at the black master sergeant before driving away.

"I'm nervous as a virgin bride on opening night," Manny said. "What do you think?"

"It's hard to believe Ghost would take on the U.S. Army."

"This is a low security post, and he's beaten bigger odds. He wants Charlie back."

Manny slowed as they approached the side gate, then passed through.

As they passed a pull-out area the odor returned for a fleeting moment.

"Where are we going?" he asked.

"Marian's place in Georgetown. The two of us are . . . uh . . . pretty close."

His mother had told Link about their arrangement.

"She has a guest bedroom set up for you. You haven't eaten, and we haven't, either. We'll pick up something on the way, then wait up for a while and see if anything develops."

"This quickly?"

"Who knows? Anyway, she's got a couple of questions she wants to ask you."

11:20 P.M.—Georgetown, Washington, D.C.

They'd long finished with the Chinese food, but were still gathered at the kitchen table. Before the television newscast had aired the first time, Marian had called Link's parents and told them not to worry about what they might see. She felt they'd be concerned and wanted them to know everything was under control.

They'd been watching a clock above the sink. The master sergeant who had tormented Link was an FBI supervisor at the Hoover Building, now agent-in-charge of the Fort Myer operation, and reported hourly to the ITF-4 comm center. The duty officers kept Judge Lindquist informed. Numerous automobiles had passed through the Fort Myer gates, but except for two forays by news reporters trying to get in to interview the terrorist, all had checked out.

Manny went to the counter for another cup of coffee. "This morning the analysts felt we had an even chance of pulling Ghost in. I think the odds are higher."

"If he's in the States," said Marian.

"If nothing happens, in two days we announce he's being extradited and the show moves to Paris. Ghost won't sit by if he believes he can bust Charlie out of jail."

Link mused. Twice they'd watched the tape on CNN, and he'd seen no obvious errors. He'd looked like Charlie. The prison uniform had hidden physical differences. His mannerisms and voice were Charlie's. If he'd seen it, it was likely Ghost believed Charlie was at Fort Myer.

He realized Marian had asked a question. "Pardon me?" he asked.

"Why did you say 'Little Crow' in front of the reporter?"

He hesitated. "It came out of my talk with Charlie in Chicago."

"Charlie *talked* to you?" Manny blurted.

"Reacted is a better word. Enough to know I'd hit a nerve."

Marian frowned. "How did you come up with the name?"

Link observed his cup. "I had a . . . dream on the airplane to Chicago."

Marian's frown deepened. "A *dream,* Link?"

He drew a fortifying breath. "My dreams have a way of coming true. It's as if my subconscious goes into overdrive and comes up with answers. Somehow I picked up on the idea that Charlie had once been called Little Crow."

"Jesus," Manny DeVera muttered darkly.

Link grew defensive. "I surprised Charlie with it in Chicago, and his expression . . . he as much as admitted it. For a minute I even thought he'd open up."

"But he didn't." Manny ran his hand through his thick hair and shook his head.

"No." Link had accepted that they'd be skeptical, but did they think he was lying?

Marian regarded him. "Did the translation of Ghost's words come from a dream?"

"No. That was from the curator of the museum in Browning. She's an expert on the Blackfeet culture and speaks the language."

"Link, a highly regarded linguist . . . a professor at the University of Wisconsin who's the foremost expert on the Algonkian language in the country . . . said the translation's wrong."

He was surprised. Marie had seemed so positive.

"Tell us more about these dreams."

Link explained how the Grandfather had appeared to him as a child, then how the apparition of his subconscious had returned to help him locate the lost tourists.

His audience remained silent.

Link wanted them to believe not that his dreams actually *foretold* anything—he had trouble with that himself—but that something useful was happening within his mind.

He tried a new direction. "I knew about the Piccadilly explosion before it happened."

Manny snorted and half turned away.

"Damn it, I did," Link said defensively.

"You told me you knew next to nothing about Piccadilly."

"A photograph you showed. I'd seen it in a dream . . . before the explosion."

Marian raised an eyebrow.

"The night before it happened we were out on the rescue I just told you about. There were two images. One of the tourists we rescued. In the other I saw the mouth of a cave.

When Manny showed the photo of Piccadilly Circus station, it was precisely as I'd seen in the dream."

"Have there been other dreams?" Marian asked. He had the feeling she was continuing the conversation not for answers but to measure his rationality.

"I get urgings, a voice in my sleep telling me to do things."

"Such as?"

Come home. Prepare yourself, the Grandfather told him.

"They're not clear," Link said. "At least I don't understand them."

Manny exhaled a sharp snort.

Link girded himself. "I've been having a new dream lately. There's a large home, then a bright flash of light and screams. It's . . . realistic."

It sounded hokey to his own ears. He wasn't surprised that they didn't seem alarmed.

Marian rose to her feet stifling a yawn. "Time to retire. Manny, would you phone the comm center and tell them to only call if they have something?"

As Manny complied, she observed Link. "Do you think our ruse is working on Ghost?"

"I don't know." He girded himself. "But I believe he's preparing to bomb a home."

"When?" asked Marian.

"Soon," he said, then wondered what had made him come to that decision.

Marian showed him the guest bedroom. When she left the room, Link knew he'd convinced neither of them. There was little wonder. How much of it did he believe?

14

Wednesday, February 1st

2:45 A.M.—Georgetown, Washington, D.C.

The Grandfather is sad tonight—sadder than he remembers him being.

The image changes, and he sees the illuminated mansion. A sudden blinding flash hurts the boy's eyes. The light dwindles.

The Grandfather's face is purposeful. "You must hurry."

"What must I do?"

"Your duty. Stop him."

The words echoed.

Link came partially awake, groaning with weariness. The dream had been repeated several times during the night.

"Got to sleep," he muttered to himself, and rolled over to try again.

3:04 A.M.—Washington, D.C.

Ghost set the limousine's parking brake and went to work. There could be no coming back, no second chance. He read the illuminated dial of the aircraft compass mounted before him on the dashboard. Two-six-one degrees. Good. He shut off the engine, lifted a surveyor's depth-of-field range finder and squinted, adjusted until the picture was in sharp focus, then depressed a button. The digital readout showed the distance as 807 feet—within tolerance.

The Lincoln was positioned at the angle and distance called for in his diagram.

He switched on the dual-frequency radio receiver. The power light illuminated. *Done.*

He'd parked in the restricted zone on East Executive Boulevard. Vehicles were promptly towed—but not promptly enough.

Ghost slid out, depressed the lock switch, and closed the door. He walked from the dark form of the limousine, briskly but not *too* quickly, casually yet with purpose—not as if he was walking *away* from something, but as if *toward* some normal endeavor. He was being watched. Infrared cameras panned the area, looking for anything out of the ordinary. If he skulked, looked nervous, or remained in shadows, he would heighten suspicion. He did none of those things.

He crossed the street, not looking at the mansion to his left, and continued north. When he reached Pennsylvania Avenue a van pulled to the curbside, and he lifted a hand as if greeting the driver. He slid into the passenger's seat and nodded for Rashad to accelerate.

"Not so fast you draw attention," Ghost cautioned.

"There's two cruisers with four cops parked near the Treasury Building."

"Did they look interested?"

"Just bored. Must be a quiet night."

By now the illegally parked limousine would have attracted sufficient attention that someone would be calling for a police car. Ghost reached onto the seat beside himself and retrieved the small Motorola cellular telephone, punched the MEM button, then 1, then SEND.

After two rings he heard, "*Washington Post.* May I help you."

Ghost felt a churn of adrenaline. "I'd like to speak with the night city desk editor."

"One moment."

There was another short wait. "Editorial," answered a sleepy woman's voice.

"The news editor, please. I believe his name is George Carter."

"He's busy right now. Would you like to . . ."

Ghost interrupted. "I've got information about an impending disaster."

Her voice changed. "Just a sec." Then, "He'll be right with you."

There was no traffic when they angled onto New York Avenue. Ghost had Rashad pull to the right, then crawl along at a snail's pace.

"Carter" came a gruff voice over the telephone.

Ghost retrieved a small box from the floor that looked like an oversize remote television tuner. "You don't know me yet, Mr. Carter, but perhaps you've heard of me. My name is Ghost, and we'll get to know one another much better. Got your recorder going?"

Ghost depressed the first switch, to arm the bomb.

Georgetown, Washington, D.C.

Link heard a single *crack!* like the distant backfire of a truck, but it hardly registered in his fatigue-tormented mind. Several minutes later he did not hear the telephone ring in the other room, or Judge Lindquist answer, or hear them leave the house in a hurry.

Later, after yet another insistent Grandfather dream, he awakened sufficiently to sense that something was amiss. He swung his feet over the side of the bed and shook his head harshly—as a dog would shake off water. He had the feeling that something momentous had occurred. He remembered Fort Myer and wondered if Ghost had gone there to rescue Charlie?

He shrugged into trousers and a polo shirt, and padded out of the guest bedroom. The hall light was on, and Marian's door was ajar. Her bed was empty, the covers awry.

Link knocked and looked into other rooms without response. The prickling sensation grew within him. *Something* was wrong! He went to the living room and switched on the television, still tuned to CNN from the previous evening.

A banner was at the top of the display: WHITE HOUSE EXPLOSION.

Link frowned and went closer, listening intently.

". . . bomb detonated at the White House collapsing columns at the rear entrance. Structural damage is reported in the . . ."

"Ghost," Link hissed. It hadn't taken the terrorist a month. It had scarcely been a week since his threat. Outrage coursed through him. It did not matter whether he agreed with the man's politics . . . his President had been attacked. Emotion welled until he trembled with it.

A mansion. A bright flash of light.

Duty. Stop him.

There was no more mystery about what his subconscious was telling him. *Stop Ghost!*

6:25 A.M.—ITF-4 Offices, Department of Justice, Washington, D.C.

There'd been previous attacks on the White House. They must determine if this was an act by an angry or sensationalist citizen, or a bonafide act of terrorism.

An IDO hurried in. "Another report from Walter Reed," the duty officer announced. "Except for the broken wrist and a few bruises, the President's in good condition. They intend to hold him for continued observation until tomorrow."

"And the injuries were the result of the bomb blast?" asked Cyrus White.

"No, sir. His wrist was broken when he was thrown out of bed, but the agents caused most of the bruises when they hustled him from the bedroom."

"Anything else?" Marian asked the IDO.

"The President's sedated, and the Vice President's temporarily assumed executive powers. He's called for an emergency meeting of the National Security Council."

"Assumed power?" Pershing Sloan asked, a look of surprise on his face. "The President's not *that* badly hurt."

Cyrus White looked at him evenly. "We can't have a power vacuum. *Someone* just tried to wipe out the White House."

"It was Ghost," Manny said with a confident nod.

"We can't assume that," said Cyrus. "The agency estimated it would take him longer to prepare. *Weeks* longer."

Slocum was called from the room. A Secret Service agent was waiting to see him.

DeVera motioned at the television monitor. "Let's watch it again."

The IDO switched the VCR to play. An infrared image appeared: a dark background with light green heat sources, taken from the southwest corner of the White House roof. The camera panned the South Lawn and—just beyond—Executive Boulevard.

A limousine eased into view and parked.

"It's in the restricted area, not the prohibited zone," Manny said. "They probably get ten of those every day. The driver knew what he was doing."

"The Secret Service picked up on the limo immediately," the IDO said. "The agent-in-charge declared condition yellow-one, a routine call to prepare to either eliminate the threat or move the President to safety. A phone call was made to the park police to have the car moved. The south gate was notified, and an agent prepared to go out when the park police arrived."

The driver emerged from the vehicle wearing a tuxedo, and walked up Executive Drive. There was no urgency to his movements.

"The AIC was watching. He said to maintain yellow-one while they waited for the park police. That's it. There's no change until the explosion." The IDO rewound the videotape.

Cyrus gave Manny a stubborn look. "I saw nothing to identify the driver as Ghost."

Slocum came back into the room brandishing an audio-cassette. "This was recorded at the *Post* at the time of the explosion."

"Jesus," groaned Colonel Sloan.

Cyrus White shook his head. "Can't be Ghost," he repeated. "We can't be that wrong."

Slocum handed the cassette to the IDO. "The tape began at zero-three-twelve hours. The night news editor at the *Post* is a white, fifty-one year old male named George F. Carter."

"Go ahead," Marian said. The IDO pressed a switch on the cassette player.

Click.

"Carter" came an abrasive voice.

The next voice was smooth and friendly. "You don't know me yet, Mr. Carter, but perhaps you've heard of me. My name is Ghost, and we'll get to know one another much better. Got your recorder going?"

"I record all calls. I was told you have knowledge of a disaster."

"Yes I do. I visited the White House a few minutes ago. The place is about to become a real catastrophe." There was a dry chuckle.

Pause. "What was your name again?"

"Ghost. You may have heard about me from your associates in Europe."

The editor's breathing sounds amplified, his voice became more alert. "We've had calls from other people saying they were him."

"Well this time it's the real thing." *A three second pause.* "I just did something, George. I set off a reaction that can't be stopped. 'Something rather momentous,' as my editor friend in London might say. You're going to be working late because of what I just did."

There was a muffled shout. *"Get someone on this line and call the police. I've got a guy here who says he did something to the White House."*

"They can't stop it, George, and they can't trace this call. You're recording, right?"

"I told you I was. Maybe we should talk about this before you do anything rash."

"I already did something rash, George. I want you to write about it, but I also want you to tell the authorities. If Charlie's not released, there'll be more."

"Who's Charlie?"

"The guy they were talking about on yesterday's news. You're probably running a story about him. That Charlie. Tell them Ghost said to let him go."

"I'll tell them, but let's talk more about this."

"Akah-ee o-match ee kay mosa."

"What was that? What did you say?"

A dial tone buzzed. The connection had been broken.

"One minute forty seconds," Pershing Sloan said, looking at his watch.

Slocum nodded. "The explosion came a minute later."

"It sure as hell sounded like Ghost," Cyrus White conceded in an irritated tone. "How did he get established in the States this quickly?"

"Perhaps he came here immediately after Piccadilly," said Colonel Sloan.

"Impossible," said Lloyds, who represented the National

Security Agency. "We've traced his last telephone call. Ghost phoned from Lisbon and relayed it through a London hotel switchboard. I was going to brief it at the daily meeting."

"Eight days," Cyrus White said in an awed voice. "How the hell did he get his hands on explosives that quickly?"

"The theft at the Rocky Mountain Arsenal," said Manny.

"That's one of the most secure bases in the country," exploded Colonel Sloan. "Who the hell is he working with that can steal explosives from a place like that?"

"J.J. Davis is there," Manny said. "He'll likely find out."

Brown, representing the Transportation Department, was a quiet, thoughtful type. He cleared his throat for attention. "I don't think the burning question is how he reacted so quickly, but what he's going to do next? And can we catch him before he does it?"

"Should we shut down the Fort Myer operation?" Marian asked.

"It's still our best bet to draw Ghost," said Manny.

"We've got to determine his intentions," said Brown. "Is he going to run as he normally does? Will he attack many leaders, or *chiefs* as his threat suggested? It's . . ."

Marian interrupted. "An expert linguist says that translation's wrong."

Brown shook his head. "Doesn't matter. We just heard Ghost says there'll be more attacks if Charlie's not released. He's not known to make idle threats. We should remember that he's normally successful when he targets someone. Will he go after the President again?"

Several voices raised simultaneously.

Marian slapped her hand on the table for silence. "Since this is likely not an isolated act, Mr. Brown is correct. We must respond to the threat."

She lifted a familiar tome. ITF-4 Emergency Plan 91-02F had been prepared at the beginning of Operation Desert Storm in the event terrorists infiltrated and threatened the national infrastructure. It had been updated five times, and they'd just completed a sixth revision.

She looked about the room. "With your concurrence, Mr. DeVera and I will present the plan to the National Security Council and recommend full implementation."

National Military Command Center, Pentagon, Washington, D.C.

With the damage to the White House, the NSC had moved its meeting to the NMCC in the basement of the Pentagon, where the Secretary of Defense had ordered execution of stage one of the DOD disaster preparedness plan. This was a precautionary step, calling for additional physical security and heightened awareness within the huge building.

Manny DeVera had played the audiotape from the *Washington Post.* Judge Marian Lindquist stood before the group—which included the Vice President—and explained that they were relatively certain it was Ghost's voice. Leonard Griggs had been uncharacteristically quiet.

Manny passed out copies of the contingency plan, then inserted a compact disk into a computer that fed an image to a projected display. He moved a trackball and selected:

ITF-4 EMERGENCY PLAN 91-02F

Marian explained the plan and its purpose. "Now that need has arrived. We find ourselves facing the sort of emergency that calls for implementation."

Leonard Griggs rose to his feet wearing an expression of disgust. The moratorium was obviously over. "This crap has gone on long enough."

"I assure you that none of this is *crap*. The emergency exists, and it's time for appropriate action. My organization has taken great effort to determine what those actions should be."

Griggs glowered. "Your organization's incompetence allowed the attack to occur."

Marian stared in amazement. "I take *great* offense with that remark." She glanced to the Vice President for support, but he was watching Leonard Griggs.

Griggs cocked his head. "Your organization was formed to contain terrorism before it reached America. Isn't that correct?"

"I've repeatedly briefed this council about the urgency of the situation."

"You also told us we had a month before Ghost could possibly strike."

"No, sir. You heard that estimate from the directors of the Central Intelligence Agency and the Federal Bureau of Investigation. Like you, we accepted it because it seemed reasonable. The estimate's been proven invalid. Now we must take the next step."

"Let's listen to what she's got, Len," said the Vice President.

Griggs huffed angrily as he took his seat and began to read from a brief.

"As I was saying," Marian continued, "we find ourselves in the very situation the plan was designed for. A terrorist organization is operating in Washington, and their leader speaks of more atrocities. We can't allow those. We've been fortunate so far . . ."

"Fortunate?" Griggs snorted.

". . . Since there've been no deaths. I'll briefly go over the recommendations, then we can discuss specific implementations."

Manny activated a drop-down menu and made a selection. The screen changed:

- MARTIAL LAW
- CURFEW

"Recommendation one," Marian read. "That limited martial law and a nine p.m. to six a.m. curfew be imposed within the metropolitan area. The Secret Service and Park Service police would establish checkpoints and limit access to the Capitol area to essential government personnel. U.S. Marshal and FBI supervisory personnel would augment police leadership. The three metropolitan police forces would be reinforced by two thousand U.S. Army and National Guard military policemen and conduct a door-to-door sweep from the Capitol area out to the beltway to find and apprehend the terrorists."

Manny clicked.

- RESTRICT AIR AND VEHICULAR TRAFFIC

"Recommendation two. That Washington National Airport be limited to essential civil air traffic and all incoming and outgoing passengers and cargo be inspected by military personnel. Also that roadblocks be established . . ."

"No!" Leonard Griggs was back on his feet, shaking his head vigorously.

Marian was startled by the force of the interruption.

"That's enough!"

"The same precautions were taken in Europe after terrorist attacks and proved effective."

"This is not Europe. The people of America will not be bullied by either a wild-eyed terrorist *or* a group of inept bureaucrats."

"The measures are designed to capture the terrorists and *protect* our citizens."

"Ghost's attack failed."

"You heard the tape. There'll be more attacks."

"If it's Ghost, he's not the only one who has failed." He looked at the Vice President. "We should examine the possibility of reining Lindquist's people in, moving the function to a more disciplined environment."

The Vice President remained quiet, his lips pursed.

Was he cowed by Griggs? Marian wondered. Even worse, did he *agree* that the attack had been made possible by ITF-4's incompetence?

She regarded the Vice President. "May I continue my briefing, sir?"

Griggs interrupted again. "There've been attacks on the White House in the past, and no one resorted to restricting the rights of citizens."

Marian shook her head. "This is not an isolated act as those were. Ghost is extremely dangerous, and we must take immediate steps to capture him."

"You already have your effort under way at Fort Myer. Anything more would be the job of the Secret Service. If they determine a threat still exists, we'll take appropriate measures. By that I mean cordon off a *small* portion of the Capitol area using park policemen. *Certainly* no military people should be involved. I can assure you the President would never allow such a thing. This is America, not a two-bit, right-wing dictatorship."

"Of course," the Vice President hastily agreed.

Leonard Griggs's voice dropped to a reasonable tone. "We can't appear to have lost control. We can't have a show of panic as Lindquist's people suggest."

The Vice President's eyes were fixed on Griggs. He nodded.

Griggs regarded Marian somberly. "We'll call if we need you."

Marian sighed audibly, then motioned for Manny to join her as she stepped from the podium. Griggs remained on his feet, saying they should immediately request airtime. A spokesman should speak to the nation to restore calm.

No one should mention Ghost or the content of the audiotape.

Marian turned. "You've got to tell the public who we're dealing with. The people must know they're extremely dangerous and to look out for them."

Griggs shook his head. "Ghost mustn't learn how little we know. That's from my own experts on the domestic terrorism panel, and I trust their insights much more than yours."

"Jesus," Manny muttered when they were in the concrete-walled corridor. "The White House was bombed and Griggs is using it as an opportunity to get even?"

"The Vice President agreed," Marian said bitterly. "Our credibility's dropped to zilch."

"No wonder. Griggs torpedoes you at every turn. And what's this domestic terrorism panel. He's making his move to incorporate the ITF, Marian."

"Maybe." She stopped suddenly and turned to him. "Link's dream. The large home and the explosion. He knew something like this was going to happen."

DeVera shook his head. "Link's part of our problem. He gave Griggs ammunition when he came up with the imaginary translation to Ghost's words."

"We should have checked it," she conceded.

"I like Link, Marian. Always have. But the strafing incident in Iraq's preyed on him too long. One nudge and he'll go the rest of the way over the edge. I just hope to hell he didn't screw up the Fort Myer operation with his bullshit about Little Crow."

Marian continued toward the escalator to the main floor of the Pentagon, wondering. She decided to double-check the translation, then have another chat with her houseguest.

Rockville, Maryland

Ghost wasn't upset with the results of the bombing. He'd known the walls of the White House were sturdy—lined with steel plate as thick as the hull of a battleship—and hadn't erred in the amount of explosive it would take to penetrate them.

He'd not meant for the President to be killed by the fiery tongue that reached forth from the limousine. His death would have been a terrible error in his plan to cast the country into disarray. He'd gained their attention, as he'd intended.

Now the next step. They'd prepositioned other devices in the past few days.

"Slower," he told Rashad, who was at the Escort's wheel. As they passed a sprawling condominium complex, Ghost lifted the multiple-frequency transmitter-receiver device and depressed the button labeled F. A green light-emitting diode above the button illuminated.

The bomb he'd placed under the rear seat of the automobile in the covered parking lot had remained undetected for the past thirty-six hours. It was now armed, as were five others.

Six LEDs glowed on the transmitter device.

"Back to the warehouse," Ghost told Rashad. He had more work to do.

Relentless.

Georgetown, Washington, D.C.

Link had spent the morning pacing restlessly and watching the news. Idleness chafed him, for he was a person who needed activity.

Periodically he'd wonder about the events that had dominated the past weeks of his life. It was not difficult to determine the watershed that divided his past life from the present. The change had come with the reappearance of the Grandfather. If he'd understood it better, he could have warned authorities about the tragedy at Piccadilly Circus and this morning's attack on the White House. If it happened again—if given foreknowledge of an atrocity—he would do his best to avert it. Yet he wondered if that was possible. Who would believe him?

He might be able to relate images; fat and skinny trees to a water tower and windmill, a cave to a subway entrance. But what about the other messages? *"Come home,"* the

Grandfather—his subconscious—kept telling him. He'd tried returning to the Farmhouse, the only real home he'd known, but he did not believe that was what the old man of the dreams had meant.

"Prepare yourself." Another puzzle . . . unless . . .

Browning, Montana

Marie LeBecque was in her office, just off the phone with her aunt when the telephone on her desk rang and she voiced her greeting. It was Link Anderson.

She found herself smiling at the sound of his voice. She'd thought of him often during the past two days. "You sound tired," she immediately fussed.

"I haven't been sleeping all that well," he admitted.

"We saw the damage to the White House. Thank God the President wasn't badly hurt."

"It was Ghost."

"No one mentioned him on the news."

"It was him. I'm sure."

"When will you be back?" She'd blurted out the words. She didn't know him well enough to reveal how much she missed him, or that her aunt had been so impressed that she'd advised Marie to pursue him. Ben White Calf had told her to watch out, though, because something troubled the young man that would not be easily healed.

Her aunt and uncle could tell she was interested in him. She wondered if *he* knew.

"I've got a question," Link said. "How did the Piegan prepare warriors and holy men?"

"How long ago?"

"In Black Wolf's time?"

"Male children were taught what would be expected of them when they were young. There was a lot of feasting and telling of stories, and the youngsters were expected to listen. When they became teenagers, some went along when the warriors made their raids. They'd help with preparations, keep the camp, and haul the battle gear, food and such. If they were helpful, they'd graduate to scouting or tending the horses. Finally they'd join in, and if they did well, they'd be recognized in the stories the warriors told and accepted at the next Okan."

"Okan. That's the name of the holy festival?" She noted skepticism in his tone.

"Yes, the Sun Dance. There they'd be recognized, given new names, and become warriors. The ritual was painful and mystical, involving piercing of flesh and public meditation."

"And to become a holy man?"

"Some just bought a medicine pipe and the trappings and went to work, hoping others would come for advice. The best ones, like Black Wolf, were proven warriors who demanded respect. They had a lot of horses and could buy the best pipes and the best medicine, which they'd hang in a bag outside their lodge. The key was the same warrior ritual I told you about. The ones who did well in battle and at the Sun Dance went on to become influential men."

"So a proven warrior could become a powerful medicine man."

"Yes, and the wisest and most powerful holy men became weather dancers at the Okan. Everyone sought their advice."

"When was this . . . Okan . . . held?"

"In the summer, around the end of June. Now we hold them in July."

He sighed. "It sounds like a bunch of stone-age bull."

"You asked the question," she answered sharply, irritated at his sarcasm.

"I couldn't wait until July," he said. "How long did it take?"

"About a week. You're thinking of going through the ritual?"

"In the dreams I keep hearing that I must prepare myself. I wondered if that's what my subconscious is trying to tell me. How close are today's Okans to the way it used to be."

"The old ways are outlawed. There's no more piercing of flesh, thank God, and from what I've found in my research, a lot of the ritual has been forgotten. What we have now is symbolism. It's become a big Fourth of July celebration. Everyone's invited, outsiders included. There are stands where souvenirs are sold. Tourists gawk. The women fix a big barbecue and the girls eye the guys. Vietnam and Desert Storm vets march, and Korea and World War two old-timers grouse about how they don't know what it was *really* like. It's fun, but it's certainly not the same as it was in Black Wolf's day."

"It doesn't matter. I don't have that much time."

"I hope you come back soon," she blurted again, and was immediately embarrassed.

"I will, just as soon as I get done with things here."

"I found something that might interest you, Link. A reference in the agency police records from July of 1968. Three children were found north of Peshan, near the Canadian border. Isn't that the same year you were adopted?"

"Yes. Who were they?"

"The police records are unclear. They just say three small children were brought to Browning and turned over to agency authorities. I couldn't find anything about them at the administrative office. They may have just been local kids who wandered off."

He sounded interested. "Can you find out more?"

"It's hard to locate anyone who remembers much about that time except the Vietnam War and flower children. The world was polarized around issues, and that's what they associate most with the late sixties. I'll try to learn which policemen were on the force then, and who worked at the administrative office. If nothing else works, there are a few farms not far from Peshan. Tomorrow I'll drive out and talk to the people . . . see if they recall anything."

"I'll call back tomorrow night, and you can tell me what you find."

"Something else, Link. There's a woman there in Washington you may want to speak to. Got a pen and paper handy?"

He paused. "Go ahead."

"Her name's Grace McNabb, a psychologist at the American Human Research Laboratory in Bethesda." Marie quoted the phone number and address.

"A psychologist?" His voice held suspicion.

"Grace specializes in neural sciences and generation of memory. You wanted to know why some of these things are happening, and she may have answers. I've worked with her and learned to trust her. I spoke with her this morning and told her what you've been experiencing."

"You told her?"

"Nothing specific. Just enough that she's interested in meeting you."

Marie heard him release a ragged breath. "If she can help explain what's happening, it will be worthwhile." He hesitated. "Marie, a linguist at the University of Wisconsin says the translation you made of Bright Flame's words were in error."

"Doctor Podvin?"

"I don't know his name, but he's an expert on the Algonkian language."

"That's him. He's studied the Ojibwa culture and language. Algonkian is a language *family,* like the Romance languages in Europe, and varies from region to region. Our vocabulary is identical among the Blackfeet tribes, similar to Cree and Cheyenne, but it's quite different from Ojibwa and the more distant Algonkian speakers."

"He said the phrase doesn't even sound like it was spoken by a Native American."

"I told you the pronunciation was awkward. If you want, I'll give Doctor Podvin a phone call and straighten it out."

"Yeah. I'd like that." He paused. "Marie, thanks for all your help."

"Just hurry and get back here." It was easier to say.

After they hung up, Marie wondered if she was in love. She missed him . . . a lot.

8:15 P.M.—Georgetown, Washington, D.C.

Following his conversation with Marie, Judge Lindquist had called to say they'd be late. Link had snacked on the cold cuts she'd said were in the refrigerator, read a *Washington Scene* magazine article about the home lives of local luminaries, then fallen asleep on the sofa.

He bolted upright when Marian Lindquist awakened him.

"Are you okay?" she asked, alarm in her eyes.

Link settled back, blew out a breath, and calmed.

"You were talking in your sleep," she said. "Something about 'hurry'?"

Manny DeVera came into the room, shucking off his suit jacket.

"A dream," Link said to Marian. "It's the second time I've had it."

She frowned. "What was this one about, Link?"

"Something hidden in wagons, then a sick man and an explosion," Link said.

"Wagons?" Manny looked puzzled. "Like kids' wagons?"

"More like horse-drawn wagons . . . with no horses." Link was increasingly embarrassed. "I can't shake the feeling . . . something else is about to happen."

Manny gave him a carefully maintained neutral look, then stalked to the kitchen.

He looked at Marian. "There's something going on. Like before with Piccadilly and the White House. I knew they'd happen. I just didn't know how to interpret the dreams."

"It's difficult to understand, Link."

"Hard to believe, you mean?"

"Let's have a bite to eat and talk about it."

He followed her into the kitchen where Manny was pulling cartons from Kentucky Fried Chicken sacks.

"CNN said the President's at Walter Reed," Link said, helping Marian with her coat.

She pursed her lips into a thoughtful pout as he sat at the table. "Did your dream have anything to do with the hospital?"

"I don't know. Maybe. There's the image of a sick man."

Manny cast him an irritated look.

Marian stared for a thoughtful minute, then picked up the telephone and spoke to an IDO at the ITF-4 communications center. "Get in touch with the colonel in charge of security at Walter Reed. I want all vehicles coming through the gate stopped and thoroughly checked."

She listened. "Then tighten security even more. Have them look in trunks, under the seats, everywhere. Tell the colonel to contact you with anything he finds." She hung up.

"Are you sure?" Manny asked her. "If Griggs gets wind of it there'll be questions."

"I'll just say I acted on the side of prudence."

"We don't need questions, Marian. There's concern about our credibility. We're in enough trouble because of the mistranslation." Manny cast another look at Link.

She retrieved plates and loaded them with food. "This morning I called Professor Podvin at the University of Wisconsin. He's the expert who'd told the NSC people the translation was faulty. I wanted to confirm his interpretation."

"Did he?"

"At first. Then late this afternoon he phoned back to tell me he'd changed his mind. The translation wasn't in error. It was just poorly spoken in a dialect he wasn't familiar with."

"Why didn't you tell me?" Manny frowned.

"Because you're so damned blockheaded," she said archly. "Last night Link tried to tell us about his dreams, and we wouldn't listen. If we had, maybe we could have put it together." Judge Lindquist was watching Link closely. "Now, tell us more about this latest dream."

"There's the horseless wagons with something hidden inside, then the sick man and the explosions. I was told to prepare myself and stop him. I think the 'him' is Ghost."

Marian took a call from the ITF-4 comm center; nothing to report.

They finished eating and waited. Manny made and poured coffee. Two more reports were made by the IDO. Nothing was happening at either Walter Reed or Fort Myer.

At eleven twenty-five Marian received a phone call relayed from Walter Reed. Grim-faced, she punched on the speaker. A bomb had been found under the rear seat of a car owned by a doctor coming in for the midnight shift. They'd isolated the vehicle and were calling in an explosive ordnance disposal team.

"There's no time, and there's more than one bomb," Link said.

"Tell the colonel to have the EOD team stand clear and have the guards keep searching vehicles," Marian told the IDO. "The staff should park well away from the hospital. Tell the hospital commander what's happening and advise him to move patients out of rooms nearest the staff parking lot." She hung up, pale-faced, and stared at Link.

"Jesus," Manny muttered.

They continued to wait. The direct line from the communications center warbled. Manny punched the speaker button. "Go ahead."

"Ghost just phoned the editor at the *Post* and demanded that Charlie be released. He said he knows he's still in Illinois."

Manny groaned.

"He says this time it's a hospital. Walter Reed's been notified."

Link looked at the clock. It was 11:46.

Georgetown was several miles from Walter Reed, but they heard the distant crack of the bomb detonation. Two seconds later there was another, then a staccato of sharp sounds.

At 11:56 they received the call from the intelligence duty officer at ITF-4—six explosions had been reported at Walter Reed, three from automobiles parked in the secluded area, three more from the parking lot. There was damage, but no one was injured.

"Recall the senior staff," Marian told the IDO.

Two minutes later the flash came over CNN. Frantic telephone calls were pouring into their Capitol office. Several explosions had been heard from the area of Walter Reed Hospital.

"Washington is being systematically terrorized," the announcer said.

"That's what Ghost's after," Manny said gloomily.

Marian looked evenly at Link. "Thank you," she told him quietly, then stood and slipped into the coat Manny brought for her.

15

Thursday, February 2nd

4:00 A.M.—Georgetown, Washington, D.C.

Ghost was irked that the bombs had been discovered. The security guards had tightened down and inspected vehicles entering the Walter Reed gate more closely. A zealous security chief? He'd know more when the wayfinder called next.

The media reported that the public was frightened. They'd seen nothing of what was to come. Today's effort would continue on schedule. *Bam! . . . bam!* A jab followed by a hard blow to the body. This time there'd be no holding back. Two chiefs would die.

Atrocities were the battles of a poor people's war, terrorists their army. His task was to arouse such feelings of fear and helplessness that the enemy gave in. After he'd bloodied the arrogant nation there would be blustering and calls for vengeance, but they *would* give in.

Ghost rolled the numbers six-four-five-two over in his mind.

"Kill the engine," he told Rashad. The ten-year-old Ford Escort was parked in shadows at the midpoint of the alley.

He eased the door open and closed it quietly behind himself. Rashad removed a bulky equipment bag, then began to pull the cover into place. Police cars patrolled the area often and might be suspicious of a parked car. If it was covered, they'd believe it was owned by a resident.

As Rashad joined him, carrying the heavy equipment bag, Ghost paused for a few more seconds to complete his orientation, then moved quietly, remaining in the shadows. Two doors down he slipped through an unlocked gate into a small backyard.

He'd been told there was no dog. They continued to the rear door. He unlocked the door and slipped soundlessly inside. The alarm had been triggered, but there was a twenty-second delay before it would sound. He entered six, four, five, two into the keypad. A green light illuminated—the system was deactivated. Cherone had obtained the key and code from the alarm installation company owned by his organization.

Ghost proceeded inside, Rashad close at his heels as they crept down the hardwood hallway on rubber-soled shoes. Ghost paused. "Two," he whispered as he pointed to a bedroom door. "One," he whispered as he motioned at another.

Rashad quietly placed the bag on the floor, removed the knife from his calf sheath, and crept to the first door. As he eased it open, Ghost went into the front room. He drew back the curtain and looked onto the well-illuminated street, then at a home on the opposite side.

There was a gurgling sound and whimper from the bedroom, but they were not loud.

The home across the street was two-story, built of aged brick, with white shutters and trim. There were four square columns in front.

Ghost heard a low metallic click and faint rustling as Rashad emerged from the first bedroom. He waited. There were drumming noises as the third victim convulsed.

Rashad reappeared. "It's done," he said in a normal voice. He switched on a light in the hall bathroom and left the door ajar for dim illumination, then grunted with effort as he hauled the equipment bag into the front room and deposited it. As Rashad removed three reshaped cones and placed them near the front door, Ghost smelled the acrid odor of tritonol.

This one was for Joseph DiFazio, but it fit nicely with his plan. Ghost continued to look out at the objective. There were four agents: two in a car, the others standing together outside, all wearing overcoats and trying to remain watchful. There were more at the rear of the home but they were unimportant.

Ghost waited for ten full minutes at the window. There was no hurry. Satisfied that there were no surprises, he went to the front door and eased it open.

They'd picked this particular brownstone due to its proximity to the objective, but also because the entrance was masked by tall shrubs. Nevertheless, Ghost moved carefully as he reached back and drew the cones outside, then pushed the door almost closed.

He watched the men again. One was yawning. The other massaged his own shoulders. The two in the automobile appeared to be talking to one another.

Ghost positioned the three cones together—they'd been reshaped to fit snugly—then shaped and smoothed with his fingers, taking his time as the focused-effect bomb took final form. The task took half an hour, but Ghost worked quietly and remained hidden behind the tall shrubs, and there was no slightest chance of being detected.

Finished with his sculpting, he pressed a single detonator fully into the compound at the rear of the enlarged cone and abutted the mass against the exposed concrete foundation. The apex was directed toward the very front of the building across the street. Ghost extracted the radio receiver from his windbreaker pocket and connected the detonator wires, toggled a switch to activate the receiver, and backed soundlessly toward the door.

Inside, he relaxed for five long minutes, allowing himself to mentally evaluate what he'd done. When he returned to the window, the Secret Service agents hadn't moved. He went to the couch and sat beside Rashad. "We've got two hours," he said, fingering the triggering device.

There was a sound from one of the bedrooms, causing Ghost to tense.

"There was a cat with the kid," Rashad said. He liked animals and would never harm one unless it was a guard dog. Those he mentally grouped on the sides of their enemies, but he was still reluctant to kill them. When he was forced to do so, he made sure they didn't suffer.

As they waited, Ghost reminisced. After he and Charlie had been rescued by the traveler, the Bull Clan elders had told them the story of Lame Bear and Black Wolf. How the two men's spirits had been strong, and how Ghost, descended from both, would gain extraordinary power. He'd been taught to live off the land and move stealthily; to fight and endure; to take from under the eyes of the most watchful enemies, as his forebears had done. To kill was not dishonorable, but it must be done well and for a purpose.

The Bull Clan had learned that old man Weiser had bought Ghost and Little Crow from a driver taking them to an orphanage in Helena. The driver had destroyed the paperwork given him at the reservation and provided forged ones so authorities couldn't trace the children. They hadn't been the first children he'd sold. There'd been records in the reservation administration office, but the driver knew to destroy those, too.

The driver had been Ghost's first kill—when he was fifteen. The Bull Clan had found him living in a hovel in Butte and given Ghost the honor of cutting his throat. He remembered feeling distaste as he'd done it, but it had been the last time he'd harbored such emotion.

His second kill had been old man Weiser. Ghost had returned to the ranch north of Great Falls for his birth certificate for it was required to enlist in the army, but the old man had refused. He'd cursed him and gone to get his shotgun, unaware of how strong Ghost's spirit had become. He'd grabbed up a butcher knife and cut the old man as he'd pulled the shotgun from the closet. Then Ghost had taken the old man's thrashing body to a pig sty behind the house and dumped it in with the lean, underfed swine. When they'd begun to feed, he'd felt only contempt. He'd cleaned the butcher knife and the blood from the house, and left a scrap of paper scrawled with the sign of his spirit. His Bull Clan tutors had agreed. It was a good kill.

He'd believed his lack of emotion was due to the hatred he'd had for the old man, but when others began to die at his hand or at his direction, he'd still felt nothing. Admiration for the bravest ones perhaps, but a void where most were concerned.

The intelligent young man named Gerard Weiser had encountered no problems with the army. He'd become an explosives ordnance expert, then attended the army linguist school in Monterey, California. Ghost had learned the rudiments of his profession from the country he despised. Sp/4 Gerard Weiser had died during a joint training exercise with Peruvian troops at Fort Chaffee, Arkansas, the victim of an explosives accident. The badly charred corpse was not associated with a farmer's son who'd disappeared the week before.

In two hours, when the woman across the street emerged to get into the government car that always came for her, Ghost would make his call to the *Post,* then leave. As soon as he was clear of the house, he'd send the signal to activate the bomb. There was no doubt that the woman would be killed . . . or that he would again feel nothing as they escaped in the confusion.

Rashad's head was nodding. Ghost jostled him harshly. "Get up and walk around."

Rashad rubbed at his eyes and got to his feet.

"Tell me when it's seven," Ghost said. He lolled his head against the couch and closed his eyes to think—of Charlie and their childhood—of how he would exact revenge upon the enemy of the People. He was the chosen one, the instrument of vengeance. Charlie would be freed. The People would be vindicated.

Link came awake with a start. It took a moment before he realized he was in Marian Lindquist's guest bedroom.

The Grandfather had visited. He groaned with fatigue, yet he knew it was important to remember. There were elusive images. Something near a bush. A man? *Crouched behind a bush. Hiding as he worked on* . . . he couldn't remember, but the man's fingers had sculpted and smoothed. Strong, sure fingers. He'd pictured them more clearly than their task. The man had gone about his work with an almost delicate touch, as if what he was doing was important.

The man waited in darkness, watching. A woman walked from a home. She was getting into a wagon-like thing. *A horseless wagon.* A tongue of flame leapt forth.

Link staggered to his feet, ran trembling hands through his hair. He squinted and blinked eyes that felt as if hot grit had been poured into them. He left the bedroom, knowing he had to tell the others. He knocked on the master bedroom door, then tried the bedroom where Manny slept. There was no response from either. Judge Marian and Manny were still at their meeting.

He remembered the direct line to the ITF-4 comm center and found the telephone.

The answerer did not tell where he was located, only responded with a last name.

"Judge Lindquist," Link blurted. "It's an emergency." He waited, trembling with fatigue.

A moment later he was told a staff car was on its way to pick him up.

6:48 A.M.—ITF-4 Offices, Department of Justice, Washington, D.C.

They were in Marian Lindquist's office. For the third time, Link described what he'd seen in the dream. Manny and Marian listened as he spoke haltingly.

"He was kneeling behind a large bush."

"Who?" Manny asked.

"Ghost," Link said. It was the first time he'd been sure. "He was hiding while he built something. Sculpted it. I remember the fingers. They were . . ."

"Where was he, Link?" Marian asked.

He shook his head helplessly. "There was a large bush." He brightened. "But that wasn't what he was looking at. There was a home. It was . . . it looked like yours."

"A brownstone?"

"Maybe." Link racked his brain, trying to recall details. "Brick perhaps, but it looked something like yours . . . with fewer plants in front. A woman lives there."

"Two story?"

Link nodded. "Two story brick." He recalled more. "It had white trim."

She pushed a pen and pad across to him. "Draw it."

Link lifted the pen, waited and tried to remember, then drew a large box. He added windows on top and bottom, cross-hatches for panes. He paused.

"The front door?"

He drew in the rectangle, hesitated. "There was something more."

Manny was watching incredulously. "Gables on the windows?" he offered.

"No." He drew in trim. "That's white," he said. He drew two rounded bushes set out from the house. He drew shutters. "Those are white, too."

The others were staring at his work, eyebrows knitted.

Link sighed and shook his head. "I can't remember."

"Is there time to drive around different neighborhoods?" Manny tried.

"No!" he said forcefully.

"Was there a porch?" Marian asked.

"I'm not . . ." he hesitated. "Yeah. There was a porch and . . ." He added an overhang and two columns, then two more. He examined and nodded. "That's it."

Marian frowned. "A woman," she muttered.

Manny shook his head. "That could be any of a hundred . . ."

"Wait," Marian exclaimed. "A woman," she breathed. "My boss!"

She dialed the attorney general's restricted-access number.

7:05 A.M.—Georgetown, Washington, D.C.

It was becoming light outside. The car would arrive, and in five minutes the woman would come out. Both the driver and the woman were punctual.

As if he'd ordered it, a dark sedan pulled in front of the house. The driver emerged and nodded at the Secret Service agents as he walked around to the rear passenger door.

"Go ahead," Ghost said quietly. Rashad walked briskly down the hall toward the back. He would go to the car in the alley, remove the cover, and start the engine.

It was time for the call. Ghost shifted the triggering device to his other hand, hefted the cellular phone, and dialed the *Post,* still staring through the gap in the curtains at the house across the street. After his message to free Charlie, the editor would receive another from the Islamic Brotherhood of Al Fa'qa taking credit for the killing of the attorney general.

"Hello?" Ghost started to respond, then stopped himself and frowned in disbelief.

"Hello?" The sedan was speeding away. The Secret Service men were hastily withdrawing down the street, and he could hear sounds of approaching vehicles.

It seemed impossible that it was happening, but . . . *The vehicle sounds grew louder.*

Ghost turned and sprinted toward the back door, slipped

on a throw rug, twisted and fell hard onto the wood floor. Both the cellular telephone and triggering device went flying.

A spike of pain coursed through his calf and ankle. He pushed to his feet and staggered, then limped as he hurried, knowing he had to escape before the area could be cordoned off. As he exited the back door and lurched down the alley toward the waiting Ford Escort, Ghost's mind worked furiously.

How had they known? Who could have warned them?

10:15 A.M.

Manny DeVera drove them to the scene in his car, Judge Lindquist in the front passenger's seat, Lincoln Anderson in back, staring out at the quiet neighborhood of stately homes.

Link exercised his overtired mind, trying to reason how he'd been able to recapture it so accurately. Although he was increasingly aware of the power of his subconscious, it was baffling how the elements had come together. There'd had to be knowledge of the appearance of the attorney general's home. That he had that information stored in his mind was not beyond reason, but the other parts—Ghost's intention and the timing of the event—were difficult to rationalize.

Manny stopped at the police cordon, and they showed identification before DeVera drove on through. The area had been evacuated, sealed, then thoroughly swept by explosive ordnance disposal teams. The bomb had been quickly found and disarmed. The task had been made trickier because Ghost used a fuze designed to detonate with tampering, but they'd carried it off.

Manny DeVera parked at the side of the street. The home with four columns was on their left, a house with large shrubs hiding the entrance was on their right.

"Look familiar?" Marian asked Link.

"The memory's faded," Link said, frowning at a slight pungent odor.

"It certainly looks as you described it," said Marian.

"Part of it's that I'm tired. I haven't gotten much rest in the past few days."

"We'll remedy that. Your health has become critical to us, Link."

He remembered that neither of the others had slept the previous night.

Manny motioned at the home on their right. "That's where the bomb was set up. An extremist group called Al Fa'qa called to take credit, but it was Ghost's bomb. He'd scratched his signature onto the radio receiver. The bomb was tritonol compound, like the ones from the automobiles going through the gate at Walter Reed."

"Are they having any luck tracing it?"

"J.J. Davis is making progress. He's figured out the who and how of getting the explosives out the gate at the arsenal."

Marian rolled down her window as an agent approached the car.

"No signs of forced entry. We're guessing they had a key. Then either the alarm wasn't activated or they had the code. The doctor, his wife, and their daughter were killed in their beds. It's not pretty. The killer didn't just cut their throats, he damned near removed their heads."

"Rashad," Manny muttered.

"We found a portable transmitter for the bomb and a cellular phone on the floor in the hall. Looks like one of 'em slipped on a throw rug and dropped them. Probably in a hurry to get out or he'd've picked them up. That means we were close."

"A cellular telephone?" Marian asked.

"The number's listed in the name of a moving company in Capitol Heights. We're checking it out."

"I'd like to go inside," Link said, looking at the house.

He shrugged. "Go ahead, long as you don't move anything."

As Link got out he stared first at the shrubs, then across at the Attorney General's home. He walked up the short sidewalk, then paused at a large, sculpted bush. The pungent odor became pronounced. The lawn area was trampled where the bomb squad had done their work.

As he passed through the open front door, Link stopped abruptly. It was as if someone was before him—breathing, functioning . . . living. The odor was pervasive. After a pause he continued into the living room where his attention was captured by the sofa—plush and comfortable, with three small throw pillows disarranged. He went closer. *Ghost had been there.*

He stood very still, ignoring the agents and policemen who filed through the room.

It was gone then. Ghost's presence left as quickly as it had come. He saw bloody smudges and a clear outline where a knife blade had been wiped on one of the throw pillows, but there was no sensation of familiarity.

He went back out—the sharp odor was replaced by a pleasant aroma of flora—and walked to the car where Manny and Judge Lindquist waited.

"I'd better find a hotel," Link said as he crawled inside. He was trembling with fatigue. If he didn't sleep soon, he would collapse.

"We were just talking about that," said Manny as he eased the car away from the curb.

"You've become critical to us, Link," Marian said. "I've called for around-the-clock protection at my house. You can continue to use my guest bedroom. I don't want you going anywhere. Just tell us the moment you have another dream . . . or whatever."

They passed through the cordon and accelerated.

"I also called for a doctor to meet us at the office. He'll give you something to let you rest. You can use a couch in one of the offices."

On the way back to the Justice building, Manny DeVera began to eye the rearview mirror. Link also became observant for a moment, then forced himself to drop it. It was no time for unwarranted apprehensions. He was so damnable sleepy!

They stopped in a long line of automobiles. Security had been tightened around the Capitol area, and only those on official business were being allowed through.

As they waited, Link lolled his head against the top of the seat and drifted off.

"Link?" A hand jostled him.

He groaned as he came partially awake.

"You've got to show your ID," Marian said.

"Your identification, sir?" asked a uniformed patrolman.

"Yeah?" Link fished out the leather folder and handed it over, still groggy.

There'd been another Grandfather dream.

The policeman handed the folder back to Link and stepped away, motioning them through. Manny DeVera accelerated.

"I just had another damned dream," Link muttered.

"Jesus," said Manny. "Another bomb?"

"I believe so." Link inhaled deeply and blew out, feeling utterly exhausted.

His head ached, and he wanted to repress the dream as he'd done as a child, but it was important that he recall details. *A large, green living thing . . . a chief . . . a bright flash.* The living thing had been noisy, rising, falling, growing, diminishing . . . The Grandfather had been unsure of what he was trying to describe. There'd been a chief. A man.

Link rushed his words as he related the dream.

"An insect?" Manny asked as he pulled into the Department of Justice parking lot.

"It resembled a grasshopper, then seemed more like a dragonfly." He felt foolish as he realized what he'd been saying.

"A chief," Marian murmured.

"I think Ghost considers all leaders chiefs. This time it's a man and his death has something to do with the . . . an insect-like thing. I don't know how it harms him, but it's large."

Manny smiled, yet Link could think of no other way to describe the image. As they walked, then took a side elevator, Link continued to reflect. There was nothing more—only the image of the grasshopper/locust/dragonfly . . . whatever . . . and a chief.

They went directly into Marian's office. Link sat on the couch trying to conjure the dream, his head feeling as if it would burst with the effort.

"The doctor's waiting to see Mr. Anderson," Mimi called from the outer office.

"Not yet," Link said. The pain in his forehead was more intense. "Where's the President?" he asked. It seemed right.

"He's being taken by motorcade to the White House," said Marian, staring intently as if wanting to crawl inside his mind. She glanced at a wall clock. "He'll be there shortly."

A motorcade? That wasn't like the dream. He shook his head. "Is anyone else traveling?"

Manny called the comm center and put the IDO's to work researching VIP schedules. A few minutes later the senior duty officer confirmed that the President had arrived at the White House without incident.

Ten more minutes passed, and Link's headache worsened. He rubbed his brow and continued to try to think of something that might cast new light on the dream's meaning.

An IDO came to the room. Link examined the list of lawmakers and cabinet members traveling from Andrews and Washington National. None of them seemed right.

Marian shook her head. "Perhaps you should rest," she said.

"Yeah." Link sighed, wondering if the headache would allow it.

Another intelligence duty officer came in and whispered to Manny and Marian.

"Jesus," Manny muttered as Marian followed the IDO out of the office.

"What's happening?" Link asked.

Color was fading from Manny's face. "The Vice President's on his way to Camp David for a meeting. The helicopter should be picking him up at Blair House now."

A large green dragonfly making a chattering sound. *A U.S. Marine helicopter.*

"Yeah. That's it." Link's headache continued to pound behind his brow.

Airborne VH-53

The controllers voice was urgent. "Marine One, this is Eagle Control. Hold in place."

The lieutenant colonel aircraft commander slowed their descent toward the small helipad on the grounds behind Blair House, the 170-year-old, government-owned mansion presently being used by the Vice President while repairs were made to his official residence.

"Confirm that, Eagle Control," said the aircraft commander. He could see the Vice President and his wife walking from the mansion in the midst of a swarm of bodyguards.

"Confirmation is Echo-Yankee-Foxtrot. Hold your altitude."

The copilot had the code wheel in his hand. He nodded. "Roger, Eagle Control. Marine One is holding."

The lieutenant colonel worked the throttle and collective, and entered an approximation of a hover. The radar altimeter showed they were 550 feet above the ground.

The meticulously cleaned fire extinguisher was secured in its bracket in the rear compartment. At its top were two small, innocuous holes. Inside one a barometric port closed as the preconditions—a period of descent followed by a period of no change—were met. The device sensed that they'd landed, although they had not. The electrical circuit switched to receive orders from the second port, preset to detect an increase in altitude. At the same time, a timer was activated. If either situation occurred—the increase in altitude, or the expiration of the timer—a signal would be sent to the detonator buried in five kilos of molded tritonol compound.

The copilot pointed. The procession below was hastening back inside the mansion.

"Marine One, this is Eagle Control. Maintain your present altitude and proceed to the Potomac. Do not descend and do not climb."

"Roger," he responded. The lieutenant colonel tautened his jaw. He'd geen given the instructions they were to follow if a bomb was suspected to be aboard. He nodded brusquely to the copilot and gingerly turned toward the river.

"Stay strapped in back there," he said over the intercom. The loadmaster and steward had been listening in on the radio conversation and didn't respond.

He flew toward the river, and when he reached it, angled leftward. "Marine One is over the Potomac, abeam the Pentagon and proceeding south over the main channel."

"Marine One, you are cleared for emergency landing at Quantico North. Pick the most deserted area of the ramp, put it down, and evacuate."

"Roger, Eagle Control."

Although it was only minutes, the flight seemed to last forever. Finally the copilot pointed ahead at the sprawling U.S. Marine base.

"I've got it in sight," said the aircraft commander in a clipped voice. "Loadmaster, open the main entry door. I'm going to put it down quickly, then I want everyone out."

"Roger, sir."

He slowed only slightly, took a short breath, and began the descent. If there was a barometric bomb aboard, it would sense the change of atmospheric pressure.

As they passed through four hundred feet, he selected the concrete ramp where he would land. There was no activity, aircraft, or equipment in the vicinity. The area had been evacuated.

"Through three hundred," said the copilot.

The aircraft commander did not respond, but concentrated on the direct-in pattern.

Within the fire extinguisher, the second port of the fuzing device continued to await on increase in altitude. The timer neared expiration.

At two hundred feet the aircraft shuddered, and the copilot tensed, eyes glued to the radar altimeter. They passed through one hundred feet.

"Prepare for touchdown," said the aircraft commander. His throat was exceedingly dry. At fifty feet he slowed the descent, then let the bird settle gingerly. As soon as the gear touched the concrete, he set the throttles to idle, disengaged the rotor blades, and keyed the mike.

"Everyone out!" He jabbed a thumb toward the rear. The copilot released his harness and scrambled. The lieutenant colonel waited for a slow count of five, until everyone should have deplaned, then slapped the electrical and engine fuel switches off and released his own seat belt.

He almost caught up with the copilot as they raced the fifty yards to where the crew had gathered on the grass adjacent to the ramp.

"What the hell was that about?" asked the steward, still panting from the run.

The timer expired.

There was the flash and sharp report. A split second later the fuel ignited, and the concussive wave from the explosion swept over them.

Bethesda, Maryland

Ghost listened as the news bulletin came over the television in the warehouse office. A marine VIP helicopter had been involved in an accident at Quantico. There'd been no casualties and no officials aboard. Military and National Transportation Safety Board authorities were en route to investigate the cause.

Ghost's eyes narrowed. He felt himself trembling with anger.

Martin Cherone was staring at the television with a brooding look.

"Who's telling them?" Ghost asked aloud, and he wasn't at all sure that his voice hadn't quavered. Three times his plan had been thwarted. The first he'd felt was chance, but three?

Ghost motioned to Rashad. They went out to the workbench, where he'd been molding tritonol for a new bomb.

Was that it? he wondered. Was he overlooking things in his new haste?

"Bad luck," Rashad mumbled.

The failure at the attorney general's home had been the worst. He'd lost the cellular telephone, but that was no problem. It had been replaced, and he'd called the Bull Clan elders with the new number so they could pass it to the wayfinder. The other was unforgivable—the triggering device and bomb had been left intact as he'd fled.

He still limped from the sprain and pulled muscle, but refused medication or wrapping. The pain helped to focus Ghost's mind . . . and remind himself of the failure.

"Think it's Cherone?" Rashad wondered, staring toward the glass office.

"Maybe."

"Want me to take them out?" Rashad did not like Martin Cherone or his men.

"Not yet." Yet Ghost knew he couldn't continue to be compromised. The public was growing more confident each time his efforts were stopped. Credit was being given to Leonard Griggs, director of the NSC. The report that Griggs was a blustering incompetent was obviously in error. Or was he receiving reports from one of Cherone's people?

The new cellular phone buzzed. He switched it on.

"This is the wayfinder" came the crisp voice. "The person you're looking for is Judge Marian S. Lindquist." He gave an address, then more information of interest.

The connection was broken.

As Ghost began to think of a next step, Martin Cherone came from the office. "That Anderson guy's back in town."

It made sense. A. L. Anderson was the only one who could have posed so well as Charlie for the television cameras at Andrews. "Where's he staying?"

When Cherone told him, Ghost's eyes narrowed at the coincidence.

"Have him followed," he said. "I want to know where he goes."

"That may be difficult. Someone's already bird-dogging him."

ITF-4 Offices, Department of Justice, Washington, D.C.

Marian Lindquist was going through the preliminary report from Quantico. The bomb had been small, secreted in a fire extinguisher. The Vice President and his wife were fortunate to be alive.

Manny had left to drive Link to Bethesda, to meet with a doctor who specialized in the formation of memories. Link wanted to understand what was going on in his head. Neither Link nor Manny understand premonition. As a woman, Marian was able to accept it more easily. She wondered if it was wise for Link to seek scientific explanation.

Mimi's voice came over the intercom. "Mr. Leonard Griggs is here."

Marian was surprised. "I'll be right there," she said.

She went to the outer office, cautiously shook Griggs's hand and smiled more than she felt. He looked about curiously as she led him into her inner sanctum.

"I've got to congratulate you on your work these last two days, Lindquist."

"We've been lucky."

Griggs took his seat, stretching his legs and crossing them at the ankles, all the while staring with a brooding expression, as if gauging her with the flat-black eyes. There was no trace of warmth in the look.

"I met with the President this morning after your people gave the advisory about the bomb on the chopper. He was impressed. Told me to give you any help you may need." Griggs pursed his lips. "The best way to do that is to bring your organization under the NSC."

She remained silent.

"I've suggested that the President be moved from the White House to a safer location. If you worked with us, you'd have immediate access. You'd remain in charge, and you'd pick up the people currently assigned to my domestic terrorism panel."

"That would be in contradiction with our charter."

"Charters can be changed. I intend to approach the President with that proposal. In the interim, the least we can do is cooperate, don't you agree?"

"Certainly." She believed she knew what he was about to ask.

"Who's giving you your information about Ghost's plans?"

"That's compartmentalized for the present time."

"Lindquist, I'm the national security adviser to the President. Who's your source?"

Marian didn't have the right to withhold critical information when the safety of the nation's leadership was at stake. But Griggs would want access to Link, and his heavy-handed tactics could turn off the flow of information.

She decided on compromise. "There's a person who provides information."

Griggs lowered his voice. "An inside source, right?" He smiled.

"There's no insider." She took in a deep breath. "This person has somehow tuned to Ghost's thoughts."

Griggs grimaced. "His *thoughts*?"

"That's the only way I can explain it. We don't know how it happens, but the information has been accurate."

"For God's sake, Lindquist. You may think this guy's getting information from moonbeams, but he obviously has inside information. Maybe from Ghost or the Al Fa'qa. Did you think of that? Did you check him out?"

"Thoroughly. The person works for us."

"He works for you? You've been infiltrated!" Griggs exploded. He rose to his feet. "The terrorists are feeding you information, and you're listening to them."

"That's ridiculous. We've saved lives. You admitted it."

"I was right all along. You're a group of incompetents and loonies over here." Griggs snorted with disgust as he stormed from the room.

3:00 P.M.—Bethesda, Maryland

"You're Marie's friend?" asked the middle-aged woman as she entered the reception area.

"Link Anderson," he said, standing. They shook hands. "I'm glad you could see me."

Doctor McNabb smiled. "From what Marie said, you're a unique young man. I've cleared my afternoon schedule. How long do you have for me?"

"A friend will pick me up at four-thirty."

She led the way down a hall to her cluttered office.

"No couch?" He smiled.

"Sorry but the chair will have to do. I'm not a therapist. I do research into what makes the human mind tick. I've been hooked on the stuff since undergraduate school." She sat at her desk, opened a notebook computer, and switched it on.

"How did you meet Marie?" he asked.

"You're not the only person with your talent, Link. Three years ago I received a grant to search for commonality, perhaps an identifying gene, a mote on the DNA strand of those who share the phenomenon. Marie LeBecque had written me about heightened perception in the Piegan culture. We worked together until my funding expired and I had to go back to a real job."

"You mean my DNA may be different from others?"

"The DNA of most humans differ. I was searching for a common thread among those with highly developed neural signaling."

"What does that mean?"

"Unique understanding. The ability to take in a vast number of inputs and use long-term memories to put the pertinent ones together in an orderly fashion. Marie told me you're educated. Do you remember the thalamus, cortex, and hippocampus?"

"Vaguely. They're areas of the brain."

"They pass neural transmissions among themselves to help with thought processes. When I was working on the project I told you about, I concentrated on an area called the limbic system, and in particular, the amygdala, where long-term memories such as associations with fear are stored. If you hear the sound of a gun being cocked, you know to be concerned. That sort of long-term memory is stored in the amygdala. The amygdala also helps generate emotion so you'll do something about it. Make a fight or flight decision."

"What does that have to do with precognition?"

"Since the amygdala is so orderly, I felt it might work with short-term memories in the hippocampus and be the key to the complex reasoning we're talking about. Then I found that highly perceptive people are also those who react best to emergency situations."

She punched a few keys on the notebook computer. "May I ask a few general questions?"

"Sure."

"I'll try to explain as I go along. Now, how would you rate your reaction to emergency situations? Calmness, or a tendency to panic?"

"No panic." He thought back. "My mind seems to go into a sort of slow-motion mode."

She made an entry. "Have any of these recent dreams turned out to be totally false?"

"Not that I know of."

"That indicates a lack of confabulation, no generation of false memories."

"False, as in hallucinations?"

"Those would qualify. In some cases, a subject has a series of fantasies and believes he's intuitive when just one turns out to be valid. That's not your case, Link." She typed on the computer. "After you've had one of these dreams, do you feel emotional?"

"Sometimes. When I do it's . . . unsettling."

"That would be the reaction by the amygdala, since it recognizes a stored threat." She made an entry, looked up again. "Do you have what people call a photographic memory?"

"Not in regard to the dreams. I have trouble recalling them."

"How about day-to-day recollection? On a scale of one to ten, how would you rate your recall of what you see."

"Eight or nine. I can recall details others can't."

"That's called hypermnesia." She punched keys. "Marie said you were a fighter pilot."

"A few years ago."

"During the study I told you about, I looked at a number of military aviators. I interviewed high achiever pilots, such as those who had shot down large numbers of enemy planes, and also those who tended to have bad luck. Guess what I found?"

That one was easy for Link. "The best pilots know their enemy's next move," he said.

"In their language it's called situational awareness. A sixth sense that draws a mental picture of what's happening about them in the sky. They grow the ability to forecast what their opponent is about to do. I use the word grow rather than develop, because I've concluded it's not something learned. It's an inherent phenomenon."

Link's eyes narrowed.

"Your situational awareness was very good as a fighter pilot, wasn't it, Link?"

"Yeah." His friends had thought it was uncanny the way he could second-guess them.

"I spoke with fighter aces like General Robin Olds, who shot down enemy aircraft in three different wars. I've seldom met more perceptive people."

"So it's not just Native Americans we're talking about."

"Not at all. Theirs is more a matter of acceptance. If you've talked much with Marie, she's told you about the differences between American Indian and European cultures. Certain tribes placed great faith in prescient ability. The Piegan were one of those. Their ceremonies, their battles and raiding parties, even their day-to-day activities, were driven by belief that the future could be accurately forecast."

"The mystical?"

"You can call it that, although that indicates a lack of understanding, and from what we know, they understood practical application very well. Same with the best fighter pilots. They may not comprehend how long- and short-term memories interact, but they know how to use it to shoot down enemy planes. My job is to demystify the process, to find out how some people can have *memories* of future events."

Link Anderson felt a calming sensation. "Then it *is* explainable?"

"Not presently but it will be. I'd like to take a blood sample, then listen to what's been going on with these dreams of yours. Marie said there are things you can't talk about. Can we discuss *any* of it?"

Link became thoughtful. "Where would the information go from here?"

"Nowhere. You're case number 96–67, not Lincoln Anderson. If I talk anything over with colleagues, it will be in the abstract with no specific references."

He paused, thinking of his official vow of secrecy. Then Link decided that he must know more. After all, it was his amygdala.

As Manny drove them toward Judge Lindquist's home, Link explained what he'd told Doctor McNabb. He was surprised when Manny DeVera approved.

"We asked the Bureau for a background check. They didn't have to look far. They use her to help with their psychological profiles, and I guess she's damned good."

"She wants to talk again tomorrow. I think she can help me understand what's going on."

"Yeah?" Manny's look held a mixture of amazement and awe. He'd worn the expression a lot that day. "So what do you think Ghost's next move will be?"

"I have no idea," Link said, watching the rearview mirror. A Ford van replaced the coupe that had followed them, three cars behind. "There's the van back there again," he said.

"I noticed. What do the people inside look like?"

"There's two in front, but it's too far back to get a good look."

They entered the Georgetown residential area and turned onto a quiet street.

"Bring your pistol?" Manny asked, staring in the mirror.

"Yes." He'd been carrying it. "Any idea who it is?"

"No. Hang on." Manny immediately turned into an alley, followed a dogleg until they were out of sight, then pulled to the left and killed the engine. They got out.

"Probably just the jangles from all that's going on," Manny muttered.

"They were following us," Link confirmed. As they waited, his anger mounted as the outrages of the past few days became focused on the van.

"Hear the engine?" Manny asked, loosening his jacket so he could get to a belt holster.

It was a low sound. The van had stopped beyond the dogleg. Link pulled a kid's well-taped baseball bat from a trash can and followed Manny down the alley toward the vehicle.

The crackle-crunch sound of gravel under tires became distinct as the vehicle was put into motion. They waited behind an aging VW camper.

The van slowly emerged into view, side windows so dark it was impossible to see inside. As it drew closer, anger continued to swell within Link. The dreams were frustrating mental games. This was something real. He hefted the bat.

When the vehicle was abeam them, Link stepped from behind the Volkswagen and swung hard at the driver's window. The impact jarred his shoulder as safety glass was punched inward. He swung again. The window broke through, and he felt contact with something inside.

There was a painful howl as the van lurched and accelerated. Link followed, fury mounting, and swung at the rear window. It shattered, and glass was still dropping free as the van picked up speed. A surprised face gawked back at them, jaw drooped in surprise.

The van skittered onto the street and was gone.

Link dropped the bat disgustedly. "They got away."

"They'll think twice before following us again." Manny was grinning.

As Link calmed, his heart suddenly sank. He wondered if they'd been police officers.

Manny chuckled as he started for his car. "The one in back was a staffer for the NSC. What you just saw was a bad case of Washington-style interoffice rivalry. They want to know how we're getting our information. Even if they knew, they wouldn't believe."

5:35 P.M.—Peshan, Montana

Marie LeBecque had spoken with several retired policemen who had served in July of 1968 when the three children had been discovered near the Canadian border, but none had been involved. Then she'd asked every adult living near Peshan. No one could recall the incident, only that an official had come by asking questions about some runaway kids.

She was determined to speak with Bright Flame again. Yet even if she should find her, Marie doubted she could carry on a lucid conversation.

Marie rapped on the door of the shack without response. Then she sat in the Jeep with the engine running and the heater blowing, wondering how long she should wait. She had no desire to hang around the spooky town in the dark, and nightfall was rapidly approaching. Also, a heavy snowstorm was forecast, and she wanted to return to town before it began.

Five more minutes, she told herself. At 5:45 she would depart. When four of those minutes had passed, she took a final look around.

A shadow flitted across the face of the shack. Bright Flame paused near the vehicle, staring toward the burial ground.

Marie shut off the engine and dismounted. "Hello," she called out tentatively as the wind blew ice needles into her face.

There was no response from the older woman. Marie noted that she was wearing the trousers and heavy coat Link had left by her door.

She approached closer. "Bright Flame?" she asked in Algonkian. Still nothing. Bright Flame continued to stare, then began trudging forward, toward the burial ground.

"May I come?" Marie asked.

Bright Flame was silent. Marie followed, but when they reached the edge of the trees, she held back. Finally she took a resolute breath, then continued down the decline and past the first dark mounds. On then, past others, and Marie wished she'd remembered to bring a flashlight. When they approached the same burial mound as before, Bright Flame stopped and slowly knelt.

"Lay-ton," she crooned.

Henry Layton? Marie wondered, recalling the man who'd disappeared.

"Lay-ton," Bright Flame repeated, then whispered the word. She drew a breath and emitted a long, low keening sound. "La-ay-ton!" She became quiet, and there was only the sound of wind blowing through the trees.

When Bright Flame began her hardly audible chant, as she had the other time, Marie held her breath in her effort to remain unobtrusive.

"I must tell my story to help my sons, Lay-ton."

Sons? Marie was half-crouching near the older woman.

She wanted to reposition to be more comfortable, but felt her movement might break the spell.

Bright Flame shook her head, and the parka hood fell back as she continued the chant. Marie interpreted her song:

The year after she'd borne Spirit of Lame Bear, a young white man had come to visit.

"You, Lay-ton."

He was good to her, kind and gentle to the child as well, and she'd come to trust him more than any person she had ever met. He'd asked her to return to Browning with him, but she was ashamed of what the Ah-but-ochsi had done. He'd come again and yet again, and brought her blankets and a crib for the baby. Each time he'd left, she'd wanted him to stay. Once she'd asked him to remain, and he'd returned more often after that. Lay-ton took away her awful fears, and finally he'd responded to her affection and they'd slept together.

Lay-ton had become her husband. She'd told him of the shame placed on the name Bright Flame, and asked him to choose another for her. He'd offered his mother's name.

"Sar-ah Lay-ton," she repeated proudly.

Marie was numbed by the revelation.

She'd borne two children by the man named Lay-ton, and each day he was gone she'd waited eagerly for his return. He'd brought her jewelry and clothing, and asked her to come back with him, but she would not and they'd become content with the life they shared.

Then the terrible day came. He was in the small building with her when the men of the Ah-but-ochsi returned for the boy-child Spirit of Lame Bear. When they'd found Lay-ton, they'd gone into a rage and killed him with their fists, boots, and pocketknives. They'd wanted to kill the children of Lay-ton, but one said they must beware the strong spirit of Black Wolf, so they took all three, as well as Lay-ton's car and the things he'd brought for his woman.

After they were gone, she'd sung holy songs and scarred her legs and cut off the ends of five fingers to show her grief. Then she'd carefully wrapped Lay-ton in a blanket and buried him in the white man's way in the holy ground.

"I have mourned for my husband Lay-ton," she whispered, staring at the mound.

A shiver ran up Marie's spine. "What came of the children?" she asked in a quiet voice.

Bright Flame nodded at the mound, as if Henry Layton was the one she spoke with, and began to rock back and forth and chant.

Not far north, the Ah-but-ochsi men had stopped to sort their stolen goods, and the three boys had run away. Just then they were almost caught by a horseback patrol of agency police. The men took Lay-ton's vehicle and fled down a gully and crossed the Canadian border, leaving the boys behind. She'd learned that from the men when they'd returned to look for the boys.

A white woman arrived from the Indian Bureau, asking questions about the children. She'd told her their mother had been a woman named Sar-ah Lay-ton.

Bright Flame paused and nodded to herself. She'd told the woman the oldest child was Spirit of Lame Bear. When she'd explained that he'd been fathered by an Ah-but-ochsi, the woman from the agency hadn't understood, but she'd finally written something down.

"Albertson," Marie whispered to herself.

Bright Flame had told her the second son's name was Spirit of Black Wolf, that the youngest was Little Crow. When the woman had left, Bright Flame continued fasting and prepared herself. Without Lay-ton and now childless, she'd wanted to die beside her husband's mound. But shortly thereafter the agency police had come and taken her to Browning, where they'd bandaged her legs and fingers and forced her to eat.

She'd gone to the agency office and asked a man about her children, but he'd rushed her out the door and told her to go away. When she'd persevered, he'd taken her out again and hissed for her to go away or he'd kill her children. She'd tried to go to the police, but the man called her a crazy woman. Wherever she went, he'd already told people to watch out for her, because she'd threatened him. He'd told the purebloods and the people at the stores, and they'd become afraid.

She'd returned to Peshan, wondering why the man had acted that way. The police had come back for her once more, but no one in Browning had listened to her that time, either, so she'd returned to Peshan again.

She'd wondered why she still lived. There was a reason, but she'd not known it.

"Now I know, Lay-ton," she whispered, rocking and staring at the mound.

Marie's heart ached. She felt she was eavesdropping on a private conversation.

"Lay-ton, we must help your first son. He is in danger from my other first son, Spirit of Lame Bear." She looked at the grave and nodded proudly. "Your first son gave me this coat, Lay-ton, so I will be warm. We must warn him."

The impact of what she'd said swept over Marie. Link was in peril.

Bright Flame began to rock and then to croon "La-ayton" in the mournful tone.

As she drove back toward Browning, Marie could not get Bright Flame's words from her mind. She decided to go to her uncle with the story. Doctor Benjamin White Calf was a prominent member of the tribal council, and one of the most astute men in her life. It was likely he would know what her next step should be. But first—and most importantly—she had to tell Link about Bright Flame's warning.

The snowstorm pitched into full fury, and she had to concentrate intently just to stay on the highway.

16

Friday, February 3rd

6:50 A.M.—Georgetown, Washington, D.C.

They were up, eating the breakfast of toast, thick-cut Canadian bacon, and poached eggs Marian Lindquist had prepared.

"Wonderful!" Manny exclaimed. While he lavished praise upon her, Marian remained cool toward him. Yet DeVera stayed in her second bedroom and seldom visited his apartment across town. It was an odd arrangement for an avowed bachelor, Link decided.

Marian glanced Manny's way without expression, then looked apologetically at Link. "I'll make you a good meal this weekend."

Link finished his glass of freshly squeezed orange juice and smiled. "I'm suffering."

He'd tried to phone Marie the previous evening, but a storm had swept across northern Montana, cutting telephone communications in its wake. He'd gone to bed and slept for the first couple of hours before his subconscious began its nightly wake-up calls.

Come home. Prepare yourself.

Doctor McNabb had told him to pay heed to every nuance of the dreams. She'd said it was unlikely there'd be false alarms. But what did the words mean?

"Was the psychologist helpful?" Marian asked, as if reading his mind.

Link finished his breakfast. "Let me show you something."

He went to the bedroom and brought back the *Washington Scene* magazine he'd looked through two nights before. There was an article on local lifestyles, and a photo of the Attorney General. Her home was shown in the background—slightly out of focus but distinguishable.

"I looked through the magazine before I went to sleep, then had the dream. Doctor McNabb says I'm hypermnesic."

Manny was frowning so he tried to explain. "Amnesia's the lack of long-term memory. *Hyper*mnesia is the ability to store and recall a great deal of it." He tapped the photo. "Like the image of this home."

Manny gave the fuzzy photograph a dubious look.

"Doctor McNabb says a few hypermnesic people are able to associate memories with inputs—what they see, hear, touch, and smell—and become intuitive. She compares it to S-A."

Manny stared at Link. "Now *that* I understand."

"S-A?" Marian asked.

Manny filled her in. "Situational awareness is a pilot's ability to see everything that's going on in the sky in three dimensions."

"But there's another element," Link added. "A pilot with good S-A knows what his adversaries are going to do *next*. Which way they'll turn and how they'll maneuver."

"How does he do it?" Marian asked.

"It's sort of a sixth sense. He can glance at one airplane and say, 'he's going to do this,' and at another and say, 'he's going to do that.' Then he positions himself accordingly."

"Isn't that impossible?" Marian asked.

"Yeah," said Manny. "But it happens. Not even the greatest fighter pilots have it all the time, just often enough to win a hell of a lot more than the others."

"And they teach that to pilots?" Marian asked.

"They try," Manny said.

"Doctor McNabb believes it's inherent," said Link. "Not learned, but born in some people. She even ran a research project to try to discover a common gene."

"Situational awareness." Manny DeVera grinned in his new understanding.

"Intuition," said Marian.

Link nodded. "I'll meet with Doctor McNabb again this afternoon. In the meantime I need to learn everything possible about Ghost. Each new factual input will help with the insights."

"That may not be easy," said Marian. "After Leonard Griggs left my office, he issued a directive to the agencies that the NSC gets everything regarding Ghost first."

"I thought your group was primary where Ghost is concerned?"

"I should be able to get his order reversed, but it's one more hassle."

"Why would Griggs interfere like that?" Link asked, remembering the van.

"It's a wearisome subject," Marian said.

Arlington, Virginia

Two workmen in green overalls walked resolutely down the hallway of the high-rise condominium. They carried toolboxes, and patches were sewn onto the left chests of their overalls reading: *"McCleery Bros. Plumbing."*

"That one?" asked the larger, darker of the men as they approached a door. The other nodded, then looked about. There was no one else in the hall. He rapped lightly and drew back a step so he could be seen through the view port.

A man opened the door, neatly dressed in dark blue suit, white shirt, and club tie.

"We're here to check the water pressure," Ghost said politely.

The man glanced at his watch as they entered. "I'd appreciate it if you could hurry. I'm about to leave for work."

Rashad broke his knee with a hard kick. Fifteen seconds later the man lay groaning on the Persian rug in the middle of the living room, his neck gripped in Rashad's steel grasp.

"Don't hurt him so badly he can't talk," Ghost instructed.

Rashad held the man's throat so he couldn't cry out as he reached down to grasp an arm. He swiveled it about, then slammed the elbow against his knee. There was a dull cracking sound from the limb. Rashad repeated the ritual with the man's other arm . . . and he was immobilized.

Ghost pulled a chair from the kitchen and set it before

their victim. He sat and watched, then questioned. Even in his pain the man remained reluctant to speak . . . until Rashad went to work with his knife. Then he talked.

He's brave, Ghost thought idly as he posed questions and listened carefully. After a period of time he learned the flaw in their operation he'd been looking for.

He formulated a plan, then began to mimic the man's voice.

When they'd finished the colonel begged for death, and Ghost considered ordering Rashad to kill him cleanly.

But Rashad preferred to mutilate, and Ghost allowed him his enjoyment.

I-76, near the Ohio–Pennsylvania border

J.J. Davis had finally used enough bullying and compromise with the contractors to discover that the people who'd taken the high explosive were likely sent by organized crime. Probably from the New York area, he'd decided. The description of the man the contractors had dealt with matched that of a businessman who had worked for the now dismantled Gambino family.

He'd traced the truck—operated by someone fronting as Oregon Building Industries, a legitimate company out of Eugene that kept more than three hundred trucks on the road—through five states. They'd shown different destinations on bills of lading at each weigh station. Yet it was the same weight and identical load of plastic-concrete building material that he'd chased from one state to the next.

Now, at the first weigh station across the Pennsylvania line, he watched as the agent with him rifled through paperwork. "Yeah," the agent muttered.

A rig had passed through on January 27th with 5,838 pounds of building materials. Operator: Bobby C. Lewis, the same as shown at Illinois weigh stations. Bethesda, Maryland was shown as the destination, and that rang true to J.J. It was in the right area, and after all the trickiness they'd likely thought they were home free. But where in Bethesda?

Call & ask abt warehouses w/loading docks in Beth, he wrote on his pad.

Twelve minutes later they had a response from the Hoover Building. There were some 450 warehouses in Bethesda, and a few were known to be used for criminal purposes.

J.J. pondered for a moment, and decided to stay on the same two tracks he'd been pursuing. One, *determine the people involved.* Concurrently, *find the cargo.*

The Buffalo bureau office was trying to locate the businessman who had set up the deal. The operator licenses of the different drivers of the rig showed various addresses, but two, issued in Massachusetts, were valid. The Boston office was working that end. With the current frenzy for results, the regional directors and agents-in-charge would bend enough rules and drag in enough markers from local officials to get timely results.

He would also order an examination of every possible location in the Bethesda vicinity where 5,000 pounds of tritonol explosives might be stashed.

He wrote a message on the pad: *Have ten 5-man srch teams formed in DC.*

"Gotcha," said the young agent, who somehow reminded J.J. of Hiram Jones even though he was pure WASP.

As J.J. waited for him to complete the call, his stomach growled so loud a weigh station operator looked about suspiciously. J.J. had lost thirty-nine pounds and felt weak from the lack of food. There'd simply been no way to get enough down to properly fuel him.

The agent finished, then followed J.J. out to the government helicopter that had been their vehicle for the past two days.

9:45 A.M.—ITF-4 Offices, Department of Justice, Washington, D.C.

Link was in the coffee room, pouring himself a fresh cup, when Judge Marian entered wearing a woolen coat.

"Colonel Sloan spoke with me yesterday," she said. "The DIA's developed a new profile of Ghost using the telephone recordings."

"I'd like to read it," Link admitted.

"I just got off the phone with him. He confirmed that it includes new insights, and feels we should definitely see it. Get your coat."

"He's not going to bring it here?"

"ITF-4's no longer on the access list, remember? Colonel Sloan talked the analyst into bringing the profile to his condo in Arlington. We'll go there and take a look."

Link wondered about the machinations of Washington politics. "This Griggs fellow's making things difficult for you."

She hmphed. "I'd resign in a heartbeat if it weren't for the emergency."

Marian drove, and they talked. "The fire extinguisher was placed aboard the aircraft three days ago," she said. "It was activated by remote control after the helicopter was airborne."

"How did Ghost know it was going to pick up the Vice President?"

"Either it was a hell of a guess or someone's giving him sensitive information. We're opening an investigation on everyone who could possibly have known. It isn't a long list."

The city seemed calmer than during the previous two days. There were more crowds, and more of the normal bustle of activity that beat like a great heart within the Capitol city.

"We're making a difference," Link said.

"I'm concerned that Griggs might convince others to stop taking our advice."

"Even though we've been successful?"

"In Washington access to the top is power. We've been calling the right shots, and we're being listened to. Len Griggs doesn't like that, and now he's found a weapon to use against us." She shook her head. "He's spreading it around that we've been infiltrated."

"By whom?"

"By you. He's saying whoever's giving us our answers about Ghost has got to be getting inside information. I handled it poorly yesterday. I'm considering another approach—to introduce you to Leonard Griggs, level with him, and try to get the NSC aboard. Let them share in the operation. It may be our only option."

While Marian was parking in a lot beside a high-rise condominium complex, Link felt a chill of foreboding and smelled a foul odor. He had trouble concentrating on the new dilemma.

"I shouldn't bother you with all that," Marian said. "I

don't want you brooding about it. Just keep making your inputs, and I'll handle the politics."

"How long have we got here?" he asked as they emerged from the vehicle and walked toward the entrance.

"Half an hour. I've got work at the office, and the analyst has to get the profile back."

They took the elevator to the twelfth floor, Link's mind still troubled by ITF-4's difficulties. As they walked down the plushly carpeted hallway, he again sensed that something was amiss. The odor became sharper.

He slowed and looked carefully about.

"Is something wrong?" Marian asked.

"I'm not sure." Link was frowning.

She stopped before a door and knocked.

The odor became overpowering, the feeling more distinct. "Marian, I don't think . . ."

The door swung open, and a man stood before them, a pistol gripped in his hand. "Inside," he said in a smooth voice.

"Ghost!" Link whispered. He weighed their odds of escape, of bolting back down the hall, but Ghost held the automatic pistol steadily, aimed directly at Marian's chest.

Link followed her into the room on wooden legs.

She gave a gasp, looking at something in a corner, but Link's eyes were fixed on the man behind the gun. It was the face he'd seen in the hotel—different from the drawings he'd been shown. The sense of familiarity returned, mixed with the dread and odor he'd sensed as they'd approached the room.

A darker man shut the door and stood behind Marian as the muzzle of Ghost's pistol shifted to cover Link. *Rashad Taylor,* Link's mind registered. He was as tall as Link, with the massive legs, arms, and barrel chest of a weight lifter.

Ghost stared into his face without betraying the slightest emotion. He was shorter than Link—compact and sturdy, with features that could be easily overlooked and forgotten. He reached into Link's coat and pulled out the Beretta.

The stench in Link's nostrils was heavy.

"Take care of her," Ghost said, his pistol now aimed squarely at Link.

Marian moved quickly, shifting away as she reached into her handbag. Rashad moved—a hardened hand, knuckles rigidly extended, hammered into the side of her head with a meaty thump—and a small handgun flew across the room. Marian staggered drunkenly, eyes unfocused and unseeing. Rashad followed, a tiger closing for the kill.

"No!" Link shouted.

"Stay still, brother," Ghost said in the smooth voice. Beyond him, Link saw the bloody, dismembered mass that had been Colonel Pershing Sloan.

Rashad formed a wide grin as he stalked Marian, shifting as she reeled, hands rigidly before himself in a karate stance.

He could not allow it! Link ignored the unwavering gun barrel and had started forward when Rashad kicked out in a smooth, fluid movement. His heavy boot caught Marian squarely on her knee, snapping it inward and eliciting a dull cracking sound.

She screamed shrilly. Before she could crumple, the dark man lashed out and up with his rigid hand, twisting the rock-hard knuckles in midair as they struck the base of her nose.

Link had learned the killing blows in military survival training. The one Rashad delivered was intended to drive the cartilage into the brain in a single stroke. Crimson spattered across Marian's face as her head snapped back . . . and she dropped like a stone.

Link cried out in horror and rage as he continued forward.

"Watch him!" Ghost said.

Link drove his shoulder hard into Rashad's side, carrying him past Marian's body. The man yelled in surprise as they fell together against a glass and wrought-iron table, shattering it. Link reached for his face, grasped, pulled, and ripped—intent on destroying him.

Rashad shrieked and twisted, freed himself, backpedaled and crouched, gasping and drooling blood. "Bastard," he cried out, but the words were muffled by a flap of flesh hanging at the corner of his mouth.

It was Link's turn to stalk, moving relentlessly forward.

"Bastard!" Rashad shrieked louder as the pain worsened, the aperture of his mouth extended by an inch, white teeth exposed through the dangling flap. He trembled violently as his hand dropped to his calf and pulled free a heavy knife with an eight-inch blade.

Link crouched, circled until he stood between Rashad and Marian's body, eyes intent on the knife. *Concentrate on the immediate threat,* the combat arts instructor had told them.

"I'm going to cut out your fucking heart," Rashad hissed. Blood ran freely from his torn mouth onto his bull's chest.

"That's enough," Ghost said sharply, moving up beside Rashad, his eyes on Link. The muzzle of the pistol was now lowered, held at his side.

"I'll *kill* him." Rashad was trembling with rage.

"No."

There was a pause of silence. Ghost's mouth was firm, his eyes so intently focused that Link felt they penetrated his mind. There was an almost hypnotic communication that Link could not comprehend. Alien fear suddenly invaded him. The smell/taste of bitter alum remained strong as he endured the emanation of the man's inner power.

Link had to force his words, "Leave her . . . alone."

Ghost's hard expression altered, softened. He nudged Rashad and spoke quietly. "Get a towel and cover your face, and go down to the car."

"I want him." Rashad's words emerged in a hiss.

Ghost turned only slightly, yet Rashad took an immediate, fearful step back. He returned his knife to its leg sheath, eyeing Link with feral hatred.

Link knelt over Judge Marian, scarcely hearing the men as they prepared to leave. Rashad's fierce blow had not struck squarely, but it had done terrible damage. Although he'd seen it, Link had not imagined the brute strength of the man. The central area of her face was sunken, the front of her skull collapsed. Her breathing was uneven, her pulse weak and unsteady. She was bleeding profusely from ears, nose, and mouth, and threatened to drown in her gore.

Ghost called from the door in his smooth voice. "You're responsible for what happened here, brother. You'll receive no more messages. There's nothing more you can do."

"I'll . . . find you," Link said with difficulty, but his voice was unsure.

"No, brother. When I've finished with my task, I'll find you."

The door closed.

Link turned Marian on her side, opened her mouth, and removed blood and matter, ensuring the passageway was clear. He tried the phone—the line was dead. He hurried out and down the hallway, pounding on each door in turn.

He had to get medical help quickly or Judge Lindquist would die.

Fort Myer, Virginia, Hospital

From the moment he'd entered the waiting room, Manny had been a basket case. Cyrus White was there, as were Slocum and Lloyds, and all wore bleak expressions, but none were as stone-faced or pale as DeVera as they awaited word from the surgeons.

Link's thoughts were of self-recrimination. If he'd acted upon his feeling that something was wrong; if he'd attacked Rashad sooner; if he'd done any of a dozen things—Judge Lindquist might be unharmed. He did not dwell on the interchange with Ghost. Something inside kept him from any slightest thought of the man.

For the first time in his memory, Link had felt fear of another man. Not simple anxiety, but overpowering and numbing trepidation. He did not want to think about it lest it return.

The doctor emerged. He'd perform an emergency tracheotomy, then hurried Marian into the emergency operating room. He was young, but possessed an efficient air.

"She's past the first hurdle," he said wearily. "Our initial prognosis is that she'll survive." The first blow, on the temporal area of her head, had resulted in a fracture and severe concussion. The second blow had been so violent that the doctor was surprised her neck hadn't been broken. He described the facial bones that had been crushed into sinus cavities.

"We've reconstructed her malar and nasal regions," the surgeon said. "Another team is about to begin on her knee. That's serious, but not life threatening."

"Will she walk again?" asked Slocum.

"Yes, assuming she'll be able to make motor-control decisions. The brain is badly swollen. We tried to relieve the pressure, but we know there's damage. There's a possibility she won't regain consciousness. If she does, she may have limited control of her functions and faculties. Those things are difficult to forecast."

As the surgeon left, White and Slocum's faces were crinkled in concern. Manny appeared numbed, as if he could not accept what was happening.

Link approached him. "I'm going to Marian's and pack my things. I'll leave my key on the kitchen table. You can reach me at the Americana."

"That's not necessary." DeVera said softly, his mind elsewhere.

Slocum spoke up. "I'll contact the Secret Service. Marian wanted you protected."

Link shook his head. "There's no need." Ghost had shown that Link was to be spared, had even stopped Rashad from attacking him.

"I'll drive you to the office," said Cyrus White. "We'll need a debriefing. Also, everything you can give us about Ghost and Rashad's appearance and mannerisms."

"The police want a statement."

"We'll take care of that."

He rode with White to the ITF-4 office and made the report, then took a cab to Marian's home. After packing his bags, Link went directly to the hotel. He did it all by rote, feeling intensely ashamed, knowing he was to blame for Judge Lindquist's terrible injury.

Ghost had said Link was responsible. Ghost did not lie.

In the hotel room he placed his bags in the closet, then went to the bed and sat.

Ghost had said there'd be no more messages. Had he meant the Grandfather dreams? How could he have knowledge of them? Had he penetrated ITF-4's security? Link wondered if the answer wasn't simpler, if Ghost hadn't indeed peered into his mind.

Link dialed the number for the American Human Research Laboratory. He'd had an appointment with Doctor McNabb for three o'clock. He told the receptionist he'd be late.

The appointment was now even more important. The dreams were his only weapon, more effective than the pistol Ghost had so easily removed from his shoulder holster.

He brooded about Ghost and Rashad, and how he'd been left unharmed. Ghost had told him why. He'd called him brother . . . and Ghost did not lie.

4:05 P.M.—Bethesda, Maryland

Doctor McNabb switched on the notebook computer and punched buttons. "I've been thinking of what you told me, Link. Your memory association is incredibly developed."

"The Grandfather?"

"I'd say he's just as you thought: an early association with a photograph or illustration. Same with the sweat lodge setting. A child's mind would be interested in such things."

"What about the rest? The dreams and images."

"As I told you, perception's a matter of associating inputs with long-term memories, but with you I have problems. The possible inputs seem too vague to reach definitive conclusions."

"Like the Piccadilly bombing?"

"That's the most difficult one. Could you have adapted the dream *after* the fact?"

"I've gone over it too many times. The dream came before."

"Which takes me ingloriously back to square one." She tapped keys. "Could I ask . . ."

"Doctor, I need answers, not more questions. This morning a man was killed and a woman brutalized because of what's been going on in my head. It was Ghost, the man I spoke about yesterday. I've got to stop him, and I don't know how."

"You seem to have done well so far."

"I failed this morning." He described the encounter. She listened intently.

Link shook his head. "It was as if he looked into my mind. The thought processes you spoke of, the activity between parts of the brain. Could they be transmitted over distance?"

"We've discovered transmitter and receptor neurons in lab rats that pass information without direct contact, but it was over small distances . . . perhaps as much as a millimeter."

"Can thoughts be transmitted between two individuals? Perhaps two . . . relatives?"

"There've been documented cases, but they're regarded as coincidental and none have been proven. We've run numerous tests on closely related perceptive humans, twins for instance, and found no incidents of shared knowledge when the subjects were isolated."

"Then whatever is happening is within our individual minds? Mine and Ghost's?"

"Anything more would be telepathy."

He remembered Ghost's eyes, the feeling he was delving into his mind. The times when he'd felt Ghost's presence. "Something like that's happening, Doctor. I have to learn to use it."

"What you're asking is beyond the scope of my research. I work in an orderly world, Link, exploring heightened perception and trying to learn how and why it happens. I can't tell you how to control it. Someday perhaps, but certainly not yet."

"Dead end," he said bitterly.

"There's still much to be learned about the brain. There are areas—within the association cortices for example—that are extremely active, yet we don't know their purpose."

"There's something I didn't mention yesterday. I'm not sure I even realized it. This morning I smelled a sharp odor and had an uneasy sensation that someone was watching me. I'd felt it before when I was near Ghost . . . and yesterday when I was driving here."

"Today, too?"

"No." Since the encounter he'd felt only anguish.

"What do you sense during the Grandfather dreams?"

"A feeling of well-being. When I see or hear the images I sometimes feel emotion, but there's no odors or feeling that someone's watching me."

"Different parts of the brain deal with different senses, Link. Sight, touch, hearing, and so forth. Smell is a special case and is processed entirely differently."

"Yesterday you said I should place faith in everything I receive in the dreams."

"They'd proven to be valid, yet you seemed doubtful. I didn't want you thinking you were abnormal in any inferior sense. Your level of hypermnesia is extraordinary."

"What if I'm encouraged to do something absurd? Go through a primitive rite I can't accept as having credence?"

"Such as?"

"An old Piegan ritual."

"You're asking another question beyond my professional knowledge."

"I'd like to hear your opinion."

She paused thoughtfully. "In many ways the early Piegans were as primitive as you say. They had little or no appreciation for pottery, basketry, boatbuilding, or many of the crafts perfected by other American Indians. Yet spiritually they were highly developed, with a strong sense of community and family bonding. And as we discussed, they believed in being able to foresee the future in dreams."

"So?"

"I can tell you the scientific bases of what happens in the human brain. Someday I may even come up with the *how* of what's happening, but I have no slightest inkling of application. If you want to learn to control what's going on in your mind, the old Piegan rituals might be the best place to start. They were experts at the game."

17

Saturday, February 4th

4:15 A.M.—Americana Hotel, Washington, D.C.

Lincoln Anderson came awake slowly. He'd dropped off to sleep hoping to dream—wanting new answers, praying he could still learn Ghost's atrocities before they were unleashed. But there was no dream, and even in his groggy twilight he had the uneasy feeling that something was very different.

He sat up in bed for a while, wondering what was happening in his overtaxed and troubled mind. Finally he lay back and evened his breath, and tried again.

The young boy is afraid in the dark, steam-filled enclosure. About him are sounds of men locked in struggle . . . grunting and hissing angrily.

An alien face rises into view, hardly visible in the gloom, lips drawn into a snarl, then disappears. An upraised hand grips a hand ax, another hand grasps and restrains it. Both are old, gnarled from age, clutching so fiercely to the ax that the tendons are prominent.

Then silence.

"Grandfather?"

There is no response.

"Grandfather?"

A new voice, smooth and confident: "There is nothing you can do."

Link came awake groaning, breathing in harsh pants, his movement restricted. The sheet had become so twisted about him that it took effort to extricate himself.

Something had happened to the Grandfather!

There is no Grandfather. Doctor McNabb agreed . . . the Grandfather was a vehicle created and used by his mind.

Link sat up, trying to calm emotions that welled inside him. Sorrow. Trepidation.

Doctor McNabb had explained them. The parts of the brain that associated memories also generated intense feelings. He had to ignore the emotions and sleep—delve into his subconscious for a message—then awaken and piece it together, as he'd done before.

He lay back, trying to will the Grandfather to return. It was another half hour before he slipped from consciousness.

". . . No more messages. There's nothing you can do."

Link reawakened, yelling hoarsely. Someone was holding him down . . . reaching, clawing at his eyes. Pain! He thrashed, wanting to fight it away. Someone was . . .

He became aware, but could not believe . . .

He held trembling fingers up before his eyes in the dim light. They were alien, as if they belonged to someone else. There'd been a single vision. Ghost's face. The confident voice had repeated yesterday's words. *"You'll receive no more messages. There's nothing you can do."*

Link rose on shaky legs and pulled back the curtains, then sat and looked out at the lights of Washington, huddled and shivered as beads of blood trickled down his face.

A shock of fear coursed through himself. There was a single, distant crack of thunder.

Link started, then wondered where the explosion had been set off—whose life had been taken. The Grandfather had not warned him. He could not, for he was gone. Ghost had won.

He went to his trousers and pulled out his wallet, then a card, and dialed the number he'd written on back. He hoped the telephone lines had been restored.

Marie answered on the fifth ring.

"I needed to talk with someone," he said.

Her voice was thick with sleep. "Are you okay?" she asked.

He nodded as if she could see him. "I'll be coming back today."

Her voice changed to happiness. "Give me an arrival time, and I'll meet you."

"My truck's at the airport. I want to make the drive alone, Marie. Maybe look out at the mountains and regain some sanity. I'll call if it's not too late when I get there."

"I don't care what time you get in, call."

Her tone was upbeat, which made him feel better. "I will."

"I talked to Bright Flame, then I went to my uncle, and together we've discovered all sorts of things. I tried to get hold of you yesterday, Link."

"I've been busy."

"I'm going to attend a meeting of the tribal council this morning. How much of your story can I tell them?"

"Anything you want. All of it. It doesn't matter anymore."

"Remember when Bright Flame told us she was raped, that her son was named Spirit of Lame Bear? I didn't think of something, Link. The words spirit and ghost are interchangeable."

"Ghost?" he muttered.

"Bright Flame also had two other children, by Henry Layton. I'll explain tonight."

"Their names?" His voice was hoarse.

She hesitated. "One was recorded as Black Albertson."

Ghost had called him brother. Ghost did not lie.

"Bright Flame's second child by Henry Layton was named . . ."

"Little Crow," Link half whispered.

Marie paused. "Yes. How did you know?"

"That's Charlie's real name." Fragments of the puzzle were coming together.

"Perhaps you should go to the authorities and tell them," Marie said.

Link remembered what Marian had told him about Washington politics. "I don't think so. Not yet anyway." He recalled something else. "Marie, what's the Blackfeet symbol for spirit?"

"Almost the same as for smoke. Two parallel vertical waves."

The signature Ghost left on his bombs. Another puzzle piece in place.

"Are you still interested in the Okan? Possibly attending a special ceremony."

"I don't know," he admitted. "My mind's pretty screwed up just now."

She spoke in a rush of words. "God, but I miss you, Lincoln Anderson."

He perked up again. Her voice affected him like that. "We'll talk tonight."

As Link replaced the receiver, a needle of pain reminded him of the damage to his face. He went to the bathroom and cleansed away blood and coils of skin. He returned to the chair and sat before the window, looking out at the awakening city.

Again he wondered whose life had been taken. He did not turn on the television to find out. It would serve no purpose. He was powerless to help.

Three hours later he was still there, still awake.

He called the ITF-4 number and was connected with Manny.

"You're at the hotel?" DeVera asked. His voice was alert. He'd returned to life.

"Yes. What happened this morning?"

"The director of the FBI and his family were killed. Their house was gutted by the explosion. We've been meeting for the past couple of hours."

"Do you need me?"

"I went over the sketches and the report, and they look complete enough. Just give me a phone call the second you have your next premonition, okay?"

"Tear up my contract, Manny. There won't be any more revelations."

Manny paused. "You're sure?"

"Yeah. The latest report from my subconscious was that it's shutting down. I'm going back." His voice was heavy.

DeVera sighed. "Damn!"

"I'll phone if there's a change. How's Judge Marian?"

"Still unconscious. They're going to wait for a couple of days and operate again."

Link took a breath. "I'm sorry about what happened."

"You did everything you could."

* * *

Link dressed in casual Western wear, packed, then returned to the telephone. This time when he dialed, he didn't need to look up the number.

"Hello," Lucky Anderson's deep voice responded

"Hi, Dad."

"Link?" There was happiness in the tone. "Are you okay, son?"

"I need your help."

Washington National Airport, Arlington, Virginia

Lucky Anderson was in the left pilot's seat of the Learjet 60, going through the cockpit preflight. He'd started the charter flight service when he'd retired from the air force and periodically took the controls of the various birds to maintain his proficiency as a pilot. This flight was unplanned. After Link had phoned, he'd called and insisted that the Learjet be diverted from a contract.

He watched a taxi pull up at the company office. Link emerged. As he pulled his bags out, Billy Bowes, chief pilot for the flight service, came out of the office and joined him. They approached the airplane, talking together.

Lucky examined his son as he walked, his sure and smooth stride like the athlete he was. Link hadn't gone through an awkward period as his friends had in their early teens. He'd never been silly or foolish as they'd been. Lucky hadn't thought of it much when it was happening. Now he wondered if Link hadn't missed out on something by being so serious about life.

When the two were aboard, Lucky yelled for them to secure the hatch and come forward.

Link entered the cockpit and gave him a quizzical look.

"You'll be copilot." His son looked bad, with heavy rings under bloodshot eyes and deep scratches on his face. Lucky took it in without comment. He motioned. "Get strapped in."

Billy Bowes took the jump seat. "We'll see if this pup of yours can still fly."

Link examined the four flat-glass displays, two in front of each flight position. "Looks like a fighter cockpit," he said.

"Flies like a fighter, too," said Bowes over intercom.

"Great stability. Good avionics, lots of power, and no unwelcome surprises," he said. He pointed out the center-console radios and nav gear, the flight instruments and the various ways to display them, and the control features.

"Time to start engines," Bowes said, and he walked Link through the steps.

Twenty minutes later, Link taxied out of the parking area. He'd slipped back into the pattern easily, making the correct calls to ground control and the tower, as if he flew every day and hadn't had a five-year sabbatical.

When they finally took the active for takeoff, Link looked over at Lucky.

He shook his head. "You've got it, son."

Billy Bowes explained the critical takeoff speeds, then sat back to watch.

Link ran up the two Pratt and Whitney engines, disengaged nosewheel steering, and released brakes. During the takeoff, Lucky kept his eyes moving about the sky before them, but he periodically glanced over at his son's guarded expression.

The tenseness left Link as soon as they were airborne. It came as no surprise. Flight was therapy for a pilot.

"Pull in a couple more degrees of angle of attack," Billy Bowes said over intercom.

As they passed through ten thousand feet, Bowes unstrapped. "I'm going back and settle in one of the VIP seats. I'll be off intercom, so if you want me make an announcement over the speaker." He pulled off the headset and left them.

"Nice guy," said Link.

"Billy's a good chief pilot. We had to bribe him away from another company." He looked across the cockpit. "He went back so we could talk, Link. He knows you didn't like him when you were young and probably wouldn't say anything with him around."

"As a kid I was hung up on the Indian thing," Link said. "When I learned he was a full-blood Cherokee, something inside just couldn't handle it."

"You weren't like that around Sam Hall."

"General Hall's black. My prejudice was only toward Indians."

"Billy's proud. Since there was no way for him to fight

back, after a couple of tries he stopped coming to our house."

"I'm over it. I just had to learn the hard way."

Lucky radioed Pittsburgh Center and told them they were climbing through twenty thousand, on their way to thirty-five.

After a moment of silence Link wagged his head wonderingly. "Nice aircraft."

"Should be. It's less than a year old, and cost the company an arm and a leg."

They talked about the bird and the weather until they passed over the Pittsburgh VORTAC. Then Link neutralized the trim and set the autopilot, and they settled back.

"You wanted to talk?" Lucky asked.

The words came easily from his son, like water spilling over a filled dam. Lucky learned about the Grandfather. The apparition had appeared after Link had come with them to Virginia, had left when he was no longer needed, then returned to help with the lost skiers.

Billy Bowes came forward, bringing freshly brewed coffee. Before he could leave, Link motioned for his attention. "I'd like you to hear this, sir."

Billy settled into the jump seat. When he came on intercom, Lucky filled him in on what his son had told him.

Link continued, telling them about Ghost, Rashad, and Charlie. Then about going to the reservation and meeting Marie LeBecque.

Lucky picked up on the change in his son's voice and asked about her.

"Marie's special" was all he would say, but Lucky sensed there was more to his feeling.

Link told them how the Grandfather's revelations had helped to outfox Ghost.

Lucky took it in quietly, as he'd once done with pilots in his squadron when they'd come down from tough combat missions. Link was as troubled as any of those had been. Lucky didn't know how much of it was real—Link certainly did not—but his son was one of the most truthful humans he'd ever known, brutally frank at times, and was telling it as he knew it. By the time Link arrived at the attack in Colonel Pershing Sloan's apartment, they were past Kansas City.

"Manny told us Marian was severely hurt," Lucky said. "He didn't say how it happened."

"I should have done more to protect her," Link said.

"Bullshit," said Billy Bowes, speaking up for the first time.

"I saw a psychologist," Link said, and explained what she'd told him.

"Interesting," said Lucky when he heard the parallel with situational awareness. He regarded Billy Bowes, who had the best S-A of any combat pilot he'd flown with. The Cherokee was still looking out. "What do you think, Billy?"

"Makes sense. What's your next move?" he asked Link.

"Try to prepare myself, like my subconscious was telling me to do. How much do you know about the Okan, Colonel Bowes?"

"Probably about as much as you. It's the biggest ritual of Plains Indians. We Cherokee have our own ceremonies. There's not much left of the old ways, and most of them have been altered as the needs and ways of our people changed. It's likely the same with Blackfeet."

"Think it's worth trying?"

"If I was going through what you are, I'd try about anything. And if a voice was inside telling me something, I'd sure as hell listen."

"You've never experienced anything like this?" Lucky asked.

"No. My Grandma Bowes was gifted, and there were times she could foretell events."

"Gifted?" Link asked.

"That's what people in our part of Oklahoma called it. I had good S-A, but I was never gifted like my grandmother. She could tell the sex of the babies women would bear, if the crop was going to make it, things like that."

"Then if you were me, you'd go through the ritual?"

Billy nodded. "This Ghost needs to be stopped." He pointed out a distant airliner high at their two-o'clock. "You two go ahead and talk. I'm going back and finish my siesta."

When Billy Bowes had left them, Lucky looked over. "Do you want me there?"

"It's going to be embarrassing enough without you watching."

Lucky chuckled. Link formed a slight grin.

From Denver on, they talked more freely than they'd done in years.

"How are you doing with the Desert Storm problem?" he finally asked.

Link looked surprised. "I guess I haven't had time to think about it. Like you told me, there's too much going on to worry about things I can't do anything about. If I could change what happened, I would, but I can't."

"Same with what happened to Marian, Link. You did your best, and it's done with."

As they began the letdown to begin a long, straight-in approach to the Kalispel airport, Lucky realized that the situation regarding Ghost and his terrorism was more dangerous than he'd imagined. It was time to call on a few friends.

8:15 P.M.—Browning, Montana

He had needed her, and she him, and neither had hesitated. After a single kiss at the door, they'd unclothed with no heed of modesty, no vacillation or making sure it was what should be.

Marie lay against him, nestling and not wanting to move away lest he'd leave her again. His strong hands moved lightly over her back, making her skin tingle where they traced.

They fit well, as they had when he'd first pressed into her body. Not gently but with need, probing tentatively, then thrusting and making her cry out with the passion that had grown inside her like a hot fire since she'd first seen him.

She'd given . . . and taken greedily. Encouraged him to push himself to his limit, to set a fast rhythm, then to slow so she could join in. She'd felt him stiffen and shudder . . . when he'd lifted his head in wonder, they'd cried out together.

There was no shame in her. She caressed his penis. He was ready once more.

"Again," she whispered. "Now."

As he rolled over her, she guided with sure fingers. He was gentler, more considerate, and they moved together, this time more necessary than the first, sealing the unspoken bond. When he began to release, she was in the midst of a shuddering emotional high.

"Link!" she whispered urgently as he continued moving—filling her with warmth that spread deliciously into every part of her.

As ecstasy dwindled, they remained coupled. They'd never been strangers, but now, regardless of where they went with their lives, they could never be less than once-lovers who had known the ultimate unselfishness; the intimacy of sharing, of allowing the other to delve into their bodies and minds.

He eased onto his side, still holding her, moving his hands over her as if she were the first woman he'd known. She wished it was true, that they'd only had one another and no one else.

He traced the scar that ran from her cheek to her chest, and Marie felt no sense of embarrassment. "Does it still hurt you?" he asked.

"I just can't let it get too much sun," she said.

His hand lingered on her breast. "You're exquisite."

"How was the drive?"

"Calming. A world of white. The mountains have never been more beautiful."

"We've had a lot of snow. Now you've brought blue sky."

"Things are bad in Washington."

Marie kissed his arm and breathed in his odors. "Tell me about it."

She was quiet for the next half hour, astounded that he'd been so involved in the events she'd heard on the news, frightened when he described the confrontation.

He finished. "Ghost won," he said.

"Was Grace McNabb helpful?" she asked, ignoring his judgment.

"She explained a scientific view of how she believes it happens. But it really doesn't matter what part of my brain's involved, it's how it's controlled."

"Knowledge is still useful, Link. If you were an ignorant person, it might be of no consequence. If that was the case, I'd never have suggested you see her."

"Did she call today?"

Marie nodded. "She said you're one of the most gifted persons she's worked with."

"Gifted is what a friend of my father's calls it. I believe it's a curse. Or it *was*."

"Nothing's changed," Marie said, studying his stern expression. "I've confirmed something."

"What's that?"

"You matter to me. I love you."

Link held her tighter.

"Know something else?"

"What?"

"If you keep blaming yourself for everything, you're going to drown in self-pity."

He frowned.

She stroked his face. "I said I love you. That means I can fuss at you."

"You think I'm feeling *sorry* for myself?"

"Ghost has you believing you're to blame. He's the one with the disorder, not you. Grace McNabb was concerned that you don't understand that. You are very rational and very gifted."

"Ghost was very intense and very convincing," Link countered. He shook his head. "He's too clever to be insane."

"Did Grace tell you about a portion of the brain called the prefrontal cortex?" she asked.

"Not as I remember."

"That's the gray stuff that allows you to judge your actions in an ethical sense. Ghost may be a genius, but he's lacking there. On the other hand, *your* sense of ethics works overtime."

"He called me brother."

"He's your half brother." She told him what Crazy Woman had related, that he and Charlie were the children of the murdered Henry Layton. "I don't know what happened, but Ghost and Charlie obviously turned bad at some point. Ghost probably didn't need much prodding. Like I said, he has an obvious mental disorder that Grace McNabb says was likely inherited. Probably from the old Ah-butochsi rapist."

"Descended from Lame Bear."

Marie nodded. "A woman from the agency tried to find out about the children, but she didn't understand Bright Flame's story. She was likely frightened of her, because she'd bloodied her legs, cut off ends of her fingers, all the traditional mourning practices. When Bright Flame mentioned Ah-but-ochsi, the woman misunderstood and listed Albertson as the last name for all three children. When she heard you were Spirit of Black Wolf, all she wrote was Black."

"Spirit of Black Wolf?"

"That's the name Bright Flame gave you. I believe she did it to balance the influence of Lame Bear, and that's precisely what's happening."

"It's damned confusing."

"When Bright Flame said the children's mother was Sarah Layton, the woman didn't realize that was the name she'd used as Henry Layton's wife. The woman just wrote it down as the mother's name."

"Ghost called me brother. He knew."

"The two of you are utterly different. Deaths of others means nothing to Ghost. He's mentally imbalanced. You are ethical to the point that you blame yourself for *too* much. See what I meant about knowledge being helpful, Link?"

"You think Ghost has me spooked."

"You're every bit as mentally strong as he is, but he planted seeds of doubt, and your outsize sense of guilt took it from there. You blamed yourself for Judge Lindquist's being hurt because Ghost *said* it was your fault. He said you'd have no more dreams so you engineered the death of the Grandfather and blamed yourself for that as well."

"In my mind the Grandfather is truly dead."

"I believe he'll return."

"With Ghost gone berserk in Washington, there's no time to wait for him. There must be another way to regain the insights."

"Are you still interested in the Okan?"

"July's five months away."

"I've got so much more to tell you," Marie said, trying to organize it all in her mind. "Yesterday and today were incredibly busy."

"Start from the beginning."

"Okay. I got up in the morning feeling wonderful because I'm in love." She pecked a kiss at his face, rolled out of bed, and began putting on her clothes.

"The party's over," Link said ruefully, pulling on shorts.

"No way." She slipped on her sweater. "But I'll keep

getting distracted if we lay around naked like that. Once we've had our chat, I'll rip your clothes off and we can start again." She admired his chest. "You'd better put on some more or I'll stay tongue-tied."

She pulled out a chair and sat.

"Yesterday," she started. "First I visited the administrative office with my uncle. He was growling orders, and clerks were scurrying. The only Albertson shown was your birth certificate. Nothing on file about the three lost children until they found a reference on a microfiche record from 1968. It was a single line on the daily log, showing C, B, and G Albertson, ages three, four, and six. But it also showed the initials of the clerk who'd made the entry, and we found her working at the community college library.

"When I tried to question her, I drew a blank. Then my uncle took over, and she recalled that sisters from a Catholic orphanage in Helena came to get the children, but they were only able to take one. I believe it was you. The other two had whooping cough. After a couple of weeks, a male clerk at the administrative office drove the other two children and their records to Helena. The following year the same clerk disappeared with ten thousand dollars of tribal council funds."

"Wonderful," Link muttered.

"This morning I attended a closed-door session of the tribal council called by my uncle, and told them everything I knew. About Bright Flame and what happened with the Ah-but-ochsi, about Henry Layton being murdered, and how the kids were found and sent to the orphanage. Then I told them about you and what you've been going through."

"Did you tell them about Ghost and Charlie, and the terrorism?"

She nodded. "Everything."

"And their reaction?"

"Outrage at what Ghost and Charlie had done. Disbelief that they could be Piegan. Then Jack Douglas stood and said he'd support you wholeheartedly. He called you a hero and said it doesn't matter whether Ghost's Piegan, just that you are and you might have a chance of stopping them. One man felt we should send men out to help you stop Ghost. Jack Douglas and a number of others offered to go."

Link was smiling, and this time she knew it wasn't mockery.

"I told them that you'd had the spiritual power to stop Ghost, but now you need the Okan to show you how to use it better. There was absolutely no argument. Although the Sun Dance is held in the summer, they agreed to a ritual now, and to use the old ways."

Link sighed. "I guess it's up to me to decide now."

"The council declared an emergency," Marie said. "The Piegan only do that in wartime. A group left for Peshan this afternoon to begin preparations. You don't have any choice in the matter. They've *ordered* that you go through it. They'll expect us there by eight in the morning. I told them we'd be coming together."

"And I don't have a choice?"

"Nope. You're about to become a Piegan warrior, my love." She grinned. "Now, why don't we go to the lounge for a drink. Just one, then we'll come back and I'll rip those damn clothes off you and you can distract me all you want."

18

Sunday, February 5th

6:20 A.M.—Washington, D.C.

Rashad used a pattern he'd perfected in Europe. He began by breaking a knee with a powerful kick to immobilize, and concurrently crushed the larynx to evoke silence. Then he'd methodically break, batter, and carve his prey. It was ultimately painful. The final knife strokes were necessary only to present a picture of horror to those who discovered the bodies.

Ghost listened but did not really hear the thrashing or muffled screams of the second victim of the night. The first had been a federal prosecutor named Ringold who'd been delving into the business interests of the Mafia. This one was a senior DEA official who had spent several months in France helping with investigations of the Marseilles underworld. The wives and bodyguards who had also died were incidental. These were for the Cosa Nostra, as the killing of the FBI director had been, in payment for the explosives and support.

No one had been forewarned. Ghost had told Martin Cherone to expect no more interference. Judge Lindquist was fighting for her life, and A. L. Anderson no longer posed a threat—although he'd disappeared and Martin Cherone's agency was unable to find him.

Beneath his confident facade, Ghost had not been sure. He'd been second-guessed on three occasions, half expected it to happen again, and had held his breath until yesterday's bombing had gone as planned. The FBI director's home had been well guarded, but a van laden with a massive directional bomb had reached out from three hundred yards and leveled the place. Rashad's hands-on operation was also proceeding smoothly. After a short respite—demanded by Joseph DiFazio while his people surveyed the reaction—Ghost would resume with focused shaped charges, reaching out to victims from a distance, as he was so good at doing.

As the final victim's struggles weakened and he came to realize death would be his only mercy, Ghost thought about A. L. Anderson, as he'd done often in the past two days. His image had loomed to interfere in his meditations, an occurrence that upset both Ghost and his helper. A. L. Anderson. So similar to Charlie that he'd not allowed Rashad to kill him . . . yet so different.

He wondered where Anderson had gone. He'd checked out of the Americana Hotel but hadn't returned to Judge Lindquist's home and had not been listed on airline flights. The telephone number of Boudie Springs hadn't been reactivated, but Ghost hadn't ruled out the possibility that he was there. Somewhere Anderson would use a credit card or a telephone calling card, and Martin Cherone would know. Ghost supposed it no longer mattered now that he'd destroyed Anderson's confidence, but it interested him nonetheless.

Rashad was almost done with the victim, who was gurgling, drowning in his own blood and vomit. He'd been particularly mean since A. L. Anderson had ripped the corner of his mouth and Ghost had been forced to suture the wound *sans anesthetique*. Rashad had lost control of that part of his face and was growing a stubble to hide the stitches.

The victim began his final throes. It was time. Ghost turned from the sight and smells of death and switched on the cellular telephone to call the *Washington Post.* He was impatient. There was important business to tend to today.

Boomtown, Washington, D.C.

"Mr. Donovan gave me this number," Ghost said into the telephone.

"I've expected your call, Mr. Hickey," replied a rumbling voice. "I've got the perfect property for you." The voice named an address and gave instructions on how to find it.

Ghost pulled on a coat and went out to the vehicle at the curb, ignoring the hard-eyed men who lounged about. Twenty minutes later he pulled into a mall parking lot in College Park, where he waited and looked for followers. None were apparent. He drove out the back end of the lot and proceeded down a quiet street, looking at house numbers. He found the right one, noted the FOR SALE sign on the lawn, and parked in the short driveway. A Cadillac DeVille pulled in behind him, and an incredibly tall, thin man dismounted. He was balding, with a prominent hawk's nose, rheumy eyes, weak chin, and protruding Adam's apple.

Ghost glanced at his watch. He didn't have long. The wayfinder was to call in half an hour with critical information. He climbed out of the car and nodded. "You're the realtor?"

"Kevin Gilroy at your service," said the tall man, smiling and nodding at the home. "I believe this would meet your family's needs. Shall we go inside and look around?"

Ghost was pleased. The IRA contact did not let down his guard prematurely.

Gilroy found a realtor's lockbox on the garage door, patiently dialed until it snapped open, then brandished a key. He unlocked the front door and ushered Ghost inside.

The house was stark and barren of furniture.

"How's my old friend Mike Donovan these days?" Gilroy asked conversationally.

"Jock, you mean?"

Kevin Gilroy eyed him. His smile faded. "Yeah. Jock."

"He was fine when I left him in Dublin."

"I heard from him a couple of days back. He wasn't happy with what you left in the guest house bathroom. Said he opened a garbage sack and puked all over what he saw."

"He let the girl see our faces after I'd told him not to." Ghost's voice turned to business. "Donovan said you'd be willing to share information about Charlie."

Gilroy examined him with the watery eyes. "He's still in Chicago. Lots of questioning, but he's not talking. They're moving him to Joliet tomorrow."

Ghost felt a flash of anger. Martin Cherone hadn't told

him. But then he wondered if Cherone had the access this man did. The tentacles of the Mafia were shrinking. The IRA had contacts in Chicago right up to the mayor's office.

"We've got Joliet covered, too," Kevin Gilroy said, as if he'd read Ghost's mind.

"Is the brigadier still interested in another Piccadilly?"

"Probably. He's impressed with what you've done here."

"What kind of information do you have access to . . . locally?"

"Government?"

"Yes." Ghost was uneasy with the present arrangement. It would be prudent to have an alternative if he had to divorce himself from DiFazio and Martin Cherone.

"Put it this way. Before you start hitting senators, congressmen, or staffers, check with me first. They may be ours. Do that again and your man Charlie may find problems."

"Do I hear a threat?" Ghost asked in the soft voice.

"You've already hurt one of our people. One's enough."

"I didn't know," Ghost said. He mused. "So you can get someone in to see Charlie. How about passing messages?"

"It's according to your arrangement with the brigadier."

"See what he thinks of a Parliament disaster. Same fee as before, and the damage could be as extensive as the *supplies* you provide."

"Jock has more Semtech, but he won't be able to get to it until the heat simmers down."

"I'm talking about a few months. When I'm done here we'll take a break, then I can do the job for your brigadier."

Kevin Gilroy mused. "I'll get back with an answer. Give me a number I can call."

"I'll do the phoning." Ghost started to leave, then turned. "How about a token of good will. Who's making problems for your people here in town? Think big."

Gilroy didn't hesitate. "Senator Smithfield."

"He's next, free gratis. I'll need information about his movements and a special rifle."

Gilroy wrote down the specifications of the firearm and ammunition.

"If the brigadier agrees, I'll want continuing information about Charlie and to be able to pass messages. I may also come to you for logistical support while I finish my project here."

"I'll have the brigadier's answer in the next couple days."

Ghost noted the time. "I've got to go." As he walked to the car, he felt it was nice to have a fall-back position. The brigadier would jump at his offer.

As he crawled inside, the phone buzzed on cue. The wayfinder's brusque voice told him to pick up a package and gave directions to the blind drop in nearby Rockville.

He drove directly there, then back to Boomtown. Inside the safe house he examined the contents: color photographs of an ornate bas-relief statue with detailed measurements and instructions. Only an accomplished artist could construct it.

Ghost smiled. The time of retribution was approaching.

ITF-4 Offices, Department of Justice, Washington, D.C.

"Meeting's adjourned until this afternoon," said Manny DeVera. The four other directors on the senior staff rose to their feet and began to file out.

DeVera was now acting chairman of the diminished ITF-4 organization and was more determined than ever that they accomplish their objective. The discussions had begun with an overview of the night's atrocities. Two Justice Department officials, one a prosecutor, the other DEA, had been mutilated and killed along with their wives and the men assigned to protect them. There'd been no doubt who had been responsible. Ghost had made his telephone call demanding that Charlie be released, and no one killed quite as horribly as Rashad Taylor.

The meeting had turned to a discussion of the victims. If the Islamic Brotherhood of Al Fa'qa was behind the killings, as the phone calls claimed, why hadn't pro-Israeli officials been targeted. A duty officer had given the backgrounds of the victims. There was a pattern in the last few—all had been helping to dismantle elements of the Mafia, both abroad and domestically.

J.J. Davis had learned that organized crime had been involved in the theft of the tritonol, and wondered if the key to finding Ghost might not be in tracing the linkage.

The final discussion was of who could have provided

Ghost with the information about the Vice President's flight. They were approaching a dead end, for only highly placed officials and the VIP squadron at Andrews had been aware. If there was a leak, it was not obvious.

In the hallway, Manny decided to call the hospital to ask about Marian's progress. Thus far there'd been little to be jubilant about. In the outer office, he found Mimi engrossed, staring at a paper in her hand. She looked up and blushed.

"This just arrived by courier, sir. It's from the Office of the President."

"Please," Manny asked, reaching out.

"Want me to translate?" came an unpleasant voice from the opened doorway. Leonard Griggs stood there with two men, one with his left arm in a sling.

"What do you want?" Manny asked, unable to mask dislike.

"Read the letter," Leonard Griggs said, unable to subdue a smile.

Manny glanced first at the President's scrawled signature, then at the contents. By executive order, all objectives and duties of Interdepartmental Task Force Four, along with all personnel and files, were to be immediately transferred to the National Security Council.

The Farmhouse, Falls Church, Virginia

Lucky Anderson had called the mid-morning meeting, and was pleased as the room began to fill.

Senator Glenn Phillips had just arrived, saying he'd left an emergency conference on the topic of the day: the continuing terrorism in the Capitol city. Like several others in the room, Glenn had served in the air force with Lucky. His fast-track career had been interrupted by six years as a prisoner of war in North Vietnam, where he'd been brutalized and left crippled.

Sam Hall had been first to arrive. He was a highly decorated retired air force four-star, now working on behalf of young farmers and small businessmen he felt were the true victims of the Washington bureaucracy. Sam believed and promoted the idea that America was indeed the land of opportunity for those who would reach out for it, but he admitted he was prejudiced . . . against sloth, easy welfare, and anyone who stood in the way of free enterprise and ambition.

Both major political parties were wooing Sam, trying to convince him to run for office under their banner. When he saw Glenn Phillips enter the room, he rolled his eyes.

"Man, this guy's following me *everywhere*."

The senior senator from Florida shook his head at Lucky. "We're offering Sam the moon, and he still won't make a commitment."

"My daddy'd roll over in his grave if I became a Republican," Sam countered.

"I didn't know you were a Democrat, Pop." Mack Hall was the center linebacker for the Redskins. He'd inherited his father's huge stature, ebony skin, and pleasant smile, and worked hard to maintain both a wholesome image and bone-crushing reputation on the football field.

"Didn't say that, son," Sam said. "But don't go giving away any family secrets."

Billy Bowes was already seated, and Manny DeVera had called to say he was on his way. Both were once fighter pilots and old comrades-in-arms. The only outsider was Doctor Grace McNabb. When Lucky had called, she'd not hesitated to attend.

"Coffee and tea are in the kitchen," said Linda Anderson to the group. "Lucky has liquor, beer, and soft drinks at the bar."

For his guests, Lucky had gathered overstuffed chairs into a circle about the large coffee table in the great room. He leaned against the bar, a bottle of Perrier water in his hand.

"With things going to hell," he said, "I thought it was time we got together."

Glenn Phillips spoke. "There are already a lot of qualified people trying to put a stop to the terrorism." He nodded at DeVera, who was just coming in. "Manny's group, for instance."

"Not anymore," Manny muttered. "ITF-4 was just disbanded and placed under the NSC. My last official act was to place myself on leave of absence. Griggs has convinced the President everything's our fault."

Phillips exploded. "They're trying to blame you?"

"They need a scapegoat, and Griggs got what he wanted. The NSC is now in charge of the entire counterterrorist effort."

"I'm chairman of the Intelligence Committee, and they didn't even have the decency to tell me?" Glenn found the nearest telephone as Manny took his seat.

The senator spoke to Len Griggs, demanding to know what was going on. He listened for a moment, then said they were to, "by God not release anything to the press. I will hold you personally responsible, and I *promise* you will not like the consequence."

Glenn's face was crimson as he stalked to his chair. He motioned to Lucky. "Go on with what you have. I've got to cool off and think of a way to get Manny back in business."

Lucky began. "Yesterday Billy and I flew Link to Montana and heard a story that got our attention. I'm going to pass it on. It's going to take faith on everyone's part to believe some of what you hear. Manny can confirm events, and Doctor McNabb can help explain them."

Lucky detailed Link's premonitions.

"The Grandfather?" Glenn Phillips asked, with a raise of eyebrow.

"Think of him as an escape mechanism," Doctor McNabb said. "And like General Anderson said, for the present add a kernel of faith."

When Lucky nodded, Manny DeVera took over. "I've been studying Ghost and his crew for the past three years." He began to detail the terrorists' backgrounds and atrocities.

Doctor McNabb interrupted. "Do you mind if I take notes?"

"Not at all, it's Leonard Griggs who doesn't want anything released about Ghost's group."

"Ridiculous," said Sam Hall. "All America should know about them."

Manny pulled drawings from his briefcase. "These are the latest composites of Ghost and Rashad Taylor. Griggs refuses to have them circulated."

"We'll see about that," snapped Senator Phillips. As the others looked at the drawings, he regarded Lucky. "I withdraw what I said. This meeting's a damned good idea."

8:30 A.M.—Peshan, Blackfeet Reservation, Northern Montana

Lincoln Anderson stood apart as Doctor Benjamin White Calf finished his briefing to the group leaders, answered a couple of questions, then motioned for him to follow.

A growing mass of pickups, recreational vehicles, campers, and trailers were parked in ragged rows in the area between the group of old buildings and the ancient gathering place.

"Nice day for it," commented White Calf as he led him to one side of the clearing. The temperature hovered at thirty degrees, but the dryness and altitude made it seem warmer.

Link looked about. "How many people are here?"

"Twenty-seven spent the night. Forty have already arrived this morning, and there'll be more. The police are spreading the word on the reservation, and I made phone calls to Great Falls and Billings. The People are damned upset about what's happening in Washington."

As Marie and Link had approached Peshan, they'd noted the flag from half a mile away. A fifty-foot steel pole had been erected, and the stars and stripes fluttered in the constant breeze.

A truck-trailer combination arrived, the diesel engine gunning and billowing black smoke that hovered in the crisp air. On back were two Sno-Cats. Another had brought a backhoe. A grader was already at work leveling and preparing the ceremonial area.

"Looks like a military operation," Link said.

A familiar figure approached wearing a heavy coat and immaculate Stetson. "How you doing, Captain?" asked the onetime maintenance man.

"Fine, Jack," Link responded. "Good to see you."

Jack Douglas stepped up beside Doctor White Calf. "The city's going to need the grader back by afternoon."

"I don't see a problem after the site's leveled. The operator ought to make another run on his way out to the highway, though. We don't want anyone stuck in a snowdrift."

"Doc, we've already got a challenge to our ground rules."

"There's only the three. No commercialism, no alcohol,

and make it as close to the old ways as we can. Someone's arguing with that?"

"A woman over there wants to set up her booth like she does at the summer Sun Dance. I told her about the no commercialism rule, but Marie stepped in on her side. She says they bartered at Okans in the old days, so we should reconsider."

White Calf sighed. "What's she selling?"

"Ornaments and silver bells for the ladies' ceremonial dresses. Let her in?"

"Leave it up to Marie. She can decide on concessions. But absolutely no alcohol. We'll set up food and soft drinks in the meal tent, paid for out of the special fund passed at council."

"That's what Marie said. Sort of like the old feasting." Jack Douglas walked back toward the cleared area, waving for Marie's attention.

A four-wheel drive pickup churned through the snow from the trees lining the creek. Three fiftyish men in camouflage U.S. Army utilities were in back, holding a stack of saplings in place. As they approached, they regarded Link closely.

"Vietnam veterans," said Benjamin White Calf. "In the old days warriors brought in a hundred willows for the sweat house. They selected each one carefully to make sure they were strong and straight, and were alive when they were cut. Some of us wanted them to use travois drawn by horses like back then, but the council decided it wasn't necessary."

"Travois?" Link asked, fighting back a smile.

"If we're going to do this, it should be done right. The Sun Dance has become a commercialized farce. This one must be as close to the old way as possible." He pointed. "They're putting up the lodge of the holy woman. She'll open and close the ceremony."

"Sort of like the homecoming queen?" Link quipped.

"She's selected for her knowledge of the ritual, her purity, and because she made a promise when someone in her family was saved from death. She's called the vow woman. Several ladies were nominated, but we took Marie's suggestion. I spoke with her yesterday evening and she agreed." He looked at Link oddly. "She said she'd known it was coming a long time ago and promised Old Man she'd do it."

Another pickup filled with fresh-cut willows and curious Vietnam vets passed by.

The two Sno-Cats headed toward the creek, those manned by younger men carrying rifles and wearing utilities of a lighter shade. "Desert Storm veterans," said White Calf. "They wanted the honor of bringing in the medicine lodge's main pole. One of them was a tank commander. He said pilots like you saved his life, so he was given the honor of selecting the tree. He went out at dawn and scouted until he found it . . . now he's going back with these guys to get it."

"A full-size tree?" Link wondered just how big the lodge was going to be.

"The medicine lodge will be as they were in the beginning. Marie told us the shape was changed after Black Wolf's death. Before that they were built with a tall and sturdy cottonwood log in the middle, and others spoking out like a giant tepee. That's what we're building."

"They're carrying rifles."

"They symbolize a raiding party and approach the tree warily. After it's down, they'll tap the branches with their rifle muzzles to count coup, and then shoot it. That's the old way."

Shoot a tree? Link's cynicism mounted. "I just want to get it over with as quickly as possible," he said as he watched the Sno-Cats approach the distant thicket.

Doctor White Calf continued to watch the erection of the vow woman's lodge.

A couple walked by, she carrying gourd rattles with handles, he with a taut-leather drum.

"All this and music, too," Link observed.

"Damn you," the doctor said, and Link was taken aback.

White Calf's voice emerged angrily. "We're holding the ceremony in the wintertime, with three feet of snow on the ground. We're starting on the fifth day of the old ceremony, ignoring the early ritual." His words were increasingly incensed. "I was hesitant from the beginning, not only about rushing things, but about you. I'm not convinced you're worth the effort. If it was a genuine ritual with self-torture, you wouldn't last, Anderson. We're making our best effort, and you have the gall to act like it's all horse manure."

"I didn't mean to disturb your sensitivities," Link said, returning the sarcasm.

"Well, you did. We will not rush things more and make mistakes to anger Old Man. From everything that's happening back east, he's obviously unhappy enough as it is."

A thin and elderly man passed, his face streaked with white paint.

"You're the boss," Link said as he examined the strange-looking man.

Doctor White Calf pushed a fat cigar into his mouth to wet it, then pulled the thing out and eyed it. "Yes, I'm in charge here, and you're the unknown element. I'll continue to help and give advice, but only because Ghost just might be Piegan—which I doubt—and what they're doing is damned shameful. If you want the truth, I wanted to send our own men to Washington."

"What changed your mind?"

"Marie convinced us you're the best hope we've got. She told us you have the powerful spirit it will take to destroy Ghost, that you'd stopped him several times already."

"Stopping Ghost had nothing to do with *spirits*. I second-guessed him. I was able to organize my thoughts and . . ." His voice faltered. ". . . Come up with answers."

"Marie said you lost that capability and wanted it back."

Link was defensive. "If I have doubts about a pagan ritual and spirits, I can't help it."

"Spirit's just a word, Anderson. A way of explaining the perceptiveness you spoke about. But after listening to you speak lightly about what we're doing, I wonder if it's worth our effort."

"If you want to call it off, that's your option. I'm skeptical. Most men would be. But if you go ahead with it, I'll do whatever's required. Not because I *believe* in the ceremony, but because it's the only next step I knew of."

White Calf chewed the cigar. "Doubt all you want, just don't belittle what we do."

"I'll try not to, not openly, but I can't get serious about grown men in war paint, and others out taking potshots at trees."

"They're doing it to help you."

Those words gave Link pause. The doctor's cigar was becoming dark and sodden. Lucky Anderson did the same, chewed on unlit cigars when he was upset. Link's voice altered. "You really think there's a possibility this can work?"

"I'll put the question to you. Would you have the balls to go through it if you were facing self-torture? That's part of what we're trying to re-create . . . going back to a time when warriors were uncommonly brave, faced death and danger with impunity, and *some* were given insight. We don't know *why* it worked but we know it did, so we're trying to do it the same way."

"What do I have to do?"

"I'll be telling you as we go along. There'll be no self-torture, because regardless of what you think, we've become rather soft and even quite civilized." Doctor Benjamin White Calf placed the cigar back into his mouth, chewed it, then walked off toward the busy Okan site.

Link wondered how a man of science could worry about such tripe as the shape of the lodge and the condition of willows for a makeshift sauna. Then, before he became more sour, he remembered that they were intent on a common objective—to stop Ghost.

The stone-age ceremony would continue, and he'd do as White Calf said. Perhaps, with what he'd learned from Grace McNabb and whatever happened here, he could regain the perceptiveness. Like the Grandfather, the Okan was not something he could believe in, but it might be a means to an end.

The various components of the medicine lodge were neatly laid out. The cottonwood log for the center pole was more than forty feet in length, with a notch at the top. Twelve tall, still-foliated saplings were to be set about a large circumference, reaching from the ground to the notch. A number of participants were confused by the old-style medicine lodge, for detailed instructions had been lost in antiquity. Marie had brought a buffalo hide from the museum with a pictograph of a lodge, and the craftsmen used it for reference. Periodically Benjamin White Calf would enter the closed lodge of the vow woman and emerge with more precise instructions.

Though the preparations were being rushed too much for White Calf's liking, Link waited impatiently as each step was drawn out. Presently everything had been halted again, and the old man with the white face was moving in exaggerated motions about what would become the inside of the structure, dipping and bowing as he rattled a gourd and grunted low words. It was only one of several times the old man had emerged from the vow woman's lodge to stop the preparations as he did his dance.

Ridiculous, thought Link. The old man looked farcical, for he had a lazy left eye that wandered, making it seem he was looking in two directions at once.

Doctor White Calf walked to Link's side, watching the man's dance.

"What the hell's he doing?" Link said impatiently.

"The vow woman's bidding," said White Calf.

"I didn't see her enter her lodge," Link said. "She's inside now?"

"You didn't see her go in because you weren't supposed to. She knows the old ways. We've got a lot to learn from her."

Link looked at the lodge. "I'd like to meet her."

"You already have. You can't go in there now, though."

"You do."

White Calf sighed. "I'm a weather dancer, like the old man in white-face, and I'm also in charge of the Okan ceremony. We'll do our best, but she knows more about it than the rest of us. That's why we ask her advice."

Link wondered. The doctor had said he'd met her. Then it came to him. He almost said Crazy Woman, but changed his words. "Bright Flame. She's the vow woman?"

"A damned good choice. She slips into her reverie now and then, but she's determined to see it through. She says your life was saved as a child, and she made a vow to have this ceremony. She's prepared for it ever since."

"My . . . mother." It was difficult for him to accept.

"She began fasting four days ago. That's why we can go ahead as if this is the fifth day of the Okan."

"How did she know?"

White Calf pursed his lips and didn't respond.

Link motioned at the wall-eyed dancer, who had finished and was walking back toward the vow woman's lodge. "What was the old man doing?"

"It's like preliminary blessings to prepare the medicine lodge to be brought to life. That won't happen until the vow woman makes her march."

"When is that?"

"Watch and listen," White Calf said, and nodded toward the vow woman's lodge. Four women approached it carrying leather bags, and went in with the white-face man. A moment later a low chant was audible from the tepee.

"The four assistants are in with her, presenting the medicine and dressing her in the holy clothing. The white-face man is acting in the place of her dead husband. I'll join them later, when it's time for another ceremony. That will take about an hour, then we'll all come out. I'll be first, then the white-face man, then the vow woman and her assistants. You should be here and watch with the rest of the People. After we've walked completely around the lodge, the vow woman will make an ancient chant while the center pole's raised and planted in a deep hole. Then she'll sip a concoction of berries and herbs while the poles are attached, and again while the attendants enter and make offerings, and the Okan lodge will become a living thing. We'd lost much of that in our Sun Dance ceremonies."

"And the medicine lodge will be officially opened?"

"It will become alive. The lodge pole will connect the heavens with the earth."

"What's next for me?"

Doctor White Calf motioned for Link to follow. He was led into a small trailer, where Ben White Calf tossed him a dressing robe and began to pull off his clothing. Link too disrobed. When naked he pulled on the robe, as White Calf did with another.

"Let's go," said White Calf, and led him out.

Both men and women acted as if it were perfectly normal for two men in flimsy robes to be walking so casually across packed snow in subfreezing weather. Link wanted to step gingerly, or at least hurry since the snow was so cold on his bare feet. Instead he stoically followed the doctor across the expanse.

Outwardly the sweat house appeared to be a haphazardly placed bundle of leafed brush with an earthen opening at one side. Steam issued from various orifices.

When White Calf ducked, shucked off the robe, and went in, Link did the same.

"Don't step into the pit," White Calf warned.

"Yeah, I know," said Link in the semidarkness, taking his seat on the earthen ledge.

"You've been in a sweat house?" White Calf asked with surprise.

"In the dreams."

"Then you know about the holy colors?"

"Black and red."

"They symbolize day and night, good and evil, light and darkness . . . sort of a yin and yang thing. There's a cup and a bucket of water next to you. Toss some onto the rocks."

Link did so, then smiled in the gloom, remembering the comfort he'd felt in his dreams when the Grandfather had been with him in another such place.

"How does this one compare with the one in your dream?" White Calf asked.

"There's more light in this one, and I remember the other one as being larger. I may be wrong. In the dreams I was a young boy."

Link relaxed as the steam gathered, and listened as Ben White Calf explained more.

"Tonight, when the medicine lodge is alive, two lines will form: the men before me and the women before the vow woman. You'll make your request—as I understand it, to heighten your awareness and return your ability to understand messages from your subconscious."

"Something like that."

"You should also ask to be given a helper, and pledge that you'll endure the pain of self-torture. That won't happen, but try to place yourself in a mental state as if it were."

"Who's this helper I'm asking for?"

"The Piegan once believed a spirit, like that of a weasel, coyote, or buffalo, would come to the dreams of a chosen few and help them. The spirits were called helpers."

Link almost asked if White Calf actually believed what he was saying, but he held his tongue. Instead he listened as the doctor explained more of the old customs.

The sweat house surroundings were familiar and pleasant, and Link half expected the Grandfather to join them. He drew fresh steam into his lungs as he'd seen the Grandfather do and felt the warmth grow inside.

19

Monday, February 6th

6:20 A.M.—Peshan, Blackfeet Reservation, northern Montana

The previous afternoon had gone as Benjamin White Calf had said. Following the procession of the vow woman, Bright Flame had bobbed and chanted as the center lodgepole was raised and slipped into the hole. She'd sipped dark liquid from a bowl as the men secured the periphery poles and bound them with leather strips, then again as her assistants and others brought and hung leather pouches from the poles. The medicine lodge had been brought to life.

Link had joined the men's queue and, when his turn had come, made his request. "I ask for the return of insight"—he'd almost forgotten the other—"and for a helper."

White Calf, dressed in beaded buckskins, his face painted white with brilliant vertical streaks of red, had reacted somberly. "And what will you give for these gifts?"

"I will endure self-torture," he'd muttered, trying to capture the spirit but feeling only self-consciousness. The ninety-odd men and women had watched closely, and from the corner of his eye Link had seen Marie and Bright Flame looking on.

"So it shall be," White Calf had responded, and Link had tried to imagine the fear he'd have felt if the torture was going to be real.

After a barbecue dinner in a tent illuminated by kerosene lanterns, where he'd sat with Marie, Jack Douglas, and his wife, White Calf had appeared and tersely shown him to the small trailer he was to share with three other bachelors.

"Where's Marie staying?" he'd asked.

"Don't concern yourself," White Calf had said angrily. "You shouldn't have eaten with her. Keep your mind on the ceremony, not your testosterone level. In the morning you'll have to go to the sweat house to purify yourself again."

The trailer was unlighted, so Link had slept for there'd been nothing else to do. There had been no dream. He woke early and lay thinking about the strange day that had been and the one to come, wondering about White Calf's urging to imagine he was to undergo torture.

A knock at the door. Link answered before the others awakened.

Ben White Calf was in his robe, the sky behind him painted with fiery streaks of morning light. "Time for the sweat lodge," Ben said, pleasantly.

Link joined him, and they walked casually across the snow in the thin robes, as if the bitter cold of the dark morning wasn't burning into the soles of their feet, the frigid air engulfing their legs and privates. There were more people up and about than Link had expected, most staring into the medicine lodge at pouches hanging from the angled rafters and center pole.

"It's going well," said White Calf almost cheerfully.

"What's in the bags they're looking at?"

"Medicine brought by the People to bless the Okan lodge and make it powerful."

As they approached the sweat house, Link realized there was something very basic he did not know. "What the hell is medicine?" he asked.

White Calf crouched and entered first. "Things that make you feel good, that symbolize your life and your achievements. Things you think might please Old Man."

Link took his seat on the dark ledge. White Calf had already been busy for the hot rocks were steaming nicely. "Cold out there."

"Yeah," White Calf said, rubbing his hands briskly together.

Link settled comfortably. "Marie stay in your trailer last night?" he asked.

"She and my wife stayed there. I slept in another. I told you before, don't let your mind become sidetracked during the Okan. You must concentrate on what we're trying to do."

"Did you feel the medicine lodge come to life?" Link asked.

"I tried to feel it. It looked different than I'm accustomed to seeing, yet it seemed appropriate. More basic . . . as things were back then." White Calf nodded his approval. "It's good to have it the way it was in the beginning."

"I'm trying, but I can't make myself believe anything more than we're seeing." Link sucked steam into his chest, held it, whoofed it out as he'd seen the Grandfather do.

"Since we're products of a different society, that's all we can ask of ourselves."

"You, too?"

"Sure. I'm just more aware that it worked for our ancestors . . . that they were able to achieve great things through the old ways. Maybe we'll never rediscover that secret, but it's worth the effort. The others out there think the same way. They don't know it will work, but they understand that it can because it has in the past."

Link thought about it. "To tell you the truth, I still don't know what to expect."

"None of us can help you there. We're not sure, either."

"So far my mind doesn't seem any clearer. I didn't dream at all last night."

"The ceremony's just begun. Today try to get the feeling of anxiety you would if you were about to suffer. This afternoon, try to imagine the pain."

"The piercing? Could you explain it?"

"A relative or close friend made incisions in a warrior's body—two vertical slices for each insertion—and a stick from a sarvis berry bush was shoved under the skin. Sometimes shields or arrows were hung from a warrior's back or sides, and he'd rip them free. Ropes were fastened high on the Okan lodge center pole and tied to the ends of longer sticks inserted through their chests. They'd lean back, hands clenched at their sides, and suffer. If the sticks didn't tear through the skin easily, they'd lean harder, adding more and more weight until the sticks ripped through the flesh. If the cuts were shallow, it happened quickly. If they were deep and the sticks passed under muscle, it took longer. Even the bravest men cried from the pain."

White Calf looked at him in the gloom. "Some couldn't endure it."

"That's understandable."

"Today we'll pass a strip of canvas around your back and under your armpits, and tie the rope to the ends. The fabric will be scored, but you'll have to lean back and strain until it tears. Try to be convincing, but don't bust your ass when you fall."

"And after that?"

"Except for a few more rituals that won't concern you directly, that will be the end of the Sun Dance. In the old days, while they were healing—which took a considerable period as you can imagine—some of the warriors would go off and build a dream house to try to contact their helpers." White Calf described the procedure they'd followed.

"But the warriors began with the promise and self-torture at the Okan?"

"Not all of them. Only the ones who felt they could endure it. What we'll do today is as close as we can come. It will look real enough."

"And you want me to imagine I'm going through the real thing? That might be difficult."

"We're trying to make everything as true to the old way as possible. The rest must come from you. Within your mind and imagination."

They were silent then as Link thought about it all.

Prepare yourself, the Grandfather had said. The Grandfather's image remained clear, and Link remembered the gnarled skin on each side of his chest. The Grandfather had obviously endured the self-torture, as Marie had said the greatest warriors and holy men must do.

Prepare yourself.

White Calf spoke. "This morning there'll be a time for warriors. Everyone will gather and the stories will begin. Two others have volunteered, and you'll be expected to join in. After all, you're the reason for it all."

"What kinds of stories?"

"Recitals of what you've done and why you deserve to be a Piegan warrior. It's not a time for modesty." He chuckled.

"Piegan men have never been shrinking violets when it comes to telling tales and boasting about achievements."

"I'm not good at that sort of thing."

"Fake it. You can emphasize, bluster and boast—in fact that's expected—but be truthful. From early childhood, Piegan men were taught to always tell the truth."

Ghost did not lie.

"I'll give it my best," he said.

After they'd breakfasted in the mess tent, the people gathered at the medicine lodge to watch Benjamin White Calf and the other weather dancer, their bodies streaked in red and white, raise hands that clutched white cattail fronds, then chant and bob and step about in exaggerated movements as they faced the bright morning sun. White Calf had explained it was to bring good weather for the ceremony. Apparently they were successful—the sky remained impeccably blue.

The holy men retreated to a small, open-sided structure in the medicine lodge and pulled blankets around themselves for warmth.

Jack Douglas, dressed in a heavy buckskin jacket and his ever-present impeccable hat, started a fire near the entrance of the lodge. When it was blazing to his satisfaction, he nodded solemnly to the three men near the entrance.

The tank commander who'd had the honor of selecting the main lodgepole was first. He strode energetically to the fire and lay a stick beside it, then turned to the crowd and raised his voice. "It happened four years ago in a faraway land called Iraq," he began in a loud, boastful voice. "My crew was the bravest collection of men imaginable, and our tank had been given the task of riding the point position, staying three hundred yards . . ."

He motioned with his hands and told of cowardly enemy soldiers fleeing—of encountering enemy armor, and how they'd broken their positions without firing as his unit approached. He told how they'd grown overconfident and overextended, and had been ambushed by a large force of enemy tanks and tank destroyers. His crew had fought furiously but feared the worst. Then a flight of A-10 attack airplanes had arrived to help. The enemy ambushers were destroyed by tank fire and the valiant A-10 pilots.

When he finished, he picked up his dry stick of wood, brandished it about, and tossed it onto the fire.

Shouts of approval went up from the crowd. As he emerged from the medicine lodge, men clapped the ex-tank commander on the back and told him he'd done well.

The crowd turned and waited. Marie smiled at Link from one side of the group.

"Your turn, Captain" came Jack Douglas's voice.

Link took a breath, picked a stick from the nearby stack, and walked resolutely to the fire. He pitched the stick on the ground, then turned and tried to smile.

Fake it, White Calf had advised him.

Prepare yourself.

He hesitated—ninety pairs of eyes fixed on him—and wanted to shrink away.

You must, came a voice from inside.

As he stared out at the mass of gathered people, the periphery of his sight became blurred until a narrow tunnel of vision formed and the only person he saw was Bright Flame. She stood stiffly erect, her expression proud, her eyes fiercely set upon him.

"It was five years ago this month," he began uneasily. "I was in a good squadron, with capable pilots and mechanics, flying A-10 Thunderbolt airplanes. I was a flight commander."

Louder, he told himself, and raised his voice. "On the morning I'll speak about, we'd been briefed that enemy armored columns seventy miles northwest of Kuwait City were on the move, protected by mobile antiaircraft fire and surface-to-air missiles. I was to take three other pilots on a patrol . . ."

As he continued, the words came easier.

The AWACS control airplane had reported that an enemy tank attack was threatening a friendly force. "After we identified them, my airplane was first to attack. As I was setting up in a thirty-degree dive-bomb, an infrared guided SAM-eight came zipping through the sky . . ."

He had his hands up, showing his airplane and the surface-to-air missile that came at him like a small streak of fire. "I pulled away hard . . . and it flashed by my cockpit, barely missing."

Link continued. "I turned back toward the target and was hit by a cloud of fire from what we called a zipper, a twenty-three millimeter vehicle-mounted cannon that fires a thousand rounds a minute. A round went through my canopy bow and barely missed my helmet. Bullets shredded my right wing and . . ."

He found himself breathing hard, speaking forcefully, remembering each detail vividly. He told of diving through another hail of bullets and then destroying two tanks with his thirty-millimeter Gatling cannon. He'd had trouble pulling up, and immediately turned for home.

"I told the others in the flight to stay and finish the other targets, and went on alone."

He described almost having to eject when he'd had control problems from loss of hydraulics. Of making it to the airfield streaming fuel and putting it down on damaged landing gear, skidding and going off the runway. Of being pulled from the airplane by crash rescue men.

Silence.

"That is my story today."

Link picked up the stick, brandished it, and tossed it onto the fire.

"Yeah," said Jack Douglas, beaming.

As Link turned to walk away he heard a shout, and the tank commander who had spoken before him rushed up to grab his hand and shake it in both of his own.

"Thanks, Captain," he said. His eyes were moist.

The applause began, followed by loud yells of congratulations. When the clamor subsided, another man stepped forward with his stick and began his tale.

When the third man was finished and had been congratulated, Doctor White Calf came from the weather dancers' enclosure and stood before the crowd.

"I spoke with Bright Flame last evening, and she told me a different version of the story of Old Man and Scarface. She said it was the way it was told to her as a child, passed down from the old days. Our traditions are very important and must never die, so I'll tell it to you, and you should tell your children and grandchildren."

As he listened, Link felt pleased with his performance. They'd approved of him. Then, although the morning was cold and the air filled with ice needles that darted into his skin, he felt a flush of apprehension as he remembered what was to come. The thought of it so filled his mind that he did not think once of the ridiculousness of the situation, or that the story White Calf told was a myth passed on from a stone-age people.

I must endure, he told himself, and wondered if he could.

10:00 A.M.—Fort Myer, Virginia, Hospital

Manny DeVera was happier than he'd been in days. Marian was aware. She looked as if she was asleep, but twice he'd spoken to her and she'd gripped his hand. Not tightly, but perceptibly. When he'd told the nurse she'd smiled, and although he knew she didn't believe him, *he* knew.

He held Marian's hand, waiting for another sign from her, and regarded the television above the foot of her bed as a special bulletin was aired.

An unsmiling woman, the spokesperson for the White House, read from notes. "In response to the terrorist acts that have shaken the Capitol city during the past days, the President has approved the following measures suggested by the National Security Council. One, that a voluntary curfew will be imposed throughout the Washington metropolitan area between the hours of nine p.m. and six a.m."

Voluntary? Manny wondered.

"Two, that the Washington area police leadership be augmented by supervisors from the U.S. Marshal's office."

One by one the spokesperson went through the precautionary steps that had been advised by ITF-4, but in each case the measures were diluted.

"It's not enough," Manny said to himself.

There was no mention of martial law or a police sweep.

The spokesperson introduced the director of the NSC.

Leonard Griggs exhibited a grim smile. "I would like to reassure you that these measures are temporary, instituted to protect our citizens and bring the terrorists to justice. We must act firmly when national security is at stake, and I ask you all to cooperate fully. We can, we *must,* prevail. Thank you."

"He damned near looked like a leader," Manny said aloud.

A television analyst regurgitated what had been said, then added that an informed government official—name withheld—had confirmed that the terrorist called Ghost was responsible for the attacks.

The analyst went into more detail on Ghost and Rashad. The same source had revealed that the NSC had recent descriptions of the two men. "We assume the new composite drawings will be released . . . for the welfare of the same public Mister Griggs says he wants to protect."

A smile quivered at Manny's lips.

TV analyst: "The source also questioned whether Ghost is working in the behalf of the Muslim extremist group Al Fa'qa, as claimed by the NSC. Due to the choice of the recent victims, he wonders . . ."

Manny switched off the set. "I have to leave you for a while," he told Marian. "Lucky's called another meeting. Yesterday's was interesting."

Again he swore he felt a slight pressure on his hand.

The Farmhouse, Falls Church, Virginia

The great room now included a four-by-eight chalkboard. The names of the players in the room were listed on the left side.

"Once we've filled in the spaces on what we'll be doing and how we'll interact, we'll have a plan of attack," Lucky said. "But first we should define what we want to accomplish."

"That one's easy," said Mack Hall. "Find and take out Ghost."

Glenn Phillips disagreed. "Too definitive. We're a small group, and we've got to limit our goals. I think our biggest contribution is going to be keeping the public informed."

"Let's not limit ourselves *too* much," said Sam Hall. "We should do everything possible to help the authorities neutralize his ability to terrorize."

At the top of the board Lucky wrote: OBJECTIVE—NEUTRALIZE GHOST

"I'd like to neuter the guy," grinned Mack.

"Me too, son," said his father. "Problem is getting our hands on him."

Manny spoke up. "That's a problem with all counterterrorist efforts. One of ITF-four's recommendations was to conduct a sweep from the Capitol to the beltway, searching for Ghost. Even if we didn't find them, we felt we'd keep them on the move and on the defensive."

"Sounds like something that should be done," said Sam Hall. "We just don't have the thousand-odd policemen it would take."

Lucky nodded. "I agree, Sam, but we have another advantage. Two of the most popular figures in Washington are here in this room. You, because of the respect you've earned in the black community. And Mack's best known of us all."

The middle linebacker for the Redskins looked embarrassed.

"What would you say to spearheading a sweep—you and Mack taking a stack of the composites of Ghost and Rashad, moving from neighborhood to neighborhood and organizing searches? Once the descriptions are out, someone's bound to see them."

Sam became thoughtful, then turned to Mack. "What do you think?"

"It could work. I'm for it, Pop."

Doctor Grace McNabb raised her hand. "I've been constructing psych profiles and behavior forecasts for various law enforcement agencies, and I have access to sensitive information. Yesterday Mr. DeVera showed me a profile of Ghost. Using that, adding what I learned from Link, what I got out of the Hoover Building this morning, I've been able to form impressions."

"Such as . . . ?" Lucky prodded.

"If Ghost is threatened, his reaction will be to try to destroy the threat. You should consider that." She looked at Sam Hall. "If you get close, Ghost will try to stop you."

Mack grinned. "I've got a few friends who can help out there."

Sam looked about the room. "We'll do it."

Lucky printed the task beside their names: ORGANIZE NEIGHBORHOOD SEARCHES

Glenn Phillips was staring at the chalkboard. "I'm pretty well tied up with meetings. About all I'll be able to offer is to run interference and try to make sure no one gets into trouble for what we're doing. That and attempt to have ITF-four reinstated."

Lucky filled in the space beside his name.

"It won't be easy to get in to see the President," said Phillips. "He's been moved to secure quarters at a location the Secret Service is holding close to their vests. We're told access has been limited, and he's canceling speaking engagements. That's damned serious considering he's at the beginning of a reelection campaign."

Manny snorted. "I'll bet Griggs has access."

"Len Griggs is close as glue to the President. He's even passing on his messages. My colleagues are concerned. Not everyone trusts the man."

Lucky regarded Manny next. "You did well with the press. You're a good leak."

DeVera grimaced. "Thanks a lot."

"Linda and I will coordinate activities and messages from here at the Farmhouse. We'll also hold a meeting each day for all who can make it."

"How about me," said Bowes, nodding at the chalkboard.

"Mack will handle security at the search headquarters, but you do your best to keep the rest of us from harm's way."

He made a few more entries on the chalkboard and stepped back. "How does that look?"

OBJECTIVE—NEUTRALIZE GHOST

PAUL & LINDA ANDERSON—HOST MEETING & COORDINATE INFORMATION

BILL BOWES—SECURITY/PROTECTION OF PERSONNEL

MANNY DEVERA—PRESS "LIAISON"/EXPERTISE ON TERRORISM

SAM HALL—ORGANIZE NEIGHBORHOOD SEARCHES

MACK H.—(GAIN POPULAR SUPPORT FOR ABOVE)

DR. MCNABB—PSYCH PROFILES

GLENN PHILLIPS—POLITICAL ACTION/REINSTATE ITF-4

Bethesda, Maryland

J.J. Davis had led the search, with teams of agents and sniffer dog teams methodically sweeping seedy warehouses that had seemed the most likely candidates. They'd started on newer structures, but those, too, proved to be barren of explosives, and he increasingly wondered if the destination was wrong. The explosives could be anywhere in the area, yet he still felt a warehouse would be the appropriate unloading place for the semi and its load of metal tubs.

The dog team had left the final warehouse, and J.J. was

contemplating their next step when the young agent hurried in.

"The Hoover Building just got a message from Cincinnati. The middleman talked."

J.J. would have grinned if his jaw hadn't been wired. The previous day they'd located the businessman—the middleman—who had paid off the Rocky Mountain Arsenal contractors.

"He got his walking orders from a man named Martin in New York. Didn't know if it was a first or last name or if it was real, but he gave a description and they're making up a composite. Martin made initial contact, then sent another guy who the middleman identified."

J.J. motioned impatiently for him to continue.

"He's Norb Maier, once errand boy for old man Gambini. When we nailed Gambini, Maier switched to another boss, name of Joseph DiFazio, who's looked clean for the last ten years. DiFazio's more or less retired." The young agent went on, mentioning more names.

J.J.'s eyes narrowed with a memory. He drooped his head, thinking, trying to recall a rumor he'd chased when he'd helped the Italian authorities after Salvator Riina, the Cosa Nostra's *capo di capi,* had been taken and Ghost's crew were on their killing rampage.

They'd had a name from an informant—of a man who had met with Riina in Palermo. The name he'd mentioned was Giuseppe DiFazio, likely a different man bearing the common Italian name, but . . . the next day the informant had been killed with a head shot by Charlie.

He pulled out his pad and scribbled: *Put a stake on DiFazio.*

The young agent went to find a telephone.

J.J. turned back to his examination of the warehouse. Another bust. The final search would be of smaller warehouses and those collocated with businesses. If those proved invalid, he would have to do some more deep thinking.

3:00 P.M.—Peshan, Blackfeet Reservation, northern Montana

Except for a lunch break, Link had spent all day in the ceremony, doing as he'd been told by Doctor White Calf, listening and watching, and wondering if he could endure what was to come.

He was last in a queue of men waiting to appear before the weather dancers in the medicine lodge, to receive guidance and make a vow that must be kept. Immediately afterward, White Calf had told him, would come Link's simulated self-torture.

Link was oblivious of the advice given to the man before him or the promise he made, concentrating intently on what he must say.

It was his turn. The older weather dancer looked at him closely as he advanced.

"You have requested much," said White Calf. "You want to be able to see the future and have a helper show the way. We cannot know if . . ."

White Calf stopped speaking. The older white-face man's eyes widened, and Link glanced to his side.

Bright Flame had approached, frowning oddly as she peered at the weather dancers.

"Go away," the wall-eyed holy man hissed, looking frightened.

"It will be," she said in a shrill tone.

"I don't know if we can promise . . ." White Calf began, then grew silent and stared.

"It will be," she repeated, louder this time, her voice cracking with the effort. She nodded to the men. There was utter silence from the watchful crowd outside the medicine lodge.

Bright Flame's eyes dimmed and grew distant, and she held up her hands and examined the missing fingertips. "Lay-ton," she crooned mournfully, and stumbled.

Marie LeBecque entered the medicine lodge and placed a gentle hand on the older woman's shoulder. "Come," she whispered.

Bright Flame blinked then drew a deep breath, as if trying to force herself back to the present. She looked at Link with a void expression, turned, and left with Marie.

White Calf watched the women depart, then turned his white-red face back to Link.

"What you ask for will be," he said, his own voice low and unsure.

"I thank Old Man," Link said, then steeled himself. "This is my promise. I will go through the old ceremony

. . . with the piercing . . . as it should be. No cloth or simulations. I will endure the self-torture in the old way."

White Calf's eyes were narrowed. "We can't. The council has outlawed it."

"Then I will do it myself, for it is my promise." He abruptly turned and left the enclosure.

Marie hurried to walk beside him.

"You must stay away from me," he told her firmly.

She faltered and then stopped as he continued walking toward the old buildings.

"Wait!" White Calf hailed, hurrying up from behind. Link turned and waited.

"That was a stupid thing to do," the doctor said angrily. "Where are you going now?"

"To carry through with my promise. If that was the way things were done in the old days and they got results, it's my only option. I didn't come here to go through with half of it."

"And how do you propose to do it by yourself?"

Link shrugged. "I'll find a way."

"You'd cut yourself?"

"That's how I understood it happened. A friend or relative was supposed to do it, but since I don't have one around who's willing to help, I'll give it a try."

White Calf ran a hand through his gray hair, looked around, then turned his eyes back to Link. "You'd likely become infected."

"I'll do it as sanitarily as I can, but I've got to go through it. I knew that from the beginning. You and these people have done what you could, but as you said, the rest has to come from me. Otherwise, we both know none of this is likely to work."

"It's symbolism, Link. Whatever happens is in the mind."

"My imagination's not that powerful. I've got to go through with it. If nothing happens, I'll know I gave it my best."

"I'm a physician. If I helped you, I could have my license revoked."

"I understand." Link nodded politely, then started to walk on.

"Wait."

"I can't waste more time, Doctor. I appreciate everything you've done, but it's got to be finished properly."

"Damn it!" White Calf exploded.

"I think you know it's the only way."

White Calf blew out a long sigh. "I'll help."

"What about the medical board problem?"

"We'll work around it. I'd prefer if the others don't see me making the incisions."

"That's fair."

The doctor grimaced, then slowly nodded. "It must be done as antiseptically as possible. I'll want you to take the precautions I suggest."

"So long as it's all done the old way. If you don't mind, I'd like to get on with it." Link smiled grimly. "The sooner we start, the more quickly it will be over."

The two men were hidden from sight in the small enclosure used by the weather dancers, the front of which had been covered over by willow branches.

"I'm ready," Link said. He looked not at all as he had an hour before. He was now clad only in breechcloth and moccasins, his face and body painted stark white, spotted with symmetrical rows of black spots and circles daubed on by the old weather dancer.

"I'll make two vertical incisions, four inches apart, on either side of your chest," said Doctor White Calf, his voice grave.

Link fought off a shiver. "Not shallow," he instructed. "I must suffer."

White Calf opened his mouth to speak, then snapped it shut. He raised the scalpel and measured his rubber-gloved hand. It was steady.

"Go ahead," Link said.

"Try to relax your chest muscles."

Link stared the doctor in the eye. He hardly felt the first cut of the sharp scalpel. By the time the fourth incision was made he discerned a stinging sensation. He could feel blood running freely down his abdomen and onto his legs.

The doctor put the bloodied scalpel aside, then reached for the first stout, twelve-inch stick. Over White Calf's objections about cleanliness, Link had insisted that they be cut from a live sarvis berry bush, as had been done in the old ritual.

When the doctor paused Link gave a terse nod, keeping his eyes on the man's face. White Calf puckered the wound with his fingers and pressed in with the green stick. Link grunted aloud from the excruciating pain.

The doctor paused.

"Go on," Link managed. "Not this . . . far and . . . stop."

Pain bolted across his chest as the stick was pushed farther and farther, then he felt a tearing and almost swooned from the nausea. He staggered once, then stood firmly in place.

"The other," Link muttered through clenched teeth.

Doctor White Calf lifted the second stick into view. This one was worse, for Link knew the pain was coming and anticipated as flesh was torn and the fire bolt passed through his chest.

"Done," muttered the doctor.

Link did not linger. He staggered once, then emerged from the weather dancer hut into the main lodge area, holding his arms wide so the crowd could see. He ignored their gasps and a sharp outcry from Marie, and walked on rubbery legs to the side of the medicine lodge.

"I suffer, Old Man!" he shouted as waves of nausea swept him.

Hands were on him, positioning him, cutting notches into the ends of the stout sticks and attaching woven leather cords suspended from the center lodgepole.

White Calf gave a slight tug on first one rope, then the others, but each movement sliced through Link as if a hot knife had carved into his chest.

"You're ready," White Calf muttered. He pushed the end of a short willow branch into Link's mouth as he might a stogie, gave a final grim look, and left him.

Link could not stop a long, low moan from emerging. He bit down harder on the resilient wood to stop the sound, and slowly backed from the lodgepole toward the periphery.

The quicker he pulled the sticks through the flesh, he reasoned, the sooner the pain would stop, but as the pressure mounted on his chest he hesitated.

Oh God! he cried out to himself, and knew he could not do it.

Why should he? It was irrational, ridiculous to suffer such torment for only . . .

A tiny gust of wind stirred across his exposed body, the

chill mixing with the agony and making him shake more violently.

Ghost's face stared. Mocking him. A lip lifted in a slight sneer.

When I'm finished with my task, I'll find you.

Link wondered if Ghost had been through the true Okan.

Prepare yourself. The Grandfather's words echoed in his head.

Link slowly leaned back, arms held stiffly at his sides as White Calf had said—the pressure on his chest muscles grew, and the pain increased.

"Stop it!" He heard the shrill voice dimly, knew it was Marie's voice, but did not look.

Another voice cried out in anguish. Bright Flame?

He leaned back, placing more weight against the cords.

"Tear, damn you!" he whispered around the wood in his mouth. Then he hissed in a long breath and fell back, hard.

The pain in his chest was overpowering. Against his will tears began to flow down his cheeks. Those tickled his face, blood his legs. He strained harder, but felt no tearing flesh—only more agonizing torment.

Discordant noise filtered through: the old weather dancer moving about, chanting and bobbing. Another sound, of Marie LeBecque sobbing.

Prepare yourself.

A dark face flickered, almost appeared, then quickly faded.

The stick fell from Link's mouth. "I've missed you, Grandfather," he said in grunted words, his voice tortured. Link wanted to plead for help, but knew it would be wrong.

He moved forward a step and began to cry, his body shuddering with continued agony.

Someone approached. "Do you want . . ."

"Move away," he shouted.

Link took a final deep breath, clenched his teeth, and hurled himself back. There was a ripping sensation in his chest . . . he fell, freed from the constraints . . . the pain pulsing, overpowering.

He heard himself screaming as he fainted from consciousness.

20

Thursday, February 9th

8:40 A.M.—Peshan, Blackfoot Reservation, Northern Montana

"How do you feel?" Marie LeBecque asked as Link slowly awakened. She'd come from the rear of the trailer soundlessly, looking concerned, as she had throughout the previous three days.

"Still like a deer that's been gutted and field dressed," he said. The pain came and went with each breath, but he'd not let Doctor White Calf sedate him . . . not even when he'd sutured the gaping wounds. He'd only been able to sleep when weariness had become overpowering. He did not know why he'd insisted on enduring the pain, only that it had seemed appropriate.

"Was Jack able to get the things from Boudie Springs?" he asked.

Marie nodded. "He checked with your friends before he went into your cabin, like you wanted. I've got it all in my car."

"Thank him for me."

"You can do that. He's been hanging around the trailer night and day. I'd better get my uncle so he can give you your morning check-over," she said.

"Not yet." Link wanted another moment alone with her. They were in White Calf's trailer. He'd refused to let the doctor take him to the hospital in town. Benjamin White

Calf had treated him on the pullout bed he lay on, did his best to reattach torn muscles, and sutured the incisions and the ragged four-inch gashes where the sticks had torn through his chest.

"Do you want me to bring you something to eat?" Marie asked.

"I'll join the others in the mess tent." The Okan was over. Today they'd all be leaving.

"I don't think that's wise, Link."

Link looked at her. "I have to get up anyway. There's something else I have to do. It's not finished yet." There'd been no insights, no visits from any so-called "helper."

"The dream house?"

He didn't answer. He was not to speak about it. In the old days, the warrior would leave unannounced, for a location only known to himself.

"Give it another week, Link. You're not strong enough, and my uncle's still concerned about infection."

"Time's my enemy. Is there any news from Washington? Any more killings?"

"None that we know of. It's been quiet. The government released drawings of Ghost and Rashad, and Charlie was moved to another prison where he can be guarded better. Maybe Ghost realizes there's no way to free him and it's over."

"God, I hope so. I've still got to finish what I've started, though."

Marie left to get her uncle. Jack Douglas peeked inside as Link struggled to sit up.

"I got your things from Boudie Springs."

"That's what Marie said. Thanks, but come on in before I freeze."

Jack closed the door behind himself. "Weather's taking a turn for the worse. We were lucky to have the good days for the Okan."

Link laboriously slipped into long underwear. "Guess the weather dancers did okay."

Jack smiled. "You, too. We're proud of you, Captain."

"I'm trying, Jack." He pulled on jeans.

"None of the rest of us know what the hell's going on inside your head, but we're all rooting. This Ghost is one bad character. Think you can stop him?"

"I'm going to try."

"Are you heading back east now?"

"In a few days. There's something else to do here."

Jack Douglas eyed his chest and the swath of bandages. "A group of us have been talking. Maybe we should tag along when you go back."

"It's a different ball game there, Jack. Sometimes you can't tell the good guys from the bad." He told him about being followed by the NSC staffers, and the confrontation.

"I see what you mean," Jack said. "Our guys aren't good at self-restraint."

Doctor White Calf came in. "Turning colder," he said. "How do you feel this morning?"

"Sore."

White Calf examined the bandages. "No use to change them for another day or two."

The two men helped as Link pulled on a cotton turtleneck, then a wool shirt.

During the final breakfast meal, Link sat with Marie LeBecque and Benjamin White Calf, and made a point of speaking to everyone who came by the table to see him. They seemed cheerful, and he felt easy with their presence for he'd become one of them.

"We'll have everything hauled out and cleaned up by afternoon," said the ex-tank commander, who was also foreman for a general contracting company. He nodded at the sky. "Another storm's on the way, so we'd best get to it."

"After the dust settles on this Ghost thing, let's get together for a beer," Link said.

"You're on. Seems we were in the same place once in the past." He looked evenly at Link. "Things were a real mess in the desert during that fight. The enemy was massed in front, then an unidentified column of armor approached from the east, firing at us on the move. We were taking hits, so our major called for an immediate air strike on the second column. Your guys came to the rescue, same time we opened fire on them."

"So that's the way it was."

"Yeah. Between the strafing and our rounds, we knocked out two vehicles before we IDed them as British and flashed for them to knock it off." The ex-tank commander's eyes were narrowed as he reflected on the day in the desert.

"Bad scene, but like the man said, shit happens. I'd like to go for that beer some day, Captain."

The man shook his hand and left, walking out to the area where the remnants of the Okan lodge were being hauled off.

White Calf spoke from beside him. "You've done well."

Link got to his feet, and Marie followed. "We'll go now. Thanks for everything, Doc. You've put on a hell of a show."

White Calf was looking out at the Okan site when they left.

Link followed Marie, walking gingerly and smiling at the people they passed. When they arrived at her Jeep, she helped him inside then went around and slid into the passenger's seat.

He recognized his pack in the backseat.

"Your snowshoes are there, too," she said, starting the motor.

"Wait," he said. Bright Flame walked from her small hut, clad in the parka and woolen trousers he'd brought her, and started toward the burial ground.

"She's not lucid, Link. She hasn't been since you went through the self-torture. It was as if she was hanging onto a thread of sanity until that was over and done with."

"My mother," he said in a wondering voice.

"She was intensively devoted to Henry Layton . . . she still is. He brought gentleness into her life when she was tormented, and while she might forget other things, that's always with her. I believe she'll continue to mourn him until she dies. For a while, though, she was aware of you and who you were. She was very proud."

"She also gave birth to two terrorists. Do you think she knows that, too?"

"I truly hope not . . . but there's some kind of contact. Remember her conversation that night, and how she knew the words Ghost used in his phone calls?"

She drove toward Browning slowly, trying to ease over the bad spots in the road so Link wouldn't be jarred.

Going to the Sun Road

Marie LeBecque tried to remain stoic outwardly, although that was not at all what she felt. The man she loved was about to be threatened again, and that dread was difficult to subdue.

Link had been quiet during the return to Browning. He'd then spent half an hour at her kitchen table going over the geodetic survey maps Jack Douglas had provided.

Finally he'd folded and put them aside.

"You know where you're going?" she'd asked, but he'd only smiled and finished his coffee. Then he'd quietly gotten to his feet and pulled on his heavy parka.

"How long?" she'd tried to ask, but he'd only smiled again, walked to the door, and left. He'd gone out to her Jeep and painfully transferred the backpack and snowshoes to his truck. She'd hardly bundled up and stepped outside when he'd pulled away, and she'd had to hurry to catch up when he'd driven out of the town.

He turned onto the road through Glacier Park, closed now as it was all winters due to heavy snows, drove around the barricade and proceeded on. She trailed at a distance, shifting the Cherokee into 4-wheel drive as they encountered snow. The accumulation became deeper as they climbed with increasing difficulty. Marie followed doggedly, unwilling to lose him.

Link finally stopped.

Marie also halted, fifty yards behind, and watched. He paid her no heed as he donned the backpack, then the snowshoes, periodically looking up at Siyeh Mountain. He stamped about a few times, as those familiar with snowshoes do to test bindings, pulled a knit cap down over his ears, then trudged upward. After he'd disappeared into the trees, she waited for a while longer. Finally she backed and maneuvered to turn the Jeep around, and began the trip home.

Siyeh Mountain, Glacier National Park,
northwestern Montana

Link had not brought his watch for he'd not wanted the distraction of thinking about time, but he estimated that he'd been trekking and climbing for more than four hours when he cautiously approached a small ledge on the sheer-sided mountainside trail.

The warriors had picked their sites for the danger they'd

presented. He peered over the side. The drop-off was several hundred feet. It would do.

He pulled off the canvas pack. As he knelt to remove the snowshoes, a jolt of pain shuddered through his wounded chest, so he waited for a few breaths before continuing. When they were off, he stuck them upright in a nearby snowbank to block the trail to animal traffic.

Link opened the pack, pulled out a three-by-twenty-inch tube, and carefully extracted, then set up a small backpacking tent. After positioning the fly over the top, he spread a waterproof ground cloth on the tent floor.

White Calf had told him dream houses were made in many ways, sometimes with gathered brush, others in caves—whatever was handy or they were accustomed to.

He added a capped bottle to contain his urine, since he wouldn't emerge for several days. Link rose then, savoring the primeval feeling that comes with establishing camp, and stood back for a moment to look out at the surroundings: the soaring granite and white mountains, the angry clouds of the growing storm. A smile formed as he continued surveying. A bighorn sheep stood stock-still on a promontory half a mile distant, likely wondering what the intruder was about.

Link almost spoke out in greeting, then paused, wondering if the old ritual hadn't included silence. He decided not.

"Hello, Mr. Sheep," he called out. "Are you my helper?"

The animal shifted slightly.

Regardless of what was to come, the beginning was both pleasant and spectacular.

He favored his chest—Doctor White Calf had told him to be careful that he didn't tear stitches—and knelt over the pack. He began to remove and spread his medicine about the interior of the tent. He smiled as he handled each item, an appropriate expression. Medicine consisted of private things that made you happiest, proudest. Medicine made you feel good.

There was a Little League trophy and completed coin collection from his youth; a photo of Lucky and Linda; his Air Force Academy ring; the pilot's wings Lucky had pinned on his chest when Link had graduated from flight school; a squadron patch from a flying unit; a ski instructor pin; one of the stout sticks that had penetrated his chest when he'd endured the ritual. He was also proud of that.

Perhaps it was a residue of a stone-age belief, but he was glad he'd done it.

He chided himself for doubting. *Believe,* he told himself.

He regarded the boiling clouds.

"I'm here, Old Man, and I'll do as I'm supposed to. I've got to have special knowledge if I'm going to stop Ghost, but the old ways say I can't get it without a helper."

He almost felt foolish, but quelled the notion.

"Now it's your turn, Old Man." Link paused to look about for a last time. "You certainly have a spectacular world here."

He pulled the last item from the pack, a survival blanket made of stitched layers of aluminized polyester. Link folded the pack and put it under the fly, then placed the survival blanket inside the tent, crawled in, and zipped the door flap closed. The interior was gloomy but not pitch-dark. He rolled down the knit cap until the ski mask covered his face, drew the parka hood into position, and pulled the drawstring until it fit around his head.

He was snug enough, he decided.

Link settled down in the tent, pulled the survival blanket around himself, and turned to face the unseen precipice outside. He would remain on that side for two days. The following two days, if he could endure for that long—and White Calf had explained it would be torturous—would be spent on the other side, all the while waiting for *helpers* to appear.

They might appear as animals, or something else. They varied from person to person, for everyone was different. He must wait here until, and if, they came to him.

The holy and mystical number was four, so he wondered if it wouldn't take that many days. The number three was considered good, but not as good. Five was too many.

Lincoln Anderson dropped off to sleep more quickly than he'd imagined.

21

Saturday, February 11th

7:50 A.M.—Fort Myer, Virginia, Hospital

Judge Marian Lindquist's head and face remained hidden beneath the same adornment of bandages she'd worn since she'd left the operating room the last time. But she was aware for short periods, for now and then her breathing betrayed emotion. At least that was what Manny believed. The doctors still weren't convinced. They'd noted little brain activity.

One thing Manny knew. The hand squeezes were real. Whenever he spoke endearing words, Marian reacted. That the doctors had observed, and agreed were positive indications.

Manny held her hand and watched the television screen, as he did every morning.

Leonard Griggs had requested time from major networks for yet another special announcement. The director of the NSC had been on television often during the past days, sometimes admonishing "certain members" of the Senate—meaning Glenn Phillips—for bringing the argument about the transfer of ITF-4 into open debate on the Senate floor.

It was Griggs and not the President who offered words of leadership to the nation. Some of Manny's government acquaintances were concerned that the President remained in the basement of the Pentagon, and had even stopped his weekly radio broadcasts.

Senator Glenn Phillips had been making a lot of loud waves in the past days, trying to encourage the President to take firmer action against Ghost. Increasingly, he said to the press, the nation was being governed by vacillation.

And by Griggs, Manny thought as the news bulletin began.

There was no fanfare, only a shot of Griggs walking up to the microphones. The director of the NSC was unpopular with the press. They called him mercurial. On two occasions he'd called news conferences and canceled—an odious offense as far as the media was concerned. He wouldn't allow questions during or following press sessions. Griggs felt he should speak to the citizens of America, with no intermediaries or arguments. He was abrasive when he dealt with producers, then put on a different face for the public.

Leonard Griggs spoke to the camera. "It's now been six days since the last outrage by the terrorist we are increasingly sure was Ghost."

Griggs shook his head sadly. "Last evening Senator David Smithfield was murdered in front of his home in Annapolis, Maryland. The President deplores this tragedy. While there was initial speculation that the terrorist called Ghost might have been involved, the NSC has determined that was not the case. Senator Smithfield was a victim of yet another mindless gun fanatic. Such incidents will continue until Congress passes comprehensive legislation for the registration, licensing, and control of all firearms."

Manny groaned. "That's called a smoke screen," he said to Marian, as if she could hear.

Griggs looked at the camera. "We've received confirmed information from authorities in Europe that Ghost has been seen at different locations during the past week. Accordingly I've suggested to the President that the precautionary measures we imposed last week be lifted."

Griggs firmed his jaw. "We will continue to pursue Ghost and all who support him with perseverance and vigor. We shall do this in Europe or wherever he may be."

The image faded.

A popular television analyst appeared. "The director appeared on behalf of the President. Some easing of restrictions will be made tonight, the remainder tomorrow. As you heard, Mr. Griggs denies that Ghost was involved in the murder of Senator David Smithfield."

The analyst looked at notes. "An informed government source claims that Ghost is still with us, that the shooting of Senator Smithfield was indeed done by Ghost. The source accuses Mr. Griggs of reacting too cautiously in the face of the national emergency, which he believes is anything but over. He feels stronger action should be taken to protect our citizens, but as you've seen, even the present efforts are being curtailed.

"My tendency is to agree. If the emergency is indeed over, why hasn't the President of the United States emerged from his sanctuary in the basement of the Pentagon?"

Good point, Manny thought as he switched off the television.

He heard something. A whisper? Manny bent close over Marian. He could see no change.

Manny sighed and sat back down. He'd spoken with Slocum and White during the night. They were disgusted with what they heard at their NSC panel meetings. There was no definitive information that Ghost was in Europe, only the normal sightings that so often proved to be false.

Another premature announcement. Glenn Phillips was right. Government by vacillation.

Another sound, like a low sigh. She squeezed his hand. Not vigorously, but he felt it.

"Marian?" he asked incredulously.

He heard her, and began to laugh with happiness.

"Are you watering my plants?" she asked again.

Bethesda, Maryland

Ghost was at the bench in the warehouse, working on the ornate bas-relief of an eagle. A fierce, grand eagle, with a wingspan of precisely six feet. Detonators and radio receiver were embedded in a core of slightly less than a hundred pounds of tritonol. The eagle's feathers were of scored titanium. The outer layer was sculptor's plaster that would set as hard as alabaster. It was a beautiful piece, and the detailed features required every ounce of Ghost's artistic ability.

It was certainly not the largest bomb Ghost had fashioned, but it was the most important. An artist had sculpted the original in the mid-1850s, when the People had been humiliated by the treaty-which-was-a-lie. The Bull Clan warriors had pleaded for the chiefs not to sign, but the chiefs had listened to Black Wolf and put their marks to the paper.

The Bull Clan had denounced the treaty that separated the Piegan. They'd become a secret society, and each new member vowed revenge. The eagle would be their vindication, wreaking death upon descendants of the men who'd cheated the People of their heritage.

The wayfinder had done well. During his tutoring the Bull Clan elders had mentioned that a wayfinder had been trained to assist him. He'd been a young boy when they'd brought the wayfinder into the cabin room and kept him in the shadows while he pledged to support the chosen one in his great task. He'd been taken away then, and Ghost had been left to wonder.

Ghost had dedicated much of the week to the sculpting effort, since Joseph DiFazio had ordered the cooling-off period extended. The directive chafed. The Mafia's timidity didn't fit with Ghost's plan, and he was increasingly tempted to change employers.

The Cosa Nostra was in such decline that he wondered how they'd even summoned the courage to carry off the bold theft of the explosives.

Yesterday Cherone had come to the house and told him about the new delay. After he'd left, Ghost had met Kevin Gilroy at another empty home in College Park. Later he'd paid his visit to Annapolis and Senator Smithfield. He was pleased with the kill shot, and wished Charlie were there so he could boast about it. His brother might have picked Smithfield off from farther away, but he'd be proud of Ghost's achievement.

He wondered if Martin Cherone suspected he'd killed the senator. He certainly didn't know about the message Kevin Gilroy's people would relay to Charlie: *It won't be long now. Be ready when I come for you.*

The IRA brigadier had agreed to provide support in return for the promised British Parliament disaster. The brigadier wanted the north wing of the House of Commons left in rubble during the current session, scheduled to end in

August. Kevin Gilroy said they'd supply as much Semtech compound as required.

Ghost had decided to use a remotely controlled vessel on the Thames, and determined where he'd focus the explosive for maximum destruction. Kevin Gilroy had already relayed his request to obtain a motorized barge.

Ghost was saddened that his relationship with the Cosa Nostra was ending. They'd once impressed him with their codes of honor and brotherhood, so similar to those of the Bull Clan. But the Cosa Nostra was a timid shell of what it had been.

He'd stepped back to examine his work when Martin Cherone came into the warehouse, flanked by the pair of ever-present bodyguards. He seemed more morose than normal.

Rashad eyed them suspiciously. He trusted none of them, and would be happy when they were finished with the alliance.

Cherone eyed the worktable. "What's that?" he asked.

Ghost did not reply.

"You were told to wait."

"We won't wait forever." Ghost looked at him evenly, wondering if he'd ask about the shooting in Annapolis.

Martin Cherone had come for another purpose. "The FBI teams are getting close. Next they'll check warehouses collocated with businesses."

The adjacent complex housed a building supply outlet for contractors.

"You ought to be safe for a couple of days, but . . ."

Ghost interrupted. "We'll move the supplies to the house." He'd already been warned by the wayfinder.

"I'll have a couple panel trucks brought around."

"I don't want any new men involved. One truck, and Rashad will do the driving."

Martin Cherone shrugged. "I've got a location on the A. L. Anderson guy. He's back in Montana. Some place called Browning this time."

What was Anderson doing on the reservation? Ghost wondered.

"Keep track of him," he said. He looked at the cones. "Now let's concentrate on getting the supplies moved before the FBI arrives."

Browning, Montana

Although the storm had passed, Marie remained concerned. Link had been gone for two days. She alternately worried that he'd freeze to death or die from some cataclysm—and she might never hear from him again. He wouldn't be the first to disappear in the glacier wilderness.

Her uncle told her to be patient and chided her for having followed him. She was gratified that he'd become so impressed with Link, yet she knew that he too was imbued with an excess of bravado—a common failing among Piegan men.

She moved papers about her office desk woodenly, uninterested that the museum's budget was being increased this year as she'd fought so hard to make happen.

"Miss LeBecque?"

A middle-aged man stood in her office doorway.

"My name's Bill Bowes, ma'am. I'm a friend of Link's from Washington."

"Oh?" She'd thought he was from the reservation. Upon inspection she found his features subtly different from the classic ones of the Blackfeet. Marie remembered the little Link had told her about Bowes. A family friend, now chief pilot for his father's charter flight business.

"Link told us about the Okan ritual when we were flying him out. What he knew about it, anyway. We'd expected him to call by now."

Marie put the correspondence aside. "Please come in."

When Bowes had taken his seat, she explained how Link had voluntarily endured the terrible self-torture. Bowes didn't seem surprised, but she'd decided he wasn't the kind to exhibit emotion. She finished by telling how Link had gone to the mountains.

"You followed him?"

"As far as I could. He parked and went out on snowshoes."

"Alone?" Billy Bowes's eyes narrowed.

"Yes." She stared. "Link told me you were Indian. What tribe?"

"Cherokee. Born and raised in Oklahoma. My grandmother Bowes considered anyone who wasn't one of the People as uncivilized, including whites and tribes like yours." He smiled. "After living in Washington, I've learned she was right about whites."

Marie laughed, then remembered the rest of what she'd been told. "Link said you were a colonel when he was young, and he treated you horribly."

"We've straightened it out. Could you give me directions to Link's pickup?"

"I'll do even better. I'll take you to it."

"I didn't mean to bother you that much."

"I've been looking for an excuse to go back there for the past two days."

He remained gentlemanly and did not raise the obvious question as she cleared her desk.

Upon her urging, Billy Bowes drove his rental auto to her house. There he parked and lugged a large duffel and a heavy kit bag to her Jeep.

"The back hatch is unlocked," she called to him. As soon as he'd deposited the bags and was inside, Marie drove westward toward the Going to the Sun highway.

"So what's this ceremony?" Bowes asked. "He only mentioned the other one."

"This one's not a true ceremony. In the old days our warriors would go out alone, pick a place that was potentially dangerous—which doesn't make me feel good about what Link's doing—assume an uncomfortable position, and fast until they were visited by spirits. I've wondered if with all the fasting and discomfort, anyone wouldn't hallucinate after a while."

"You've got doubts about it?"

Marie was unable to provide an accurate answer.

"We met your friend Grace McNabb in Washington. She explains it all in scientific terms. Do you feel the same way? That everything's explainable?"

"I'm really not sure. I've always believed the self-torture in the Okan ceremony was just a way to get the warriors' attention focused. Certainly intense worrying and pain might do that."

Bowes looked thoughtful.

"Yet there've been things that certainly seem unexplainable. Some of Link's insights, for instance. And a woman has been telling us some startling things."

"His real mother?" Bowes asked.

"Link told you?"

"Some of it," Bowes said, looking out at the mountains as they turned onto the closed, snow-covered road. "Did the ceremony give him a better handle on what's going on?"

"He's trying hard. Link's a realist, utterly unimpressed with hocus pocus, so he's doubly disturbed by the things happening in his head. For most of his life he rejected the childhood visions, even denied they'd happened. Now he's in the position of trying to get them back."

"My Grandma Bowes would have told him to just accept what he's given."

"She believed in dreams?" Marie asked.

"She was gifted herself, but she never made a big deal of it."

The road began to climb. Marie stopped, shifted into low range, then continued. "A storm passed through since Link went up. It was down to twenty below last night. I hope he was okay."

"We learned about winter survival in the air force."

"Link mentioned you were military, too."

"A fighter pilot, like Link and his father. That the pickup up ahead?"

"Yes." Marie continued until they were close, then stopped and let the engine idle. The truck was covered with six inches of new snow.

"There's a spare key in a magnetic box hidden in the wheel well," she said.

Bowes went to the rear and opened the hatch, and removed his bags. He busied himself with the duffel—pulled out a rifle and checked it over.

Marie rolled down her window. "Are you going up after him?"

"No. I'll be staying for a while, though."

"It's awfully cold," she said.

"We went through all the right training for this sort of thing." Billy Bowes continued to observe the surroundings. "Do you have the phone number for Link's parents?"

"Back at my house."

"I'd appreciate it if you'd give them a call and tell them what's going on."

"Certainly. Do you have food?"

"A few candy bars. Anyway, this place is a supermarket.

So far I've seen two rabbits and a ptarmigan. Do me good to camp out for a while."

When she left him a few minutes later, Billy Bowes was squinting up at the mountain.

7:00 P.M.—Boomtown, Washington, D.C.

The move to the house had gone as planned. The tritonol cones were stacked neatly in the garage, the bas-relief carefully placed on a workbench there.

Ghost had applied the first coat of metallic gold paint to the eagle. As he waited for it to dry, he read the *Times* article about announcements made by the director of the NSC with mixed emotions. The killing of the senator was seen as the obvious work of a professional, but was pointedly blamed on someone other than Ghost. That was good. Yet he was disturbed that things were being reported as normalizing, brought on by the lull of terrorist activity.

He decided to immediately begin another project. His campaign of relentlessness would remain stalled if he abided by Joseph DiFazio's rule, and all he'd gained would be lost.

Martin Cherone entered the room with his bodyguards.

Ghost lowered the newspaper. Rashad looked up sharply from the television.

"We've got another problem. Ever hear of a football player named Mack Hall?"

"The big guy who plays for the Skins?" asked Rashad.

"That's him," said Cherone. "He and his father are organizing a search to find you."

"They're not authorities?" Ghost asked. "And they're searching?"

"Super citizen types. Mack brings in crowds—men, women, you name it—and the old man organizes 'em, and sends 'em out to look. Won't be long, and they'll be here in Boomtown. Jesus," Cherone grumbled, "if it isn't one thing it's another."

"And there's no police with them?" Ghost asked again.

"They don't need 'em. They've got mobs taking your drawings everywhere, carrying handheld radios and talking to operators at their headquarters who're talking to the cops."

"Where are they?"

"North side, in a gym on tenth. They get much closer, we'll have to move. *Again.*"

"Or stop them," Ghost said.

"The boss says to cool it. The feds are crawling all over New York, and it's gettin' serious. Since the FBI asshole was hit, our people are being hauled in—and we don't always know what the fuck they're saying."

Ghost tried to reason with him. "If we don't keep up the pressure, they'll have time to regroup, and I have more work to do. We've already delayed too long."

"Have you?" Cherone shifted his eyes to the rifle in the corner, then tried to pin him with a look. "No more until the boss gives the word. Period."

Ghost didn't take the effort to reply. He was more sure than ever that he was working with the wrong people. If not for his reluctance to turn on an employer, he would have already made the switch.

"I've gotta go," Cherone said. "Thought you oughta know we may have to move again."

When the three men had left, Ghost motioned at Rashad.

"Get your coat. We're going to take a look at the gym where they're operating."

"How about the curfew?"

Ghost smiled. "Mr. Griggs has announced we're not a threat any longer. The more I hear of the man, the more I like him."

22

Sunday, February 12th

9:00 A.M.—Washington, D.C.

Not much more, Mack Hall thought, and they'd be finished at the Freedom Gymnasium. Then they'd leave the supervisors and team leaders in charge and move on to the next neighborhood.

The police considered this a mean part of town, but when they'd gathered the community leaders together and told them the purpose of their search there'd been no hesitation. This morning's response was as overwhelming among the down-and-outers, welfare mothers, and corner rappers as it had been in the plush neighborhoods. Small businesses let a percentage of their employees off to join the search. Bars and restaurants provided food.

A street map was displayed at the gym, the "neighborhood headquarters" where five men and women were assigned as supervisors. Operators relayed their instructions to search teams, each of which consisted of a leader who carried a radio, an assistant, and twenty searchers who worked in pairs and remained in contact with one another and the leaders. Different teams were assigned different blocks or apartment buildings. They missed very little. If Ghost and Rashad were hiding in the neighborhood, they'd be ferreted out.

Sam Hall had established the minimum age for volunteers at eighteen. Since it was Sunday there were hordes of kids available, so Sam declared that those from fourteen to seventeen could help with logistics, carrying coffee and boxed meals out to the volunteers and running messages to and from the groups without radios. A dozen mothers were in charge of the runners, and thus far they'd behaved themselves.

On Friday, Motorola Corporation had loaned fifty portable FM radios, extra batteries and rack chargers, and four base stations to the cause. They were already running low on portables, but not because of theft. Only two were missing, and those had been at Georgetown. The others were in use. Four hard-eyed mothers signed them out at the Freedom Gym, and gave an admonishment to each recipient to take good care of them.

Mack wondered if the neighborhood operations weren't similar to those of the U.S. Army, because his father tended to pick veterans as team leaders. Three hundred and fifty people had already been sent out of the gym, and Sam was now speaking to the leaders he'd selected for four new search teams.

Except for a handful of Latinos and whites, everyone in the group was black. Yet neither race nor gender seemed to matter with the people they'd worked with. Sam had picked blacks, whites, Latinos, men, and women to lead the various teams, and no one complained. All seemed to just be pleased to join in the effort to find the terrorists. They were tired of sleepless nights, waiting for another distant "crack," then wondering who it had been this time. Few believed Leonard Griggs's telecasts that Ghost had left and the situation was back to normal. Sam and Mack Hall said the terrorists were around, and their words held the sincere ring of truth.

Mack looked about the room. Two of his friends, rookies with the Redskins, were at the door, looking out to see if anyone was watching the building. Mack didn't believe there'd be a problem. The locals would tear anyone apart who threatened.

He glanced to the front of the room. The man with the stubble was standing near Sam, who was finishing with his briefing. Mack examined him, wondering where he'd seen him.

"You kids hush up," said a woman near the radio counter, speaking to two teenage boys who'd begun to argue. One glanced toward the front of the crowd, then turned back and raised his voice louder.

Mack looked toward the front, wondering who the boy had looked at. Pop was walking through the open door of a back room, probably to get more circulars and composite drawings.

The stubble-faced long-haired man followed Sam into the room.

Mack started forward to investigate.

The two teenagers near the radio counter started to yell at one another, then to scuffle.

"Hey, cut that out," Mack yelled, but they continued. He sighed and started over, then stopped and turned toward the front. He glanced back at the kids, who were pushing their way through the crowd. Trying to get away? *From what?*

"Pop!" Mack yelled out hoarsely as he spun about, then ran toward where his father had disappeared behind the closed door. As he pushed two men aside, Mack thought of how there'd been something familiar about the long-haired man—not apparent or glaring, but . . . *Oh Christ!*—who'd followed Pop.

The door was locked! Beyond he heard a raised voice.

Mack slammed his shoulder against the door and fell through as the hinges splintered.

Sam Hall was in the process of crumpling, clutching his throat, his knee bent unnaturally. The stubble-faced man was pulling a knife from his leg sheath, eyes on the doorway and Mack, backing toward the exit door.

Mack bellowed in anguished rage, and rushed forward.

The attacker whirled, lashed out with a foot that caught Mack squarely in the ribs. Mack fell past him, reaching out but grasping only air.

The stubble-faced man was out the exit door.

"It's Rashad," Mack yelled out to others rushing into the room. "Get him."

He bent over his father who lay like a fallen giant, bloody-faced and badly hurt and trying to draw breath into his blocked throat.

Mack cried out: "Pop!"

A woman knelt beside him. "Move aside," she said. "I'm an RN."

Mack staggered toward the still open exit door where

Rashad Taylor had disappeared, ignoring the pain that coursed through his rib cage.

"We've called for an ambulance," someone said, and Mack went back to stand protectively over his father.

Bethesda, Maryland

J.J. Davis watched the dogs sniffing excitedly around the workbench where the bombs had been constructed. J.J. didn't need dogs. He could smell the stuff.

Question the staff, he wrote on the pad to the young agent, and nodded toward the business in the adjacent building. As the agent gave instructions to the others, J.J. walked about, looking at the layout. He was angry that they hadn't found the terrorists or explosives, frustrated because Ghost had anticipated that they were closing in.

Two agents were excited about finding crumbs of explosive on the floor near the bench. He ignored them and walked toward the big cargo door opened by a supervisor from next door. The place had been sublet to a door and sash company, a start-up company that was new in the area. The lessor had been a smallish, quiet-spoken man.

One of the men they were searching for, the one who'd called himself Martin when he'd made initial arrangements for the theft of the explosives, matched the description.

Martin was believed to work for Joseph DiFazio. They'd ask more questions and look harder there. But the other half of it, finding the explosives, had just taken a step back.

An agent came in with news that a sedan and two different vans had been seen arriving and leaving the previous few days. A light-colored panel truck had hauled away a load the day before. Of those noted in the area, a reddish-hued black man with long hair and stubble-beard had been seen, accompanied by a compact man whose features no one could quite recall.

They'd continue to collect facts and descriptions, and search for another location where the tritonol might have been moved. The panel truck had been unloaded somewhere with room for a bomb lab. It could be in a house or place of business. A garage. A shed. Almost anywhere.

One thing was certain. The NSC announcement was wrong. Ghost and Rashad were still around. J.J. decided to make sure his superiors understood that, even if the NSC had them effectively gagged. He would also notify Manny DeVera, as he'd done with other discoveries.

The Farmhouse, Falls Church, Virginia

Lucky opened the front door for Doctor Grace McNabb, took her coat, then led her into the great room where the others were already seated.

"Sam Hall was attacked," he told her. "He's at Walter Reed in serious condition."

"I heard it on the news. Ghost?"

"Rashad Taylor. Mack got to him before he could finish the job or Sam would be dead."

Doctor McNabb sighed. "I was worried something like that might happen."

"You warned us. Mack thought he had it covered, but Rashad by his men."

"Anything new in your analysis?" asked Glenn Phillips.

"Not really, Senator. Just more confirmation that Ghost is without conscience."

Lucky leaned back against the bar and faced the group. "We now know two things. One, Ghost and Rashad are still around. Two, they don't like us looking for them. That means the neighborhood searches are effective. I suggest we replace Sam and Mack. Volunteers?"

Manny DeVera immediately volunteered. "I've got nothing better to do." Manny had been upbeat. Marian was aware now, even talking some. Her speech was halting, but she was awake for short periods and the doctors were encouraged.

Mack Hall hesitated as what Lucky had said sank in. He bolted to his feet. "Don't even talk about replacing me. I'm in for the duration . . . until we find Rashad."

Lucky shook his head. "You're too emotionally involved, Mack. We don't want people out there with blood in their eye. Someone will get hurt that way."

Mack set his jaw. "Things will go on just like Pop set them up. None of the teams are armed. Their instructions are to pass out composite drawings and flyers, and gather information. If someone sounds fishy, the neighborhood headquarters calls in the police. It's going to work. That's why Pop was attacked."

"Are the authorities cooperating?" asked Senator Glenn Phillips.

"An FBI agent came by and told us to lay off, that the federal authorities would handle it. Pop told him to take a hike. The local police think what we're doing is great. We're getting the cooperation of people they can't work with."

Lucky mused. "Do you mind if one of us works with you?"

"I don't want anyone else getting hurt."

"I'd like to give it a try, Mack," said Manny. "If they come around again, we'll be expecting them. I know them better than anyone here, and you've seen Rashad Taylor."

"I noticed something familiar, but it just didn't register. He didn't look like the drawing. He had long hair, sort of stringy and bushy, wore eyeglasses, and had a week's beard."

"That'll change. They're chameleons."

"There's one thing I don't think he *can* change. One side of Rashad's mouth droops."

"Link thought he did some damage. We'll add it to the descriptions."

"How about the kids who started the scuffle?" Lucky asked.

"A couple of local junkies," said Mack. "Rashad had paid 'em twenty bucks each. Told 'em he was a friend of mine and it was a joke. They didn't think it was serious and needed to make a buy. I should've been on my toes instead of talking so much."

"That's what's keeping the neighborhoods on our side, Mack," Manny said. "You keep on talking. I'll fill in for Sam and do the organizing."

Mack started to argue, but Lucky cut him off. "That's the way it is, Mack. None of us can work alone for security's sake." He regarded Doctor McNabb. "Will Ghost attack them again?"

"He may, but I spoke with Mr. DeVera and there's another consideration. Ghost may be cheating on his employers, not telling them everything—such as the shooting of Senator Smithfield. That will create inner conflict. His odd sense of honor doesn't allow him to lie, and that includes lying by omission. If he's troubled by it, he'll be more volatile than normal."

Manny raised a hand. "J.J. Davis confirmed Ghost is working with the Mafia, but with all the present heat the mafiosi are holding him back. That explains the lull. J.J. thinks it was Ghost who hit Senator Smithfield, and he was a thorn in the side of the IRA, not the Mafia."

"So Ghost may be about to switch employers," said Lucky.

"Back to his sense of honor," Doctor McNabb said. "If he's going to switch, he'll have to manufacture a reason. That may mean he'll go counter to his present employer's wishes."

"Like what?" asked Glenn Phillips.

"Something awful I'd guess, since that's what he does, but more spectacular than usual to make his employers react and give him a reason for dropping them."

"J.J. Davis had some good news," Manny said. "They discovered where Ghost unloaded the explosives and built his bombs. Ghost and Rashad were seen there just yesterday."

Lucky cocked his head. "Then Griggs has to realize they're here and they pose a threat."

Manny shook his head. "The NSC has a muzzle on the FBI, and Griggs has a group of incompetents telling him Ghost is in France. I stopped off and told my friendly reporter the attack on Sam was made by Rashad, and that Ghost and Rashad were seen yesterday. That'll be on the news, but it likely won't be enough to change Griggs's mind."

Lucky frowned. "Why's Griggs being so hesitant about Ghost? He's taking flak because of the vacillation and confusing announcements that the emergency's over. Hell, why hasn't the President replaced him? The man's destroyed the credibility of the administration."

"I'll try to speak to that one," said Grace McNabb. "Since he seems to be central on all this, I've begun a profile on Leonard Griggs."

Lucky nodded.

"He came here from Canada in 1970 for his law degree, and joined the Students for a Democratic Society, the rabid activists against the Vietnam War. To them the cause was holy and people like yourselves were the enemy. He was jailed for severely beating two policemen during a demonstration, and again for burning a chemical plant. Both times he took the rap for others and gained the support of a number of grad students, including the current President and First Lady. When Immigration tried to ship him back to Canada, the students rallied until a group of congressmen blocked the action and sponsored him for citizenship."

"That was a time of unrest," said Senator Phillips. "A lot of kids were involved."

"Perhaps," said Doctor McNabb, "but most mellowed when the war ended and they were faced with the realities of making a living. Len Griggs simply changed causes. He's supported movements to legalize drugs, halt forest harvesting, give homelands back to Native Americans, unplug all nuclear reactors, and disband the military."

"I remember," said Linda. "It hasn't been that long since he was a radical activist. He's altered his appearance dramatically."

Grace McNabb nodded in agreement. "Four years ago he made an abrupt change. T-shirts to button-downs. Negativism to avid support of all social programs embraced by his college buddy, the candidate for the White House. During the campaign he concentrated on the once-hippie-now-yuppie-still-liberal crowd. When his friend won, he asked for an obscure appointment as an assistant deputy in the State Department. Six months ago he convinced his friend a change was needed at the NSC."

"So what does all that tell us?" asked Glenn Phillips.

"One, he holds influence over the President, which may involve some unpaid debts. Two, which Leonard Griggs is real? The destructive radical or the concerned citizen?"

"Which do you think?"

"Neither. He's an actor playing a role. An opportunist with an agenda. But there's one constant. You're still the enemy, just as you were when he was in college."

"So what does that mean?" Glenn asked.

"He'll never compromise with you."

"Jesus, we've got a psycho on our hands."

Grace McNabb smiled. "Leonard Griggs believes the same about you."

4:30 P.M.—Glacier National Park, northwestern Montana

"I brought hot coffee and sandwiches," Marie called out to the man who walked toward her.

Billy Bowes smiled. "Think I couldn't hack it on water and scrawny rabbit?"

"I felt since you Cherokee were so civilized, you might get tired of killing bunnies."

He chuckled. "I tried one last night. You're right. The rest of 'em are safe."

She pulled the thermos from inside the Jeep. He poured a cup, held it in both mittened hands, sipped, and ahhed.

"No sign of Link?"

"No." Bowes looked up a mountainside.

"Were you warm enough last night?"

"I built a fire and rigged a parachute panel reflector. I actually got too hot."

"You are trained, aren't you."

"So is Link," he said, sipping coffee.

"Then why are you here?"

"Not because I'm worried about the cold or an animal mauling him."

"You're worried about someone trying to get to him?"

Bowes smiled. "Not anymore."

After examining Mr. Billy Bowes, Marie had to admit she wasn't, either.

"Did you get through to Link's parents?" he asked.

"I spoke with his mother. I travel to the Smithsonian periodically on museum business, and we've agreed to get together for lunch."

"You'll like her."

Marie smiled. "I think she knows I'm in love with Link."

Bowes didn't change expressions at the revelation. Marie wondered if she was that easy to read, and decided she was.

She nodded toward the mountain. "Will you check on him?"

Bowes shrugged. "I'll wait here and hope whatever he's doing works." He glanced at her. "You didn't answer yesterday. Do you believe in all this?"

She hesitated, sighed. "I don't know. We talk about this at work and all, but . . . I really don't know. But on one thing I'm sure. I don't want Link hurt."

23

Monday, February 13th

2:50 A.M.—Siyeh Mountain, Glacier National Park, northwestern Montana

Four days and nights had passed. The gnawing hunger had left, and he'd become unconcerned about any of it except the torturous position and the thirst. His throat was so parched, he had great difficulty summoning sufficient moisture to swallow.

The Grandfather had visited often, clearer than ever before, but he'd pushed him away. It was the *helpers* he waited for, and he was determined to continue until they appeared. Several times he'd had senseless hallucinations and babbled in his sleep, and partially awakened hopelessly stiff and numb from lying so relentlessly on the same side, all for naught.

The Grandfather returned again and again, each time more persistent.

Link tried to use reason, tell him he must leave so he could find his helpers. He did so again, his voice emerging in a dry crackle. The Grandfather's image persisted, and as Link struggled in the twilight of senses between sleep and awareness, knowledge flooded over him.

Black Wolf, most holy of Piegan medicine men—the Grandfather—was his helper.

He took a sharp breath as he recognized truth.

* * *

He is a young man, sitting in the sweat lodge. The Grandfather is beside him, his eye twinkling capriciously. "Preparation has made you no less stubborn."

"Why did I go through it, Grandfather?"

The Grandfather looks at him with surprise. "That is the way of young men."

"I am pleased you are my helper."

Was he awake or asleep? Speaking aloud or in a dream? He decided it was unimportant.

The Grandfather pulls in a deep breath of steam and whoofs it out.

The young man does the same, and the Grandfather looks on proudly. Then he frowns in concern about another matter.

Images come and leave, shown clearly. The Grandfather describes his understanding—a great medicine lodge built of stone is to be destroyed—but the young man needs no explanation. He knows what the flashing, fading, repeated visions mean.

"I must go," the young man says.

"Yes." The Grandfather nods.

Link's eyes blinked open, and he came awake. Not slowly, but as with a snap of his fingers. He knew his surroundings, for it was as if he had just crawled into the tent. He lifted himself, turned, and lay panting for a moment—his side aching from deep inside.

There was little time!

He pushed painfully to his knees. Ice had formed in a thick sheath on the fabric of the inner tent, condensation of four days of his breathing. Link removed the mittens so he could work the zipper, and with difficulty opened the flap. Delicious fresh air rushed inside.

The moon was partially cloaked by clouds, but cast sufficient light for him to avoid the precipice as he crawled from the tent into the bitter cold.

Link staggered to his feet, almost lurched into the abyss, and—pulling the coat tightly about himself—began to slog through heavy snow down the windblown path. He was overcome by a sluggishness caused by lack of water and body fuel.

He found the snowshoes stuck upright on the narrow trail, knelt, and struggled to put them on. The task was difficult. Periodically he'd stop and huff, then try again with cold-numbed fingers. The snowshoes were critical. Their web would help to negotiate deep snow, and the metal claws on bottom would allow him to walk better on ice. When he at last succeeded with the bindings, it took a mighty effort to gain his feet.

He pulled the mittens back on, then broke off an icicle hanging from a ledge and pushed it into his mouth. The first trickle of icy water entered his throat. It would take time for the dryness to be alleviated. He continued sucking on the ice as he continued downward, unable to hurry on the sheer mountainside trail.

Link lurched and fell, thankfully into the mountain, then carefully reattached a loosened binding and continued. When he finally emerged from the steep and narrow mountain trail onto a gentler area, he was utterly exhausted.

No time, his mind told him. *Keep going.*

Twice he was forced to stop, remove the snowshoes and strap them to his back, and let himself down rock faces. When he'd climbed them he'd left lengths of rope attached to pitons to make the task easier in his weakened condition, but he'd not imagined he would be so fatigued.

On the second face, he slipped, dangled and almost caught his right leg in a granite crevice. He grasped the rope and lowered himself, ran out of energy and dropped the final ten feet. The impact knocked the breath from him, and he groaned and wanted to lie there forever.

He remained immobile for several long minutes before rising, reattaching the snowshoes, and plodding on. After fifty yards his feet became lead weights.

How much farther? he wondered. It seemed he'd already walked for far too many miles. Could he have somehow missed the highway?

He staggered through a narrow defile and came onto a field that seemed larger than anything he'd encountered on the trip up the mountain. He stopped for a moment, puzzled, but knew he must continue. Somewhere at the bottom of the mountain he must encounter the road.

Would he? The road was snow-covered. *Had he passed over it?* Link went on, looking about, and did not see the drop-off as he stepped forth. He fell, tumbling helplessly, and yelped at the sharp pain as his shoulder struck a rock. He grasped tightly to the outcropping, and cautiously peered over the sheer ledge at the deadly rocks far below.

He rested for a few seconds, then stood on shaky legs.

"Here," someone called out, and he saw a shape across the dark field near a tiny, twinkling fire. Beckoning to him with a waving arm. A rifle in the other hand.

Danger! He turned and started back over the rise.

"Link?" the voice called. He paused, looked back suspiciously. The shadowy figure beckoned again from across the field, then came toward him, slogging through deep snow.

"Billy Bowes here," the man called out.

Link turned and lurched in that direction. As he drew closer, Bowes stopped and waited. "You've got the snowshoes. I've gotta get back through this stuff."

"I didn't know you'd be here," Link managed to croak.

They approached a makeshift camp. A small fire was flickering, casting radiant heat and light into a shelter, as Link had been taught to build in survival training.

"I've got to get to a phone."

"Let me break camp," Billy said. "Just take a minute." He motioned. "Thermos there with coffee, in case you're interested."

It was hot, wet, and wonderful. As Bowes rolled up his sleeping bag, then the parachute panel, Link walked a few steps farther. The highway was just beyond the trees. He saw the shape of his pickup and couldn't contain a grin. No road had never looked so good.

"Here," said Bowes, handing him a sandwich. "Your girl brought the food out."

Link took a single bite and was instantly ravenous.

"Better go easy."

"If I puke, I puke. I'm *hungry*!"

Billy Bowes led the way to the road. When they reached the truck, he dropped a duffel and pilot's kit bag in the rear and held out his hand. "Keys?"

Link produced them.

As Billy drove, a pink glow grew in the eastern sky. It would be light within an hour.

"Well?" Bowes asked. "Did it work?"

"We'll see when I make the phone call."

"Marie told me about you leaping around, trying to tear your chest apart. Know why they call us Cherokee civilized? Because we don't do crap like that."

Link finished the coffee and sighed, content. "I think it's probably just you who thinks the Cherokee are civilized."

"Nope. The U.S. government called us that just before they marched our people a thousand miles across the country in the dead of the winter."

They arrived at Marie's, and Link was quickly out of the truck. He knocked insistently. She glanced out the window only once before opening the door.

"Thank God!" she cried out, and rushed into his arms.

"I've got to make a phone call." Link's voice was urgent.

Washington, D.C.

The city news editor listened to a too-familiar voice, one he'd not heard for more than a week.

"This is Ghost." The voice was light and conversational.

"What have you got?" asked the editor, forcing himself to maintain a neutral tone.

"Looks like the weather's going to turn cruddy again."

"That's why you called?" His voice had almost cracked.

"I got up this morning and I said to myself, 'I've been ignoring my friends too much.' We need to talk more often, old buddy. I'll be calling you a lot in the days to come. I'll keep calling until Charlie's released."

The editor felt his throat tighten. "Where are you, Ghost?"

"I've just come from the Supreme Court Building. Big place. Grand, sanctimonious, more than a little ostentatious. Filled with all sorts of useless old documents and scruffy old lawyers. They need a change. Renovation. New people. I hear they're in special session this morning."

The voice paused. "I just pushed a button that's going to change all of those things."

[illegible]

[illegible]

[illegible]

[illegible]

[illegible]

[illegible]

[illegible]

[illegible]

BOOK THREE

Spirit of Black Wolf

24

Tuesday, February 14th

10:00 A.M.—The Farmhouse, Falls Church, Virginia

Link had been unable to get enough of cleanliness or eating. He'd showered and breakfasted at Marie's. After Doctor White Calf inspected his wounds and removed the sutures, he'd showered again, listened to Marie's happy chatter during the drive to Great Falls, and ate again at the airport. He'd nibbled snacks en route, and when he'd arrived home, taken a sudsy bath then devoured the bountiful dinner prepared by his mother. He'd awakened to a huge breakfast.

During the ordeal at Peshan and Glacier Park, he'd lost fourteen pounds. This morning, he wondered if they hadn't been replaced. He also felt gloriously clean.

On the flight out, Billy had told him about the Farmhouse strategy sessions.

Link knew the people gathering in the great room. Manny DeVera, Billy Bowes, Glenn Phillips, and—surprisingly—Doctor Grace McNabb.

They drank coffee and chatted. Manny said Marian's condition was improving daily. She was sitting up, talking, and was eager to rejoin the human race. She was concerned that Link felt responsibility for what had happened.

"She wants you to know she's grateful that you saved her life."

Before Link could respond, Lucky asked for attention.

"Let's open with a discussion of yesterday's show. Link called me at eight-thirty in the morning with the warning. I contacted Glenn at eight-thirty-three, and he took it from there."

The Senator nodded. "I phoned an acquaintance in Secret Service. His people commandeered a large truck parked next to the Treasury Building with a load of furniture, and pulled it up on the sidewalk in front of the van while the buildings were being evacuated."

Lucky smiled. "Lots of flying truck parts and government furniture but zero casualties."

Glenn continued. "An FBI team dropped by my office to ask how I'd gotten my information. That was a consideration I'd overlooked."

"What did you tell them?" asked Manny DeVera.

"The truth. I'm working with a network of observers who'd rather remain unidentified, and one called about a suspicious van."

The front door chime sounded. A moment later Linda led Mack Hall inside. Link had known him throughout his childhood. Mack was several years younger, but he'd always been large, agile, and athletic. Link hadn't been surprised when Mack had become an outstanding college football player, nor when he'd been signed by the pros.

Link got up and shook his hand. "I heard about Sam."

Mack looked around grimly. "I just left Pop at the hospital. Not much improvement yet."

As Mack took his seat, Linda filled him in on the discussion.

"You've got the floor," Lucky told Link. "What happened in Montana?"

Link spoke of the proud Piegan people and what had happened at the Sun Dance, including the storytelling, which drew chuckles, and the self-torture, which drew uneasy frowns.

"I was the biggest doubter of all," Link told them. "Maybe I still am. But since we were trying for realism, I went for the piercing. When the Okan was over, all I had to show for it was a sore chest. Still no dreams or insights. So I figured if you want dreams, you go to the dream house, which was a more private ritual. I guess it worked. Yesterday morning I dreamed about a white van and a stone building, and there was absolutely no doubt it was the Supreme Court."

Grace McNabb looked on avidly. "Did the Grandfather reappear?"

Link nodded. "He's the helper they talked about."

"That's logical," Doctor McNabb said. "And you think he'll return?"

"It's likely. I feel more in control of the dreams. More focused. Colonel Bowes gave me good advice on the flight out. He said not to question, just accept it and try to save lives. That's what I'm doing. I don't care if the Grandfather is a tool of my subconscious, an Indian myth, or something else. You can attempt to explain the dreams, Doctor. Just now I don't care which part of my brain is doing what. I'm going to continue working with whatever I'm given."

"I have no argument. If what you're doing works, do it."

Link's father asked if anyone had questions.

Glenn Phillips spoke. "The minute Link gets another of his insights, call so I can alert the appropriate people. We'll keep an unlisted line open. If I'm not in, tell Erin. The rest of my staff are efficient, but they talk too much and we don't want our source compromised."

"Especially to Leonard Griggs," Manny DeVera said with a sour look.

"Or Ghost," Doctor McNabb added.

Glenn Phillips was reflective. "Ghost's still got the initiative. If we'd been just a few minutes later, there'd have been another disaster." He turned to Grace McNabb. "What can we expect from him next?"

"Ghost failed, so he's in turmoil. He may blame it on the situation with his employer and break away. If he realizes he was second-guessed, he may try to eliminate the source again."

"Will he continue with the atrocities, or can we expect another period of respite?"

"What did he say during his latest call to the newspaper?"

"The transcript hasn't been released outside the NSC. Not even to the Intelligence Committee. All we know is that a call was made."

"During this period of worsening relations with his employer, he'll try to rationalize everything. It will be more important than ever that he tells the truth. Ghost isn't as complex as many would believe. He's quite predictable. Ghost will do whatever he said."

"Is there a way to get our hands on the transcript?" Lucky asked.

Manny mused. "J.J. Davis might be a bet, but he's out of town."

"He's not investigating the explosion?"

"He took a look and wrote there was nothing new about the bomb. 'Classic Ghost,' he wrote. Now he's in New York chasing a lead. By the way, J.J.'s a different man. He doesn't look like a beach ball any longer." Manny grinned. "More like a football with skinny legs."

Lucky wasn't smiling. "Glenn, how about your effort?"

"I'm taking a Senate delegation to meet with the President day after tomorrow. It wasn't easy to set up since he's been damned near incommunicado to everyone, Congress included. One of our goals is to convince him to reinstate ITF-four."

"Good luck on getting past Griggs," Lucky said. "Next issue. Security of our people."

Colonel Bowes was thoughtful. "Doctor McNabb says Ghost may look for the reason he failed. He figured it out before. Is there a way to get federal protection for Link?"

Manny snorted. "Not with Leonard Griggs in charge. He'd respond with sarcasm."

Glenn Phillips agreed. "Griggs has a lock on the Secret Service and the FBI."

"Then we should keep Link here at the Farmhouse. How many can you sleep, Linda?"

"There's four unused bedrooms. Three now that Link's here."

"My house is available," said Senator Phillips, who lived two miles distant.

Billy shook his head. "I can set up security better here, where we've got a view of the surrounding area. I'll move into one of the bedrooms."

Mack Hall stirred. "Same here."

Billy regarded Lucky. "I'd like to hire a couple of security guards for night patrols. They're at a premium around Washington, so we'd have to fly them in from out of town."

Lucky nodded. "Go ahead." He looked at Mack and Manny DeVera. "Next subject: the neighborhood searches. Is everything back on track?"

Manny smiled. "Mack packs 'em in. We set up an entire search effort yesterday, and it's going like clockwork. After yesterday's attempt on the Supreme Court, Motorola offered fifty more radios, and they'll be on the streets today."

"This afternoon we're setting up in an area the locals call Boomtown," said Mack. "I dropped by their meeting hall last night. A pair of FBI agents showed up and tried to discourage them, saying counterterrorism was a federal matter. The local leaders said, 'counter-huh?,' told them to butt out, and invited me onstage. They expect four hundred searchers by noon."

Lucky looked around. "Anything we haven't covered?"

There was no response, so Lucky adjourned. As they filed from the room, Lincoln Anderson felt a glow of happiness. They were finally on the offensive.

2:00 P.M.—Teaneck, New Jersey

J.J. Davis looked out at the home from the rear seat of the unmarked government sedan, thinking about the various vague indications that Joseph DiFazio might be involved. Since his name had arisen in the investigation, a dozen others had surfaced. Families of wise guys intertwined, but no one at the pinnacle. The office had been inundated, sinking in a quagmire of connections when J.J. had decided to fly up for a look.

They'd shown him spiderweb matrices they believed were organizational charts of the New York Mafia. When he'd asked where Joseph DiFazio fit in, they weren't sure. Two supervisors believed he was retired from the scene.

"He was never a mover and shaker," one said. "Came out of the Roslyndale section of Boston in the fifties and hung around the fringes here. Did a lot of traveling to Italy—maybe as a messenger. Never associated with the airport or waterfront rackets, or a single murder. We watched him because of his association with the Gambinos, but then he started keeping his distance from them, too."

They'd been ready to write him off. Yet J.J. remembered the informant in Rome who had said Joseph DiFazio had met with Salvator Riina. The man named Martin, who had set up the theft of the explosives, had worked with another who worked for DiFazio. So Martin likely worked for DiFazio, too.

Let's take him in 4 a closer look, J.J. had written on his pad the previous evening. J.J. Davis watched the two agents ring the doorbell. An elderly man in shirtsleeves answered. He looked bewildered, like someone's elderly uncle might if confronted by federal agents. He went back for a coat, then followed them out, smiling nervously, and was helped into a dark sedan.

The agents would take him to the Newark office. Question and answer sessions often revealed a lot about men living in the netherworld of crime.

The sedan across the street pulled away. J.J. waited. Two minutes had passed when the garage door opened and a car pulled out. As it accelerated past, J.J. saw two men in front.

Recognize them? J.J. wrote on the pad.

The agent driver from the New York office had fixed both men. One had been a top lieutenant for the Gambinos, the other a known but unindictable killer. Both were important in the Mafia, now relegated to being bodyguards for the man who looked like someone's uncle.

They drove to the Newark FBI office, hurried upstairs, and entered the interrogation room where two agents had Joseph DiFazio seated and were reading his rights. Before J.J. settled, a team of four lawyers was making their way into the room.

The questioner waited until they were seated. "Do you know a man named Martin?"

"Martin who?" answered DiFazio.

Little things, J.J. told himself. Martin was likely a first, not a last name.

"Do you know a man called Ghost?"

"What I see on television, he's an asshole. Blows up people."

"Do you know anything about the theft of explosives at the Rocky Mountain Arsenal in Denver, Colorado?"

DiFazio frowned, looked toward the lawyers, then back to the agent.

A lawyer raised a manicured hand. "What is the purpose of this . . . intrusion?"

"We have reason to believe Mr. DiFazio is aware of how the theft was set up."

"I don't understand how . . ."

The FBI questioner cut him off. "The explosives were

used on the White House and at Walter Reed Hospital. They destroyed a helicopter that was sent for the Vice President. They killed the director of the Bureau, and almost blew up the Supreme Court Building yesterday. *That's* the purpose of this intrusion on Mr. DiFazio's home life."

The lawyer glanced at his colleagues, then whispered to his client, drew his ear close to Joseph DiFazio's mouth and listened. When he spoke it was in a low voice. "Mr. DiFazio hasn't been out of Teaneck during the past month."

"I been at home," said DiFazio, trying to smile.

J.J. watched closely. The man was shaken, but the questioning went nowhere. Half an hour later, Joseph DiFazio left with the lawyers after refusing a ride home courtesy of the FBI.

The interrogator looked at J.J. "Bingo," he murmured.

The regional director burst into the room. He'd watched from the other side of the glass. "Each of those lawyers run five hundred per. He blew five grand having them sit there with their fingers in their noses."

The agent who'd accompanied J.J. in the sedan told about the men who had followed DiFazio from his home. "He has high-powered help."

Keep watching! J.J. wrote on his pad. Then he added, *Make sure he knows U'r doing it.*

The regional director thought over J.J.'s suggestion, then nodded to the agent-in-charge. "Do it. In the meantime keep looking at the smoke screens. Maybe we'll get someone to crack and explain why so many people are ready to take the fall."

Find out who Martin X is? J.J. wrote.

The regional director added the instruction to the agents. J.J. followed him from the room. "Heading back to D.C., J.J.?" the man asked happily.

He nodded.

"I don't envy you. With the director gone, Leonard Griggs is knee-deep in our business there. Any leads on who'll take over the Bureau."

J.J. shook his head in the negative.

"Got time for dinner before you leave?"

J.J. wagged his head again. The food in the area was great. In normal times he could not imagine turning down a meal, but with the pap he was limited to, it didn't matter where he ate. He hitched up his trousers. Since the shooting he'd gone through six new pairs, diminishing from size sixty-four down to size forty-two.

But J.J. Davis was pleased. The wires on his jaw would be removed the following week, and he was a step closer to Ghost.

8:00 P.M.—Boomtown, Washington, D.C.

Martin Cherone was livid as he slammed into the living room. Two days ago he'd berated Ghost for Rashad's attack at the Freedom Gym, but he'd been conspicuously absent following the attempt at the Supreme Court. Ghost had wondered if he wasn't awaiting new instructions.

"You were supposed to lay off, for Christ's sake," Cherone screamed.

The two men behind Cherone looked around suspiciously with their careful eyes.

"What you wanted wasn't according to my plan," Ghost said in his soft voice.

Cherone pointed a trembling finger. "It didn't even work, you crazy asshole. You blew up a fucking truck."

Ghost gave him a thin smile. The employer had finally crossed the line.

"You fucked it up, and they've got feds watching the boss."

"*Your* boss," Ghost corrected in a soft voice. He could no longer work with them. Unfortunate, he thought, but they'd brought it on.

Cherone turned to eye his men. He was, Ghost knew, trying to decide on the best course. There was only one way the partnership could be dissolved.

Rashad entered silently, stood just inside the door to take in the situation, then stepped farther into the room on cat's feet, remaining behind the Mafia men.

"Is everything packed?" Ghost asked him. An hour earlier the wayfinder had called. The search teams were closing in.

The mafiosi whipped their heads about. One touched his jacket with his right hand, reassuring himself, poising it there. The other scowled.

"The statue's done like you wanted," said Rashad. "I'm not finished moving the cones."

"Thinking of going somewhere?" Cherone asked sharply.

Ghost stared at Rashad. "It's cleanup time," he said.

Rashad smiled, reached down with his right hand.

Cherone's face flushed as he regarded Ghost. "'You're not going anywhere," he snapped, unaware that Rashad had lifted his pant leg. "That's an order."

The razor-sharp blade flashed, slid cleanly into the first gunman's kidney. Rashad swept the hand in a violent arc, slashing the second man's throat as he reached into his jacket. Both men staggered. One fell. The other slowly knelt, and the blade flashed again. He dropped, almost decapitated. It was over very quickly.

Cherone's mouth drooped, his face turned chalky white. He eyed Rashad and back-pedaled. "Jesus," he whispered.

Rashad followed, the crimsoned blade held upward in his grip, eyes unwavering on Martin Cherone's face.

"Not me," Cherone pleaded to Ghost. "You promised."

"You broke the agreement," Ghost said calmly.

Cherone's eyes were fixed on the knife blade, his chest rising and falling dramatically. He cautiously reached into his jacket, as if by moving slowly Rashad might not notice.

Rashad turned, kicked hard, snapping the knee. Cherone's squeal was cut off by a knuckle-blow to his throat. He grasped at a chair then dropped to the floor, mouth opening like a just-landed fish, unable to utter meaningful sounds, fingers grasping at his damaged throat.

"Finish him," Ghost said, then frowned and looked up at the curtained window.

Rashad tossed the knife to his killing hand and lashed out in an arc. Cherone's fingers were severed in the same sweep that cut his throat.

"Hurry," Ghost said quickly, avoiding the newest spout of blood and thrashing body as he started for the door. He could sense imminent danger.

"How about our clothes?" Rashad asked.

"No time." Ghost led the way out, then to the rear garage door and inside. A Ford van waited, the third that had been provided them.

The eagle was crated and nestled in one side of the van, but Rashad hadn't finished loading the cones. The feeling of urgency was growing. Ghost slammed the cargo doors closed.

"Drive," he called out sharply. He opened the garage

door, then hurried back to climb into the passenger's seat as Rashad gunned the engine to life.

"Now!" he said emphatically.

The heavily laden van roared backward, spewing gravel on the driveway. One of the watchers scurried to keep from being run over. "Hey!" he yelled angrily.

"Keep going," Ghost breathed. The feeling was pronounced.

He saw them. Two groups coming down either side of the street to their fore, another from their rear.

A nearby woman gawked and peered into the van. "It's them!"

"They've seen us," Rashad said, looking about at the converging groups.

"Straight ahead!" Ghost said forcefully.

Rashad accelerated, almost hitting a man who rushed onto the street to stop them.

"Faster!" Ghost urged.

They squealed around the first corner, sped for two blocks, then turned again.

"Get onto the Beltway," Ghost said, his heart pounding. Kevin Gilroy would meet them in College Park. They'd just changed employers.

As Rashad drove up the ramp leading to the Interstate Beltway, Ghost counted the numbers of tritonol cones. There weren't as many as he'd hoped. Rashad had remembered to bring the rifle, but Ghost would much prefer more explosives. Kevin Gilroy would be able to augment it, but that would take time.

In the meanwhile he'd be frugal, use less compound and focus the charges carefully. Ghost took heart. The bas-relief statue was safe. The wayfinder's phone call had warned them in time, and now they were done with the reluctant employer. He could concentrate on the relentless campaign. *And* on another matter, for someone had forewarned the Secret Service and stopped the van bomb from destroying the Supreme Court Building. That someone was likely A. L. Anderson. The wayfinder had learned of his activities at the reservation. The Piegan had held a holy Okan for A. L. Anderson and now he'd returned.

The Bull Clan had decided Ghost needed no such ritual. His senses had been focused during his time with old man Weiser. He heard the urgings of his helper very clearly.

As Rashad continued toward College Park, Ghost's mind turned to an idea he'd been thinking about to reach out to the next victim on his list. Although it was mid-February, the day had been unseasonably clear and warm, and tomorrow was forecast to be the same. On such days the minds of a number of Washington's less-than-sane citizens turned to golf. Local clubs and public courses remained open year-round and were used on all but the stormiest days.

Kevin Gilroy should have no trouble getting his hands on the things he'd need.

Ghost's concern was that A. L. Anderson might interfere again. He thought of a way to delay him, if the IRA had a sympathizer within the proper organization. It was unfortunate that he had to go to such lengths, but Ghost had not been sufficiently persuasive the last time he'd confronted Anderson. His helper had been angry with him for not destroying his brother.

The helper was always right.

Ghost would have to deal with A. L. Anderson.

25

Wednesday, February 15th

8:29 A.M.—The Farmhouse, Falls Church, Virginia

"I made more coffee," Lucky said as he joined the other men at the kitchen table for the eight-thirty news special. Mack Hall and Billy Bowes had joined them at the Farmhouse.

"You're the star this morning, Mack," said Link. The report would likely be about yesterday's discovery of Ghost's hideaway.

The familiar face of the news analyst appeared. His words were clipped and neutral. "The following video is *said* to be of a press conference recorded this morning, although we weren't informed of any such conference. The tape was provided to all major networks by the executive branch. We will air it unseen, as requested, but reserve the right to comment."

The analyst's image faded, replaced by Leonard Griggs, seated at his desk with U.S. and Executive Branch flags on either side. Opposite him sat the spokeswoman for the White House.

Griggs smiled warmly. "I'd like to open with an announcement. Last evening, acting on leads provided by my staff, the Washington Metropolitan Police discovered the home used by terrorists to construct explosive devices and plan the recent atrocities."

Mack Hall frowned. "The NSC didn't have anything to do with finding it."

"At the scene we found clothing, maps, electronic equipment, and the bodies of three men yet to be identified. Most importantly, we recovered the remainder of the stolen explosives."

Griggs turned to the spokeswoman and introduced her, saying she'd pose questions suggested by various of the news media.

"Mr. Director, is the President aware of this latest development?"

"The President was briefed immediately after the hideout was located. He's relieved that the worst of the crisis is now over and would have conducted this conference himself if he weren't inundated with the day-to-day activities of world leadership."

"Were the dead men found at the scene members of Ghost's Gang?"

"As of yet, we have no idea. Unfortunately, they were killed by a vigilante group."

"That's a lie," Mack Hall cried out. "The search teams waited for the police. *They* went in and found the bodies."

The spokeswoman went on. "Can we be sure the home was used by Ghost's group?"

"FBI criminalists have confirmed their fingerprints. Also, two persons matching the descriptions of Ghost and Rashad Taylor were reported leaving the home in a blue van. Last night we located such a vehicle gutted by fire some twenty-five miles away in rural Maryland."

The spokeswoman nodded. "And how would you describe the present situation? Should the citizens of Washington continue to be concerned?"

Griggs smile was fatherly. "The terrorists are no longer in Washington. Throughout the night we've followed reports of two men matching their descriptions fleeing the area. They were almost captured in a roadblock in western Pennsylvania. At my direction the FBI, in conjunction with local authorities, are mounting an intensive manhunt."

"Thank God," said Lucky.

Mack shook his head. "He lied about the rest of it. I don't believe anything he's saying."

Old composites of Ghost and Rashad were shown. The spokeswoman recited: "These men were last reported between Harrisburg and Mifflintown. Citizens should consider both to be armed and dangerous. Sightings should be reported to the number shown on the screen."

An 800 prefix telephone number flashed at the bottom of the screen.

Griggs smiled. "Ghost no longer possesses tools of destruction, and we'll soon have him in custody. I implore our citizens to ignore those who would have them take the law into their hands, and ask the vigilante gangs roving the streets of Washington to immediately disband."

Mack was outraged. "They're working their butts off, and he calls them vigilantes?"

"Mr. Director, do you have a message for Ghost if he's watching this broadcast?"

"I certainly do. Revolutionaries are in themselves not evil. Americans revere patriots like George Washington, Martin Luther King, and the brave men and women who dared to become fugitives within their own country to resist the evil war in Vietnam."

Mack exploded. "Now he's comparing terrorists and deserters with George Washington and Doctor King!"

"Ghost, I implore you to turn yourself in. I understand how you may have come to distrust authorities and their misuse of power, just as have many others before you. Call the number shown below, and I *promise* you will be received with due fairness and respect."

"I can't believe this guy," said Mack, livid.

The spokeswoman sat back. "Any final comments, Mr. Director?"

Leonard Griggs smiled. "With these developments in mind, the President has directed the National Security Council to lift the remainder of the state of emergency. Although Ghost and Taylor must still be considered dangerous, they no longer pose a threat to Washington citizens or the national infrastructure."

"Thank you, Mr. Director," said the spokeswoman.

Griggs's face faded, and that of the network analyst reappeared. After a few seconds of thoughtfulness, he shook his head somberly. "I am appalled that Mr. Griggs chose to call his soliloquy a news conference. I assure you the questions we would have posed would have been different from those so obviously staged. Such as why the director insists on repeatedly making announcements that the nation is no longer in peril when Ghost remains at large? Why he attacks the laudable efforts of retired General Sam Hall and his popular son, football player Mack Hall, in organizing the citizens of Washington to seek out Ghost and Rashad?"

"That's better," Billy Bowes told Mack, who was still seething.

"There will undoubtedly be numerous polls conducted today, and more than a few will ask the nation's response to Mr. Griggs's newest statement that the emergency is over, and whether stringent measures shouldn't be imposed to protect us until Ghost is apprehended. Mr. Griggs's abhorrence of all things reeking of the establishment, or of the willingness of citizens to pitch in and help, does not extend to the rest of the nation as he seems to believe."

"Yeah!" said Mack. "I like this guy."

"This reporter is beginning to smell the distinct aroma of rotten fish coming from the National Security Council. I wonder how long it will take the American people to come to the conclusion that enough is enough. Whether or not Ghost and Rashad Taylor are on the run in the Poconos or anywhere else should be thoroughly investigated, but so should the too-often unfounded statements of the esteemed director. Thank you, and good morning."

Lucky muted the sound. "With Griggs so unpopular, why does the President keep him around?"

"That one's easy," said Manny. "Who's giving the President his briefings?"

Boomtown, Washington, D.C.

J.J. Davis stood near the sidewalk, watching as yet another crew went through the garage. They'd examined both the house and the garage throughout the night and morning. In a corner of the garage 1,800 pounds of tritonol cones rested on the floor.

The newly appointed FBI deputy director, criminal division, walked from the open maw of the garage door. He smiled. "We finally got it, eh, J.J.?"

Davis showed him his pad. *There's 800 to 900 lbs missing.*

The deputy director chuckled. "We had five positive sightings of Ghost and Rashad in Pennsylvania last night, driving a Ford Escort. There's no way they could have packed that much explosives in the thing. And . . ." he nodded toward the garage, "I've got two men over there who say that's all of it. You're putting in too many hours, J.J."

Davis pulled back the pad and scribbled.

An agent hurried up to the deputy director. "They just found the Escort."

"Where?"

"Thirty-five miles from Mifflintown. They blew the engine and abandoned it on a back road on Jack's Mountain. The state troopers are bringing in bloodhounds."

"Did they find explosives in the car?"

"No, sir. But they left a valise with a false bottom and two passports. The photos show Ghost and Rashad in disguise."

The deputy director's eyes glittered. "Tell the state troopers to get the hell out of the way. This is a federal matter."

"We're sending a new agent-in-charge by helicopter." He named a man-tracking expert from the Quantico training program. "We'll have fifty agents on the scene within an hour."

"I want our people to make the capture . . . period."

"Yes, sir." The agent left them, looking pleased with himself.

The deputy director grinned at J.J. "Now what do you think?"

J.J. showed him what he'd written: *I know Ghost. We R being scammed.*

The deputy director's smile faded. He turned and stalked toward the garage.

J.J. sighed heavily as he went to his vehicle. He had to take his knowledge to someone who would listen.

1:34 P.M.—The Farmhouse, Falls Church, Virginia

Link was experiencing an undercurrent of emotion that increasingly pervaded his thoughts. For the past hour he'd sensed something was wrong but couldn't comprehend the source. He walked almost aimlessly through the house, wondering if it was something he'd forgotten.

"You okay, pard?" asked Billy Bowes. He was upbeat.

Two security guards were being flown in with German shepherds, and would arrive within the hour at the airport.

Link went to his room, took a chair near the window, and stared out at the open field. A 12-gauge pump shotgun leaned in the corner, a box of double-aught buckshot beside it. Billy Bowes had positioned similar weapons at strategic locations throughout the house.

He observed the large field below, saw Billy driving his parents' minivan down the lane, on his way to pick up the guards. There were no strange vehicles in the area, but it wasn't worry over their personal security that bothered him. Something less definable niggled at his mind.

A car pulled into the lane—Link recognized Manny DeVera's sedan—and the driver stopped and chatted with Billy before proceeding. There was a passenger.

The odd feeling of something amiss lingered, grew stronger. Link leaned his head back and closed his eyes, wondering. His mind slowed.

Chevy Chase, Maryland

The truck driver, a burly black man with long, braided hair, wearing large-framed sunglasses, went to the rear and slid open the door, then pulled down twin ramps. Inside was a golf cart. He climbed into the cargo area, and a moment later drove the cart down the ramps, trying not to jostle it too harshly. He'd been told there'd be no problem, even though 300 pounds of explosives were packed into the rear of the cart. He had faith in the man who'd told him.

He drove onto the side of the fairway, stopped, and waited.

Of all humans, golfers were craziest. It was February, for God's sake. There'd been two days of sun, and even with the chill factor lingering near forty, the place was crowded with idiots.

Nearby, three members of a foursome huddled in heavy jackets, discussing the lie of a ball and whether the man should use a three wood rather than the iron he'd selected. He ignored them, set up, and drove the ball . . . and squealed in anguish as it swerved leftward.

"The unhappy hooker," one called to the golfer, who responded with a scowl. He took off at a brisk walk, the others following in an identical cart to the one at the side of the fairway.

Rashad pulled his golf hat lower, swiveled his head, and saw the green Suburban pass by, then pull into an empty spot some two hundred yards from the truck.

The Farmhouse, Falls Church, Virginia

Link bolted upright in the chair, eyes alert. The images had come and left quickly, clearly, urgently. There was little time! He pushed to his feet and hurried from the bedroom.

Two men were in the kitchen with Lucky, one of them a shell of the man who'd been J.J. Davis. The other was Manny DeVera, speaking angrily about federal agents who had broken up Mack Hall's latest neighborhood search effort.

"We tried to ignore them," Manny said, "but they showed a cease and desist order."

"Who signed it?" Lucky asked.

"The U.S. District Court. Mack's there now, along with half of the Washington city council, raising hell and trying to get it reversed. It's Griggs. I know it."

Supervising Agent Davis nodded his agreement.

"J.J. says Ghost's still around and he's got explosives. He thinks someone's leaving a fake trail in Pennsylvania, but no one will listen. Griggs has the FBI and the Secret Service walking in lock step."

As he approached, Link felt another wave of foreboding. "I've had another input. Ghost is about to bomb another home."

"Damn!" exclaimed Manny DeVera.

"Where?" Lucky asked.

"Large. Lots of greenery around." Link closed his eyes, then nodded. "Maybe a park. Something like that." He opened his eyes. "There's not much time."

Chevy Chase, Maryland

Rashad fastened rods to brackets at either side of the steering wheel, and finished by connecting a dangling RCA jack into the base mount of a small radio antenna.

A twosome stopped nearby. "Having trouble?"

"I've got it fixed," Rashad said, smiling his thanks.

When they'd left, he turned toward the parked Suburban, then looked back at the golf cart. Although there was no driver, he heard a clicking sound. The electric motor whined to life, and the cart moved forward a few feet. The steering wheel moved first right, then left.

The radio control was working as advertised. Ghost was in the Suburban, observing both the cart and the objective, pushing buttons and moving small levers on an RC box.

Rashad went back to the truck, slid the ramps up and into position, closed the cargo door, then walked forward to the cab. Before he climbed into the driver's seat, Rashad looked back to where he'd left the golf cart. A group was directly in front of it, another foursome just behind.

Ghost would have to delay until the golfers moved on.

The Farmhouse, Falls Church, Virginia

"The house," Manny blurted. "Describe the house again."

Link's eyes were closed, the clear image before him. "White. Dark trim. Large, with gables on the second floor." He was concentrating hard, his speech erupting in rushes of words like machine-gun bursts.

"More," breathed Manny.

Lucky remained watchful and quiet. J.J. Davis looked on in disbelief.

"Lots of flora. Not a park, though. The house is beside . . . a golf course?"

"Who lives there?"

"A man and a woman . . . they're downstairs." He huffed a breath. "We've got to hurry."

"Draw it," said Manny.

J.J. Davis pushed his pad and pen across the kitchen table.

As Link bent over the paper his hand trembled, not from fear but from anxiety that he might not be quick enough. He drew lines. "Grassy areas, like fairways." He drew the box of the house, then the gables and entrance. He added windows and lifted his hand. "Recognize it?"

"Keep going."

"The man's got . . . white hair."

J.J. snatched up the pad and stared at the drawing. He scribbled on the side of the drawing: *CHEVY CHASE. SPEAKER OF HOUSE.*

Lucky lifted the phone and punched the speed dial button.

"I'd like to speak with . . ." He drew back and stared at the phone, then punched the second line button.

"It's dead," he announced. "The damned telephone's dead."

CAR PHONE? J.J. scribbled.

"Yeah," said Lucky as he started for the door. The others hurried behind him.

Let it be in time, Link pleaded as they ran toward the automobile.

Chevy Chase, Maryland

The Speaker of the House of Representatives, second in line in the hierarchy of the succession to the presidency of the United States of America, was in his living room with his wife, finishing the speech he'd give that evening to a joint session of the House and Senate, called in response to Leonard Griggs's latest announcement and the current crisis of government.

He looked up in anticipation. "What do you think?" His wife was his most trusted critic, as she'd been since he'd first run for office thirty-two years before.

"It's good," she said, "but do you really want to come down that hard on them."

"The President acts as if he's paralyzed, won't even come out of hiding, and Len refuses to take appropriate action. Something has to be done."

The telephone rang, but it was a muted sound and he waved his hand in dismissal.

"The entire nation feels that way, but you should still temper the rhetoric. Hit them with the old velvet hammer, not a cudgel."

The telephone in his office began to ring. His *utterly* private line.

"Damn," he muttered. He sighed. "I'll be just a moment." As he started to turn away, he glanced out at the side lawn and the fairway beyond, and frowned. One of the

golf course's electrically powered carts was moving directly toward the house. He peered closer.

"No one's in that golf cart," he muttered to himself.

The cart continued, passing a Secret Service agent who began to lope after it, yelling out.

He paled. "Get down!" he yelled and dove for his wife.

"What are you doing?" she screamed as he pulled her off the easy chair and sprawled atop her on the floor.

Nothing happened.

He continued to crouch protectively over her.

"What's happening?" she huffed from beneath him, her voice now unsure.

He felt increasingly foolish, wondering if he'd seen what he'd believed he had, yet he didn't want to move too soon. It was likely explainable, but . . .

They did not hear the massive explosion that ripped through the central portion of the house facing the fairway. The Speaker's limbs were torn away, as were those of his wife. Their torsos were blown a hundred yards through the back of the home and came to rest at the edge of the fourteenth fairway in a mass of shredded furnishings and building debris.

Kevin Gilroy's face was blanched as he drove from the golf course, unable to restrain himself from looking back through the mirror at the column of dark gray smoke.

"Don't speed," said Ghost as he lifted the cellular telephone.

Ghost had delayed the call, making sure the cart was not somehow intercepted. In the interest of conserving explosive, he'd wanted the bomb to be detonated very near the objective. The golf cart had worked precisely as he'd planned.

"I'd like to speak with Mr. Carter in your editorial department," Ghost said to the *Post* receptionist. "No. It's quite a serious matter, but I'll hold for him."

They were in a nondescript nine-year-old green GMC Suburban, and had not been challenged. The emergency in the Capitol city had been lifted. The Pennsylvania mountains were swarming with searchers, though, looking for two men who resembled Ghost and Rashad. That had been the wayfinder's idea. Kevin Gilroy had found and paid the men, and was impressed. The wayfinder had also advised

Ghost to make an addition to his normal phone call to the *Post.*

"Jesus," Gilroy muttered for the third time since the explosion.

"Mr. Carter," his passenger said into the mouthpiece, "This is Ghost." He chuckled. "No, I'm the real thing. Are you having trouble with copycat calls?"

Gilroy looked at Ghost incredulously. It was as if he were chatting with a friend.

"Let me prove I'm really who you don't want to think I am. Precisely one minute and ten seconds ago I set off one of my toys at the home of your esteemed Speaker of the House. Now, got your recorder going? Good. This morning I heard Mr. Griggs tell us the emergency is over. I agree and *strongly* suggest that there be no more foolishness about curfews, military police, and such. They won't do any good, and it's an utter waste of taxpayers' money."

Ghost covered the mouthpiece and motioned. "Slower. Rashad's parked up ahead on the right. Pick him up, don't run over him for Christ's sake."

He spoke to the editor again. "Still there? Now here's another suggestion. Charlie's at Joliet, in isolation. He's to be *immediately* moved to a more civilized and private room. Within the next two days, I would also like the President to announce on national television how he will unconditionally release Charlie and guarantee his safety."

Rashad Taylor opened the back door and crawled into the seat. Kevin Gilroy pulled back into the traffic.

"If those things are not done, I'll go to the next person on my list." He listened politely and smiled. "Sure I'll tell you. It's the President. I was only trying to get his attention before. This time I won't miss."

26

Thursday, February 16th

8:00 A.M.—National Military Command Center, Pentagon, Washington, D.C.

Glenn Phillips and six other senators approached the National Military Command Center. Two men in open-neck shirts and sport jackets guarded the entrance.

As they showed their identification, Glenn frowned. "Isn't the command center normally guarded by military policemen?" he asked.

"We're army, sir," said one of the guards. "Director Griggs says the President doesn't like uniforms around him. Says they make him nervous."

"Thank you," Glenn said grimly. He'd graduated from West Point and served in the military for seventeen years. Only a medical discharge after being brutalized as a POW had kept him from serving longer. The fact that Leonard Griggs and the President were serious when they disparaged military personnel wasn't lost on Lieutenant Colonel (USAF, Retired) Glenn Phillips.

"The senators are here," said the second guard into a telephone receiver.

The door opened, and they were met by a young man in a dark blazer. "I'm Captain Doyle Baker, U.S. Marine Corps." He spoke the words tersely, as if challenging them to remark about his affiliation. "I'll be your escort officer. This way, please."

He stopped at an inner door with a red light glowing over it. "Inside is the new domestic situation room. Beyond the DSR are remodeled private sleeping quarters, a new recreation facility, and a kitchen for the President's family, staff, and NSC members. The DSR opens onto the emergency tunnel connecting with the primary government facilities in the Capitol area."

"How long will we have to wait?" asked a senator, eyeing the red light.

"The morning situation briefing should be over shortly."

Glenn leaned toward the captain. "Could we speak in private."

"Certainly, sir."

Glenn stepped a few paces away. "You're one of the briefing officers?"

"Yes, sir. We provide intelligence and situation reports for the senior staff."

"You brief the President?"

"Sometimes." He looked as if he were about to add something, then stopped himself.

Glenn looked around. "I worked in a command post similar to this in Wiesbaden, Germany as a captain."

"You're highly regarded here, sir. Not many are supporting the military these days."

He looked at the marine captain. "The country's in a mess, Baker."

The captain pursed his lips thoughtfully.

"Is the President getting the straight word about what's going on in the outside world?"

The captain paused thoughtfully, then shook his head. "That's according to your perspective, sir. They talk as if Ghost is ten feet tall and can choose his victims as he wishes, that they don't dare let the public know how bad it is or there'd be chaos."

"What do you think?"

"We should declare martial law to button the city down, put a fighting vehicle on every corner to protect the citizens, and send out military police patrols to capture the bastards."

"What did the President say when you told him that?"

"When we're asked a question, we write it down and give the answer to the White House briefing team. They make most of the presentations, too."

"Does the President leave the building often?"

"Neither he nor the First Lady leave the shelter area at all. They're told it's unsafe."

"Do they have access to television and radio?"

"Their briefers go through all the newscasts and record highlights, then Director Griggs holds a dog and pony show each night at eight o'clock. The joke around here is they make ice cream out of horse manure."

"Green light," called out one of the senators. "They're ready for us."

"Thank you," Glenn said to the captain. He turned to rejoin his colleagues.

"One last thing, sir. The President may be in the dark about some things, but he sure isn't trying very hard to find out more."

In contrast to the stark NMCC, the DSR was sumptuously appointed. The walls were oaken wainscot, topped by Williamsburg-blue wallpaper adorned with expensive abstract art. Overstuffed leather chairs were set about a glistening teak conference table.

At the head was the President. On his immediate right was Director Leonard Griggs. Six other men and the White House spokeswoman sat about the table.

The President smiled as they entered. His right forearm was still in a cast, his once-youthful face etched with worry lines.

Leonard Griggs rose to his feet. "Gentlemen," he said in greeting. His eyes and expression were carefully neutral.

Glenn started for one of the dozen empty seats at the conference table, but an aide quietly said, "Over here, sir," and led them to chairs set up at one side of the room.

Glenn Phillips remained standing as the others took their seats.

Griggs spoke first. "I apologize that the President couldn't work more time for you into his busy schedule. There's only twenty minutes until his next scheduled meeting."

"We asked for an hour."

Griggs lifted his shoulders helplessly.

Glenn began. "Mr. President, our group is bipartisan, formed by direction of two standing committees. I'm from Intelligence. My cochairman is from Judicial, and as you know is a member of your party."

Glenn's cochairman nodded from his chair. "Good morning, Mister President."

The President raised his good hand, holding the smile.

Glenn looked at Griggs. "We'd prefer to speak *privately* with the President."

The President glanced about the table. "I asked Len and his team to sit in."

"You may wish to reconsider," said Glenn.

Leonard Griggs cleared his throat. "I believe the President can determine whom he wishes to be present."

"Of course." Glenn Phillips's voice was steady. "Mr. President, our constituents are demanding we take action to end the crisis, and the same is happening to our colleagues in the House. But each time we try to see you, Len Griggs tells us you're too busy."

The President sighed. "We've been meeting almost constantly," he explained.

"Out first agenda item is to ask you to reinstate the recently dismantled Interdepartmental Task Force Four. ITF-four was on the right track with their suggestions about how to handle the emergency."

"We don't agree," said Griggs.

The President appeared surprised. "I had them moved under Len to provide emphasis, not dismantle them." He looked at Griggs. "Have the members complained?"

"Certainly not."

"The organization has been emasculated," said Glenn.

"I'll look into it," said the President.

"We're demanding action, Mr. President, not promises to look into things."

"Demanding?" asked Griggs with a raise of his eyebrow.

"If they're not immediately reinstated, we will reconstitute the task force by act of Congress and place them under *our* authority. If you try to veto it, we'll override you."

"We're out of patience," said the cochairman. "So is the House."

Griggs shook his head. "If you send us such a bill, the President can sit on it for ten days. By then all of this will be over."

The cochairman sighed in exasperation. "You've said it was over too many times, Len. No one believes you anymore. Not us. Not the people. No one."

The President's voice emerged in a strained tone. "It's over. I'm doing my part."

Griggs regarded the President with an annoyed look, as if he'd revealed something he should not have.

"What do you mean?" Glenn challenged the President, wondering if they weren't about to say the emergency was over, as Griggs had announced so many times.

"Len evaluated Ghost's requests and found them not all that unreasonable."

"Requests? From Ghost?" Glenn sputtered.

"Ghost wants his man moved. Len's convinced me that's not asking much."

Griggs's jaw drooped.

"You'd give in to a terrorist's demands?" the cochairman asked incredulously.

Leonard Griggs found his voice. "Reasonable men don't resort to knee-jerk violence to solve problems. They talk."

"This is outrageous!" said a member of the subcommittee.

"What other demands has he made?" asked the cochairman.

Glenn remembered something. "We'd like the transcript of Ghost's phone call."

Griggs shook his head. "That's privileged information."

The cochairman lurched to his feet. "We'll have a subpoena here within an hour!" he exploded. "You can't ignore that, by God."

"When are you planning to move Charlie?" Glenn asked Griggs.

"He was transferred at seven this morning."

The President swallowed uncomfortably. "Now if you'll excuse us, we have work to do. Len wants me to go on national television this evening."

Griggs swiveled his head and frowned at the President's words.

"Is that in response to Ghost's phone call, too?" the cochairman asked the President.

"He's threatened to kill me." The President's voice trailed off, then was filled with new bravado. "Of course, that's not my primary concern. The country needs . . ."

"For God's sake, sir. You're in the most heavily defended fortress in the world. He can't touch you. Now precisely what did Ghost say, and how are you going to respond?"

"Len wants me to ask, on behalf of the American people, for Ghost to stop his killing."

"You'd *plead*?" the cochairman asked. "What else?"

"Len feels I should consider his other . . ." The President frowned oddly, then looked at Griggs as if realizing what he was being asked to do for the first time.

"Release Charlie?" Glenn Phillips asked. "Is that what you're considering?"

The senators were all standing, staring at the President, who turned to Griggs with a questioning look.

Leonard Griggs recovered slowly. "In time's such as these, when the very fabric of our nation is at stake . . ."

"Are you suggesting that the President meet the demands of a mass murderer?" the cochairman asked incredulously.

"We feel it's time for compromise, not further confrontation."

The cochairman pointed a trembling forefinger. "Mr. President, do you realize what's happening to the nation? While you've hidden in this grand basement, the country cried out for leadership, and Mr. Griggs fed them pap. Yesterday fewer than ten percent of the public believed his carping that the emergency is over, and they were proven right when the Speaker of the House was killed."

"Tragic," said the President in a sorrowful tone.

"Your approval rating is lower than that of any president in history. Only one person is held in less esteem, and that's Len Griggs."

"But . . ." The President appeared confused. "My reelection committee . . ."

"Mr. President!" interrupted the cochairman. "There is no campaign. Members of your own party are speaking about having you declared mentally incompetent. There's talk of impeachment, but certainly not reelection."

"I . . ." The President stared, then frowned at Griggs. "What have you done to me, Len?"

A grimace formed on Griggs's countenance.

The President drew himself up. "I agree to reinstate ITF-four."

"You must also take the steps they recommended."

"*What* steps?" the President asked.

"I told you about . . ." Griggs began.

"Leave us," the President interrupted harshly. "I'd like to speak to the senators privately."

As Griggs stalked away, trailed by the confused NSC members, Glenn spoke. "When you were in the hospital, Judge Lindquist proposed strong action to protect the city and find Ghost. Griggs threw her out of the meeting."

"I didn't know."

"You've begun to compromise with a killer," said the cochairman. "That too must end."

"Of course," the President said.

The marine captain was waiting outside the door to escort them through the NMCC. Before they left he gave Glenn Phillips a tiny nod, an unspoken communication between military men.

As the senators walked down the hallway toward the escalator, Glenn wondered about what they'd witnessed. Had Leonard Griggs pulled the wool over the President's eyes, or had it been a case of adroit maneuvering by the President, who claimed he'd been hoodwinked?

He trusted neither of them.

The Farmhouse, Falls Church, Virginia

When they'd returned to the house from calling Senator Phillips on the minivan car phone the previous day, the lines had been restored. The telephone company hadn't been able to offer a reason for the interruption. They now had two cellular telephones available for use in the house.

Lincoln Anderson stood in the great room, staring out at the pastures, feeling the odd sensation he'd had all morning. He'd been visited by the Grandfather during the night, but the message had been subtle. There'd been an eagle with outstretched wings. It hadn't appeared real—more like an ornate decoration—yet it had seemed important and was troubling.

When the Grandfather had gone, the sensation had come to him. It had nothing to do with the Grandfather or the eagle. It was more like . . . someone was watching.

Although Link had experienced the feeling before, his normally crisp memory balked.

Was Ghost posing a new threat?

He didn't believe they were in danger at the Farmhouse. The security guards had patrolled the grounds through the night. Now their dogs were in one of the runs outside, and the two guards were in the kitchen taking a snack before turning in to bed. They'd reported nothing of interest during their tour of duty, no vehicles or people stopping near the property. All morning, Billy Bowes had taken frequent strolls around the property, and had seen nothing.

Link shook his head, wondering.

Mack Hall came into the great room with Billy. He'd left early to visit his father at Walter Reed. "Pop's better," he said. "He's eating and functioning, even talking some."

"Good news," said Billy.

"They've moved Judge Lindquist to Walter Reed for therapy on her knee. She's down the hall from Pop. I dropped in to see her and talked with Manny DeVera."

"Manny's got a terminal case of love," Billy said.

"Pop says he's been a bachelor since forever."

"Manny's pleased his share of the ladies, but he never came close to any altars."

As they talked, Link wondered if he shouldn't call Doctor Grace McNabb and ask about the feelings. She'd said the areas of the brain reacted in different ways to stimuli.

So what was the variation. *How* was it different?

He tried to describe his present sensations. Uneasiness, like someone was watching. A faint yet distinct odor. Otherwise . . .

The odors! "Ghost is nearby," he muttered.

Billy came over and squinted through the window. "Out there?"

Mack joined them. "Where?" he prodded, his voice an angry growl. He'd simmered with anger since the attack on his father.

"I can sense Ghost. Like now. Very faint, but it's there. He's not close . . . the sensations aren't strong . . . but he's not far, either."

He turned to Billy and Mack. "I've got an idea," he said. He was tired of worrying about what Ghost would do next. Link decided upon a more direct approach.

11:05 A.M.—Annandale, Virginia

They were at the outer edge of the urban sprawl, in an isolated house set discreetly off the road by some two hundred yards. Kevin Gilroy had found it for them.

The endgame had begun. Early that morning Ghost had gotten a call from the wayfinder. Gilroy's people were now delivering the crated eagle to the Government Services Administration warehouse as the wayfinder had suggested. Tonight the President would announce that they would release his brother.

Ghost watched the television set in the sparsely furnished living room, waiting for word about the President's speech. Rashad sat beside him; they were turned to CNN.

At the sound of a vehicle, Rashad went to the window. "Gilroy," he said.

Ghost was still watching the screen when Kevin Gilroy came in.

"We dropped the crate off. More good news," said the IRA conduit. "Our contact at Joliet says they moved Charlie to minimum security this morning."

Ghost felt an inner glow flush through him. The government had blinked.

"Now the bad news. They've declared martial law, and the army's sending military policemen to help the local cops."

"It doesn't matter," said Ghost. He was extremely tired, pleased that the operation was about to be concluded. The remaining step was also crucial, though, for when Charlie was released he had to be contacted, hidden, then moved to safety before the eagle did its duty.

They would go home. It would be good to be with Charlie as they walked the mountains and fished the ice-cold streams.

A small shudder of uneasiness swept over him, but he easily pushed it aside. Things were proceeding too well for last-moment apprehensions.

"I'm going outside," Ghost said, rising to his feet.

Kevin Gilroy wanted them to remain in the house, but Ghost craved fresh air, and the house was hidden from the view of neighbors. He pulled on a heavy coat—the warm period had ended, and the weather had turned blustery during the night—and went out.

11:20 A.M.

They were in Mack's Lincoln Towncar on Interstate 496, Mack driving, slowing at each off-ramp so he could take it if necessary. Link was in the passenger's seat with his eyes closed, trying to interpret the sensations as they became stronger. Billy was in back with the shotguns.

"We just entered Annandale," Mack muttered in a low voice.

"Keep going," Link breathed. His eyelids fluttered open, and he looked about. They were approaching the turnoff to State Highway 236.

The others were silent, hardly drawing a breath that might interfere.

"Turn there!" Link jabbed his forefinger.

"Damn," Mack Hall muttered as he swung the wheel, crossed a lane, and entered the off-ramp. The driver of the car behind them braked and swerved, honking loudly.

Billy Bowes laughed. "Ride 'em cowboy," he yelled as Mack squealed around the loop.

We're close, Link thought. His senses were so tuned that he could almost *smell* the way.

"Slow down," Link said, and Mack eased off the accelerator.

11:23 A.M.

Ghost walked to the large shed, entered, and switched on the light. The twelve tritonol cones were set out neatly in a corner. If things went as anticipated, there'd be no need for them.

Of course, there was the possibility that the President would balk and he would have to use them. He hadn't decided that one yet. It would be dangerous to venture near the Pentagon where the President was in hiding. He doubted . . .

Ghost stiffened, the uneasiness so distinct that he could no longer ignore it.

Was his helper calling for him to meditate? He half turned, wondering, plagued by the growing sensation.

He's coming.

A shudder coursed through Ghost. He sprinted out of the shed toward the house.

As Ghost burst through the door, Rashad lurched to his feet.

"We're leaving," Ghost announced. "Now!"

Kevin Gilroy came from the kitchen. "Is there a problem?" he asked.

"Don't question the man," Rashad snapped.

Ghost grabbed the rifle from the corner and trotted out to the Suburban. He tossed the firearm into the rear seat, started to crawl in, then paused. "The tritonol," he called to Rashad.

Gilroy manned the driver's seat and started the engine. Ghost opened the cargo doors and stepped aside as Rashad hurried up with a cone. Ghost scrambled into the shed to help. After two trips, he shouted "No more time," and crawled into the rear as Rashad slipped into the front.

"Go!" Ghost shouted hoarsely, praying he'd not judged the margin too closely. Gilroy jabbed the accelerator to the floor. The Suburban fishtailed down the lane toward the road.

11:27 A.M.

Link stared about, then pointed left. "Turn there."

Mack swung the steering wheel.

"Not far now. Load 'em," Link said. When the Lincoln settled on the new course, Billy Bowes began thumbing 12-gauge shells into the three shotguns.

"We're damn close," Link muttered. His eyes narrowed when he saw an unpaved side lane. He jabbed his forefinger. "There!"

A pall of dust was settling on the long driveway as Mack turned off. He slowed to a crawl, and all three men stared. As they approached, Link could distinguish the open maw of a shed, offset from a small clapboard house.

They got out together.

"Here," said Billy, offering a shotgun.

"There's no need," Link said in a heavy voice. "They're gone."

Mack took a gun anyway, then cautiously led the way to the house. The door was ajar. As the others examined the living room and kitchen, Link looked into the first small bedroom. A suitcase was opened on the floor. He knelt and fingered a woolen shirt.

"Ghost's," he muttered. There was a faint, lingering odor.

Link went through the living room and back outside.

Tire tracks led toward the lane. He could see where the vehicle had fishtailed as it sped to get away. When they'd arrived, the dust of Ghost's departure hadn't yet settled.

"We almost had them," he muttered as the others joined him.

Bowes went into the shed and knelt over seven cone shapes placed in a neat row.

Mack frowned. "What are these?"

Link stared out toward the road for another moment. He sighed, then joined them and took his own look. "Ghost's explosives?"

Billy rose. "I'll call Manny on the car phone. He'll know who to contact."

8:05 P.M.—Motel Eight, I-95, Maryland

They'd taken adjoining rooms. Kevin Gilroy had gone to a restaurant across the parking lot to get food for himself and Rashad, who was watching television in the next room.

Although he'd not eaten, Ghost had no stomach for food.

The headline news was an announcement by the President about imposing martial law and a strict curfew in the city—nothing indicating Charlie would be released. Ghost wasn't surprised. With the discovery of the second safe house and more explosives, the President would be imbued with new courage.

The fact that he would be untrue to his word was troubling, yet Ghost could not think of a way to carry through with his vow that the President would die. He might somehow *damage* the Pentagon, but even that was doubtful—and there was no way to destroy his target.

That they'd almost been caught was even more worrisome.

Ghost knew who they were, the ones who had come for them. The wayfinder had told him several men had gathered at the home of A. L. Anderson's stepfather, a retired general who lived outside Falls Church. Now A. L. Anderson was leading those men to them.

Ghost considered destroying the home and all who were

inside. He'd given the address to Kevin Gilroy to have the telephone disconnected at the strategic moment before he'd killed the Speaker of the House. Gilroy had learned more about the house and the men, and Ghost still had explosives. Yet if he went there, he wondered if Anderson wouldn't sense his presence.

A. L. Anderson had second-guessed him before. Yet while a part of Ghost despised him, he remained reluctant to kill the brother who was so similar to Charlie.

Ghost switched the lamp to its dimmest setting and lay back on the bed. It was time for meditation. This time he would follow whatever advice his helper gave him.

The same words had been pounding at Ghost since they'd fled the safe house in Annandale: *Destroy Black Wolf.* He did not know what the words meant. Black Wolf was the name of an ancestor, half of the source of the powers the Bull Clan said made him so special.

Ghost closed his eyes and evened his breathing to meditate. He was tired, bone-weary from the exertions of the past weeks. As Ghost tried to summon the helper, he quickly dropped into deep sleep. *Destroy Black Wolf.* He almost surfaced, then drifted once more.

An aeon passed. Images came and left. Words and meanings.

Destroy Black Wolf. Ghost groaned, then slowly sat up and wearily swung his feet over the side of the bed. He was still groggy as he shook his head and struggled to fully awaken.

He knew the meaning of the message.

Ghost stood, then took a deep breath and sat at the desk. It took two calls to Calgary, Alberta before he had the number of the man in Browning, Montana.

"Hello" came an elderly, crackling voice.

"Is this the traveler?"

A drawn breath. "Yes," the voice whispered. Ghost envisioned the man he'd known as a child, who had come to rescue him and Charlie. The man with the eye that wandered, and which the Bull Clan members felt made him able to see more than others.

"This is the chosen one," Ghost said.

"It's been so long," the old man said, "I did not believe I would hear your voice again."

"I have a place you must go and a task you must do."

Ghost closed his eyes, remembering what he'd learned from the helper. For the next five minutes he gave directions.

"Go there now. Tonight." He gave instructions on what was to be done.

"It is cold here," the traveler complained. "Even colder in the mountains."

"It must be done *now*." Ghost waited.

"I will try," the traveler said in his old man's voice, and Ghost knew he would. The Bull Clan elders did not lie.

"There is something else," said the traveler. "Lincoln Anderson was here. He attended a special Okan, given in the old way. I was a weather dancer and saw it. He was prepared. The elders believe he learned the old secrets. Some think he is your equal."

"That's foolish. I am the chosen one."

"I know, but beware him."

"Go do your task, old man," Ghost said, but he was troubled by the traveler's words.

He hung up the telephone knowing his helper was right. He could no longer afford to ignore his advice. A. L. Anderson must be dealt with.

Destroy Black Wolf! Everything about him.

The cellular phone buzzed. "Go ahead," Ghost answered calmly.

It was the wayfinder. The President had changed his mind; there'd be no deal to release Charlie. Ghost must not venture inside the Beltway. The city was swarming with MPs.

Ghost told him he'd be leaving and explained where the wayfinder would find the transmitter for the final bomb.

"You know what to do," Ghost told him, and shut off the connection.

He went into the adjacent room. Both men were there, seated at a small table, eating food Gilroy had brought and watching an old movie.

Ghost switched off the television and stood before them. "Tell me again about the place called the Farmhouse," he said to Kevin Gilroy.

"A large house on a hill, with pastures all around. My source said there's four men and a woman inside. They've hired two guards with dogs to patrol the grounds at night."

The information tracked what Ghost had seen in his meditation. He outlined the first part of his plan. Kevin

Gilroy grew silent and reflective. Rashad grinned in anticipation.

"How many men will you need?"

Rashad thought. "Two, three at the most."

Rashad sometimes underestimated the strength of adversaries. Ghost turned his eye upon Gilroy. "Get him four."

"They won't be easy to find, with all the recent excitement." He wilted under Ghost's gaze. "I'll find someone."

Rashad continued to smile. It was an audacious plan, and he particularly liked his part.

27

Friday, February 17th

5:30 A.M.—The Farmhouse, Falls Church, Virginia

Link awakened feeling troubled, as if someone close to him was in peril. He got out of bed, still weary and half-asleep, and looked through the window. Billy Bowes was outside, caught in the illumination of the floodlights he'd installed, talking with a security guard. Since all seemed to be in order, Link lay back down and relaxed. Finally he slipped into deep slumber.

Steam issues from rocks piled at their feet in the center of the small hut. The Grandfather is there—serious as always—speaking the strange, yet understandable words to the young man beside him. The visions are clear.

The image of the eagle appears. Golden and grand with outstretched wings. It adorns a great lodge, silent and unmoving as a group of chiefs enter and talk together.

The image fades, replaced by that of an old man struggling up a mountain path. He stops and pants. His left eye wanders oddly. He lowers his head into the stiff wind and continues.

Jeopardy!

Link came awake with a start, sweating profusely, wondering what the strange visions had tried to tell him. He knew it was not himself in danger, but someone close to him. He needed more . . . another visit from the Grandfather so he might understand. He lay back and evened his breathing, willing the Grandfather to return. So troubled, it was difficult to fall asleep again.

It was another hour before he rested.

Wood smoke is mixed with the steam. The Grandfather speaks and an image appears.

The eagle is changed. It is badly tarnished and seems uglier than before.

The gathered chiefs sit in a great circle, unaware of the eagle's existence.

The Grandfather's presence returns. He looks at him with a nostalgic stare.

"You are prepared."

The other image flickers. The circle of chiefs. The eagle has become hideous and threatening. A flash of light. Deadly feathers shower down upon the chiefs.

The grandfather returns and nods gravely.

"The rest must be done by you alone."

A beam of light is rudely cast into the enclosure, interrupting him. The Grandfather looks beyond the young man and glares as an intruder comes inside.

"Go away!" the Grandfather says angrily.

"Go away," cries the young man.

An ax appears in the young man's vision. Lifts and strikes.

"Go away!" Link shouted, as he turned and struck out at the intruder.

"Grandfather?" the young man asks cautiously.

There is no response. Something terrible has happened to the Grandfather, to Black Wolf, to his helper.

"Damn you! Go away!" he shouted.

Someone grasped him. Link turned and lashed out again.

"Whoa!" yelled a voice, and laughed.

Link blinked, then came awake.

Mack Hall was standing over him, huge, with his hands held out defensively.

Link expelled a breath and settled back onto the rumpled bed.

"I heard you shouting and thought you might be in trouble. Another dream?"

"Yes." Link's chest was rising and falling dramatically. He tried to calm himself.

"Are they all that violent?"

"No." He tried to remember, but for the moment could not.

"Another warning?"

"It wasn't like the others." Link frowned, wondering what it had been about.

"Sorry to intrude," Mack said, and left to return to his bedroom next door.

It was light outside, a typical dreary winter morning in the Tidewater. Link went down the hall to the bathroom, where he shaved and then stepped into the shower, all the while wondering about the strange Grandfather dream.

Some of it came back. A hideous eagle. Had it exploded? An attack on the Grandfather?

The Grandfather was only a manifestation. Even if he was as the Piegan believed . . . Link's helper . . . he remained only a vision. Yet he felt profoundly sad.

The eagle had appeared threatening.

Link wondered what Ghost was up to. The odors and the feeling of being watched were gone. If the senses of yesterday were a gauge, Ghost was not nearby.

J.J. Davis was trying to determine the quantity of explosives, if any, taken by Ghost before his hasty withdrawal. It was important. Even with a single cone of tritonol, Ghost could wreak terrible destruction. But if he was gone . . .

When he'd dressed, Link went down to the kitchen where the others were gathered—joined by Manny DeVera, who had driven over to join them for breakfast.

They were more cheerful than Link had seen them. Linda gave him a smooch on the cheek as he came into the room. "There's scrambled eggs and ham warming in the oven."

Manny filled him in. ITF-4 was returning to their offices at the Department of Justice. They'd meet that afternoon to regroup and discuss new actions to find Ghost. The President had ordered his administration to provide full cooperation with the task force. If Link had another revelation he was to call the duty officers at ITF-4, and they'd respond immediately.

Linda answered the warbling telephone. "Manny, it's for you. It's the special agent working with J.J. Davis."

Link scooped breakfast onto a plate, adding two of Linda's special-formula, melt-in-your mouth biscuits that he craved every time he left home.

"I'm going out to talk with the security guards," Billy said, and went out the back door.

"Colonel Bowes is mad as hell," said Mack Hall. "Last night he caught one of the guards curled up in the barn. He said the guy's dog was sleeping as soundly as he was."

"Are you seeing Sam this morning, Mack?" Linda asked.

"Yes, ma'am. Afterward I'll drop by all the neighborhood search headquarters and thank them for their work. They'll cooperate with the army MPs. The locals like the idea of having control of their neighborhoods."

DeVera hung up and returned to the table. "J.J.'s at the Annandale house. It looks like Ghost and Rashad departed in even more of a hurry than last time."

"Do they still have explosives?" Linda asked.

"J.J. estimates Ghost has three hundred pounds of tritonol, plus or minus fifty."

"Damn" was muttered around the table.

Link finished a biscuit. "I don't believe Ghost is in the area."

"Could it be over?" Linda asked, wanting to believe.

"I don't know. Despite what Doctor McNabb said, the dreams aren't right all of the time. Last night's was a meaningless jumble. And I don't trust Ghost worth a damn."

"We can't afford to let our guard down," said Manny.

As Link finished his breakfast, Manny DeVera and Mack Hall left for the city.

The telephone warbled. Linda smiled at Link. "It's Marie."

Link picked up on the extension in the great room.

"When will you be back?" she blurted. "I miss you, Lincoln Anderson."

He started to tell her what he felt, then held his tongue. *Why was it difficult to speak his heart without becoming embarrassed?*

"Have you seen Bright Flame?" he asked.

"I go up there every other day to take food and make sure she's okay. Jack Douglas and some of the men want to renovate her shack, but I guess that has to wait until spring. In the meantime Jack's installing a wood-burning stove."

"Is she well?"

Marie sighed. "Not really. It's as if all she was waiting for was the Okan, and to make sure you were prepared.

Most of the food I take to her isn't eaten, and she's thinner than ever. I believe she'd purposefully starving herself. My uncle wanted to bring her into town for a physical examination, but she wouldn't cooperate."

"When I get back, I'll see if I can reason with her."

"You can try," Marie said dubiously. She had a visitor at her office and had to hang up.

Link put down the receiver, feeling better than he had in days.

Indianapolis, Indiana

Kevin Gilroy was driving again, still on Interstate I-70 as they entered the city. He and Ghost had taken turns at the wheel of the Suburban since early morning.

Gilroy was nervous about the cones jostling about in the rear of the van, regardless of how harmless Ghost told him they were.

"I guess if they ignited somehow, we'd never even know it. Just a big boom."

"Yes," Ghost said without a smile. He picked up the cellular telephone and entered the number he'd learned the previous night.

"This is the chosen one," he said when the traveler answered.

He nodded at the man's words. "I'll see you in three days." He punched the END button and replaced the telephone on the seat.

"Chosen one?" Kevin Gilroy asked with a raised eyebrow.

Ghost didn't respond, just stared ahead at the highway for a while so Gilroy would know he didn't intend to answer. "What can we expect where we're going?" he finally asked.

"The Irish settled in Chicago when the town was born a hundred and fifty years ago. Boston, New York, and Chicago are where we get most of our support."

"Jock Donovan said he'd spent time in those places."

"He came over on a fund-raiser when the cease-fire started breaking down. Told 'em how he was on the front lines of the fight. The money trickled in from everywhere, but *especially* from Chicago."

"What was their response to Piccadilly?"

"There were bad reactions from Boston, but not Chicago. Al Capone's one of their revered historical figures. If a politician's not on the take, he's boring and probably can't deliver. Chicago's tough."

"Pragmatic," Ghost said.

"Yeah, and there's a large element who aren't turned off by violence."

"Including your guards at Joliet?"

"We've got an assistant warden and a number of correctional officers here. Two are especially dedicated. A captain and a lieutenant working in minimum security. That's why we wanted your brother moved there."

"And on the outside?"

"A couple of state cops. I'm keeping the number to a minimum like you said."

"How's Charlie holding up?" Ghost asked.

"He's got a private room, good meals, and access to a recreation room that he refuses to use. He doesn't answer anything anyone asks him, including our people. Even when they told him what you said, that it wouldn't be long now, all he did was stare at a wall."

Ghost nodded. Charlie would never talk. "How about these people who are cooperating? What do they think about what I've done in Washington?"

Kevin Gilroy drew back in mock amazement. "You aren't the one doing it . . . it's a bunch of wild-eyed Arabs. You're being blamed because of your connection with the IRA. It's a plot set up by the FBI." He grinned. "None of 'em like the Bureau, because they send information to the Brits about their meetings and contributions."

Ghost motioned. "Turn right here."

"Gotcha." The overhead sign read I-65. Chicago.

Gilroy reached for the cellular telephone and punched buttons, calling the Chicago number he'd been in contact with since morning.

After a brief conversation he nodded to Ghost. "They're ready."

11:10 P.M.—Falls Church, Virginia

Rashad didn't trust any of the four men. They were silent and brooding types, dedicated only to the money they'd receive. Kevin Gilroy had said they'd not been told the purpose of the operation. They'd not asked when Rashad had briefed them on specifics and what he expected.

Rashad pulled the Honda well off the road and killed the engine. "We walk from here," he said, then switched on the overhead light, pulled his weapon—a Smith & Wesson 9mm semiautomatic—from his shoulder holster and checked it. He replaced it, reached down and patted the knife in its sheath for final assurance, then turned off the light and crawled out.

Each of the men had a three-foot-long steel bar he'd issued at the motel. All wore dark clothing, and he'd briefed the value of silence. Two had wanted to bring pistols, another an assault shotgun, but they'd been left behind. He didn't want the sounds of a firefight broadcast across the countryside, regardless if the nearest army patrols were miles away in the city.

"Keep to the trees," he said gruffly, and led the way. They were a quarter mile from the house and would approach from the rear, not from the road in front.

There were only three who must be killed, but Rashad intended to take out everyone. Not out of blood thirst, but because it would make withdrawal easier. Allowing even one to live could make things difficult, and Ghost had impressed the importance of the withdrawal phase.

First the security guards, next the others. Then he would perform cleanup—another task he looked forward to since he disliked the men he worked with—and return to the car to make the cross-country drive to rendezvous with Ghost and Charlie.

Ghost hadn't been specific about how he'd remove Charlie from prison, but Rashad didn't doubt it would happen. He didn't much care for Charlie, but he understood Ghost's concern and his efforts to free him. He'd do the same for Rashad, which was a reason he felt dedication to Ghost. That and because he was the only living man Rashad was afraid of.

Ghost knew things that were impossible to know. Like when they should get the hell out of a place or when they could stay. Rashad was even afraid to think bad thoughts about him, because he was certain Ghost would look right into his fucking brain and *know*.

"Wait here," Rashad said to the others as they came to the edge of a thicket of trees.

"How long?" one asked.

"Until I come back," Rashad said. "Move from here or make any noise, and I'll personally take you out. That's a promise."

He didn't wait for an answer, but crouched and moved toward the fence to begin his reconnoiter. It took seven minutes to get a position on both dogs and handlers.

One team was in the open, walking a field near the front of the property. The other took longer to pinpoint, because the guard was in the shadow of the big house, leaned back in a lawn chair, his dog at his side. Rashad took them out first. He was angry because he had to kill the dog, happy it hadn't put up a fight. Neither had the man who'd died in his sleep. Except for a single yip from the shepherd and some trashing from the guard, it was done silently.

He waited eight more minutes for the second guard to complete a long beat around the front of the property. Rashad struck as he came by the side of the barn, the dog whining and trying to tell the silly asshole he was there. He hit the guard once, then sliced the shepherd's throat. The dog was flopping around, so he jabbed the blade deep into its chest until it was still, then grasped the still-moaning guard by the neck and dragged him across the field.

Rashad the puppy killer, he raged inwardly. *Jesus!*

"Come on," he growled in a low tone, and pulled the guard along. The twit tried reaching for his pistol, so he whacked his arm with the heavy knife-butt and the gun went flying. Rashad dragged him on, until he reached the edge of the field near where he'd left the others.

He motioned for them to come out to join him, and began to ask his questions of the guard, keeping his voice low. "What's first inside the back door?" he asked.

The security guard balked, so Rashad grabbed his hand and lopped off two fingers. When the man started to scream he cut off the sound with a hand gripped around his throat.

"You want to lose more fingers?" Rashad loosened the grasp on his neck.

The guard lifted his bloody hand and began to cry.

"How about your whacker? Want me to cut off your cock?"

"No," the guard wailed.

"Keep your voice down," Rashad hissed. "What's first when you go in the back door?"

It took five minutes to get the entire layout of the house. By the time the security guard finished, Rashad knew the rooms and where everyone slept, and where the alarm panel and yard floodlight switches were located.

"You guys hear all that?" he asked.

"Yeah," they answered one at a time.

"Need anything else from this man?"

"How about dogs?" one asked. "I don't like fucking dogs."

"I took them out," Rashad said, and lifted his knife.

"There's . . ." the guard began, but Rashad had already begun his swipe across the man's throat. The guard fell, gurgling blood, and one of the men with him muttered "Fuck" when he was kicked and almost knocked over by a drumming leg.

"You and you," Rashad said to two of them. "You'll come in with me like I said before. We'll take them out, one bedroom at a time. I'll use the knife and do the killing. Just make sure I'm not blindsided. One of you in the room with me, the other in the hall. Bring your flashlights, but don't use 'em unless I say to. Same with pistols. No lights and no noise. Period."

The men looked at the objective. Floodlights remained on outside, illuminating the area around the house.

"Follow me and don't make any fucking noise. You kick something over, I'll leave you flopping like that dumb shit there. Got it?"

"Yeah." Now they'd seen his work, he'd gained their attention.

"You other two hang around outside next to the doors, one in front and the other in back. Anyone comes out, hit 'em hard with the bar. I don't want any fucking noise tellin' the others we're there. And don't hit us when we come out, for Christ's sake."

The rain began to fall harder. Winter rain that chilled to the bone.

"Let's go," said Rashad.

They moved out toward the house.

Mack couldn't sleep. He kept thinking about Pop. How Rashad had savaged him, and how he'd missed grabbing him when he'd been so close. The whining didn't help, either.

He was in the downstairs guest bedroom, and General Anderson's two English setters were just outside in a kennel run, more nervous than normal.

One barked, and the other whined louder.

Mack got up and looked out, but there was nothing except the kennel run and darkness beyond the area illuminated by the floodlights. Rain was falling, the drops streaking the window.

He started to get back into bed, when something caught his attention. He turned back to the window. The floodlights had been shut off.

Mack pulled on a robe and went out into the darkness. As he walked down the dark hall toward the kitchen, he heard a noise from the other wing. One of the others was up.

He fumbled, found the switch, and turned on the kitchen lights.

"Hi there," said a voice, and he whirled about.

"Sorry," Billy Bowes said, grinning as he came down the stairs.

Mack blew out a breath. "Scared the pee outa me."

"Thought I'd come down and check on the guards," Billy said.

"The outside lights went out," Mack said.

"I saw. Probably one of the guards turned 'em off," Billy said, pointing to wet tracks on the floor. "This time I'm going to have their asses." He went to the switch panel, flipped the appropriate one for the floodlights, then peered out the window.

Mack heard a sound, slight but audible, from the hall leading to General Anderson's master bedroom. Then he saw outlines of damp footprints on the hall carpet.

"Something's wrong here," he said in a low voice.

"Yeah." Billy Bowes drew back from the door. "Someone's out there, and it's not a security guard." He reached into the pantry and pulled out a shotgun he'd left there.

There was a muffled outcry from down the hallway. Mack didn't hesitate, but began to hurry toward the source.

A shadow moved a dozen feet in front of him.

"General?" Mack asked, slowing.

The shadow raised its hand in a threatening gesture. "Move back, asshole," the shadow said in a wavering voice.

A scream came from the master bedroom. Linda Anderson's voice.

Mack rushed, lowered, hit the shape hard, and heard a loud grunt. He grasped and lifted. Something heavy fell to the floor. Mack threw him against the wall, slammed an elbow into his chest, then kept moving toward the black maw of the open bedroom door.

He felt beside the jamb, found the switch, and flipped it. The room was illuminated.

The general was out of bed, struggling with a black man in dark clothes. Another man held Linda Anderson, mouth drooping as he stared at Mack's huge figure.

A loud boom sounded from outside, then another.

Mack grasped for the man holding Linda, clutched the shirt, and swept his right fist in a roundabout as the man tried to dodge away. The head snapped back hard, making a cracking sound, and Mack immediately turned toward the other assailant.

The long-haired black was grappling with the aged general, shoving a knife blade into his midriff.

Rashad!

Mack could not contain an outraged roar as he swept forward.

Rashad sidestepped, lips drawn into a lopsided snarl as he lashed out.

The blade sliced an inch-deep gash in Mack's chest, but he continued moving forward.

He grasped and lifted, still roaring his rage, wanting to squeeze the life from the man he despised. A pistol skittered across the floor. Rashad emitted a loud groan.

Mack needed a better grip, shifted his grasp, but the man was muscular and strong and his writhing drew Mack off balance.

The change of position freed Rashad's knife hand. He swung wildly, although without force, and the blade jabbed into Mack's left buttock.

Mack stumbled, releasing his hold. He smacked headlong into the wall and fell with a crash, stunned by the impact.

Sound filtered through the roar in his head, and Mack was slow regaining his feet.

Rashad was there! Mack shook his head to clear it, then

saw him, halfway across the large room by the opened window, chest heaving as he eyed Mack with a pained expression. Then Rashad Taylor disappeared headfirst over the sill.

Mack hobbled in pursuit, stopped at the window, and tried to follow, but he could not nearly fit in the opening.

The sound of Billy Bowes's shotgun reverberated from outside, and Mack prayed it was Rashad Taylor in his sights.

"Dad!" Link Anderson cried out hoarsely from the doorway.

Mack turned and limped forward to help.

28

Saturday, February 18th

7:20 A.M.—Joliet Facility, Illinois State Prison, Federal Wing

Charlie sat on the bunk, anticipating the call to breakfast. Things were different in medium security. Here there were real doors, steel reinforced but the kind that swung open and didn't slide when electrical motors were activated. Here there were bars only on the windows.

The only difference between Charlie's treatment and the others' was an ever-present armed guard who remained just outside his room and followed wherever he went. Presently it was the lieutenant from the graveyard shift, who had several times acted as if he was passing messages from Ghost.

Charlie didn't trust any of them, regardless if the lieutenant had whispered that Ghost was on his way. He longed to be free, to walk the mountains as Little Crow and watch the animals going about their business. He wanted to be back with his brother and talk about the things they savored together. To laugh and not worry about the next operation.

Ghost knew the killing troubled Charlie and was careful not to mention the victims after a task was done, only tell him when he'd done well. The first ones had been hardest, when he'd had to make himself continue the trigger-squeeze until the bullet was released. After the fourth one they'd been easier, for Ghost had turned it into a game.

Charlie had killed old man Weiser over and over, and soon it hadn't been hard at all. Faces and mannerisms had been transposed to those of the man he hated. From five hundred yards and farther he'd been able to hit the target . . . then again, and yet again.

Perspiration grew on Charlie's face as he stared at the wall and remembered the old man, and wished he had a rifle in his grasp. He was still deathly afraid of him.

The door opened, and the florid-faced lieutenant entered.

"Here," he said, and placed clothing on his lap. It was a guard's uniform.

"Put 'em on. Yer friend's comin' like I said."

Charlie looked back at the wall, wondering if it wasn't true.

"Put 'em on, damn it!" The correctional officer pulled him harshly to his feet.

Charlie did as he was told. The lieutenant pulled the belt buckle squarely to the front.

"Ye don't want to be a sloppy guard, do yer?" The lieutenant grinned, then pushed something into his hand. "That's a stun gun. Hits 'em with twenty-five thousand volts an' stops 'em cold. Don't use it unless ye have to."

Charlie nodded his understanding, and for the first time since the man who was his mirror's image had visited, his heart began to race. It was real!

The lieutenant placed the stun gun into a leather pouch on Charlie's belt, rearranged him a bit more, and looked at his watch. "We're okay on timing. Wait here until I return."

An eternity passed in the next few minutes until the door swung back open.

"It's clear. C'mon."

Charlie followed the lieutenant out, then down the corridor, trying to act as if he belonged. *You are whatever you believe you are,* his brother had counseled.

I am a prison guard, Charlie told himself, and his step became more sure.

"Hey lieut," called out a prisoner from the view port of a door. "I got the diarrhea. Been shittin' all night. I gotta see a medic."

"Morning meal call's in twenty minutes," said the lieutenant. "Ye can hold it until then."

"No way, man. Put clothes on and shit in 'em already. I need somethin' to stop it."

The lieutenant grinned as they continued past. "Keep yer pants on."

The prisoner was still complaining as they continued out of earshot.

They turned a corner, and the lieutenant guided him into an empty guard post position, then stepped in beside him. "It's steel reinforced." He looked at his watch, appearing only slightly nervous. "Six minutes to go," he said.

They waited.

"Better hold yer ears," the lieutenant finally whispered, and knelt.

Charlie crouched beside him. Waiting, hands covering his ears, eyes glued on the corridor. Wondering if another guard would discover them.

Even with his ears covered the sound was enormous. A brilliant flash of fire flickered like a great tongue through the nearby passageway, followed by a rush of smoke and debris.

The lieutenant was immediately pulling at Charlie's arm, mouthing unheard words, hardly visible in the thick smoke. As they reëntered the passage, Charlie glanced back at the now-obscured section where his cell had been located. A faint, agonized scream pierced the air, the first sound to penetrate his deafness.

The lieutenant pulled him on, stopped and unlocked a door, then stumbled, coughing, into a larger room.

"You guys okay?" yelled a senior correctional officer.

Charlie joined in, coughing and holding his hand over his mouth, covering as much of his face as possible.

"Go on out," a captain yelled into his ear. "Follow the lieut." His eyes were knowing.

Smoke and dust hung in a heavy pall as they continued across a small clearing and entered the gatehouse.

"Jesus!" a guard asked them. "What the hell was that?"

"Dunno," shouted the lieutenant, obviously deafened. "Maybe a gas explosion, like back in '79. I was in that fucker, too." He shook his head and continued coughing. "We're going through," he yelled, and pushed Charlie toward the huge steel door that barred their way.

The door trundled open.

Charlie and the lieutenant stepped into the entrance mall, then hurried, staggering slightly as if still suffering from smoke inhalation, toward the parking lot.

"For Ireland," hissed the lieutenant as he pushed Charlie toward a waiting police cruiser.

A cop opened the door for him. As soon as he was inside the driver sped away, siren blasting and joining the cacophony of a dozen others.

Charlie was dropped off in a small, empty parking lot a mile distant.

The cop in the passenger seat rolled down the window, grinned. "Go on back and kick more British ass until they get the fuck out of Ireland." He waved. The cruiser turned and sped back toward the prison.

Less than a minute later a green GMC Suburban pulled into the parking lot.

Falls Church, Virginia

No one at the Farmhouse had slept during the night. There'd been an endless procession of local and state police, FBI agents led by J.J. Davis and his assistant, and reporters from every segment of the media. Those last were discouraged, and information withheld at J.J. Davis's suggestion. He told them the next of kin must be notified before names could be released.

Billy Bowes had handled the policemen's questions while the others trekked to and from the Falls Church hospital. Linda had suffered a broken left arm. Link's father hadn't been so fortunate. There would be a second emergency operation to try to repair damage to his abdomen. He remained in grave condition.

Mack had received a nasty slice across his chest and a painful jab in the buttocks, but he'd been patched up and was back on the scene at the Farmhouse. Billy had been struck with a steel pipe, but he'd been moving away and it wasn't serious.

As Link drove up the lane toward the Farmhouse, the mob scene was continuing. He had trouble finding a place to park amid the police cruisers and official vehicles. The press had been told to keep their vehicles on the road below or the parking area would have been filled.

Billy Bowes emerged from the house. "How's Lucky?" he immediately asked.

Link told him as they went in together.

"Wish to hell we'd been quicker about it last night."

"Thank God you and Mack discovered them when you did."

Four men had died. The two security guards and two of the bad guys—one done in by Mack when he'd broken his neck in the master bedroom; another by Billy's shotgun near the front door. Two were badly hurt. The man in the hall was suffering from a crushed chest and concussion, and remained unconscious. Bowes had shot the other, who wasn't expected to live.

Rashad Taylor had gotten away.

Link was putting away his raincoat when Mack Hall yelled out from the kitchen. There was a news flash on CNN.

J.J. Davis and his assistant were watching with Mack when Billy and Link joined them.

". . . where at least nineteen prisoners were killed in the explosion. Charlie, co-conspirator of the terrorist called Ghost, is believed to be among the dead."

"No loss," said Mack.

The camera shifted to a point outside Joliet prison, focused on a gap in the fences and the crumbled brick building beyond. "Authorities are exploring the possibility of a gas line explosion such as happened in 1979. In that one there was no loss of life."

J.J. Davis leaned closer to the television screen, peering hard. The camera panned from the fence to the prison building. He pulled out his pad and scribbled words.

His assistant became grim-faced.

Link touched the agent's arm. "What did he write?"

"The blast came from outside the building."

Billy Bowes frowned. "Ghost?"

"Doesn't make sense," Link said. "Why would he want to kill him."

When the station turned to other news, a reporter stated that the President had promised continuing vigorous action to apprehend Ghost. Recent polls revealed that his popularity had surged dramatically during the past two days.

Link went to the great room to get away and think, inexplicably saddened by the death of Charlie, the man he'd learned was his brother.

8:00 P.M.—St. Cloud, Minnesota

Ghost smiled happily as he looked at Charlie in the passenger seat. He'd left Gilroy in Chicago, and now it was only the two of them, traveling west on I-74 in the green Suburban.

Charlie was staring out the window. "We're not going home?"

"We've got unfinished business ahead," Ghost said. "We've been given a task. Rashad will join us in a few days."

Charlie remained quiet. The two men had never been fond of one another. Rashad was tougher, physically and mentally—Charlie smarter but more vulnerable.

Ghost had searched the radio dial, but there'd been no word about Rashad's success or failure. The newscasts were filled with reports of the efficiency of the troops who had finally brought a sense of security to Washington citizens.

"What was his name?" asked Charlie. "The one who came to see me?"

"Abraham Lincoln Anderson." Ghost had avoided discussion of him.

"I couldn't believe it when he sat across from me. It was like looking into a mirror. And when he called me Little Crow?" Charlie shook his head. "Who is he?"

Ghost hesitated. "Our brother," he finally said.

"I thought so," Charlie said. "I remembered you'd told me we had a brother, and after he left the prison, I thought how nice it would be if we could all be together. Maybe walk in the mountains like you and I do. I don't think we should do the operation in London."

Ghost looked over sharply. Charlie had never questioned before.

"Tell me about him again," Charlie said.

"I only remember him from when we were very young and some men were taking us away from a woman."

"Our mother?"

"The Bull Clan elders would never tell me. I think so, though. The men who took us stopped the car, and we tried to run away. The men started after us, but some others came on horses so they left in the car. The three of us kept running, but after a while the men on horseback caught us."

"Did they give us to old man Weiser?"

"Another man did that later."

"Why didn't our brother come with us?"

"Someone took him away first."

"What was he like?"

"All I can remember was that he was the quiet one." He paused. "I told Rashad to kill him, Charlie. His stepparents, too. Rashad will join us when it's done."

Charlie looked alarmed. "Why?" he cried.

"He was dangerous. Rashad was going to kill him once before, but I stopped him. I wanted to let him live. If he'd left us alone, I would have, but he kept interfering. He even tried to lead them to us. It's better this way."

His brother grew quiet.

Destroy Black Wolf, the helper had ordered. *Everything about him.* His helper had demanded that he destroy Anderson and his stepparents and all that were close to him, and this time Ghost had not dared go against him.

"Take a look at the rifle in the back," he told Charlie. "You can have it. I used it once, but it's like new."

Charlie switched on a dome light, then lifted the Sako from the rear seat and looked it over.

"We'll need warmer clothes," Ghost said. "We'll stop and buy them tomorrow. It will be cold where we're going."

Charlie examined the rifle in silence.

"We'll drive all night, taking turns," Ghost said. "Get some rest now."

Charlie did not question. It was good to be with him again.

29

Monday, February 20th

7:00 A.M.—The Farmhouse, Falls Church, Virginia

The explosion at Joliet Prison had nothing to do with a gas main. A focused-effect bomb had been detonated near the prison's west side parking lot. J.J. Davis and his team of FBI investigators were on the scene, and estimated that two hundred pounds of shaped explosives had been buttressed against a concrete slab, the blast reaching out in a channel of fury that had cut through the reinforced concrete walls like butter.

It was likely the bomb had been placed early Saturday morning, yet none of the guards remembered seeing anyone in that brightly illuminated area.

By the morning of the second day after the prison disaster, the FBI team had narrowed the field of candidates to C-4 or tritonol. The announcement was carried on CNN. After three weeks of reading about and watching analyses of various explosive compounds, burn rates, and bomb construction, the American public had become familiar with those terms.

The people around the farmhouse breakfast table looked at one another.

"Ghost," said Manny DeVera, and no one argued. They'd all wondered since J.J. Davis's revelation that the explosion had come from without.

"That's why you haven't felt him around," Billy said to Link.

"Probably." But Link had had no contact from the Grandfather, either, and was increasingly convinced his insights were a thing of the past.

Last night Manny had come by for another meeting at the Farmhouse, called by Senator Glenn Phillips to bring them up to speed on what was happening in the city.

Leonard Griggs had appeared before his committee to explain the NSC's role during the period of indecision—and had been composed, even called senators by their first names. When he'd been scalded with criticism, he'd become the martyred saint.

"I've done my best to ensure the security of my country," he'd said. "We felt it was crucial that the public not be led into panic. If we erred, it was in the interest of serving the citizens of this nation." And so forth, never quite answering the questions posed to him. Glenn had finally dismissed him in utter disgust.

There'd been no comment about Griggs's dismal performance from the President, only another appearance where he iterated his firm actions to combat domestic terrorism. While there were no words about his bid for reelection, his popularity continued to rise as memories of the atrocities faded. Doctor McNabb said it was natural for the public to shut out bad memories and move on to more pleasant things.

The manhunt by the hosts of police, MPs, and federal agents was continuing; but they'd turned up nothing new, and it was increasingly felt that the terrorists had indeed left the city.

After the Farmhouse meeting, Link's mother had retired. Glenn Phillips had sat up with Manny DeVera and Billy Bowes in the great room, sipping whiskey and talking about the days when they'd flown together, and about Sam Hall's and Lucky Anderson's exploits.

They'd not been concerned about another attack. The Farmhouse was guarded by a host of Virginia state troopers, one of whom had driven the inebriated senator to his nearby home. Since Manny had farther to go, he'd spent the night.

This morning Link and Mack Hall had risen early, and

the others had been lured to the kitchen by smells of bacon, eggs, and pancakes.

"How was your night?" everyone had asked him. When Link answered that there'd been no dream, they responded with pleased looks. No one wanted more bad news.

The television announcer's report that Ghost might be involved in the bombing at the prison spoiled their pleasure. The same report carried news that Charlie's body hadn't been found. There was speculation that he'd somehow escaped.

"If it was Ghost, and he's got his brother and Rashad with him, we're back to square one," Billy said darkly.

"Maybe not," Manny said. "J.J. says they can't have more than a hundred pounds of explosives left, and with everything tightened down, he'd have trouble getting his hands on more. They may be trying to get out of the country."

Mack Hall scowled. "I want another chance at Rashad."

Link took a platter of pancakes from the warmer and set it in the middle of the table.

"When Marie arrives, I'll tell her you're a wonderful cook," Linda said.

"False advertising. What you see is the limit of my culinary capabilities." Link couldn't help smiling. When he'd invited her, Marie hadn't hesitated.

Mack added platters of scrambled eggs, bacon, and Polish sausages to the table. "So we finally get to see your lady."

"I'll pick her up at Dulles tomorrow."

"Billy wanted to fly out to get her in one of the Learjets," Linda said, "but Marie said it was out of the question. She's money conscious." She motioned for the men to begin.

As they ate, they talked.

"You still aren't getting any vibes about Ghost?" Billy asked.

"Nothing," said Link. "For the past two nights, I've slept like a rock."

7:25 A.M.—Browning, Montana

Marie puttered about the kitchen, cleaning up after her breakfast of a single English muffin. Although she had never tended to be overweight, she'd been especially conscious of her figure recently. Love had done that, she decided.

She'd spend the day at the museum, come home and pack, then go to her aunt and uncle's for dinner. Tomorrow she'd drive to Great Falls and take a flight that would end up at Dulles. Where Link would meet her! He'd sounded as excited about it as she'd been, even offering to have a private jet sent to pick her up, but she'd chided him for his extravagance.

Marie was frugal, and he might as well get accustomed to it. She didn't care if his parents lived in a grand Virginia home and owned a charter airline. She and Link would live well, too, but she was determined not to throw their money away.

Marie grinned at her foolishness, acting as if they were already living together. He hadn't asked her—they weren't to that stage yet—but she was sure the question would come, as certain as she'd ever been about anything in her life. If he delayed too long, Link would soon learn just how determined Marie LeBecque could be.

She thought about their conversation, when she'd steered the theme away from his sadness about the attacks on his father and others she was growing to know from his descriptions. Marie had wondered if either of them would be able to wait or whether they'd make love right in the terminal before hundreds of aghast passengers. He'd joined in, wondering how they should spend their time while they waited for her baggage.

Marie was still smiling at the silly thoughts when the doorbell rang.

"Be right there," she called out, then glanced out the window. A dust-laden Suburban was parked at the curb behind Link's truck. Odd, she thought.

When she opened the door she wanted to shout with happiness, for Link was standing with another man, wearing a bright blue parka.

As the two pushed their way inside, Marie realized she was mistaken and that something was terribly wrong.

1:00 P.M.—Washington, D.C.

The wayfinder looked at his watch. Not many blocks distant workmen would be busy installing the bas-relief in it's position of honor. Carefully, of course, for it was a work of art, replacing a much older one that was cracked and crumbling with age.

The new one would be hardly noticed by the hypocritical men and women who gathered in the large room, as if such works of artistry should be their due.

"To your deaths," the wayfinder silently toasted.

Ghost was smart; he was everything the Bull Clan elders had hoped he'd be. Even more than the wayfinder had imagined when they'd begun the long journey so long ago. Then he'd believed he'd be able to do it himself. Bring the nation he despised to its knees. Humiliate the leaders and slay the descendants of those responsible for the treaty-which-was-a-lie.

Now he admitted he could not have done it alone. There was an audacity and air of sureness about Ghost that no other man possessed. He was indeed the chosen one.

The wayfinder wondered what Ghost was doing while he remained behind here, basking in the hatred of a nation.

An assistant came into the room and deposited a new stack of correspondence. "You're in a good mood, sir."

"Why shouldn't I be?" he asked.

The assistant frowned in his lack of understanding, thinking he gave a damn about what was going on with Congress or the press.

The wayfinder wondered how long the workers would take to install the eagle. When they were done, he decided to go there and view the majestic symbol that would wreak such vengeance for the people.

10:05 P.M.—Falls Church, Virginia

Link left the others in the great room and went to the kitchen where he tried to call Marie, as he'd done several times. Again there was no response. There was no cause for concern—she was likely at her uncle and aunt's home—but he wanted to hear her voice.

His mother came in and gave him a peck. "I'm going to bed," she said. She gave him a wry look. "I'm looking forward to meeting Marie. This home has been male-dominated entirely too long."

Link evoked a smile. "With you around? I don't think there's a man alive who could dominate you."

"Your father could. He just doesn't choose to." She released a breath. "I miss him."

"The doctors were encouraging today. He'll pull through just fine."

"He's not as young as he once was."

"No more worrying. That's an order." He gave her a mock glare.

She fluttered her hand and walked toward her bedroom.

Link returned to the great room and joined Mack and Billy Bowes. He decided to have a single cognac, and try phoning Marie once more. He would call again in the morning before she left for the airport.

And tonight he would try to summon the Grandfather, although he doubted there would be a response. It was as if a switch had been turned off.

30

Tuesday, February 21st

8:40 A.M.*—Lewis Range, Rocky Mountains, Montana*

Charlie remembered when they'd discovered the old cabin. They'd been at their home near Calgary, resting after an intense training session in Libya, when Ghost decided they should trek southward through the mountains to search for old Black Wolf's secret burial place. They'd not found Black Wolf, but they'd used the cabin as a base camp, for Ghost had believed they were close.

The cabin had likely been built by a white prospector a century ago, after the Piegan had been forced to sell off the westernmost region of the Montana reservation to avert further starvation after the buffalo had been depleted. The Bull Clan had told them about the terrible time, relating how the once-proud Piegan had been reduced to begging for handouts from the government. In trade for their continuing loyalty, the U.S. government had reneged on every promise, had been late with every shipment of food, and had sent corrupt agents to rob them. It had begun with the Treaty of 1855, the terrible treaty-which-was-a-lie, when the People's leaders had first accepted the word of the American government.

One day, the Bull Clan elders had told them, his brother

would gain vengeance upon that terrible government, and the People would again be proud.

Ghost had brought the U.S. government to their knees. He said they must be patient for only a little longer, for a final bomb would bring full retribution.

"We need more wood," his brother said in his authoritative voice, and Charlie immediately pulled on the new, brightly colored parka, and went out.

The air chilled him. He decided the temperature must be ten below, perhaps colder, and he was pleased Ghost had bought him the coat with its sheepskin lining and fur-lined hood when they'd stopped in the small North Dakota town.

He'd also given him the Sako .22-250 rifle, with its Leupold ten-power scope. Ghost said he'd killed a man with it, but Charlie had decided there would be no more of that for himself.

He was done with assassinations. He could not even think of such things, for he'd finally become part of a real family. The thought warmed him so thoroughly that he hardly noticed the cold as he gathered the armful of wood and went back into the cabin.

Ghost and the woman were there, the woman huddled in the corner as she'd done since they'd first arrived. When they'd taken her from her house, Ghost had allowed her to bring only a jacket on a peg near the door. It wasn't nearly enough in the bitter cold, and by the time they'd arrived at the cabin she'd been half-frozen. Charlie eyed her as he put down his armload.

"Are you warm?" he asked. She gave a nod and pulled the blanket he'd provided close around her shoulders.

Ghost was in the opposite corner, staring at the skeleton they'd brought from the mountain cave the day before. He'd rearranged it several times, and appeared fascinated but uneasy as he cautiously handled the old bones.

Charlie had asked who the bones had belonged to, and when Ghost told him he'd wondered, for they'd searched for Black Wolf's remains for many years without success. How had Ghost found them so easily this time?

Ghost said he'd been told in his meditation. "Black Wolf's spirit was active," he'd said. "My helper told me where to send the traveler."

Many of the bones were crushed, and Charlie asked about that, too.

"Some were broken by my helper when he killed him," Ghost had said. "The others were shattered by the traveler when I sent him to the cave."

Charlie had been wary of the old, wall-eyed man called the traveler when they'd gone to his home in Browning, but Ghost had needed to speak with him. After he'd learned what he wanted, like where A. L. Anderson's woman lived and where Rashad would be staying, Ghost had sent Charlie out to the Suburban. A while later he'd emerged with an armful of groceries, and they'd gone on to the woman's house. Ghost said he'd silenced the traveler.

Cleanup, Ghost had taught them, was important. The traveler had known too much.

Charlie watched as Ghost went to his bunk and lay down to rest. He said the power of his meditations had faded. He needed rest so they would return.

Charlie wondered. The Bull Clan had told them Ghost's spirit was so strong because he was from the seed of both Lame Bear and Black Wolf, the two most powerful Piegans of all time. With Black Wolf's spirit diminished, wasn't Ghost's also?

It was difficult to even imagine those things. Charlie had never been gifted as Ghost was, and A. L. Anderson had obviously become.

Several times Ghost had queried the woman about A. L. Anderson, but she refused to speak about him. He'd not forced her to talk, just went about other things, like ordering Charlie to repair the cabin's deterioration.

Ghost was lying very still on his bunk, so Charlie was quiet as he stoked the fire. He opened a can of hash, emptied the contents into a saucepan they'd brought from the woman's house, and set it at the edge of the hearth for it to heat.

They'd left a cache of dried and canned food at the cabin the last time they'd used it, but someone had obviously discovered the place and used it, for most of it was gone. Whoever had found the cabin had left the door open, and bears and small animals had been through. There'd been droppings and damage, and it had taken hours to clean up the mess.

Ghost had taken the food from the woman's place before they'd left Browning, as he'd done at the traveler's. They'd left the Suburban burning on a back street and taken an old Dodge four-by-four pickup that they'd found parked in front of the woman's house. Before they'd left, they'd loaded a snowmobile from the woman's garage.

They'd trekked up from the snowbound mountain highway on showshoes, then Ghost had returned for the snowmobile. That had been the first time Charlie had spoken alone with the woman. Since then, Ghost had periodically gone to the mountain to meditate, and Charlie had found her to be as friendly as she was pretty.

Her name was Marie, and Charlie felt an emotional tug each time he looked at her. There was no lust in his emotion, it was more like she was family. She'd been the woman of his brother, and one Rashad had been left to kill.

He stirred the hash in the pan with a large spoon so it wouldn't burn and stick to the metal. Divided into thirds, it would make a satisfactory morning meal.

Charlie wondered if there'd be enough food for a whole month for all of them, or whether they shouldn't get more when they went to pick up Rashad.

Ghost had treated the woman well enough so far, if somewhat like furniture, but Charlie had made sure she had blankets for warmth and food to sustain her. Ghost allowed her no privacy—she held a blanket about herself as she washed or relieved herself into a chamber pot—but she hadn't been abused.

His brother said they'd stay a month, then head to Calgary before the thaw—cautiously and making sure no one was looking for them. Charlie felt his excitement mount as he thought about showing the woman their home in the foothills of the Canadian Rockies. It was similar in ways to this one, but larger and nicer. The Bull Clan elders looked after it when they were away.

He wondered if she liked walking in the mountains.

Charlie pulled the pan back and smiled at the woman. "It's ready," he told her.

Marie LeBecque sat quietly in her corner, suspiciously eyeing the others as she finished the hash on the small plate. Ghost had awakened while Charlie brought her the food.

"When will Rashad get here?" Charlie asked Ghost.

"Not for another day," Ghost said. "The traveler left a message for him at the motel."

Marie looked across at the stack of old bones and suppressed a shudder. From overhearing their conversation, she'd learned they were the remains of Black Wolf, or at least that was what Ghost believed. Periodically Ghost would go to the corner and examine them, then lean down and solemnly rearrange them. And Marie would again feel as if she was in the cast of a shoddy horror movie. But if that was so, she certainly wasn't the heroine, for she only felt a deep sense of terror and wanted to awaken and find herself back in her own bed.

They talked about Link periodically, and her heart grew heavy, for they spoke as if he'd been killed. It was a nightmare of the worst kind and seemed to be without end.

Ghost finished with his food, then set his place aside and walked over to examine the bones of Black Wolf once more. He knelt and stared.

Charlie picked up his brother's plate, then came and retrieved Marie's, offering the calf-eyed look he often wore when he regarded her.

Marie smiled back, wondering if there was a way to put his obvious puppy love to use.

11:50 A.M.—The Farmhouse, Falls Church, Virginia

Lincoln Anderson paced the floor of his bedroom, then sat on his bed and waited.

There'd been no answer when he'd tried Marie's number well before she should have left to drive to Great Falls. He'd called her uncle. She'd not come to dinner the previous evening, and when they'd called her home there'd been no response.

Doctor White Calf had gone to check her house, then phone back. Marie was not at home. "I've called the police," White Calf had said in a heavy voice.

After pacing and staring out for a while longer, Link watched Mack Hall's Towncar pull into the long drive, halt at the state trooper barricade, then come on. The car parked below, and Mack and Manny DeVera dismounted.

Link stood at the window for a while longer, waiting for the extension phone to ring and provide news about Marie. Finally he sighed and went down to join the others. He was greeting Mack and Manny when his mother drove in. She'd been at his father's bedside all morning.

"How's Lucky?" Manny asked.

"Better. The doctor says he's in good condition for his age. Did you see Marian?"

"Yeah. She's taken more than a dozen steps so far this morning," he said proudly.

The telephone sounded inside. Link hurried through the door.

"Anderson," he answered gruffly.

"Ben White Calf. She didn't show for work yesterday and there's still no sign of her. The police are here in her house. Her refrigerator and cupboards look like they've been cleaned out."

Link frowned, puzzled.

"Did she have keys to your truck?" White Calf asked.

"Sure. I left them with her so she could move it."

"Her Jeep's here but your pickup's gone. People saw it parked in front until night before last. They wondered if you hadn't come back."

"Check at Peshan. She may have taken food out to Bright Flame."

"Jack Douglas was up there installing a stove in Bright Flame's shack. There was no sign of your vehicle. One more thing, Link. Marie's snowmobile's missing from the garage. The police thought she may have taken it in your truck."

"It weighs three hundred pounds. She couldn't have loaded it."

"They're checking with neighbors to see if any of them helped her." He paused. "They're beginning to suspect foul play. There's some odd things going on in town. This morning someone called the police about one of our senior citizens who wasn't answering his telephone. You remember the other weather dancer at the Okan?"

"The old guy with the lazy eye?"

"That's him. The police went in and found him dead. They thought it was a heart attack at first, but I just got a call to go over and examine the body. There's a bruise on his throat, and his cupboards were stripped, like someone removed the food."

Link made up his mind abruptly. "I'm coming out."

"I expected that. I'll have you picked up at the airport."

The others had gathered, listening in on the conversation.

Link hung up, feeling the blood leaving his face. "Someone may have taken Marie," he said in a low voice.

"Billy's at the airport." Linda picked up the telephone and dialed, wearing a resolute expression.

While she arranged for a flight, Manny regarded Link. "It was Ghost's bomb, and now both he and Charlie are missing." He paused meaningfully. "We know Ghost's not fond of you. Could they be in Browning?"

A chill ran through Link. It had been Marie who had discovered Ghost's origins, and the terrorist was vindictive. He shook his head then. "It's doubtful." He did not want a swarm of federal officers nosing about and endangering Marie.

Mack Hall looked evenly at Link. "I want to go along."

Link knew his mind-set. He wondered if Mack's desire for vengeance might muddy the water. Yet he understood. Lucky—the only father he'd known and loved—had also been savaged by the monster called Rashad.

Link nodded at the hulking football player. "Bring warm clothing."

4:45 P.M.—Browning, Montana

The 3,000 feet of gravel runway at the Douglas Ranch wouldn't have been suitable for the jet in the summer months, but after a phone conversation with Jack Douglas prior to takeoff, Billy had decided to give the now-frozen field a try.

The Learjet 60 kissed down gently. Braking was adequate on the snowpack surface.

Billy pointed as they came to a stop beside a parked twin Cessna. A pickup and a Ford Explorer were approaching from the ranch house. "You've got a greeting party."

"We'll stay in touch," Link told him.

"I'll stay at the Farmhouse a while longer and keep my eye on the home front." Billy looked out over the fields at the high mountains. It was a vast area to search. "You guys watch your asses. Give a call when you're ready, and I'll have someone swing by to pick you up."

They trouped back and retrieved their bags. When the copilot swung open the entrance hatch, a frigid gust of wind brought notice of the subfreezing temperature.

Jack Douglas stood outside the hatch and took bags as they were handed down. Mack went out first. Link followed, and the copilot pulled the hatch back into the closed position.

When they were clear, Link gave Billy and his copilot a wave. The Learjet's engines rumbled louder, and the craft began to taxi away.

Benjamin White Calf had dismounted from his white Ford Explorer, and stood nearby. Link introduced Mack Hall to both men.

"We'll need a ride to town," Link said as they shook hands.

Jack Douglas nodded at his house. "You're welcome to stay here. We've got room."

"We'll be coming and going a lot, and it'll be handier at the motel. Any developments?"

"Nothing about Marie, if that's what you mean. And no sign of your truck."

"Why would someone take her, Jack?"

"We've all wondered, but no one's come up with anything we want to hear."

"I'll run them into town," said Doctor White Calf. His face was impassive, his eyes narrowed and dark in his weathered face.

When they'd loaded their bags into the back of the Explorer, Jack held them up. "If there's anything I can do to help, let me know and I'll be there."

Link thanked him again, and crawled into the passenger's seat.

As Benjamin White Calf drove away toward the access road, he looked back toward Jack. "He means it. The people here like Marie, and they're concerned."

"Did you get a look at the old man's body?"

"He was strangled. The marks weren't that apparent. Likely a policeman's chokehold, with pressure on the carotid to cut off blood flow to the brain."

Rashad Taylor had been a martial arts instructor, Link remembered. He tried to cast the notion from his mind. There was no basis for the idea. The old man could have been murdered by anyone with appropriate military or police training.

"Anything else," he said.

"Maybe. Yesterday the police discovered a burned-out

vehicle on the south side of town. A GMC Suburban, almost out of gas and filthy inside. Clutter, Coke bottles, things like that. The thing that got their attention was the remains of a stun gun under the rear seat."

Like Charlie might have gotten from the prison, Link thought.

"The plates were removed, and the vehicle identification number's been altered. The state bureau of investigation's sending an ID team from Helena to go through the truck, Marie's house, and the shack the old man lived in."

White Calf pointed out vehicles cruising the access roads, each carrying two persons. "They're looking for Marie," he said. "We're asking everyone to go out armed and in pairs."

The doctor took them directly to Marie's house. It had been a beehive of activity, White Calf said, but now they were waiting for the state ID team. A policeman sat in a marked Bronco parked in the driveway beside Marie's Jeep Cherokee.

Doctor White Calf got out and spoke with the cop, then motioned to Link. "He can't let anyone inside until the ID team's gone through." He handed Link a set of keys. "For Marie's car, so you'll have something to drive while you're here. She'd approve."

After transferring their bags to the Jeep and turning down an offer of dinner at White Calf's home, Link agreed to meet the doctor back at Marie's in the morning.

"Got any ideas where you'll be starting?" White Calf asked.

Link shook his head, wishing he did.

Benjamin White Calf gave a last solemn glance at his niece's house, then left them.

"Where now?" Mack asked as they crawled inside the Jeep and adjusted seats.

"The motel." Link started the engine, gave the cop a wave of his hand, and backed out of the driveway. By the time they arrived at the Outlaw Motel, it was dark.

Linda had telephoned ahead to reserve adjoining rooms, and they were fortunate enough to get them on the ground floor. As Link signed the forms, the Indian girl at the desk eyed Mack Hall like he was from another planet.

"Let's meet in my room in half an hour," Link said when

they'd driven around and lugged the bags to their respective doors.

Link called Linda and told her they'd arrived intact. There were no messages.

By the time Mack rapped at the interconnecting door, Link had changed into jeans and boots. Mack brought in a stack of composite drawings of Ghost and Rashad Taylor, and placed them on the desk.

"I brought a bunch of those, in case someone's seen them around."

"That's a gamble. There's no reason for them to be here." Link prayed he was right.

Mack Hall placed a huge finger on the drawing of Rashad Taylor. "I want the man. I may not find him here, but I'll find him."

"That's your priority. Mine's to find Marie."

It had been a long day and they were tired, and neither could think of a logical first step to take in their search. After eating supper in the adjoining restaurant, they'd come up with nothing better than to drop by the police station, learn which areas and back roads hadn't yet been searched, and drive and look like the rest were doing.

31

Wednesday, February 22nd

9:00 A.M.—Lewis Range, Rocky Mountains, Montana

Black Wolf's bones lay in the corner of the cabin; broken, disarranged, and defiled. Their condition saddened Ghost, for the legendary holy man had been powerful and brave. He was an ancestor, and as the Bull Clan had taught them, blood is important. But his helper had been adamant that he destroy Black Wolf, and had even detailed how it was to be done.

The burial cave had been violated, and the bones had been attacked with a hand ax, as Ghost had ordered. The traveler had left the ax imbedded in the ancient corpse. The helper had told him to remove the bones from the cave and strew them in the four holy directions. Ghost had brought the bones to the cabin and would do as the helper said. There was no hurry about it. Black Wolf had rested for a hundred and thirty years in the cave. A few days in the cabin shouldn't matter.

He examined the ax closer. It was common enough—the kind that could be purchased in any hardware store—with a hickory handle and a wedge to hold the head in place. Yet the common ax had destroyed the powerful spirit as another had killed the once-great man.

Destroy Black Wolf!

His brother, the man named A. L. Anderson, had received strength from Black Wolf's spirit. Ghost had ordered the death of Anderson, just as he'd ordered Black Wolf's bones defiled.

Yet now Ghost's own meditations were difficult to comprehend, the messages not nearly as clear as they'd been. He'd never questioned his visions or why they occurred. They'd been with him since he'd been taken north and the Bull Clan elders taught him the ancient secrets.

He stared at the bones longer, gently placed the ax on them, then looked at the woman.

Destroy Black Wolf!

There was another, the helper had said, a descendant of Black Wolf. The traveler said her name was Bright Flame. He was fearful of her because she walked among the dead.

Ghost had told the traveler to include her in the instructions he'd left for Rashad. He wondered who Bright Flame might be, since she, too, was a descendant of Black Wolf. *Blood is important,* the Bull Clan had taught them, and Rashad would not be merciful when he killed her.

Ghost felt a cold shiver race along his spine. But Bright Flame must die, just as Anderson's woman must die . . . for she too was a part of the whole. Killing this one would be of little concern to him, not like ordering the death of A. L. Anderson or the unknown Bright Flame, who were of Ghost's blood.

Charlie was infatuated with Anderson's woman. This morning when they'd gone outside and Ghost had mentioned that she must be dealt with, Charlie had objected. He'd given him a stern look, but his brother hadn't understood and offered to drive into town for more food. He wanted her to go to Canada with them, so he could show her their home.

Ghost couldn't allow her to live much longer. He'd only delayed this long because she'd not seemed unimportant and he'd wondered if Charlie might want her for diversion. But Charlie was speaking with her now, treating her special even though he knew what must be done. Ghost thought of walking over and taking a whack at the woman with the ax to provide a lesson to his brother.

He decided to wait, to give her to Rashad after he went for him tonight. Rashad would use her properly, and Charlie would see she was only a woman. When Rashad was sated, Ghost would take her outside and demand that Charlie accompany them, then kill her in front of him.

11:00 A.M.—Browning, Montana

They'd gone by Marie's house but the Montana SBI identification team had still been inside, so they'd returned to their rooms, exhausted after the long night of riding the roads and dropping by the police station to hear the latest disheartening news . . . no sign of Marie.

Two hours of sleep hadn't been nearly enough, but it would have to suffice.

When they returned, Doctor White Calf was outside, speaking with an investigator from the state bureau of investigation. He motioned for Link to join them.

As Link approached, he noted circles beneath the doctor's eyes. He'd not rested, either. White Calf introduced the lieutenant, who led the ID team, then left them to go inside the house.

"The doctor says you may know more about all this."

"I wish I did. What have you got so far?"

"There's no indications of violence, if that's what you mean. We've lifted a few prints besides Miss LeBecque's. We'll fax them to Washington. Some of them yours?"

"Possibly. I've been here before."

The lieutenant looked at the house, and Link could tell he was sifting through his mind, trying to think of the right questions.

"You can go on inside," he finally said. "Just don't touch the white stuff. Our technicians powdered the place for prints, and it's hard to get the crap off."

Link went through the front door and joined White Calf, who was peering into the cupboard. Link knelt with him. Everything was missing, even canisters, spices, and bags of salt and sugar. Someone had purposefully removed it.

Why? he wondered as he looked into the refrigerator and found the same condition.

The thieves had needed food where they were going. If that was so, why take Marie?

Link checked the hallway closet. Her Kelly green parka and snowmobile suit were still there. If she was in the open, she'd freeze without proper winter wear.

He went to her bedroom, then to her dresser and opened a jewelry box. Most of it was costume, but there were a few expensive pieces.

A thief who'd steel food from the cupboard but not jewelry?

"Find anything?" White Calf asked from the open door.

"Her jewelry's still here." Link blew out a tired breath, then walked back to the living room, shaking his head. It was all very puzzling.

He stared at the wall behind the couch, observing the artifacts. An old Piegan warrior's headdress. An ornate blanket tacked to the wall. She'd said it was more than a hundred years old—a five-star Hudson's Bay blanket traded for beaver pelts and buffalo skins.

White Calf joined him. He pointed to a segment of raw-hide stretched in a frame. "I don't remember that."

"It's new," Link said. Marie had found it in the corner of a curio and antique shop off the reservation—bought it for ten dollars from a woman who had no idea what she had. There were old markings made with yellow paint from crushed buffalo gallstones, and black, made from charcoal paste—daubed on with a porous bone by a long-dead-and-forgotten record keeper.

Link scanned the room carefully, looking for anything out of place, anything that didn't belong. Except for the white compound left on items on the coffee table, which he'd been warned to avoid, everything seemed as he'd last seen it.

He returned his attention to the historical ornaments, remembering how Marie had described each carefully, as a connoisseur of other art might explain a Raphael or Picasso. She'd been especially proud of the story pelt.

Link started to turn away, then stepped closer. There were two small marks at the bottom of the story pelt that weren't like the others. These were in blue ink from a ball-point pen, and hadn't been there when he'd last seen it.

Two symmetrical curved lines. Squiggles, Manny DeVera called them. Ghost's signature.

White Calf frowned. "See something I don't?"

Link's mind was racing.

"I've got to go," he said, and turned on his heel toward the door.

Somewhere, Ghost had Marie. Why?

Riddles within riddles.

Black Wolf. The Grandfather. The helper.

Ghost. Spirit of Lame Bear. His brother. The terrorist.

Rashad had tried to kill his stepparents. Ghost had taken the woman he loved. He had spared him, but now he was trying to destroy those near to him.

Billy Bowes had said understanding wasn't necessary, but now understanding had become essential.

As he slid into the driver's seat, Mack Hall bolted upright, stretched and yawned. "Guess I nodded off," he said sheepishly.

Link shoved the lever into gear and accelerated slowly from the curb, buying time to think of what he should do next. Driving the back roads was like searching for a single thread in a massive quilt. The big sky country was vast. There were too many gullies and hills, too many hiding places to have faith they could find them in time. If he could only get a tiny clue, anything to tell him where to begin.

Could Bright Flame help? he wondered.

He had another thought. "Get the composite drawings from the back. Show them around town and see if anyone's seen Ghost or Rashad."

Mack blinked and frowned. "I thought you said it wasn't likely?"

"I've changed my mind. I'll try to be back by dark. If I'm not, don't worry. Just see if anyone's seen those two or another guy who would have looked like me. He's a little skinnier and his hair's longer. That would be Charlie."

"Where are you going?"

"Up north a few miles. There's a woman I want to talk to."

Link dropped Mack off in town, made a U-turn, and hurried westward.

A police car sped up behind him and flashed its lightbar. After he pulled over, the cop eased up beside him and gave him a hard look, then smiled and waved him on. Link remembered him. One of the Desert Storm vets from the Okan.

He drove at a more nominal speed, turned right at the intersection outside town, and hit the accelerator. Thinking. Heart pounding. Marie was with the man Doctor McNabb had described as being abnormally without remorse.

At ninety miles per hour the Cherokee's tires chattered on the washboard highway. He kept the speedometer needle firmly pinned there.

Ghost sometimes gave women to Rashad and Charlie. Link prayed that was all, that she was only being violated, however brutally. He would get her through that trauma. Patience and love could do that. But he could not bring her back to life, and Manny had told him about their horrendous *cleanup*. He drove faster yet, for every minute might matter.

Link saw the turnoff in the distance and began to slow. He braked but still took the turn too fast, skidding onto the old Peshan road.

A familiar pickup was approaching. The driver waved.

Link stopped and rolled down the window.

Jack Douglas peered out at him. "I just came from Peshan. Checked on a stove we put in a couple of days back, and looked around for your pickup again. Nothing there, Link."

"Did you see Bright Flame?"

"Only saw her once in all the times I've been here since the Okan. She avoids people."

Link glanced behind Douglas at the gun rack on the rear window.

"I carry a rifle wherever I go these days. There's two here. Take your pick." There was a high-gloss Browning bolt-action and a Winchester model 94 carbine.

"Which do you favor?" Link asked.

"Doesn't matter. I've got a gun cabinet full of rifles at home."

"The thirty-thirty."

Jack handed it across butt first, then fished in the glove box and came up with a gold-colored box of Federal Premium ammunition.

Link placed the rifle and ammo at his side. "There's something you ought to know, Jack. Ghost has been here. He left his sign in Marie's house."

Jack's eyes narrowed. "Marie tried to tell us Ghost is Piegan. None of us would listen."

"He's my half brother by birth. He's also damned dangerous. If a couple hundred agents and state troopers came swarming anywhere near, he'd kill her."

"You don't want me to tell anyone?"

"Just get it across that we're dealing with dangerous people."

Jack nodded. "I'll see to it."

"I'm going to try to find Bright Flame. See if she can tell me anything."

"I wish you luck, but I think she's lost touch with reality."

"Mack's in town, handing out flyers and trying to see if anyone's seen any of them."

Jack Douglas nodded. "I'll give him a hand. Good luck."

As Link continued toward Peshan, his thoughts were grim. Talking with Jack had verbalized his fears. Marie had been missing for two and a half days. He was increasingly concerned that they'd already killed her.

Browning, Montana

Mack had looked up and down every aisle of the small hardware store when an elderly man emerged from the rear. His eyes widened as he took in Mack's size.

"Ask a couple of questions?" Mask said amiably.

The clerk hadn't seen the men in the composites, but said they looked familiar. Since the drawing had been broadcast on television screens for the past week, Mack wasn't surprised.

"Thanks," he said, and went out to go to the next place of business. It was damned cold, and he huddled in the overcoat.

A pickup pulled up, and the driver hailed him. "Get in and warm up," Jack Douglas said.

Mack crawled inside and luxuriated in the warm air blasting from the heater.

"Guess you're not used to our Montana heat waves," Jack said.

Mack held his hands over the heater duct. "I've got more to get cold than most."

"Link told me what you're doing. Having any luck?"

"Not yet."

Benjamin White Calf pulled in beside them.

Jack dismounted, and the two men talked. Mack overheard the words "Bull Clan," "Disgrace," and "Ghost." They were grim-faced.

Jack crawled back in beside him. "Let's get a bite to eat and talk this campaign of yours over. Maybe try the gas stations and convenience stores outside of town."

Peshan, Blackfeet Reservation, northern Montana

Link had searched the area, but had seen no sign of Bright Flame. He'd tried her shack. The place was warm from the fire Jack Douglas had built, but she wasn't inside.

He'd stood outside and called her name, then gone to the burial ground. There'd been footprints in the snow near the grave of Henry Layton, but no sign of his biological mother.

Crazy Woman, Bright Flame, Sarah Layton.

He stood in front of the old buildings beside Marie's Cherokee, wondering if he shouldn't return to town. Perhaps go to his room and try to evoke the Grandfather.

But that would be no use. The Grandfather had left him. He remembered the final dream. The eagle exploding, killing important people . . . the struggle and the death of the Grandfather.

Forget your doubts, he told himself. *Think as a Piegan.*

If the Grandfather was truly a spiritual helper come to guide him, *then* what could the dream have meant. He thought back to the ending. The man with the wandering eye had been coming for the Grandfather ... getting closer ... then attacking with the hand ax.

He saw the ax clearly as it was raised. A common hand ax, no different from others you could buy in any hardware store.

The ax had fallen, and contact with the Grandfather had been lost ever since.

Someone had strangled the old weather dancer, the man with the lazy, wandering eye. Ghost? Rashad? Not Charlie. It wasn't his style.

Charlie, Little Crow, his brother. Riddles within riddles.

Link took a last look around, then reached for the Jeep's door handle.

He paused as he heard a faint, echoing sound. A wind noise? He turned toward the burial ground, walked forward a few feet, and listened intently.

It was distant, low, and sorrowful. "La-ay-ton," the wind crooned.

Browning, Montana

He lay half-clothed on his bed, breathing harshly, a sheen of sweat glistening from his muscular body. The agony within his chest was consuming. Not sharp jolts of pain, more like a bone-deep ache emanating from deep in his core.

When the fucking football player had grabbed hold and squeezed, he'd almost done the job. He'd estimated six ribs were broken . . . when he'd been able to feel there. Now that region of his chest was swollen and throbbed, and made him constantly nauseous.

A couple of times during the endless drive he'd coughed. God but how it had hurt, and he'd tried to avoid it. But he'd coughed before he could control it, and tasted blood.

He'd known the taste of blood. He'd been bathed in the stuff as he'd dissected and slashed, but it had been the blood of others. He'd wondered if something inside his chest had been punctured and decided it was probable. Whenever he'd turned the wrong way or assumed the wrong position, the pain had been most intense, so he felt it was likely that a shattered rib was pushing into a lung or whatever.

He'd stretched as he'd driven, and never allowed himself to slump again.

It was healing. He visualized scar tissue growing over the sharp end of the protruding rib. There'd been no more bleeding, so he wondered if the inner organ wasn't healing, too.

Life was a crapshoot. You won or you lost, or muddled around somewhere in between. He was recovering. Winning. Ghost had told him you could will such things to happen if you concentrated hard enough. Scar tissue was forming. Tomorrow Ghost would find a doctor.

Ghost took care of them. He'd promised, and Ghost didn't lie. When he'd checked into the motel, there'd been an envelope with a note. Tonight Ghost would come for him.

There'd been a cleanup task in the note, along with directions to a place north of town, but regardless of how he'd wanted to, Rashad had been unable to comply. After a period of deep sleep, which he'd only been able to do because he'd been without rest for days, he could hardly stand. To drive anywhere and chase down even an old woman was out of the question.

Ghost would understand.

The torment continued. He endured, but only because he knew that it would not be for much longer. Tonight.

Peshan, Blackfeet Reservation, northern Montana

Link approached quietly, drawn by the soft crooning of Bright Flame's lament, and watched from the growing shadows as nightfall descended.

He was startled by the change. Even though she wore the parka and bulky clothing, he could tell she was stick thin, so frail she could hardly keep her head erect. She knelt by the grave, making the eerie sounds that combined with those of the wind rustling high in the trees.

"La-ay-ton," she crooned, then released a long, shuddering sob.

Bright Flame's voice dropped to a whisper, so he drew closer.

Algonkian Blackfeet words he could not comprehend.

He drew closer yet, in plain view now but she seemed not to notice. She became silent and stared at the mound, her face lost in the shadows of the approaching night.

She peered sidelong at him. He could not see her features, but knew her burning eyes were upon him. She began to chant, some of it in English, but her voice was muffled.

He distinguished the word *son,* then *Spirit of Lame Bear.* Something about *Black Wolf.* More unintelligible words in Algonkian.

An eagle . . . many chiefs . . .

He struggled mentally, and as she continued he began to understand more.

Spirit of Lame Bear was killing Black Wolf.

Everything about him.

Bright Flame stared in the darkness and whispered a final word: *Everything.*

A chill coursed through Link.

She sobbed, and the sound was like a catch in her throat.

"Where is Spirit of Lame Bear?" he asked.

He wasn't sure of the response for it was so softly spoken, but he thought he discerned, *With Black Wolf.*

As he waited for her to continue, she leaned forward and carefully positioned herself on Henry Layton's grave, arms outstretched, hands clutching at the carefully tended mound.

"Where is Black Wolf?" Link cried out.

She sighed, then giggled suddenly, as if she were a child . . . or a lover being teased.

"Where?" he asked.

"Lay-ton?" Her voice was gentle, no longer sad. A murmur.

"Please," he pleaded.

"I see you, Lay-ton," she whispered playfully, and her voice was younger. The voice of Sarah Layton? She released a long sigh of breath.

She was still. There was no more crooning.

He waited for a while longer, but there was no slightest movement.

He started to go to her, but stopped himself. A low sound issued from the treetops. He lifted his eyes but there was nothing there.

Lincoln Anderson rose to his feet and started back. He turned once and looked, but could only discern the mound of the grave. It was as if she'd become one with it.

Link sat in the Jeep, staring out at the darkness. After all the tragedy, Bright Flame had known a moment of happiness.

Perhaps longer than a moment.

Henry and Sarah Layton. Together through eternity. It was a matter of belief.

With effort he pulled his mind away, and was faced with the burning question of Marie LeBecque's location.

Riddles within riddles.

A matter of belief!

He began to go through it again, trying to look at it with the eye of a believer.

Where was Marie?

Marie was with Ghost. And, according to Bright Flame, Ghost was with Black Wolf.

Ghost was destroying Black Wolf. Everything about him.

Spirit of Lame Bear, Ghost, the terrorist, son of Bright Flame.

Black Wolf, the Grandfather, his helper.

Ghost was destroying Link, and everything about him. His new parents. His woman.

Abraham Lincoln Anderson, Black Albertson, Spirit of Black Wolf, son of Sarah Layton.

Lincoln Anderson and the Grandfather's spirits were connected. Black Wolf was the Grandfather was his helper. To destroy everything about Black Wolf, Ghost must also destroy Link . . . and everything about him.

Where was Marie? With Ghost.

Where was Ghost? With Black Wolf.

Where was Black Wolf?

The person to ask was not Bright Flame. He should go to Lincoln Anderson, who knew the Grandfather who was Black Wolf.

Okay, buddy, Link demanded of himself, *where the hell is the Grandfather?*

After a few more minutes of plaguing himself, he got out of the vehicle.

The old buildings were silent, dark, and brooding. There was a faint rustle in the distant treetops, but he knew it was not Bright Flame. She was with Henry Layton. Safe.

He walked past the buildings and the once-parking lot to the Okan site, then searched until he found the very spot where he'd stood in anguish and endured the suffering.

He closed his eyes tightly. "Where are they, Old Man?"

A chilled gust of wind swept over him. Link shivered with the cold, but did not move.

"I did as you wished. I prepared and proved myself. Where are they?"

Browning, Montana

Mack had tried the various businesses suggested by Jack Douglas, but no one had seen anyone resembling the men in the drawings. He was exhausted, his weariness worsened by the lack of sleep, when Jack dropped him off at the motel room door.

"We're both tired and out of ideas," Jack said. "Maybe a night's sleep will make us smarter. Pick you up in the morning for breakfast?"

"Sure." Mack had grown to like the rancher, once airplane maintenance supervisor.

"I won't be able to help you tomorrow, Mack. After we eat breakfast I've got a trip to make." Jack Douglas touched his hat in salute, and drove away.

Mack looked about. The nearest vehicle was a dusty

Honda parked a few rooms down. Link was still not back. Probably still out roaming the back roads, he guessed. He'd opened the door and was about to enter his room when he remembered a last place he'd not tried.

He'd asked the day clerk at the motel desk, but not the people on at night.

He huffed a shiver and walked toward the office, wondering if he should have come. Pop was still in his hospital bed at Walter Reed. If Link didn't need him tomorrow, he wondered if he shouldn't return.

What if you miss Rashad?

Mack grimaced at the thought as he entered the office and waved a greeting to the Indian girl at the counter. Her eyes widened at his size, a common reaction throughout the day.

Mack spread the drawings on the countertop. "Know either of these guys?" he asked.

"Sure. They're on television every time I turn it on. The terrorists, right?"

"You haven't seen them?"

"If I had, I'd of let the police know."

He pushed the drawings across to her. "Keep those, just in case."

She'd hardly listened. "Are you the football player we heard was in town?"

"Yeah." He flashed his smile.

"And you're staying here? We don't get many celebrities. We don't even get two black men staying at the same time."

"There's another black man here?"

"Yeah. We normally don't have many of those around."

"Who's the other guy?"

"The man in one-five-two. I admitted him. He's not as dark as you, and not quite as large, but he's a Negro . . . oops . . . sorry. That word's out these days, isn't it?"

"How big is he?"

"He's . . . you know . . . fat." She was still concerned that he'd taken offense.

"People can make themselves look fat, and Rashad wears disguises."

"This one sort of hobbles and acts like he's in pain when he walks."

Mack remembered having him in his grasp and thinking . . . *hoping* . . . he'd hurt him.

"He's sick. He went straight to his room last night and didn't come out all day. When one of the maids tried to get in to clean, he told her he was down with the flu and not to disturb him."

"And he doesn't look like the drawing?"

She looked again. "Nope. He's fat, bald, and has a heavy beard."

"A man could shave his head and not his face."

She looked closer. "You know, the features are *sort* of similar. Our guest has a funny mouth like that. One side sort of droops."

Mack felt a jolt of excitement. Words tumbled forth. "Did he use a credit card?"

"He paid for two days in cash." The girl frowned. "Think I ought to call the police?"

"Which way's his room?"

"I'd hate to disturb his privacy."

"If it's not him, I'll apologize and go straight to my room. Which way?"

"Room one-fifty-two. Four doors down from yours."

"His name?"

As she looked it up, he noticed that her fingers trembled. "J. Pittman."

When Mack left the office he couldn't hold himself to a walk, but found himself loping. He passed his room and slowed, telling himself not to do anything dumb.

He stopped in front of 152, glanced at the curtain and noted a dim light inside. Mack hesitated, then knocked. Not a hard rap, but enough to get a sleeping man's attention.

He held his ear close to the door. There were no sounds.

He knocked again. The light went off. He heard a slight noise, of someone moving inside.

"Who is it?" The voice was low and rumbling.

"Motel manager, Mr. Pittman. The maid said you were sick, and I wanted to make sure you're okay. It's our policy."

There was a long pause. "I'm fine. I just need rest."

Stirring noises from inside. The sound of a human grunt.

"I'm sorry, but I must insist."

Mack saw the curtains shift slightly then drop back into

place. The man inside had seen him. If it was Rashad Taylor, he'd remember the one who'd attacked him.

"Open the door," he demanded.

More slight noises, then the sound of a door closing. The bathroom?

Silence. Mack felt his panic rising, drew back, and lunged hard with his shoulder. The hinges gave way, and the door crashed open.

He fumbled for the light switch, adrenaline creating a roaring sound inside his head. A lamp illuminated. There was no one in the room.

Get him! Mack's mind shouted as he hurried to the bathroom door and tugged—it was locked from inside. He hit it with another hard block, and it fell inward.

A dim figure was struggling, already halfway out the bathroom window.

Not again! He grasped a leg and tugged mightily. The man came back with him, and Mack stumbled and fell through the bedroom doorway.

Rashad turned, crouched, mouth open and breathing with difficulty, not so maimed that he couldn't pull a knife from the sheath on his calf.

Mack scrambled upright, stood back, and held out his arms.

"Come on," Mack said, beckoning, feeling a smile form. "I've got work to finish."

Rashad assumed a wider stance—held the knife forward, blade up.

Mack stepped closer, leaned away as Rashad lunged, and swiped with the knife.

He groaned with the effort. Mack saw blood at the corner of his mouth.

"I thought I might have got a couple ribs," Mack said happily. He feinted forward. Rashad swung, and missed again.

"You're a dead man," Rashad muttered. "I got your old man. Now it's your turn."

Mack grinned. "How're your ribs?"

Rashad shifted the knife to his left hand and extended the knuckles of his right, poised, ready to attack, hatred glittering from hard eyes. Blood trickled from the drooping mouth.

He was still deadly, still dangerous. But how quick and how lucid was he?

Mack shifted forward slightly, darted his left hand out.

When Rashad followed the motion with a parry, Mack slammed his right hand down, contacting the forearm. The knife flew into the bathroom, clattered there.

Rashad turned and painfully knelt to retrieve it. Mack scooped him from behind, lifted, and held tightly as he carried him into the bedroom.

"Aaannghh!" Rashad groaned.

Mack tightened more. "Where's Ghost?" he panted.

"Fuck . . . aanghh . . . you."

"Where's Ghost?" Mack repeated, then squeezed and felt ribs begin to give.

"Angghhh," Rashad groaned. "I don't . . . angghh!"

"Police!" shouted a man peeking around the door. "Drop him!"

"He's yours," Mack muttered, gave a final shuddering squeeze, and released his hold.

Rashad fell into a still heap, blood dribbling from his mouth onto the carpet.

The policeman entered cautiously, revolver drawn. Another came in behind him.

"He attacked me with a knife," Mack said pleasantly. "It's in the bathroom."

Two hours later, when they'd finished questioning him at the police station, Mack was driven back to the motel.

"I still wonder what the hell he was doing here in Browning," the driver said.

The second cop spoke up. "The captain agrees with Mack. Rashad holed up on his way to Canada, trying to get out of the country."

Mack Hall was the newest local hero.

Before he got out of the cruiser, a report came over the radio. Doctor White Calf had examined Rashad Taylor. He was still alive.

"Bullshit," said the driver, who'd just gotten Mack's autograph. "You should have squeezed a little harder."

Policemen were still searching Rashad's room when Mack stopped off to tell Link the news. The Jeep was still missing, and there was no response to his knock.

When he'd settled on his bed, Mack decided to wait up

for his friend. After an hour, when Link had still not returned, he was concerned. Ten minutes later he fell dead asleep.

11:50 P.M.

The driver kept to back streets, yet had to turn off twice to avoid vehicles coming slowly, as if the people inside were searching for something.

He was unafraid. Ghost did not know fear. Yet he was increasingly cautious as he approached the motel from the rear. He doused the lights and drove closer, until the pickup was in deep shadows, then parked and killed the engine.

"Wait here while I get him," he told Charlie as he quietly dismounted, uncaring that the door remained cracked open for he'd removed the bulb from the overhead lamp.

Slowly then, he moved forward until he approached a stairwell at the back of the motel.

All was not right. He sensed the presence before he saw the shadow figure ahead.

A door opened, and he clearly saw the room number—the one the traveler had reserved for J. Pittman. A man in uniform came out and stood beside the first as he lit a cigarette. Another joined them, and they conversed in low voices. One laughed.

Ghost moved closer, listened as they smoked and talked about the man who had been in the room. Then they spoke about other things that were happening in town. Finally he moved away. Quietly and with stealth, as he knew to do.

A moment later he slid back into the Dodge pickup and started the engine.

Charlie spoke from the darkness. "Was Rashad there?"

"They have him."

"Will we go for him?"

"He's no use to us any longer."

Charlie looked at him. "You said you'd protect us."

"He failed me. A. L. Anderson is alive."

32

Thursday, February 23rd

6:45 A.M.—Lewis Range, Rocky Mountains, Montana

Charlie yawned and stretched. He slept well in the high country, with its clean, rare air.

Ghost was up, observing the old bones with a troubled look. Periodically he'd glance at the woman, Marie, asleep where she'd curled up on the floor in the corner.

Charlie swung his legs out of bed and began pulling on his trousers.

"Rashad will talk," Ghost said, coming closer. "He'll tell them everything."

Charlie felt the day was too fresh to be spoiled by pessimism. Rashad despised authorities and was terrified of Ghost. He couldn't imagine him telling them anything.

"He'll try to save himself," Ghost insisted.

"He doesn't even know where we are," Charlie reasoned, keeping his voice down.

"He's been to the cabin up north. We can't return there. Rashad will tell them about the Bull Clan and about the employers we've had."

Not return home? Charlie was distressed. "Did your helper tell you all that?"

Ghost's look became troubled. "I'm having difficulty with my meditations. In the visions I'm in a high place, then I'm flying. Like a bird."

Charlie pulled on his shirt, feeling sad. "We can't go

home? Where will we go?" He stepped into open-laced Sno-Paks.

"We'll stay here for a while."

Charlie was somewhat mollified. He was content, sharing his time with Marie, who played a good hand of gin rummy and was uncanny at cribbage. He looked forward to the time when Ghost would ease the restriction, and they could bundle up and go for walks together.

Ghost looked at Marie, who stirred then went back to sleep. "His woman will draw him."

"Our brother?"

"I've angered my helper." Ghost stared evenly at Marie. "Now she'll draw him here."

"No," whispered Charlie, almost under his breath.

"I saw him in my meditation last night, searching. I asked, but my helper wouldn't tell me what to do. He's angry because I didn't do as he told me."

"If he didn't talk to you, you should leave her alone."

Ghost looked irritated that Charlie would argue.

"There's no reason to kill her." Charlie made his statement as strong as he dared.

"My helper told me to destroy everything about Black Wolf and A. L. Anderson. We shouldn't have brought her here. I shouldn't have delayed spreading Black Wolf's bones. When those things are done, the helper may be satisfied."

Charlie opened his mouth to argue, then closed it. It would do no good.

Ghost looked at the door. "I'll go up on the mountain. I can think better there. The mountain makes me feel more alive."

"The three of us should walk there together. We could talk and explore, watch the winter ravens like we did when we were young. I told the woman about them and . . ."

"No." Ghost's voice was short. "You shouldn't become close to her, Charlie. She's not your friend. She just wants us to put off what must be done."

A sour lump grew in Charlie's throat. He wanted to ask "when?," but he knew. It would happen when his brother returned.

Ghost looked at Charlie. His look softened. "It's for the best. There really isn't enough food, and we can't be seen in town."

Charlie was distraught. It wasn't at all what he wanted. He'd been speaking with Marie, playing card games, and entertaining her. He'd never rebelled against Ghost's wishes. He knew his brother loved him, for he'd shielded him from suffering since his earliest memories. But the girl shouldn't have to die.

He couldn't bring harm to Ghost. There had to be another way.

Marie had feigned sleep since she'd awakened and heard the men whispering. She hadn't been able to make out their words, but knew they were discussing something momentous.

She sat up and stretched.

"Good morning," said Charlie.

"Want me to make breakfast?" Marie asked.

"Sure," Charlie said, and formed the lopsided grin that reminded her of Link.

Ghost studied her wordlessly, then turned and pulled on his white, down-filled parka. He drew up the hood, slipped on woolen gloves, and left without speaking.

A shudder coursed through Marie. Not at what she'd seen, but what had not been there. There was no compassion in his eyes, no slightest human communication, not even as if between captor and hostage, master and slave. There had been only a void; he'd regarded her as if she might be a weed, without even the warmth one might exhibit if observing a dumb animal.

She went to the fireplace, wondering what to prepare. There wasn't a great selection.

"Marie?" Charlie asked tentatively. He approached hesitantly.

"Is everything okay?" she asked.

Charlie heard a noise outside and cast a worried expression at the door. Then he drew a sharp breath, as if he'd made up his mind about something.

He spoke in a faint whisper, as he'd done with Ghost. "We'll leave as soon as he's gone."

Marie's heart trembled. *Was he talking of escape?*

"We must," he whispered, as if convincing himself, maintaining his fixed stare on the door. He looked increasingly troubled as they waited.

"Where's he going?" she finally asked.

"The mountain."

When Ghost had gone there on previous occasions, they'd been left alone for two hours or more. They'd have time to get to the road. Ghost had the truck keys in his pocket, but Link kept a spare in a box hidden in the wheel well. She'd thought of it often during the past three days, trying to think of a way to get to the highway and the pickup the men had buried under branches cut from trees.

The previous night they'd left for several hours, and she'd almost loosened her bindings sufficiently to wriggle free. She'd despaired at the sound of the returning snowmobile.

That's it! Ghost wore snowshoes when he went on the mountain.

"We'll take my snowmobile," she breathed happily. They could take the snow machine and be down in twenty minutes.

Charlie nodded vaguely. There'd been no noises from outside for the past fifteen minutes. He removed his new parka from where it hung on a rusted nail and handed it to her. Marie had been allowed only a light jacket, and she'd almost frozen when they'd come up.

"Thank you," she said as she wriggled into the bulky parka. She meant it.

He gave her his glove liners, keeping the leather shells for himself. "Pull up the hood," Charlie cautioned. "It's important that your head doesn't get cold."

She positioned it, and he fastened the Velcro strap at her chin. He shrugged a bulky sweater over his thinner one, then donned a knit cap, which he pulled over his ears. Finally he stood by the door and listened.

"We'll have to hurry," he told her, and she could hear unsureness in his voice.

Don't back out, she silently pleaded. "We'll make it just fine, Charlie," Marie said. "I'll take you to my house and feed you a good meal, and get some hot chocolate down you."

A wistful look twitched at his face. "They're looking for us. I'll drop you off near town and come back for my brother. Just don't tell them where we are."

"I won't." She'd make a pact with the devil if necessary.

Charlie hesitated, looking at the rifle. He huffed a sigh.

"Who would I shoot?" he muttered, and pushed open the door.

She felt they should at least disable the rifle but held her tongue, unwilling to push him too hard lest he change his mind.

Marie followed him out hesitantly. Her heart was pounding, the sense of urgency accentuated by a pulse that roared in her ears. She took several cautious steps, her first time outside the cabin since they'd arrived, looking toward the mountain where Ghost had gone, half expecting him to be waiting for them. Although the morning was gray and overcast, the light reflected from the snow was blinding. She squinted, saw only the imprints of the snowshoes.

Charlie looked about nervously. He'd confided that he'd been frightened of Ghost since they'd been children. He'd called it respect, but his change of expression when he referred to his brother made the truth apparent. She prayed he wouldn't lose his nerve.

Marie approached the snowmobile, hoping . . . She rejoiced! *The key was in the ignition!*

It was her machine, and she knew it well. She crawled aboard, wondering if she shouldn't leave both men behind. Just get to the road and *escape!*

She pulled the choke fully out—paused, willed her hands to stop their violent trembling—pushed the key, and turned it.

The starter chugged, slowly at first then more rapidly, but the engine didn't catch. Marie's heart crawled toward her throat as the raucous noise corrupted the still morning.

The engine could be cantankerous. *Please!* she pleaded to the great snowmobile deity, then tried again, this time with the choke pushed halfway in. There was no ignition. She smelled the odor of gasoline. Again she tried. The starter motor was incredibly loud in the stillness, but the engine gave no sign of willingness to cooperate.

"Here," Charlie cried, and pushed snowshoes toward her. His hands were trembling.

Marie dismounted, hurled the snowmobile key as far as she could throw it, and bent to attach the snowshoes.

Ghost stood very still, listening to the grinding sound of the snowmobile starter.

Was the woman trying to escape? He waited for a moment longer, then started back, worrying that she'd harmed Charlie.

He delayed to negotiate a small downward climb, replaced the snowshoes, and trekked faster. Even for a person in good condition, the descending journey in heavy snow was difficult. Although he hurried, the trip took fifteen minutes.

Ghost approached the clearing cautiously, moved to the back of the cabin, paused, and listened. He left the snowshoes at the side of the building, and slipped around to the front.

The snowmobile was there, as he'd known it would be. Snowshoe tracks led down the mountainside, but Ghost knew to not trust such signs. Charlie had been trained in deception.

He flattened himself against the cabin, reached with a single hand, pushed open the unlatched door, and waited. There were no sounds of movement. After several seconds he observed through the doorway, confident he would have heard them.

It was empty. Charlie and the woman were gone.

He went inside. The rifle was in place beside the bed. Ghost hefted and examined it, thinking his brother was likely okay, probably just trying to save the woman. He went to the bunk and searched beneath, where they'd hidden the ammunition.

It was foolhardy of Charlie to leave the rifle. He was obviously not thinking clearly. His brother attached himself easily to people who acted as if they cared, and the woman had been working to win him over so she could save herself. Few people really cared about Charlie. In fact, he could think of no one but himself.

Old man Weiser had despised Charlie. Even Rashad had belittled him until Ghost had made it clear he would accept none of it, that he alone was to correct or chastise his brother.

The Bull Clan had thought Charlie too weak in spirit to become a warrior. But Ghost had noticed how well his brother could shoot and had driven him to practice and continue, and he'd mastered the art of assassination. Charlie had become a feared instrument of death, just as had Ghost and Rashad. He should have been proud, but Charlie remained reluctant. Charlie wanted it to end. But Ghost knew many truths, and one of those was that for them it could never end.

Although he'd trusted him, Rashad had only been a tool. Like the traveler. Like Martin Cherone. Important for their contributions, but dispensable after they'd served their purpose.

But not Charlie.

Ghost opened the rifle's bolt and loaded the magazine with three rounds, then another in the chamber. He closed it and slipped off the safety. Four rounds went into the pocket of the white parka, although he knew they wouldn't be necessary.

He went outside. Their tracks led away, downhill toward the highway.

Predictable. Charlie should know better.

Ghost went to the snowmobile, lifted the hood, and pulled an ignition wire from the pocket of his parka. He replaced it, checked that all was in order, then closed the hood. He opened the small emergency toolbox at the side of the foot well, withdrew a screwdriver, and with a single levering motion, popped out the ignition sleeve. After twisting two wires together, he touched the third to the first two. The starter growled.

They'd thought removing the key would slow him. Charlie was not thinking properly. The woman had destroyed his reasoning.

He crawled aboard, balanced the rifle on his lap, and touched the wires together again. The engine sputtered and caught on the third try, chugged a bit, then came roaring to life.

Ghost did not wait for the engine to warm. It would take them an hour to walk to the highway, but he was determined to teach Charlie his lesson as quickly as possible.

Marie halted and turned, and saw that Charlie had done the same. They listened to the faint sounds of the snowmobile's engine as it came alive.

Why didn't I think to disable it? she admonished herself.

Fear twisted at Charlie's face. "There's not enough time," he said, his voice high.

"Hurry," she cried, and turned and shuffled faster.

Marie heard the sounds of Charlie's snowshoes behind

her. "We'll never make it," he breathed as he hurried. He fell, but she continued on.

She heard him release a sob.

The sound of the snowmobile engine grew louder.

Ghost followed their trail easily, not going fast—not having to—balancing the rifle on his lap with his left hand as he accelerated with his right.

He scanned the area before himself carefully, wondering why they hadn't gone for difficult terrain the moment they'd heard the engine fire.

Neither of them thought of such things, he decided. In their fear of him, they'd forgotten that to survive one must use every wile. Charlie had learned that—he'd received the finest training available to men in their calling—yet he'd never been a natural.

A professional would never have allowed feeling for a woman to cloud his judgment. When the lesson was taught, Ghost would tell him about his mistakes and explain how he should have done it. Then they'd walk and speak of old times. Charlie would come around as always.

Ghost slowed the snowmobile, knowing he was getting close. He crested a small rise, braked to a halt, and scanned, then saw them moving toward the trees below. Ghost shut off the engine and crawled off.

Predictable.

"You should know better, brother."

He knelt and rested the rifle's forestock on the snowmobile seat—set the magnification to times four as he preferred, and sighted. He could see the two figures plainly, going down the gentle slope. The .22-250 would be deadly at this distance, and it was easy to differentiate between the two. He moved his point of aim from Charlie to the other figure, and with a finger-wheel set bullet drop compensation for 250 yards.

It would have to be a perfect shot if he was to show Charlie how it should be done.

The second figure disappeared behind a tree, still trailing behind Charlie.

He waited, breathing normally, inhaled and released half the breath, held it. When the woman emerged, he let the crosshairs settle and began the trigger squeeze. Slowly, like the range instructors had said to do. Taking up the tiny slack—still dead on target—continuing, with only the meat of his forefinger in contact with the metal of the trigger.

The rifle bucked slightly in his grasp. He looked through the scope. The figure lay sprawled on the snow, partially obscured by a tree branch.

He sighted on Charlie. His brother hardly looked back, paused only for a scant heartbeat, then shuffled on, using longer strides.

"That's your lesson today, Charlie," Ghost murmured, then crawled aboard the snow machine, restarted the engine, and turned to go down the mountain.

He followed Charlie's progress as he disappeared into denser trees, but continued toward the woman's body. He neared to within ten feet, then stopped and killed the engine.

Ghost stared, recognition slow in coming for he refused to believe what he saw.

He dismounted and walked forward on shaky legs, stopped and knelt.

It could not be.

Ghost drew in a short breath, then bowed his head and clenched his eyes tightly together. He remained still for several long moments, shoulders periodically heaving spasmodically. Finally he held his head back and released a long and loud bellow of mourning.

Hatred welled and coursed through him. The woman had tricked him into shooting Charlie by wearing his parka.

He returned to the snowmobile, started up, and went after her.

Marie was trembling with terror as she continued to shuffle forward. Periodically she'd stumble and sometimes fall, but each time she scrambled to her feet and went on.

The snowmobile engine had died behind her, where she'd left Charlie's body, and there was only silence, only the crunching sound of her snowshoes.

Stay back there, she pleaded with the unseen man. *Be drowned in your grief.*

Could a man such as Ghost know grief or sorrow?

There was a bellow of outrage that hardly seemed human, that swelled louder and louder.

Marie raced faster, in near panic when she heard the snowmobile engine roar to life.

Ghost was coming for her! The man responsible for taking untold hundreds of lives was closing in. She felt insignificant and helpless. She stumbled, righted herself, and hurried on legs that were leaden weights. A man's voice penetrated her consciousness, and she cried out.

"Marie!" came another shout, and she slowed, for it was in front of her.

Yet the snowmobile was growing even louder from the rear.

She looked about wildly and saw Charlie, not twenty yards before her. Then she began to sob, for she recognized the man coming toward her, slogging through the snow, a rifle clutched in a gloved hand and a look of relief flooding over his tired face.

Lincoln Anderson's heart filled his chest as Marie's eyes widened and she sank almost to her knees. She lurched back to her feet then, and came on.

When he'd heard the crack of the rifle's report, he'd feared the worst.

He called to Marie again, his voice hoarse with emotion. The sound of the snowmobile engine was loud as she collapsed into his arms, sobbing with terror.

There was no time. "The snowmobile?" he asked. "How many?"

"Only Ghost," she panted. "He killed Charlie. Rashad was captured in town."

Link pulled her upright and motioned down the slope. "Your Jeep's directly below us on the road." He handed her the keys. "Head back to town. Don't wait. Don't even slow down."

"But you . . ."

"I don't want to have to worry about your safety, Marie," Link said, his eye on the source of the snowmobile's sound. "Now, go on. Please."

Marie caught a breath. She looked at him, storing a memory, then left.

Link wanted to watch her, if only for a few steps, but didn't dare. He continued forward. It was time for his destiny with Ghost.

As he cleared the first rise he saw the snowmobile less than fifty yards distant, coming slowly, paralleling a sheer drop-off.

Link moved left, then stopped near the precipice in the snowmobile's path. He lifted the Winchester to his shoulder. Link had him fixed in the buck-horn sight. It would be an easy shot.

The driver slowed, stopped—slid back the hood of his parka, and sat looking at him, the snowmobile engine idling.

They eyed one another, both men stock-still, neither shifting his gaze.

The driver revved the engine and came on. Link kept him squarely in the sights. He was close, and there'd be no bullet drop.

Ghost came to a halt ten yards away and shut off the engine. The silence was loud.

"Charlie's dead," Ghost finally said. He spoke as if they'd been together all of the years since they'd been separated.

"You killed him?"

Solemn nod. "It was a mistake."

"Why did you kill the others?" Link honestly wanted to know.

"In Europe? For money and to learn."

"But here in your own country?"

Ghost shrugged. "They killed our people before. I killed them now. They destroyed our nation. I destroyed theirs. You know how it is. I was told you've been in war."

"It's not the same. I fought for my country."

"Old man Weiser said it was no crime to kill an Indian. He was an American."

"Was he one of them you killed?"

Ghost smiled, as if at a particular fond memory.

"So many. For what?"

Ghost laughed bitterly. "I evened the score some, didn't I, brother?"

Link stared, then shook his head. "It's over."

Ghost raised an eyebrow and formed a mocking expression. "Is it?"

"Yes." Then he remembered the vision of the eagle, the death of chiefs.

Ghost moved a dangling wire, and the snowmobile roared to life. Link moved the carbine's muzzle only slightly and fired a single round. The engine immediately died.

The sound of the rifle shot echoed from the mountain.

"It's over," he said again, ratcheting another round into the chamber, lifting the carbine and tucking the stock to his shoulder.

Ghost lunged for the rifle propped at his side. Link fired another single round—the bullet struck Ghost's forearm. He stiffened as crimson blossomed on the white coat sleeve. The rifle slid from his grasp. Blood seeped from the parka, saturating his woolen glove. Ghost stared at his hand, blew out a painful breath as he exercised the fingers, then looked at him.

Link levered a new round into the chamber, shaking his head. "It's over."

Ghost dismounted, then turned and faced him squarely. He stood as erectly as possible, took a tentative step forward, scarcely breathing as he stared at the gun barrel.

Link kept the muzzle trained on the terrorist. "Tell me about the eagle."

Ghost looked mildly surprised. "You know of it?"

"I saw it in my dream."

His brother laughed, a low mirthless sound that cast a chill through Link.

"Who will you kill this time?"

"Long ago a group of men tried to destroy the People. Cowardly men who'd never met a warrior or woman of the People, who sent others to do their work. The men killed with a piece of paper. Their descendants will be destroyed by their own symbol."

"The eagle?"

Ghost smirked.

"Where is it?"

Ghost's voice emerged in a low whisper. "My spirit is stronger than yours, brother. I was firstborn. I am the chosen of the Bull Clan."

"You're a disease that must be stopped."

Ghost stared hard. A fervent expression formed—eyes intense, mesmerizing—he took another step. Link felt a wave of overpowering emotion. The eyes were the Grandfather's.

The face was younger, but someday it, too, would be much like the Grandfather's. Black Wolf's. Their common ancestor's.

Why hadn't he noticed it before?

Another step. "You can't stop me." The words were soft, the expression gentle—the same as the Grandfather's when he'd looked at him in the dimly lighted sweat lodge.

Ghost pushed the barrel aside, and began to remove the rifle from Link's grasp.

"No!" Link cried, summoning the will that had left him, and struggled to pull the rifle back. They held it, athletes at a deadly game, the muzzle twisting one way then the other.

They moved closer to the precipice, muscles straining as they fought for control.

Link twisted toward Ghost's wounded arm, and the barrel turned. He pulled the trigger, and the rifle erupted. The round went harmlessly into the snow at Ghost's side.

"Don't make me kill you, brother," Ghost panted as they continued, neither daring to release his grip, moving again toward the ledge.

Link didn't answer. He knew—they both knew—it had become a struggle to the death.

Ghost released the grip of his right hand and slammed hard knuckles into Link's face, trying to ram the nasal cartilage. Link felt an explosion of pain—his eyesight tunneled as he fought for consciousness. Blood ran freely—he spat it from his mouth.

Link twisted and almost yanked the rifle free. They fell together onto the wind-hardened snow near the ledge, still holding to the rifle.

Ghost drew back the knuckles.

He wouldn't remain lucid if another blow landed. Link jerked his head to one side, and the rock-hard knuckles slid off his blood-slicked cheek. They began to slide together, ever closer to the edge, clutching the weapon in death grips.

Link tried to dig in his heels, but the purchase swung him about and they continued to slide. He struck headfirst into a granite outcropping at the precipice—groaned with pain and slipped toward senselessness. Only animal instinct, the knowledge of sure death if he failed, allowed him to maintain the grip on the rifle.

His head cleared slightly, and he turned, staring down on craggy rocks far below. Only the providence that they were lodged against the jutting granite kept them from going over.

Link summoned a vestige of strength and pressed forward with the rifle. Ghost bellowed in pain as the rifle pushed into his throat. Link pressed harder, nearing the end of his strength.

Ghost twisted, repositioned, and twisted again. Link slipped free of the outcropping and began to slide over the precipice.

Marie had gone on as Link had told her, running, her heart pounding wildly from the effort and surging emotions of fear and concern.

She'd heard the snowmobile engine shut off, then three separate shots.

She hurried on, trying to keep her imagination from overwhelming her as it had done so often during the three days of terror. She burst from the trees onto the highway.

The Jeep was there, as Link had said. Marie started for it, then slowed; she stopped beside the car door, keys clutched tightly in her grasp, chest heaving with the effort of the long trek.

There was an angry, distant roar . . . Ghost's voice . . . and she turned toward the source.

Link had told her to keep going, regardless. If it had all happened another way, she might have been able to. But not now, not after the terrifying time in the cabin when she'd realized how much she felt for him.

He'd come for her.

Henry Layton had continued returning to Peshan to succor Bright Flame, and when he died the holy woman's life had become meaningless. Marie understood. Life without Lincoln Anderson would not be worth living.

Her man might need her. Marie set her mouth into a firm line and began walking back. When she'd passed the first trees her eyes lifted, drawn to a high, sheer cliff.

Two distant figures struggled there, as if locked together.

"Oh, God!" Marie cried out. She hurried forward, her mind numbed, eyes glued tightly on the spectacle as Link Anderson slipped and dangled over the precipice.

Link could not stop his momentum. He slid farther, clutching desperately to the rifle, until only Ghost's grasp kept him from dropping into the chasm. Ghost anchored his legs against the rock, huffing as he held to the rifle, Link kicking and clawing with his feet for the icy ledge.

Ghost's voice emerged in a whisper: "My spirit is too strong. No man can stop me."

Link paused in his vain struggle. They stared at one another, Link's death plunge delayed as Ghost savored his victory.

It had to end. He must stop Ghost even at the cost of his own life.

Ghost, Charlie . . . Lincoln Anderson. Lives and spirits intertwined.

Riddles within riddles.

No more.

He fell back with his full weight on the rifle, kicking hard against the cliff side.

Ghost was wrenched from his foothold. He emitted an angry shriek as he tumbled over the precipice with Link.

As they fell, Link reached out wildly, made arm contact with a ledge but the impact hardly slowed the momentum. Link struck another outcropping and screamed in agony as his side slammed against the rock face. He plummeted, grasping wildly at the side of the sheer cliff, continued clawing, and again made contact . . . slid along the face for a few feet, clutching with bloodied fingers, slowed, and found the branches of a small bush.

The free fall had stopped. He held on desperately, left hand on a tiny, half-inch ledge, the fingers of his right hand grasping the fragile cliff-side growth, feet dangling into space.

He angled his head and looked down. It was twenty more feet to the jagged rocks, where Ghost's inert body lay directly beneath him. His brother's eyes were wide, unbelieving, his mouth opened in a stilled scream.

The small bush began to pull loose.

Marie had watched in horror as Link had kicked against the cliff side and Ghost had been wrenched free. They'd fallen from her view, disappearing into the void trailing an echoing shriek, a sharp outcry of pain . . . then . . . quiet.

She was numbed as she began to run toward the base of the cliff.

Closer . . . ever closer . . . drawn but not wanting to see what she knew she'd find . . . on until she saw patches of color where the bodies had fallen atop one another on jagged, icy crags.

They'd died together.

As she drew closer her loss swelled within her, clutched and caught in her throat.

The clothing stirred. Caught by the wind? A final convulsion of death?

Another movement! She held her breath, unable to believe that what she'd prayed for was happening. Then Marie heard a painful sigh of breath that was not the wind.

A cry of joy escaped her throat as Lincoln Anderson rose painfully to hands and knees.

He was alive! The enormity of her emotions and of all she'd been through descended and overpowered her. She began to cry uncontrollably.

Too much! Her body convulsed. There was no strength remaining. She began to crumple, but Link gained his feet and staggered to her, and was gently supporting her. She clutching him tightly, never wanting to let him go. Never! She bawled louder and pulled him closer yet.

He said something and she hiccuped, then laughed joyously at the sound of his voice. He laughed, too. She babbled nonsensical words—her emotions rocketing from one high to the next.

They grew quiet, savoring one another's existence. A thousand questions and words of love passed through Marie's mind, but she hesitated to bring them to voice for fear the dream would vanish and she'd be cast back into grief.

"We've got to get you back," he said. "People are looking for you."

"I don't want to face them. Not yet." She drew back slightly and fixed her gaze on his bloody, battered face. "I just want to be alone with you and forget."

33

Friday, February 24th

Early morning—Boudie Springs, Montana

Link had driven to his cabin in Boudie Springs, with Marie huddled close the entire way. When he'd cajoled her into bed and covered her with the down comforter, he'd intended to call Browning and tell them she was safe. With his phone service shut off, he'd have to go to a neighbor's, and she'd been fearful for him to leave her for even that short period. He'd held her and waited for her to sleep, and dropped off himself.

He was wakened by soreness—throbbing from bruised muscles and the broken nose—and by the urgency of another matter. Link extracted himself from Marie carefully so she wouldn't be awakened, and walked quietly to stand before the fire. He'd lost his watch during the struggle on the mountain, but the hour did not concern him.

He heard her sounds as she got out of bed and came to his side.

"Ghost planted a final bomb," Link said. "It's in the form of an eagle. A statue, or something similar. I saw it in a dream, and Ghost confirmed it. I've got to warn them."

"Who?"

"I don't know. He wouldn't tell me, and the Grandfather dreams are gone now." Link turned to Marie. "Ghost said the eagle would kill descendants of men who'd shamed and killed the People. Does that make sense?"

Her brow furrowed with thought.

"He mentioned the Bull Clan. Tell me about them again."

"They despised white men and any who would deal with them. Lame Bear was their leader. After his death no one listened to them. The society died out a hundred years ago."

"I don't think so. If they were still around, who and what would they hate most?"

"They felt the Treaty of 1855 was shameful. They called it the treaty-which-was-a-lie."

"That sounds right. Ghost said the victims would be descendants of men who'd never met the People . . . who killed with paper. Who was responsible for the treaty who never saw the Piegan? The President? Someone in the State Department or the Bureau of Indian Affairs?"

"Governor Isaac Stevens of the Territory of Washington was there for the signing, but he wouldn't qualify because he met with them. Possibly all of those others, though."

"How would he kill their *descendants*? And with an eagle?"

"How much time do we have?"

He released a defeated breath. "I don't know, but I'd guess not much."

Marie went to the kitchen. "Then we'd better wake up. Why don't you shower while I fix coffee and find us something to eat. Then we'll brainstorm together."

"Yeah." Link liked the idea of working together. He watched for a moment as she began to look into cabinets, then walked painfully toward the bathroom.

10:55 A.M.—Senate Chamber, Capitol Building, Washington, D.C.

Senator Glenn Phillips limped down the aisle of the historical room, then stopped and was caught up in his surroundings. He was a patriotic man, and it was not the first time he'd paused to look about in silent awe.

The chamber was not as massive as that of the House of Representatives on the southern side of the Great Rotunda, but it was less crowded and in ways more impressive.

The senators' positions were set in a semicircle. At their

fore was the raised dais with the chairs of the Vice President and the majority leader. The gallery for the press and interested constituents was above, facing them. Most business that went on in the room was not clearly defined, being of the ambiguous nature called *implied* powers by the Constitution. Few democratic nations had a similar institution with such a sweeping agenda, for their decisions were rendered by a single parliamentary body. The same had been true of the Continental Congress and Congress of the Federation, unicameral bodies that had ruled the nation for the first years of its existence. In the constitutional debates of 1787, the smaller states had argued—fearing they'd be ignored if representation was by population alone. The dispute had continued until they'd balked and refused to sign. The deadlock was broken by the Connecticut Compromise, which called for a second, equal body of Congress.

The Senate could not introduce bills raising or expending revenues—that was left to the House—but it could initiate all others. And they alone could approve nominees to major office forwarded by the President . . . or ratify treaties.

They could also debate and censure those who held government office, and although the act would not remove a person from office, it cast a shadow on the holder's reputation.

The previous day they'd done just that to Leonard Griggs, director of the National Security Council. They'd brought all the dirty linen out for debate, ignoring dire warnings that such were classified and disclosure might cripple the executive branch. The warnings had only added fuel to the fire. Senators from both parties had joined in, jockeyed for time before the television cameras to bring evidence of malfeasance of office. The vote for censure was eighty to seventeen, with three abstentions. By the time the session closed, rumors swept the city that the president was scrambling to find a replacement for Griggs.

Today the Senate would meet again to flex their muscles, and pass an emergency bill forwarded by the House, withdrawing funding to the NSC until its membership was changed. Another symbolic slap. The President could easily divert funds from other pots.

Glenn looked about the almost-deserted chamber, hearing the echoing voices of such predecessors as Daniel Webster, John Calhoun, and Henry Clay. Those men and others had been equal to challenges that rocked the republic. At noon the room would fill with the current crop, most of whom were as honest and capable as the best of those who'd gone before. Slow to act, perhaps, but now determined to lead their nation from the precipice of disaster. He was humbled and proud to join them in the grand adventure of democracy.

His eyes raised to the forefront of the gallery above the Vice President's chair, and the prominent, intricately carved gilt eagle at its center. It fairly shone, for it had recently been refinished: the majestic symbol of the Senate and the nation the members swore to serve.

A page approached from behind. "You have a telephone call, sir."

Glenn frowned at the interruption. "I'll return it when I get back to the office."

"Erin says it's one of the people on your special list, sir. A Mr. Lincoln Anderson."

11:58 A.M.—North Parking Lot, Capitol Building

The wayfinder sat in his automobile, staring at the huge building. His time here was almost finished. In little more than a minute his task would be complete.

The chosen one had served beyond expectation. They would soon meet when they gathered with the Bull Clan elders to recount their exploits.

Ghost would get primary credit, as he should, but the wayfinder would also be extolled. He'd traveled a long, hard road over the past twenty-five years. Had gone from obscurity to become a household name. It was good to be so despised by one's enemies, yet he envied Ghost, for it would have been even better to be feared.

He raised the transmitter, then turned it on. A green light illuminated. The power supply was designed to radiate two bursts of energy, sufficient to carry from the official parking position his automobile was occupying to the bomb. No more, no less.

The wayfinder filled his chest with air and slowly released it, giddy with the power in his hand as he fully depressed the first button. The arming signal had been sent.

Ninety seconds after the second button was depressed the eagle bomb would explode, spraying deadly shards of metal throughout the lower level of the packed Senate chamber.

He started the automobile's engine, gunned it once, and let it settle to an idle.

"One and a half minutes," he whispered, and depressed the second button.

A wave of euphoria swept over him as he backed out of the space and drove through the parking lot. A dozen soldiers, a HUM-V utility vehicle and an olive-drab truck with an oblong box mounted on its rear, were gathered near a north-wing rear entrance. They posed no concern. The army had been conspicuous since the imposition of martial law. He avoided the vehicles, wanting to be clear of the lot before the explosion drew unwanted attention.

The wayfinder reached the gate, then accelerated past the attendant and military guard onto East Capitol Street, visualizing the fury about to be unleashed. The chamber would be packed with senators and staffers, the gallery filled with reporters from the television networks and major newspapers. Due to Ghost's genius, the deadly spray of shrapnel would be directed at the Senate floor. Most of the media would survive to report the carnage.

He was wondering how loud it would be, if he'd be able to hear it, when it came—a muffled, low boom. He laughed giddily, and would have had to restrain himself from dancing with delight if he'd been afoot.

"We did it!" he yelled in the confinement of the automobile. Retribution was sweet. The People . . . the Bull Clan . . . a century and a half of injustice . . . were vindicated.

The FBI would trace the bas-relief and discover who was responsible for the contract. The wayfinder had anticipated it and knew he must leave immediately. He'd packed two garment bags. One contained the disguise he'd change to in the long-term parking lot at Dulles. The other held all he'd take from the city he despised so thoroughly.

The midday traffic was atrocious. He crept toward the Beltway, listening to the radio for news of the explosion. By the time he turned off toward Dulles International, he was wondering.

There'd been no mention of a disaster. Was someone suppressing it?

* * *

Senator Glenn Phillips waited while the ATF agent made his way toward him across the Capitol Building parking lot.

"You've checked all traffic leaving the area before and after?" he asked.

"Yes, sir. All the vehicles had valid stickers, and we identified the occupants."

"Damn it, *someone* set the bomb off."

"Yes, sir." The agent pursed his lips as he looked at the Capitol Building. "And according to the bomb disposal people, they had to be close. We blocked the exits as soon as the bomb was triggered. Everyone inside checks out clean."

"Have you got the list of those who went out just before the blast?"

"Right here." He handed it over.

Glenn was reading it when Manny DeVera arrived and came over, acting in his official role as deputy chairman of ITF-4. Glenn told him what they were looking at, and they perused together. The list was extensive: two pages of printed names and license plate numbers. Some they knew well. In the minutes before the explosion, two representatives, a large number of staffers, a deputy secretary of state, and the director of the NSC had exited the lot.

"What was Griggs doing here?" Manny asked.

"Likely taking a look at the enemy. We roasted him thoroughly yesterday."

Manny grinned.

Glenn handed over the list. "J.J. Davis is over at the bang box, trying to determine what was in the eagle before it was set off. He'll want this."

He watched as DeVera walked toward the steel-walled blast containment unit in which the eagle had been placed half an hour before it had been detonated . . . by someone. If Link Anderson hadn't called when he had, there would have been a tragedy of immense proportion.

Not bad work for a Montana ski bum, Glenn thought with a smile. Link hadn't told him how he'd gotten his information—had asked that he not tell others it had come from him.

After the bomb had been placed in the containment box, Manny DeVera had convinced the host of ATF, FBI, and

Secret Service agents and the U.S. Army EOD team to call it a routine disaster preparedness exercise.

A good trade, thought Senator Glenn Phillips. Link's secret wouldn't get out.

An ABC reporter approached and motioned at the Capitol Building. "I can't get anything from them over there, Senator. Can we get a snapshot interview about the exercise?"

"Not much to say except everything went as advertised. We'll be holding these drills periodically. Can't be too prepared to divert a disaster, can we?"

7:25 P.M.—Calgary International Airport, Alberta, Canada

The Canadian Pacific Airlines flight from Toronto landed on schedule, but one of the passengers remained unhappy. There'd been nothing announced on either of the flights taken by the wayfinder. Surely they would have told the passengers about a disaster in the Capitol Building.

He'd called the Bull Clan number from Dulles, and told the answerer that he'd been successful. The elder had responded in Algonkian, as they used to establish identity. They'd pick him up in the usual place—in front of the arrival baggage area.

He'd worried that a passenger might see through his disguise—a pair of horn-rimmed spectacles, a wig providing a lush head of hair, and a soiled running suit—or that a customs official might question his identity. Neither of those things happened. He shouldn't have worried. He was the wayfinder and moved among the enemy unseen. He was returning to the People in triumph. The trip had been made in complete anonymity, to which Len Griggs had grown unaccustomed.

He made his way out of the terminal and waited on the sidewalk, standing apart from the other arriving passengers as he examined each approaching vehicle.

A dark sedan stopped at the curb before him. When the passenger's window was rolled down, Len ducked down and peered inside.

There were three men, Native Americans but with faces he didn't recognize.

"Get in back," the passenger said. He had white hair, and a strong face with a prominent Roman nose.

Len frowned, wondering.

"Ok-yi," urged the passenger in their language. *Come on.*

Len relaxed, then told him he needed to put his bag in the trunk.

A man emerged from the backseat, roughly pulled the garment bag from his hand, and unceremoniously tossed it onto the floor. He wore an immaculate Stetson hat with a cattleman's crease, and tersely motioned for him to get in.

The Bull Clan elders were obviously displeased. Len Griggs wondered what could have gone wrong as he took his seat, his feet wedged uncomfortably against the bag.

The man in the Stetson slammed the door. "Let's go."

The driver pulled from the curb into the flow of airport traffic.

"Have you heard anything?" Griggs asked. "I set it off, for God's sake, and I *heard* it."

The others remained silent as they drove toward the freeway.

The man in the passenger's seat turned and regarded him in the darkness.

"It's been a long time," said Len, looking out. "Four years since I visited here last."

"So we heard," said the passenger. "Now tell us everything."

"Shouldn't it wait until we join the others?"

"You'll be with them soon enough," said the man in the Stetson.

"Is anything wrong?" asked the wayfinder. Something didn't seem right.

"The Bull Clan elders were brought before the combined council this afternoon. It was a long session," he said grimly. "They finally told us what they'd done . . . and about you."

Griggs looked about the interior as the words sunk in. They weren't from the Bull Clan!

"The council passed judgment," continued the man in the Stetson. "Before we carry it out, we want to hear it all from you."

"I don't know what you're talking about," Len blurted, eyes darting as he looked for a route of escape.

"That's what the elders said at first, but after a while they told us everything. It was easier for them that way."

Len's voice trembled. "We did it for the People."

"You brought *shame* upon the People," exploded the white-haired passenger.

Len Griggs began to plead for mercy, but none of the angry men listened.

34

The Week of February 27th

Washington, D.C.

The week was eventful. On Monday the President made a speech from the White House, the first time he'd done so since the explosion. He declared the emergency over—there'd been confirmed sightings of Ghost and Charlie in the Middle East—and thanked the citizens of Washington for their forbearance. The citizens remembered similar previous announcements by administration spokesmen, and were annoyed and disbelieving.

That evening retired General Sam Hall and his son Mack were interviewed at the Falls Church home of a friend where Sam was recuperating. Both men expressed firm opinions that the emergency was indeed over. Thanks to Mack's efforts, Rashad Taylor was in custody. The FBI thought he'd been on his way to the West Coast to meet with Ghost and Charlie, who had somehow escaped. Both Sam and Mack were trusted and believed.

In his Tuesday speech, the President announced the restructuring of the NSC. Leonard Griggs had disappeared, last seen leaving the Capitol four days earlier, his automobile found abandoned in the Dulles Airport long-term parking lot. Those things were not announced, for the FBI had quietly initiated a nationwide search for Griggs. Supervising

Agent J.J. Davis had discovered a radio transmitter left on the floorboard of the abandoned vehicle, with two symmetrical squiggles engraved on its side.

Also on Tuesday, the *Post* carried a story that the bodies of twelve Native American cultists had been discovered in a burned cabin near Calgary, Alberta. At first the RCMP had felt it was mass suicide, but then they'd discovered that some had died before the fire was set. A team sent from Ottawa was having difficulty identifying the charred remains.

On Wednesday the President announced the de facto resignation of the missing Leonard Griggs. The post was offered to a woman, a college classmate of the President's wife.

That day, Manuel G. DeVera revealed to friends that his proposal of marriage was being considered by Judge Lindquist, who would soon be released from the hospital.

On Thursday, after receiving much pressure to run for office, General Sam Hall, U.S. Air Force, retired, issued a statement from the Falls Church home. With a capricious twinkle in his eye, Sam said he would not enter politics but would support Senator Glenn Phillips in his bid to become the next President of the United States.

In an immediate reply, Senator Phillips stuttered that he had no intention of seeking the Presidency. It was not long thereafter that he changed his mind.

On Friday Marian S. Lindquist accompanied Manuel G. DeVera to the hospital cafeteria, walking that distance unaided for the first time since she'd been hospitalized. There she joined several friends who interceded on Manny's behalf, asking if she wouldn't consider him as a life mate. She blushed like any woman in love and said she would, and the cafeteria exploded with congratulations. But although he asked then and later, Marian refused to tell Manny DeVera what he'd said that had infuriated her so.

As Linda Anderson was about to leave with her husband, who was unable to stay up longer for even that happy occasion, she winked at her good friend and whispered, "It worked."

Boudie Springs, Montana

Lincoln Anderson and Marie LeBecque spent their return to civilization in his cabin, touching often and sometimes holding fast to one another.

Link borrowed a snowmobile and sled attachment from Jim Bourne, head of the North County Search and Rescue Team, and returned to Siyeh Mountain. He searched, and it did not take long to find the cave where Black Wolf's body had been laid to rest. It was as if something had drawn him there, not far beyond the dream house he'd set up on the mountainside.

The dream house tent had collapsed, but someone had placed Link's "medicine" in a neat bundle nearby, in the way of the Blackfeet. He wondered if Ghost had known he would come for it.

He retrieved the bodies of his brothers and the bones from the cabin and one-by-one carried them up to the cave. There he solemnly arranged them, as Marie had told him was due great men, with Black Wolf's skeleton in a position of prominence and a young warrior at each side. He left his medicine on a ledge in the chamber and resealed the entrance with large stones.

As Lincoln Anderson started down the mountain, a sense of serenity filled him. He stopped and stared out across the high, snow-covered peaks, and remained there until late.

While Link was busy at Siyeh Mountain, Marie LeBecque returned to Browning and apologized to the police, telling them she'd gone to Link's cabin in Boudie Springs to get away for a short while. She'd taken the food to stock the place. No, she'd not been threatened.

The local press media were uninterested, still busy with the events that had held Washington captive and regurgitating how the nationally known figure, Mack Hall, had found and severely injured one of Ghost's gang right there in Browning.

Marie's uncle and aunt were overjoyed that she was safe, although Benjamin White Calf was quieter than normal. She went by Jack Douglas's to tell him Link had damaged the Winchester but would have it repaired. Jack, too, was oddly quiet.

Finally she drove back to Link's cabin in Boudie Springs and waited for him to return.

Although Abraham Lincoln Anderson retained his astounding memory and ability to place seemingly minor details into meaningful conclusions, he did not dream of the Grandfather again. He continued to believe that the revelations had been creations of his subconscious, but he never lost pride in the fact that he was Piegan, or that he'd endured the most ancient and demanding of their rituals.